SPIDER-MAN: THE VENOM FACTOR by Diane Duane

THE ULTIMATE SPIDER-MAN, Stan Lee, Editor

IRON MAN: THE ARMOR TRAP by Greg Cox

SPIDER-MAN: CARNAGE IN NEW YORK
by David Michelinie & Dean Wesley Smith

THE INCREDIBLE HULK: WHAT SAVAGE BEAST by Peter David

SPIDER-MAN: THE LIZARD SANCTION by Diane Duane

THE ULTIMATE SILVER SURFER, Stan Lee, Editor

FANTASTIC FOUR: TO FREE ATLANTIS by Nancy A. Collins

DAREDEVIL: PREDATOR'S SMILE by Christopher Golden

X-MEN: MUTANT EMPIRE Book 1: SIEGE by Christopher Golden

THE ULTIMATE SUPER-VILLAINS, Stan Lee, Editor

SPIDER-MAN & THE INCREDIBLE HULK: RAMPAGE
by Danny Fingeroth & Eric Fein (Doom's Day Book 1)

SPIDER-MAN: GOBLIN'S REVENGE by Dean Wesley Smith

THE ULTIMATE X-MEN, Stan Lee, Editor

SPIDER-MAN: THE OCTOPUS AGENDA by Diane Duane

X-MEN: MUTANT EMPIRE Book 2: SANCTUARY by Christopher Golden

IRON MAN: OPERATION A.I.M. by Greg Cox

SPIDER-MAN & IRON MAN: SABOTAGE
by Pierce Askegren & Danny Fingeroth (Doom's Day Book 2)

X-MEN: MUTANT EMPIRE Book 3: SALVATION by Christopher Golden

GENERATION X by Scott Lobdell & Elliot S! Maggin

FANTASTIC FOUR: REDEMPTION OF THE SILVER SURFER
by Michael Jan Friedman

THE INCREDIBLE HULK: ABOMINATIONS by Jason Henderson

X-MEN: SMOKE AND MIRRORS by eluki bes shahar

X-MEN: EMPIRE'S END by Diane Duane

UNTOLD TALES OF SPIDER-MAN, Stan Lee & Kurt Busiek, Editors

COMING SOON:

SPIDER-MAN & FANTASTIC FOUR: WRECKAGE
by Eric Fein & Pierce Askegren (Doom's Day Book 3)

X-MEN: THE JEWELS OF CYTTORAK by Dean Wesley Smith

SPIDER-MAN: VALLEY OF THE LIZARD by John Vornholt

UNTOLD TALES of SPIDER-MAN

STAN LEE
&
KURT BUSIEK

Editors

BYRON PREISS MULTIMEDIA COMPANY, INC.

NEW YORK

BOULEVARD BOOKS

NEW YORK

UNTOLD TALES OF SPIDER-MAN

A Boulevard Book
A Byron Preiss Multimedia Company, Inc. Book

Special thanks to Ginjer Buchanan at Berkley Books; Stacy Gittelman, Ursula
Ward, Mike Thomas, Steve Behling, John Conroy, Ralph Macchio, Tom
Brevoort, and Glenn Greenberg at Marvel; and Carol D. Page, Michelle
LaMarca, Emily Epstein, Howard Zimmerman, and especially Steve Roman
and Keith R.A. DeCandido at BPMC.

PRINTING HISTORY
Boulevard trade paperback edition / October 1997

The Putnam Berkley World Wide Web site address is
http://www.berkley.com
Check out the Byron Preiss Multimedia Co., Inc. site on the World Wide Web:
http://www.byronpreiss.com
Make sure to check out *PB Plug*, the science fiction/fantasy newsletter, at
http://www.pbplug.com

ISBN: 1-57297-294-7

BOULEVARD
Boulevard Books are published by The Berkley Publishing Group,
a member of Penguin Putnam Inc.,
200 Madison Avenue, New York, New York 10016.
BOULEVARD and its logo
are trademarks belonging to Berkley Publishing Corporation.

PRINTED IN THE UNITED STATES OF AMERICA

10 9 8 7 6 5 4 3 2 1

CONTENTS

INTRODUCTION

Stan Lee

Illustration by Ron Lim

What a sensational idea!

Just imagine the undiscovered bounty of thrills and surprises we're about to encounter as we recklessly plunge back to the early days of Spidey's super-villain–smashing career, from shortly after Uncle Ben's death to a few months before Kraven the Hunter departed this mortal vale.

When Steve Ditko and I started the icon-smashing saga of your friendly neighborhood web-spinner way back in the early sixties, there was so much that we left out, so many other tales we could have chronicled. But at that time we were a much smaller company, operating with a much smaller staff, and we didn't have the manpower (or womanpower, for you political-correctness buffs) to enable us to publish additional stories of Spidey's adventures each month. We had to select episodes that were only the tip of the legendary Spider-Man iceberg.

But what a difference a few decades can make. Today Marvel sits at the very pinnacle of comic-bookdom, with a coterie of talented writers leaving no stone unturned and no computer keyboard untapped in a herculean effort to bring you a spellbinding account of each and every adventure that has ever befallen our web-swinging wonder. After all, who are we to deny a breathlessly waiting world the indescribable pleasure of increasing its fund of knowledge about the planet's most popular costumed cavorter?

Thus, it is with a pardonable portion of pandemonious pride that I welcome you to the most eagerly awaited anthology since *A Treasury of Aunt May's Favorite Recipes*. Indeed, when I first set eyes on the Marvel comic book title *Untold Tales of Spider-Man*, written by the titanically talented Kurt Busiek, I knew that Marvel had once again come up with a concept to bring tears of gratitude streaming from the eyes of literature-loving fans everywhere.

So, what could be more natural than for Kurt himself to join me in this momentous literary achievement by writing the Retroduction to the book you now so gently hold and cherish? Who better to share the editorial credit of this watershed volume than the man who first opened the imaginative vault of Spidey's hitherto undiscovered tales?

And what tales they are! Chronologically arranged so as not to shatter the authentic timeline of Spidey's career, you'll start with Will Murray's account of our hero teaming up with none other than the astonishing Ant-Man as they battle the ruthless Egghead! Then, before you can catch your breath, Marvel's ex-editor-in-chief (and a chronicler of Spidey's current monthly adventures in *The Amazing Spider-Man*), Tom DeFalco, tells you of the first time one of Spider-Man's battles resulted in another man's death. Prepare yourself for a real heart-tugger.

Now the tales come at you fast and furious. Christopher Golden and José R. Nieto cook up an exotic concoction featuring the Human Torch, a gorgeous fashion model, and the sinister Sandman. Add another beautiful female, toss an unsuspecting Peter Parker into the mix, and watch the fireworks.

Can you imagine Spidey unable to use his webbing because he ran out of polymer? What a time to be in the middle of a rampage by the deadly Looter. Only authors John Garcia and Pierce Askegren know how it ends—as will you, once you've savored every word. Then, Michael Jan Friedman recounts how the Green Goblin decided to learn Spider-Man's true identity, causing pandemonium inside a great metropolitan newspaper. The excitement never stops.

A glimpse into Peter Parker's personal life comes from ex-Spider-Man editor Danny Fingeroth, as Peter must choose between continuing his wall-crawling career or caring for his ailing aunt May. Then we get a story from Aunt May's perspective by John S. Drew, which deals with a move that changes our hero's life, and the lives of those who love—and hate—him.

We get even more personal, as ex–Marvel staffer Ann Nocenti tells what happened after a stunned Peter Parker learned that his parents had been spies, and Richard Lee Byers probes the death of Gwen Stacy and its emotional aftermath, with the shadow of a serial killer called the Ripper hanging over the tragedy like a pall of doom.

Change of pace is provided by Ken Grobe and Steven A. Roman as they tell of the time the son of Fancy Dan of the Enforcers was kidnapped and only Spider-Man could help his avowed enemy. Then, the suspense continues as Glenn Greenberg describes the panic when Peter's Empire State University classmate commits suicide—with the savage Shocker on the loose! Not to be outdone, Steve Lyons describes how ESU performs an experiment on the evil Electro. When the experiment is sabotaged by one of Steve Hopkins's practical jokes, Electro is out to destroy the campus—and, to no one's surprise, that's where Spidey comes in.

Our final three thrillers are equally compelling. (I know it's hard to believe that there are actually three more stories in store after all the literary treasures we've already discussed, but, hey, nothing's too good for you Spideyphiles!)

Keith R. A. DeCandido pens a minor masterpiece about Dr. Octopus, comicdom's favorite six-armed villain, in which a professional biographer opts to write Ock's biography! (Try saying that phrase five times fast!) Then, Eric Fein tells how J. Jonah Jameson wins a Humanitarian of the Year award (proving that anything's possible in New York). But no award ceremony can run as planned when Spider-Slayer creator Alistair Smythe and the sinister Scorpion decide it's time for vengeance.

Finally, before you can catch your breath, Adam-Troy Castro wraps everything up with the tale of Dr. Gwendolyn Harris, who encounters a peculiarly paranoid young man with super strength in the emergency room's psycho ward. This one involves scorpions, rhinos, octopuses, and a mysterious hunter . . . and that's just for starters.

I'd better not tell you more, lest you think I'm resorting to hyperbole. Suffice it to say that over the years Peter Parker has become a true flesh-and-blood human being to me and, I'm delighted to say, to millions of others as well. Now, thanks to Kurt Busiek and the wonderful array of authors represented between these covers, Spidey's legend continues to grow and flourish as we learn ever more about the untold tales of everybody's favorite web-head, the always-amazing Spider-Man.

Excelsior!

Stan Lee

RETRODUCTION

Kurt Busiek

Illustration by Scott McDaniel

How do you follow Stan Lee?

That's actually a question I've got to ask myself on a monthly basis, as I write the *Untold Tales of Spider-Man* comic book, weaving new stories into and around the original Spider-Man adventures by Stan Lee and Steve Ditko that first brought Spidey to life and made him the American icon he is today. But there, I've got the advantage of having a couple of decades between Stan's stories and mine, so maybe people don't make a direct comparison, and I don't look quite so shabby by comparison. Here, though, I've got to follow him directly.

And of course, he gets all the good stuff.

Can I tell you the idea of the book? Nope. Can I talk about the stories? Nope. Stan got all that. He did it. It's done. I've got to find something else to talk about. Like, uh, what?

Well, one thing I can talk about, something I share with most of the writers in this book, is the fact that, by necessity, we have a different perspective on Spider-Man than Stan does. We have to.

See, I was born in late 1960. A little after my first birthday, Stan, working with artist Jack Kirby, sent four ordinary humans into space, bathed them in cosmic rays, and turned them into the Fantastic Four—and what's come to be known as the Marvel Age was born. A little while later, just before my second birthday, Stan and his other main collaborator of the Marvel Age, Steve Ditko, told a story about a teenager who got bitten by a radioactive spider, learned that with great power comes great responsibility, and took on the lifelong burden of being not just Peter Parker, but Spider-Man.

I missed it all, of course. I was two (almost). I wasn't reading yet, and even if I was, my parents didn't think much of comic books. So I learned to read on other stuff, and didn't see many comics at all, and by the time I read a Spider-Man story, it was 1975, I was fourteen years old, and the comic was *Amazing Spider-Man* #143.

And truth to tell, I didn't like Spidey all that much.

I mean, here I am, I'm fourteen, I've recently discovered girls, and I'm reading this comic about a good-looking guy who's built like a lifeguard, he's got super-powers, he's got a cool job—in that story, he jetted off to Paris, of all places, on *Daily Bugle* business—and he recognizes one gorgeous, curvaceous gal in the subway as an old girlfriend of his (it turns out to be a clone of the late Gwen Stacy) and another equally stunning gal kisses him good-bye at the airport hard enough to remember when you're ninety-nine—

—and this guy thinks he's got problems!

I found it a little hard to sympathize, you know? I figured that if I was in his shoes, I'd be lovin' the job and the powers, I could solve the girl problem just by picking one of 'em—it doesn't matter which, since they're both winners—and my life is fabulous. Certainly better than the one I was actually living, and you didn't see *me* hanging around rooftops moping about what rotten luck I had . . .

So I paid more attention to other Marvel books for a while, like *Daredevil* (who didn't mope about the gorgeous Russian ex-spy he was involved with), and *Avengers* (where I latched on to Hawkeye as my favorite Marvel character, a rank he still holds today), and eventually I learned about Aunt May and the death of Uncle Ben and Flash Thompson and J. Jonah Jameson's vendetta against Spidey and Betty Brant and Spidey being blamed for the death of Captain Stacy and Gwen's death at the hands of the Green Goblin and—

—and, man, what a great character this Spider-Man was!

It was the history that hooked me. Not just the great stories and art, though individual epics like the Master Planner trilogy will always have a place in my heart—and not just the great assortment of villains, from Dr. Octopus to the Green Goblin to the Lizard and more; to my mind, the single best rogues' gallery in comics—but the sweep of it all, the fact that this was a kid who lived through high school and college and several tragedies along the way, a kid who screwed up and learned from it and tried to do better, who got knocked down and picked himself up and kept going, a kid who grew and learned and changed. . . . It felt like a life, and Spidey felt like a person. And *that,* I could identify with.

It was the history. A rich, involving history, full of drama and comedy and passion and romance and more. That's what hooked me into Spider-Man.

And that's something I'll always see from a totally different perspective than Stan.

Stan was there. He cocreated Spidey, he orchestrated the adventures, he made it all happen—and the question he always faced was, "What happens next?" What's the next story, what's the next event, what's the next crisis? To him, Spider-Man is something he made happen, something that wouldn't exist if he and Steve Ditko (and later John Romita and others) hadn't been answering those monthly questions, coming up with new characters, spinning out adventures, trying new things and building on them if they worked or going in a different direction if they didn't. It was a blank slate, and it was up to Stan and crew to fill it up.

But to me, it's history. When I write an *Untold Tales of Spider-Man* story, I've got anything but a blank slate—I've got all that Stan did, and everything that came after. Far from being confining, the challenge of working within the parameters of what's gone before makes it fun. I feel, at times, like a historian researching World War II, or Napoleonic France, and figuring out what happened in between the stuff we already know. It's just that the history I'm researching is fictional, and instead of finding out what happened in between the stuff we already know, I get to make it up. I get to say, "Hey, when Peter stopped wearing his glasses, did Aunt May kick up a fuss? You know how concerned she is about his health!" I get to figure out more about Betty Brant's family, or Ben Parker's career, and weave new stories about it that fit into that history I find so involving, while standing on their own as (hopefully) thrilling super hero adventures.

And it's a blast, let me tell you.

And I suspect that, for all the writers whose work appears in this volume, it's a similar thrill. They may have encountered Spider-Man earlier or later than I did—but still, like me, they were watching a life unfold before them, watching a history progress, and now they get to pick their favorite times, their favorite characters, and explore that history, finding just the right new adventure, just the right twist, to give you a story that stands on its own, but that nonetheless grows out of that history built by Stan and Steve and John and Gil Kane and Gerry Conway and Ross Andru and Roger Stern and David Michelinie and Todd McFarlane and so many others over the years.

So, yeah, Stan got there first. And he got to make it all happen.

But we get to wander around in what Stan built, and we get to poke through the rooms and check under the rafters and root around at the foundations and find just the right bit to build on to with our own discoveries about Spider-Man and his supporting cast—and that's a whole different kind of fun.

We had a great time. I hope you enjoy reading it as much as we enjoyed putting it together for you. And, Stan—sorry about the noise, sir. I hope we didn't make too much of a mess. . . .

SIDE BY SIDE WITH THE ASTONISHING ANT-MAN!

Will Murray

Illustration by Steven Butler

Henry Pym was worried about spiders.

Normally, arachnids did not fall into his area of expertise, neither as Henry Pym, nor as his colorful alter-ego, Ant-Man. Biochemist, entomologist, adventurer, Pym had discovered a serum that shrank him to the size of an ant. After a nightmarish journey through the maze of an anthill, Pym managed to restore himself to his normal size. Many would have suffered recurrent nightmares about the experience. Pym strove to duplicate it.

Perhaps it was their sophisticated social organization. Or their uncanny ability to communicate with one another through antennae and scent signals. Perhaps it was the loneliness the young blond biochemist endured after the untimely death of his wife, Maria, at the hands of foreign agents. But Pym perfected his formula into an inhalant giving him the power to change size at will. He then immersed himself in the ant world.

Months of experimenting paid off in the form of a cybernetic helmet that converted his thoughts into electronic impulses ants could understand and obey.

Henry Pym was wearing that helmet now as he toiled in his instrument-packed private lab near New York City. An aluminum shell covering most of his head, it boasted twin needle antennae and a microphone pinched before his mouth by two stylized mandibles. He looked like a human being burdened by a stylized ant's head of surgical chrome.

For weeks, there had been reports in the press of a strange costumed entity known as Spider-Man. Some thought him a criminal. Others, a genetic freak. A few reports insisted that with his ability to mimic a wall-crawling spider, he could only be the product of an alien planet of evolutionarily advanced insects.

Henry Pym could glean nothing from these conflicting reports. But whatever Spider-Man was, it seemed a strange coincidence that he should appear at the same time Ant-Man debuted. Perhaps he was some evil mastermind determined to challenge Ant-Man. Ants and spiders were natural enemies, after all.

Whatever the truth, it was time to alert his faithful ants to be on the watch for this mystery figure.

Concentrating, Pym formed a mental image of Spider-Man and transmitted it to the ant world through his cybernetic helmet. The impulses had a limited range. But the request, he knew, would pass from ant to ant, anthill to ant's nest, until virtually every ant in the five boroughs would be watching for signs of a blue-and-red human spider.

Satisfied that the most sophisticated information-gathering network in existence was on alert, Henry Pym returned to his morning coffee, never dreaming he had set into motion events that would lead to the most bizarre encounter of his still-young career.

At a darkened electronics nest at an undisclosed location, a bulky figure hunched over a screen, his bullet head clamped by over-sized earphones. The words spoken by Henry Pym and converted into ant-understandable impulses were unscrambled into a weird electronic approximation of a human voice.

"Report any Spider-Man sightings to Ant-Man."

And on the screen a jittery image of a spider in human form flickered.

"So," he muttered, "the Ant-Man is interested in this new creature, Spider-Man. Here perhaps is the opportunity I have been waiting for. . . ."

The tarantula appeared after midnight two weeks later.

No one saw the tarantula climb the Excelsior Building in mid-town Manhattan, despite the fact that it was as large as a bus. There were no witnesses when it spun its immense untidy web between the Excelsior Building and the adjoining Good-man Towers. It was a Sunday evening, and that part of midtown is all but deserted in the quiet hours before the work week begins.

A panhandler named Oleck, scrounging for deposit bottles inside a service-alley dumpster, did take notice around three A.M.

What he saw brooding against the moonless night sky made him scurry away to the nearest subway entrance, there to spend the night clutching a bottle of cheap red wine. He told no one.

For the balance of the evening, the arachnid hung suspended, patient yet expectant.

When dawn broke, so did a kind of pandemonium.

"Peter! Don't be late! It's a school day!"

Peter Parker jumped out of his bed and his pajamas as the

age-cracked but warm voice of his aunt May, with whom he shared a modest clapboard house in Forest Hills, Queens, shattered his sleep. He had been dreaming about spiders. He had been dreaming a lot about spiders since the accident at the Science Hall four months ago—dreaming he was one of them.

"Coming, Aunt May!" he called down as he dressed. Fumbling on his wire-rimmed glasses, he faced the first crucial decision of the day: whether to wear his Spider-Man costume or not. No gym today, so it seemed a safe bet. He drew on the skintight blue-black pants and scarlet jersey with its orb-web pattern running down chest and arms. A black spider sat in the center of the chest web.

Modeling on the color scheme of the black widow spider, Parker had designed it to catch the eye back in the early weeks of his career as Spider-Man, when his only thought was to cash in on his newfound spider powers via TV and public appearances. Now the bizarre design better served to unnerve the criminals he fought in his new role as secret adventurer.

His outer clothes concealed the high-sleeved uniform perfectly. The long gloves, boots, and mask folded neatly into a hollow book in his book bag, as did his collapsible wrist web-shooters.

Aunt May was waiting for him, umbrella in hand, at the door. Her eyes glowed with pride in her long, careworn face.

"Oh, I wish you'd eat something, Peter," she said.

He gave her a peck on the cheek and said, "No time, Aunt May." And he was out the door. Without the umbrella.

Walking brisky through residential Queens streets, Parker wore a worried face. Household finances were getting tight. His dreams of earning big money as Spider-Man had come crashing down the night police broke the shattering news of his uncle Ben's murder at the hands of a common burglar—a thug Parker had callously allowed to go free, thinking it wasn't his problem. In the aftermath of that tragic error, he had decided to turn his invented persona of Spider-Man into a force for good.

After school, he would go into the city with the miniature camera that had belonged to Uncle Ben and try to snap some newsworthy photos for the *Daily Bugle* and its cheapskate publisher, J. Jonah Jameson. It was his only way to make money and still stay in school.

Turning a corner, Parker came to the quadrangle of Midtown High. Behind it was silhouetted the ever-growing Manhattan skyline.

And there, spaced between two tall buildings, was an outline that sent a shiver through his lean frame.

"Tell me I'm back in bed, still dreaming!" he said.

An insistent *bap-bap-bap* coming from his ant lab brought Henry Pym running from his breakfast nook, morning coffee forgotten.

The always-running ant communications gear was in full warning mode. Rushing to the screen, Pym donned one of the oversized high-gain cybernetic helmets he used when not in uniform.

His ears were immediately assaulted by a cacophany of tiny ant voices repeating the same alarm.

"Spider! Spider! Spider!"

On the screen a visual readout showed a section of skyline, a giant spider silhouetted against it. An ant's impression of Spider-Man prowling Manhattan's rooftops, Pym assumed.

Hurriedly, he donned his ant-bite–resistant mesh uniform with its stylized representation of a segmented ant's body. Composed of unstable molecules, it was designed to shrink with him. Affixed to the belt buckle were two vials of gas: one for reducing, the other, enlarging. Finally, the ant-form helmet fitted over his head, bulky but amazingly light.

Triggering the reducing gas vial, Pym stood stock still and waited for the astringent vapors to creep into his nostrils. The instant they hit his lungs, the potent mix was carried into his bloodstream, igniting the sudden cellular compression that transformed him from man to Ant-Man.

In seconds, he stood but a quarter inch tall. Rushing to a tiny trapdoor in one corner of the room, he entered a chamber no larger than a matchbox. There stood the powerful catapult he had designed to convey him to the city in the shortest possible time.

Punching in the coordinates, Pym climbed in. The catapult operated by compressed air, much the way a human cannonball is shot from a circus cannon. His feet flat against the spring plate, legs bent slightly to absorb the sudden shock, Pym reached over to hit the firing button beside the muzzle.

With a *whoosh*, the catapult let go, and the Ant-Man was propelled into the air at high velocity. If a full-sized human were to be shot out of a comparably sized cannon, he would be turned to jelly. But through a quirk of the reducing gas, Pym retained his full human strength even at ant-height.

Eyes pinched tight against the slipstream, he broadcast a steady electronic signal to his faithful ants who were even now converging at a predetermined point to cushion his landing.

Peter Parker took in the sight of police helicopters orbiting the giant tarantula and ducked into a thicket of privet hedge, before any of his classmates could see him. He was in the act of shucking off his shirt, when he smacked himself on the forehead.

What am I thinking of? he thought. *If I show up as Spider-Man, the authorities will think I'm mixed up with that overgrown nightmare. They'd probably shoot me on sight!*

Rebuttoning his shirt, Parker ran to the nearest subway stop. Taking the E train wasn't the most heroic way for a super hero to make his entrance, but Spider-Man wouldn't exactly be welcomed on the scene.

On the other hand, Peter Parker might just be in a great position to snap some juicy shots. . . .

The police commissioner of New York City rushed through congested traffic to personally take command of the deteriorating situation. And he was *not* happy.

It had started with a report from the Midtown South precinct.

"I know what this sounds like, but there's this giant tarantula suspended between the Excelsior Building and Goodman Towers."

Commissioner Maneely had grown pretty blasé about the unusual ever since the Fantastic Four and Spider-Man had appeared in his fair city. Instead of ordering Captain Grobé committted for observation, he asked a logical question.

"What's it doing?"

"Nothing. It's just *hangin'* there."

So he ordered in police helicopters. The first one came in too close. The tarantula twitched in its web—or maybe it was the wind buffeting it. But without any other warning, a strand of spider silk as thick as a tow rope shot out and tangled up the main rotor.

The rotor blades twisted like so much tinsel. The rotor shaft continued to spin. Centrifugal force threw the chopper body into a spin that severed the tail rotor. And the helicopter came crashing down to the roped-off concrete of Simon Plaza with a deafening *thud* and a *boom* of exploding fuel.

With that, Commissioner Maneely ordered the surviving helicopters pulled back to safe orbits. The damn thing was alive!

Once on the scene, he got his first look at the beast in the flesh, or, rather, hair. The tarantula was covered with bristled black hair. It hung head down so that its eight round eyes coldly regarded the gathering crowd of New Yorkers pushing against the straining police lines like fools.

The commander on the scene came up, saluting.

"It's just waiting, sir."

"Waiting for what?"

The commander shrugged. "We tried calling Reed Richards over at Fantastic Four headquarters. No answer."

Commissioner Maneely blew out an exasperated breath. "Then I guess it's up to us. . . ."

"Do you think this has anything to do with that Spider-Man?"

"What do *you* think?"

"I think it probably does."

"Then I guess we wait for Spider-Man to put in an appearance—unless you have a tactical solution that's not obvious to me," Maneely said bitingly.

"I don't, sir," the commander admitted.

Peter Parker couldn't get close to the police lines. Half of Manhattan seemed to be jostling for a glimpse of the hairy monstrosity that dominated the skyline of New York like nothing since an ICBM had thundered out of the Baxter Building without warning the previous spring.

Snapping a couple of framing shots, Parker circled the multiblock area looking for a path though the police cordon.

The ants were waiting for Henry Pym, as always. They had never failed. It was like hitting a springy trampoline. Pym struck the living net, rebounded, and snapped to his purple-booted feet.

Off to one side waited a flying ant, wings poised for flight.

Mounting it like a horse, Ant-Man took off into the clear light of morning.

He hoped his steed could handle the sight of the gigantic arachnid when it came into view. Ants were temperamentally stable, but even they knew fear.

Peter Parker couldn't find an opening in the crowd. So he improvised.

The side of the Goodman Towers opposite the tarantula was cordoned off, but deserted. There was no view of the big spider from that side, so no one bothered.

Slinging his book bag over his shoulder, Parker stepped up to the wall and set his fingertips against the smooth, glassy surface. Stepping out of his shoes, he began to climb the sheer face with his spidery fingers and toes. He still didn't understand how the bite of a radioactive spider had communicated its powers to him. But all he had to do was touch any surface, and he adhered to it.

Silently, nimbly, he slipped up the sheer face of the building, shifted sideways around two corners, and came down on the inside of Simon Plaza. He was within police lines but out of their line of sight—and fire.

Crouching in a doorway, he began snapping shot after shot.

Above him the eight-orbed arachnid moved its head this way and that, but seemed to take no notice of him. Which was just fine with Peter Parker. He was used to spiders looking up at him, not the other way around.

Guided by thought impulses, the flying ant zipped easily between Manhattan's spires. Then the tarantula loomed ahead.

"Steady," Pym told his steed. "Steady."

Abruptly, the ant began to buck and convulse. Squeezing its thorax with his knees, Ant-Man held on.

"Easy, boy. Easy."

The ant twisted. It executed a long, discouraging loop. The concrete-and-glass forest of skyscrapers spun wildly around.

Holding onto its neck with one hand, Pym used the other to fine-tune his helmet frequency. Different ants responded to different adjustments in his helmet. Maybe this one wasn't receiving clearly.

"Do not be afraid," he repeated. "Do not—"

And in his helmet, Pym heard a weird humanlike voice unlike any ant voice he had ever encountered.

"Spider-Man. Spider-Man. Where are you? Come join me. Come join the Tarantula."

Whether it was a spasmodic bucking jolt of his steed or the insistant message in his head, Henry Pym lost his perch. Tumbling off, he spread his arms. Hard concrete rushed up to welcome him. He was light as an ant in this size. If he could only catch an updraft, it would buy him time.

And through his helmet he called for any ants in the vicinity to form a net below him. Even as he knew that here in the concrete of midtown, ants were few and far between.

One roll of valuable film shot, Peter Parker was about to load a second when he glanced up at the sky.

Something was making his spider-sense tingle. The giant tarantula continued to scrutinize its surroundings with methodical head movements. It seemed to be searching for something.

Then, Parker caught a glimpse of sunlight glinting off a falling object. His spider-sense continued to cry out in alarm. Was the tarantula about to strike?

Ducking back into the doorway, he stripped off his outer clothes. From the book bag came the scarlet gloves, boots, and finally pullover mask that made Spider-Man such a fearsome apparition. Strapped to his wrists were the web-shooters of his own design that provided the one ability not conferred by the dying spider that had granted him his weird powers.

Reaching up, Spider-Man attached himself to the archway over his head. A curling forward flip brought his boot soles into contact with the vertical face of the building. Scuttling around, he began climbing. His was the nervous speed of a daddy longlegs spider.

Reaching the fifteenth story, he clung there in a protective spidery crouch, keeping arms and legs close to his body.

The steely glint that had caught his eyes was still tossing about. He could see it clearly now: a red and purple costumed figure in miniature, falling in stages like a leaf.

Ant-Man!

Snapping out an arm, Spider-Man pressed down twice on an

electrode concealed in the palm of one gloved hand. From the thin aluminum nozzle peeping from his inner wrist came a spray of fine webbing.

It spread outward in a silvery-gray mesh, enveloping the falling figure.

Snapping the web back, Spider-Man sought the ground once more. While not many yards away, the giant tarantula fixed its many eyes on him. It began to stir on its disordered web. . . .

It happened too swiftly to resist. One moment, Henry Pym was a helpless human leaf drifting on ever-changing air currents, the next he was ensnared in a sticky mesh of spiderweb.

He fought as it enveloped him, but soon subsided, realizing that to tear free would only send him plunging back to earth.

His spider-silk–enmeshed form fell onto hard concrete. Pym looked up.

Kneeling over him was a bizarre figure, his head encased in a red pullover mask dominated by an orb web radiating out from between a pair of inhuman insectoid eyespots.

Spider-Man!

Webby fingers approached.

Reaching for his enlarging gas canister, Pym activated it.

Hissing gas spewed out, seeking his dialated nostrils. Whatever Spider-Man wanted with him, he was about to discover that Ant-Man was much *more* than he seemed. . . .

Spider-Man watched the tiny figure struggle in his web, fascinated. He had heard of the crime-fighting Ant-Man, but never imagined he was so tiny. How was it possible? He reached down to disentangle him from the web.

Without warning, the diminutive figure was enveloped in a whitish vapor. The webbing began to stretch and tear.

Like a high-tech genie erupting from some impossibly tiny lamp, a colorful figure exploded ito view. And Parker found himself looking up at an Ant-Man who now towered *over* him.

"Good grief," he blurted. "You grew!"

Ant-Man flung aside the clinging remains of webbing and blocked his fists. His voice was edged in steel.

"I don't know what you're up to, but you're about to meet your match in Ant-Man!"

"I don't want to meet my match," Spider-Man protested. "I just saved—"

A roundhouse right came flashing his way. Spidey's superior reflexes enabled him to dodge it easily. Then it was battle.

Ant-Man expected the element of surprise to vanquish his foe. A roundhouse right on the heels of his sudden expansion to man size would have taken any other foe off guard. Not this one.

Spider-Man jumped back with amazing speed. Pym recovered and drove in again. A haymaker this time.

A scarlet wrist blocked his blow. An irresistible force sent him spinning away with effortless ease.

Bouncing off a wall, Pym came on again.

He got a better sense of his foe in that moment. Spider-Man looked thin and undersized. More like a teenager than a man. Yet his speed and strength belied his slight frame.

Fists cocked, Pym feinted left. He never connected with the right.

Spider-Man jumped back like a jumping spider. His ready fists abruptly rotated 180 degrees, showing slivery gleams at each wrist.

Then Pym had a face full of webbing to contend with. The sticky strands clogged his helmet eyeholes. A blow he never saw coming sent him sprawling and a cocky, angry voice said, "That should teach you not to say thanks with your fists, chrome dome. Next time I'll just *let* you fall."

Reeling, helpless, Pym fumbled for his reducing vial. His one hope to escape the punishing blows lay in shrinking under them. . . .

Spidey saw Ant-Man's purple gauntlets grope for the set of canisters at his belt and said, "Not so fast, my friend."

Capturing Ant-Man's wrists in the long spidery fingers of one hand, he took hold of the vials with the other. A distinct click was followed by a ghostly vapor. It permeated his mask with its stinging odor. Recoiling, Parker held his breath, hoping he wasn't too late.

He was. At first, he had the sensation of his heart and lungs squeezing down. His panicky thought was: *poison gas!*

His brain went into freefall, like an elevator dropping. He tried to run, but his sense of balance was gone. He stumbled. There was no avoiding it, so he let himself fall.

When he recovered, Parker found himself looking across an expanse of concrete at a dazed-looking Ant-Man picking himself off the pavement. Between them lay a common, ordinary object. A shirt button. Only, it was the size of a manhole cover!

"Don't tell me . . ." he groaned.

Parker looked around. Up. Then down. And his heart sank. It was true. It was impossible, but it was true! Somehow, he and Ant-Man had together dwindled to the height of a fingertip!

"The gas . . ." he whispered. "It must have been the gas."

Spider-Man climbed to his feet, anger rising in his voice, "I don't know how you did that, buster. But I know one thing. You're going to undo it right *now*."

Splat!

A long coil of silvery material struck the spot between them, throwing off sticky white beads like Super-Glue.

Spider-Man looked up.

Far, far above, the giant tarantula clambered awkwardly down its web, eight glassy burning eyes fixed on them.

"Every man for himself!" Spider-Man cried.

He leapt. It was, considering his present size, the most spectacular leap of his life. He cleared the sidewalk—now as big as a football field—and landed splayed against the Goodman Tower.

Behind him, another strand of webbing struck with a ringing finality. Parker looked down from his spider's perch. Ant-Man was scrambling out of sight. But Spider-Man had no time to concern himself with the tiny super hero. At this size, the winds whipping through the plaza threatened to tear him loose.

Crawling around to the lee side of the building, Parker found the going was no better. Discovering a crack in a window, he slipped into that, thinking, *What am I going to do now? I can't go home to Aunt May like this. I should never have become Spider-Man.*

The thought had no sooner struck him than a smooth black head poked out of a cracked piece of window molding, and he found himself face to face with a carpenter ant which tilted its shiny eyes this way, then that, then advanced with sharp mandibles clicking angrily. . . .

•   •   •

Henry Pym felt the cool shadow looming over him like death descending. Eight burning eyes seemed to be seeking him. He stood rigid. A spider's visual acuity was good. If he played possum, maybe he would have a chance.

Down, down slipped the hairy monstrosity. . . .

If there was ever a time to think fast this is it, thought Spider-Man.

The ant was out of his nest now. Two more had appeared. They studied him with beady alien eyes.

"If Ant-Man can talk to ants, maybe I can too," he thought.

Lifting his hands in a gesture of appeasement, he said, "I come in peace. Savvy?"

The lead ant showed his understanding by rearing up on its back legs. It lunged. A set of mandibles clacked for his neck.

Holy smokes! He's trying to decapitate me! Spidey thought, ducking away. He tried climbing down onto the building's face, but whipping winds forced him back onto the ledge.

They circled him.

"All right," he growled, "I tried to be nice about this."

Spider-Man brought down his arms, dropped his hands, and curled his middle fingers to his palms.

From each wrist zipped a spray of gray threads that bloomed and expanded in contact with air. . . .

The tarantula's descent did not go unnoticed by the orbiting police helicopters. Word was relayed to Commissioner Maneely. He gave the order to open fire.

From the gingerly circling police choppers came the percussive rattle of automatic-weapons fire. Steel-jacketed slugs pummeled the thing's hirsute abdomen, to no effect. Some dark, oily leakage occurred. A few web strands dropped loose. But the giant arachnid continued working its ungainly way down to hard pavement, unfazed.

In the tumult of that first pass, Henry Pym saw his opportunity. Racing across the plaza, he reached one of the now-slack hanging web strands. He took hold of it in his mesh gloves and began climbing hand over hand.

With the tarantula this close to the ground, it wasn't an impossible climb. . . .

•   •   •

The ants recoiled under the spray of webbing. Twisting and struggling, they retreated. But Spider-Man had no time to catch his breath, much less congratulate himself.

For out of the nest poured six replacement soldiers. They fanned out, mandibles sprung wide apart.

If this keeps up, I'm going to be out of web-fluid before they run out of ants, he thought, panic rising in him.

Another helicopter pass made the tarantula shake dumbly in its web. Henry Pym clung to the fiercely vibrating strand too. Another foot and he would reach the brute.

If only the monster remained distracted long enough not to notice him. . . .

They were pouring toward him, pincerlike mandibles scissoring in a mechanical fury. Spidey took out the lead soldier with a jet of webbing. It stumbled blindly past him, going off the window ledge. Its faint squeal trailed off into eternity. The sound made Spider-Man shiver. It was only an ant, but its cry of distress had sounded so . . . human.

The strand broke. It simply parted with a snap and a snarl and in that instant between both warning sounds, Ant-Man launched himself at the hairy leg that quivered just out of reach.

It was the hairiness that saved his life. His fingers came into contact with a clump of bristle, closing desperately. Pym scampered up the leg even as the tarantula, apparantly wounded by the assault of police bullets, slowly, painfully backed up in its sky-spanning web, assuming a horizontal position.

The dorsal side was literally a forest through which Ant-Man trekked, searching for any sign of exploitable weakness.

The ants had surrounded him. Parker had pasted three more with his web-fluid, then his right web-shooter ran dry. The left was good for one last sticky shot before they came pouring over him. There wouldn't be time to load replacement cartridges from his undercostume utility belt. His heart pounded in his chest.

Wait a minute! I'm as small as a spider now, but maybe I still possess the proportionate strength of a spider. If I can reach that window, and wrench it up . . .

He set himself for an ant-clearing leap.

Then, his spider-sense began to tingle. The sensation was concentrated at his back. Heart in his mouth, he whirled.

And hovering there, menacing as a hornet—a flying ant.

Henry Pym's great love was hexapods. But in a larger sense all of the insect kingdom interested him. His knowledge of spiders was comprehensive. He knew the tarantula was native to South America and while they grew to startling size compared to spiders of the northern hemipshere, normally they did not achieve the size of this freak of nature whose hairy back he prowled.

Nor did they spin webs. They were burrow dwellers.

Ergo, this tarantula was not what it seemed.

It did not come as a great shock to Ant-Man when he found himself walking through oily black pools as he worked his way around the arachnid's strangely quiescent body. Machine oil.

He found a crack in the root of a rear leg made by a ricocheting bullet. The bristling hair—it felt like black Astroturf—had peeled away to expose a silvery fish-skin gleam.

Pym slipped into the crack, unnoticed.

The first thing he sensed was a constant throb. He worked carefully down a conduit of smooth plastic toward a greenish glow that pulsed in time to the throbbing. The tube terminated in an open space where a power plant pulsed and hummed, shedding a greenish glow.

It was a solid-state device, gleaming like a block of machined titanium. No wires or cables to pull. Nothing to break or shatter. Even if he reverted to full height, there were no loose objects to attack it with unless Pym wanted to sacrifice his fragile helmet.

Ant-Man worked his way forward to the tarantula's head.

Coming to a cloudy Plexiglas port, he saw on the other side a hulking figure hunkered in a complicated nest of communications gear and although he couldn't see clearly, the bullet shape of the head looked distinctly familiar.

Turning on his cybernetic helmet, he got a rush of static. Interference.

That was all he needed to know. Pym began to wend his way out. To do what he had to do, he would need help. . . .

• • •

They were nipping at his ankles now. Kick as he might, Spider-Man knew the ants were determined to protect their nest at all costs. And behind him a more nimble foe hung on fluttering transparent wings. There was no reaching the window now.

He dropped into a coiled-spring crouch, and executed a tumbling backflip that took him high and back over the infinite abyss that was a twenty-story drop—magnified to Grand Canyon depth by his tiny size.

If he calculated right . . .

He had. His legs dropped on either side of the ant's midsection. Clamping his knees, he took hold of the feelers for want of reins and pulled back sharply.

The flying ant reared back. It bucked. All six legs kicked in six different directions. It tried to bite him. Spider-Man yanked its head around, and with his superior strength, he held on.

"Git along, little doggie!" he yelled in exhilarated relief.

Wings buzzing, the ant began climbing and Parker started wishing ants came equipped with saddles. The body was not as smooth as it looked to the naked eye.

He forgot his discomfort when he saw where the ant was taking him: straight toward the waiting tarantula!

"Out of the frying pan . . ." he muttered.

Crouched on the tarantula's back, Ant-Man roved the dial of his cybernetic helmet. The ant-frequency interference was heavy. But somewhere on the band there had to be a clear channel.

In his ear, he heard a tiny, staticky, *"I come."*

And a moment later, his nameless flying-ant steed fluttered into view. And not alone either.

It settled atop the mechanical spider, and there sat Spider-Man looking at him, blank eyed.

Ant-Man said, "Don't move. We're getting out of here."

"What you mean 'we,' paleface?"

But the weirdly costumed man held his position while Ant-Man climbed in front of him.

"Hang on," Pym warned.

"Do I have a choice? You're my only hope of ever wearing my shoes again, as opposed to living in them."

The ant lifted, zooming clear of the brooding arachnid that seemed completely oblivious to their presence.

Back on the ground out of sight of the police, Spider-Man and Ant-Man dismounted. An awkward minute passed while they sized one another up.

"So you're Ant-Man," Spider-Man said at last. "I thought you were some kinda kooky myth."

Ant-Man shook his helmeted head. "No myth. Just a man."

Spider-Man jerked a webbed thumb skyward. "I have nothing to do with that thing up there."

"I know."

"You do?"

"I know what that thing is now. Together we can defeat it. But you'll have to trust me."

"Trust *you*? Hey, pal, I'm Spider-Man. Thanks to J. Jonah Jameson's *Bugle* editorials, I'm wanted from here to Timbuktu."

Ant-Man patted the flying ant's head. "My friend here vouches for you."

"You really speak ant? This is getting nuttier by the minute."

"Settle down a minute, son. That tarantula is radiating a signal that prevents me from controlling my ant allies. Listen to my plan."

Moments later the two adventurers were standing back to back.

"No peeking, now," Peter Parker was saying as he removed his spider mask and tossed it over his shoulder. The spherical ant helmet dropped into his hands. He set it on his head.

Ant-Man—wearing the all-concealing mask of Spider-Man now—stepped into view, showing him the cybernetic helmet controls.

"I've tuned it to the arachnid wavelength," he said. "Just visualize what you want and repeat it into the mike."

"What do I say?" Parker asked.

"Try, 'Come here.' "

"Come here," Spider-Man said.

It didn't take long. Up from a sewer grate emerged a spraddle-legged zebra-striped spider. It crawled creepily toward them, its mouth parts twitching hungrily.

"Yeoow! Look at that thing. How do I make it go away?"

"Concentrate. Say, 'Go away.' "

Spider-Man said, "Shoo! Get lost. You're not wanted here."

The spider hesitated, then began retreating like a rejected puppy.

"This is one spider power I never dreamed of," Parker said, awe in his voice.

"It's one you'll need if we're to defeat the mastermind behind that tarantula. Are you ready?"

"Ready as I'll ever be," Parker said shakily.

Ant-Man seemed to start. "Spider-Man . . . afraid of spiders?"

"I'm not afraid of spiders," he snapped. Under his breath, he added, "As long as I'm bigger than them. . . ."

In his robot-control cockpit, a bulky figure angrily snapped switches. His voice was growing hoarse as he spoke into the impulse-converter mike.

"Spider-Man. Can you hear me? I have chosen this elaborate method of attacting your attention for a purpose. I wish to join forces with you against our common foe, the Ant-Man. Spider-Man, I know you are in the vicinity. Show yourself to the Tarantula."

Camera ports at various points about the robot tarantula's hide showed a three-hundred-and-sixty-degree view of his surroundings. There had been no sign of the colorful human spider since he and Ant-Man traded blows just before vanishing in a swirl of vapor. . . .

Camera #13 showed movement. Behind the roof parapet of the Goodman Towers, a scarlet face peeped. Dominated by oblique blank eyes, it was featureless except for its orb-web pattern.

"Ah, there you are." Into the mike, he said, "Welcome, my future partner in mischief. Do not be shy. The Tarantula is delighted to make your acquaintance at last."

Peter Parker didn't know whether he was leading the line of spiders up the web strand or being pursued by them. Every time he looked back over his shoulder, he felt a chill as their myriad eyes regarded him with an alien light. But they had come when he summoned them.

"Keep marching, you guys," he called into his mike.

Under his feet, the metallic web strand began to wobble.

"Don't tell me the cops are taking potshots again," he groaned.

It wasn't the police. The tarantula was moving, reorienting itself on its bouncing web to face the Goodman Towers.

Looking up, Parker saw a familiar face peering over the rooftop. His own.

No wonder the police are out to get Spider-Man, he thought to himself. *I look as friendly as a Halloween goblin.*

He kept climbing. If Ant-Man kept their mutual foe distracted long enough, this would all be over soon.

Reaching the tarantula's head, Parker picked a glassy eye at random and kicked at it. It spiderwebbed, appropriately enough. A second kick opened a crack. Small to a human, it was large enough to admit him.

Well, what do you know about that? Ant-Man was right. I do retain my full strength at this size.

Pointing to the crack, Parker said, "All right, men. Get in there and go get 'em—whoever they are."

And as the column of spiders scuttled in through the hole, Parker moved to the rear of the hairy behemoth, happy to leave his eerie allies behind.

The leg joint seam was exactly where Ant-Man had said it would be. Parker slipped in, made his way down the conduit, and found the power plant, pulsing with an eerie emerald glow.

Around his waist, he wore Ant-Man's vial-carrying belt. He found the stud of the right vial and pressed it.

The gas hit his lungs like a shot of ammonia. He jerked in response before surrendering to the exploding sensation that told him every cell in his body was expanding to its natural size.

Once more his full height, Parker went to work on the power plant. His first punch brought a satisfying crunch. The engine's steady throb skipped a beat. So he followed up with a one-two punch that made the entire tarantula shudder. Still, it defied his spider-strength. He redoubled his efforts.

The bullet-headed man concealed in the tarantula's head paid no mind to the first bite. He thought he had sat on a Plexiglas shard that had fallen from one of the robot's many overhead eyeports of two-way glass. He was too intent upon communicating with the maddeningly unresponsive Spider-Man to wonder what had caused the damage in the first place. A bullet strike, probably. One was bound to do minor damage.

The second bite made him slap at his pudgy fingers. At the third, he slapped at the rolls of fat on the back of his thick neck. Creepy, thready fingers seemed to be playing over the apex of his bald head.

He jumped to a logical conclusion: ants! But how could that be? He had the ant frequencies jammed.

Then a lazy spider slipped silently down a thin thread of spider silk before his widening eyes, triggering a primal fear. Certain spiders are venomous.

"Get away from me!" he hollered, swatting at the one before his eyes with his mike. "I did not summon you, but Spider-Man!"

Others dropped onto his skull.

And at his back came the dull thud of a blow. Another. He looked over his shoulder. Through the cloudy Plexiglas, he saw a bizarre figure in the engine room. Ant-Man. No, Spider-Man. No, Ant-Man! The intruder wore Ant-Man's helmet. But he was the size of an ordinary human, and was making a shambles of the power plant with his scarlet—*webbed?*—fists.

All at once, the control board went dead and his skin was crawling with vermin.

It was an old-fashioned kick that silenced the power plant. Parker had skinned the knuckles beneath his red gloves raw trying to knock it out. A final frustrated furious kick finished the job.

The engine room went dark. He fumbled for the reducing vial. "Gas, don't let me down now. . . ."

The tarantula shook, shuddered—and the floor seemed to drop out from beneath his boots.

No time for a careful exit, he thought. Climbing atop the wrecked power plant, he felt around the roof. His questing fingers found a rivet head. Then a seam where two plates joined.

Two hard upward blows popped rivets and buckled the seam. A third broke through to daylight. And taking hold of the tear with both hands, Parker ripped downward with all his might.

A pure vertical leap brought him to the top of the hairy back.

The air was filled with police helicopters. They rattled around like flustered ungainly pelicans. Unseen hands thrust automatic weapons into the side doors.

The muzzles began stuttering fire and noise.

Parker shot a web-line from each wrist. They struck Goodman Towers with a satisfying smack.

Then he stepped off into space, praying a stray round didn't snap his lifeline. . . .

The last thing the man calling himself the Tarantula concerned himself with was the hammer of bullets. There was no power. Stuck in his cramped control nest, he had no defense against spiders. In fact, he thoroughly detested spiders.

The robot tarantula suddenly listed. It dipped alarmingly.

"What's happening now?" he moaned.

Out one of the overhead eyeports, he spied Spider-Man. No, it was Ant-Man. No, he was wearing Ant-Man's stylized costume— and Spider-Man's mask. And pulling loose one of the mooring strands anchoring the robot tarantula in its suddenly percarious position.

A moment later, a full-sized figure wearing Ant-Man's helmet but Spider-Man's costume began attacking another anchor cable on the opposite side.

Slapping at a spider tormenting his throat, he groaned. *I miscalculated. They are not enemies, but obviously in league with one another. I have failed. And so must save myself.*

Reaching under the control board, he found a mechanical lever, and yanked hard.

The seat gave an upward slamming kick. The multiple-eyed canopy over his head popped off just in time to prevent his pointed head from being pulped.

Atop the Goodman Towers, Peter Parker saw the tarantula's head come apart. Propelled by a battery of rockets, a broad thronelike seat roared out of the exposed cockpit.

"Now I've seen everything," he exploded. "A robot tarantula equipped with optional ejection seat!"

The seat soared into the sky. Parker caught a fleeting glimpse of a green-clad frog of a man with a bald, egg-shaped skull looking like an unhappy Humpty Dumpty come to life.

The ejection seat climbed the sky until its rockets shut down. Then rear-mounted thrusters kicked in, and the fantastic figure went screaming out over the Atlantic—making his escape.

• • •

Joining Ant-Man on the roof of the Excelsior Building, Parker asked, "Who was that joker?"

"He calls himself Egghead," Ant-Man explained.

"That tells me a lot."

"He's a nuclear scientist who went renegade. I fought him once before. He cracked the secret of my abilty to communicate with ants, and attempted to turn them against me. He failed because my ants are my allies, not my slaves."

"So what was his game?"

"He thought he could team up with you to defeat me."

"What gave him a crazy idea like that?" Parker exploded.

Ant-Man touched the Spider-Man mask on his face.

"You don't exactly come across as someone children and dogs easily warm up to."

Behind the microphone suspended before his mouth, Parker grinned sheepishly. "Point taken."

Spider-Man looked out over the horizon where a burning red dot was fast dwindling.

"I have a hunch he'll be back," he said.

"I'll be waiting," Ant-Man said grimly. "Now we have an exchange to make."

Back to back, they traded headgear. When they were once more caparisoned in their correct uniforms, they stood regarding each other.

"I've had some wild adventures before," Parker said, "but this one takes the cake. Never imagined it was possible to communicate with spiders."

"Nor did I until I stumbled across the frequency." His blue eyes narrowed. "You know, I could rig up a spider-helmet for you—"

Parker threw up his hands in mock horror. "Thanks, but no thanks. The truth is, up close and personal, spiders creep me out."

Smiling, Ant-Man put out his hand. Spider-Man took it. Their handshake started tentatively, but was firm as they unclasped.

"I have a hunch we'll meet again," Ant-Man said.

"We make a good team, all right. Despite what you might read in the *Daily Bugle*, I'm on your side."

With that Spider-Man turned, shot out a string of webbing, and launched himself out into space.

Ant-Man watched him go. Then, looking to the sky, he sent out the signal that summoned his faithful flying ant as he again inhaled the gas that made him one with the ants.

AFTER THE FIRST DEATH...

Tom DeFalco

Illustration by Ron Frenz & Patrick Olliffe

He was twelve stories above East Twenty-seventh Street, upside down, and in midswing between two silken strands of artificial webbing when it began to rain. Beneath his mask, frustration lit the face of Peter Parker. It was going to be a long, cold night.

In the months since the teenager had gained his amazing abilities from the bite of a radioactive spider, Peter Parker had come to enjoy being Spider-Man. He thrilled to the *thwip* of his web-shooters and the satisfying *splat* as the webbing anchored itself upon a distant ledge. He reveled in the dizzying heights that would have once terrified him. He delighted in streaking across the New York skyline with an effortless grace envied by even the greatest Olympic gymnasts. He loved the rush of the wind, and the occasional gasps of people on rooftops startled by his sudden passing. Yes, there were times being Spider-Man was an absolute blast.

Tonight wasn't one of them.

The prospect of spending the next few hours in a soggy costume held little appeal to Peter. Under normal circumstances, he might have given up as soon as the first raindrops tapdanced down his back. Not tonight. He had a job to do, and his sense of responsibility would not allow him to quit.

The night had started routinely enough. After eating dinner, completing his homework, and chatting with Aunt May for an hour or so about his day in high school, Peter had given her a quick peck on the cheek, and headed off to bed. She retired to her own room about twenty minutes later.

Napping until midnight, Peter finally forced himself awake, slipping out of bed and into the web-covered costume he kept hidden beneath his mattress. The sleepy streets of Forest Hills were soon far behind as Spider-Man employed his unique style of commuting, swinging from rooftop to rooftop toward the brighter lights of Manhattan.

Peter was anxious to get started. The final deadline for last month's mortgage payment on the house in Forest Hills was fast approaching. So was the first deadline on this month's. So was Aunt May's birthday. And Peter was flat broke.

His plan was simple enough. Dividing the city into a grid, he'd swing overhead until the extrasensory danger instinct—which Peter had dubbed his spider-sense—began tingling at the base of his skull. Though he still didn't understand exactly how it worked, this sense somehow warned him of the potential of immediate danger. It was invaluable during a fight, combining with his extraordinary reflexes to help him avoid injury. Peter had also learned over the past months that he could use it to detect the presence of dangerous individuals. In the angry hours before dawn, he was hoping to find a few.

Though he felt more than a little guilty about wanting to run across a crime in progress, Peter was desperate to score a few action shots of himself as Spider-Man, photos taken by the automatic camera presently attached to his belt buckle. He'd try to peddle them to J. Jonah Jameson, the publisher of the *Daily Bugle.*

Jonah was no fan of Spider-Man. The blustery millionaire was the web-head's most outspoken critic, often denouncing him as a freak and a public menace. Unfortunately for Jonah, a mathematical correlation existed between the wall-crawler's presence in the *Bugle* and an increase in its newsstand sales. As much as he hated Spider-Man, Jonah had a greater love for money and the *Bugle.* He proved a voracious market for Peter's pictures, especially shots that helped reinforce the less-than-flattering image Jonah kept pitching to the public.

Peter couldn't worry about his public image now. He was cold and wet, and his costume was starting to sag, bunching in most uncomfortable ways.

Arcing toward Madison Avenue, he directed his swing westward, intending to edge up toward Broadway and the flower district. That's when he first noticed it, a familiar and welcomed tingle which seemed to be urging him southward.

A restless scowl simmered on the face of Kent Weisinger. Hunching his massive shoulders, the great bull of a man tried to prevent the rain from seeping past the collar of his leather jacket and splattering down his neck. Though hardly the happiest of individuals under any circumstances, his less-than-sunny disposition had more than sufficient justification tonight. He didn't like standing on a rainy rooftop in the middle of the night. Nor was he particularly fond of playing pack mule and lugging nearly a hundred pounds of burglary equipment up a fire escape. But, mostly his annoyance riveted on his brother Wayne.

Older by two years, Wayne had always been the brains of the pair. He had planned their first burglary many years ago, a break-in through the back door of a supermarket which had netted them eight six-packs of beer, ten cartons of cigarettes, a family-sized bag of pretzels, and a half-dozen cupcakes.

Cupcakes, Kent remembered, still harboring a grudge from that long-ago night. Cupcakes that Wayne had hogged all for himself, not even offering to share.

Sure, Wayne had picked out the store and cased the layout, but it was Kent who had smashed in the door. Kent who had hauled away the heavy stuff. Kent who had supplied the muscle. And Kent who always finished a job with the feeling that he had been cheated.

Kent's eyes flashed with animosity as he watched his brother disassemble the rooftop alarm system of Stockbridge Jewelers. Following their familiar routine, Wayne had targeted and organized this heist. He had somehow gotten hold of the jewelry store's security plan, and had dragged Kent out into the night, making him stand in the cold and the rain.

And why? Kent asked himself. *So that he can shaft me again!*

He had little choice, though. Kent had been fired from the latest in a series of crummy jobs—which Wayne knew full well. Even the lousy cut Wayne gave him beat nothing at all.

Still, Kent desired nothing more than to smash his brother's wolfish face, to revel in the snap of his bones and the anguish of his cries. He restrained himself. His temper was what kept getting him fired from every job he'd ever had.

"Almost ready," Wayne mumbled.

"About time, mastermind," Kent said. "I'm gonna catch pneumonia if you don't hurry up."

"I've got good news for you fellas."

The unexpected comment had come from somewhere behind Kent, and he immediately whipped his head in its direction. His eyes bulged when he recognized its speaker.

"You don't have to stand out in this cold rain any longer," Spider-Man said. He squatted on the building's most distant parapet, one hand perched between his legs, keeping balance on the barrier of brick and mortar. "I've come to wrap you in some nice, warm, water-resistant webbing and bundle you off to the nearest police station."

Without another word, the super hero sprang from his position, his legs catapulting him into the air like twin pistons. Cartwheeling across the roof, he planted both feet in Kent's stomach, greeting the massive Weisinger with more than sufficient force to send him sprawling.

"Get up, you idiot," Wayne growled. "We gotta flatten this little freak before he ruins everything."

"Many have tried, chum," Spider-Man said as he backflipped out of the path of Wayne's hastily thrown haymaker. "Few have succeeded."

Spider-Man pushed off the roof with both hands, leaping away from the smaller of his two opponents. Peter had already positioned his camera on the ledge of a nearby building which overlooked the rooftop of Stockbridge Jewelers. Hoping his relatively inexpensive equipment could snap clear pictures despite the ever-increasing rain, Peter deliberately sought to stretch this fight for as long as possible. He couldn't return to Forest Hills empty handed. While the capture of two would-be burglars would never be front-page news, Peter believed he could still con Jameson into buying a snapshot if it was dramatic enough. The longer the battle lasted, the more photos would be taken by his automatic camera, and the greater his likelihood of scoring a saleable shot.

Relying on his spider-sense to warn him of danger and his incredible reflexes to keep him out of harm's way, he carefully planned his moves like an experienced chess master. With lightning speed, Spider-Man sprang over one thief and darted behind the other. He backflipped and ricocheted off the roof. Forced to react to his flurry of activity, the two befuddled burglars were easily maneuvered into the proper positions for the greatest visual impact. Neither was aware that they were being photographed, nor could they lay a hand on him.

"What's wrong with you, Kent?" the small one asked. "Why can't you tag him?"

"You're such a genius, Wayne, tell me how," said Kent. "The guy's faster'n a snake."

"Boys! Boys! I hate to interrupt your friendly banter, but I'd appreciate it if you'd focus your attention on me for the next few minutes," Spider-Man said. "After we've finished here, I'm pretty sure the state will be glad to provide you with plenty of free time to resolve your personal issues.''

Launching himself off the building's chimney, Spider-Man rocketed toward Wayne. The man barely had time to plant his feet in preparation for the impact. He was totally unprepared when Spider-Man somersaulted directly in front of him. Instead of trying to knock the burglar backward, Spider-Man had positioned himself so that his downward momentum would drive his feet into Wayne's shoulders, propelling the man to his knees and facefirst into a growing puddle of murky rainwater.

Then the big one, Kent, unleashed a hail of punches, none of which found their intended target. Spider-Man nimbly leapt out of range, bounded off the nearest parapet, and returned with a flying kick to Kent's jaw.

"Do something, Kenny!" Wayne begged. "You're supposed to be the muscle, but the web-head's wiping the floor with you!"

"Give the big guy a break, pal," Spider-Man said as he pivoted back toward Wayne. Beneath his mask, Peter's eyes darted toward the building that held his camera. There couldn't be much film left. Time to stage a big finish and wrap things up.

"You're useless, Kenny!" Wayne shouted as he backed against the parapet. "Always were and always will be!"

"Shut up!" Kent responded, splitting blood as he struggled to his feet. "I'm gonna end this once and for all!"

With a bestial roar, Kent charged forward.

Though distracted by thoughts of his last few photos, Peter immediately sensed the danger rushing toward him. Without a moment's hesitation, Spider-Man instantly sprang twenty feet in the air, casually backflipping well out of Kent's path.

However, the enraged burglar didn't stop, didn't even attempt to slow his forward momentum on the rainslicked rooftop. He crashed into his brother, hurtling Wayne outward. Out beyond the building's parapet. Out into the gaping chasm which terminated five stories below.

Gasping and cursing, Wayne clawed the air in futile panic as he tumbled toward the impassive ground.

Reacting with the speed of thought, Spider-Man covered the distance to the building's edge with a single leap, his webshooters poised to snatch the plunging figure. But, even as he aimed, even as his fingers instinctively closed upon the palm switches to unleash his webbing, he realized that he was already too late. He could only watch in helpless horror as the panicked cries abruptly ended with a sudden and sickening finality.

With the slow and deliberate movements of a man who desperately wished he were anywhere else, Spider-Man shot out a web-line, and lowered himself to the ground. A small crowd of early risers had already begun to gather by the time he reached the street.

The rain and cold slashed across Spider-Man. Silent, his emotions hidden by an expressionless mask, he stood before the bloodied and twisted remains of what had once been a living, breathing human being.

Though his mind was a maelstrom of what-ifs and might-have-beens, he eventually began to hear the whispers. They flickered at the edge of his consciousness, leaping wildly among the onlookers who surged forward for a closer view of the tragedy.

"Did you see?"

"He hurled that poor man off the roof!"

"Murdered him in cold blood!"

"Jameson's right!"

"He's a freak!"

"A menace!"

Then, off in the distance, the wail of an approaching police siren suddenly jolted Spider-Man from his stupor and galvanized him into action. Even as he turned toward the safety of the beckoning rooftops, he noticed the crowd shrinking away from him. They eyed him nervously, fearfully, as if half expecting to see him begin foaming at the mouth.

Spider-Man darted up the side of the building that held his camera. He ran from the police, from the the anxious men and women who viewed him with growing apprehension and desperate accusation, from the broken body of a man named Wayne. He attempted to escape the guilt that hammered at his mind and ripped through his soul like a great spiked mace.

He was halfway back to Forest Hills before he remembered that there had been a second burglar.

Jeannette Weisinger tried to ignore the pounding at her door. Someone had a lot of nerve, and could just take a flying leap. It was much too early for company.

"Open up, Jeannie! It's me! Kenny!"

Recognizing her brother-in-law's voice, Jeannette slowly attempted an upright position. "Wayne ain't here, Ken. The cheating bum don't live here no more."

"I *know.* Something happened, Jeannie. Something bad. You'd better open up. We gotta talk."

"All right. I'm coming already." Jeannette wrapped herself in an old cotton robe, and was soon stumbling out of her bedroom.

"How about a cup of coffee?" Kent asked as he scooted into the apartment, trying to avoid Jeannette's pointed stare.

"You want coffee? Go down to the deli. In the meantime, tell me about Wayne. Where's my husband?"

"He's . . . dead."

"You kidding me? This some kind of con so that he can skip out on money he owes?"

"Come on, Jeannie, don't be that way. I'm telling you straight. The two of you might have had problems, but you were still married. He's really dead," said Kent. "I wanted to warn you before the cops came."

"Cops?"

"A job went sour, and Wayne . . . well . . . he was in the wrong place at the wrong time."

Jeannette steadied herself against the kitchen table. She had last seen Wayne two days ago for the first time since she kicked him out three months previous. He had the same wolfish grin, spoke the same stale promises, and ran through the same tired routine.

"What about me? Let's be practical, Kenny. Wayne may be gone, but I still got expenses. He was your brother. Your partner and your blood. You got a responsibility to make good."

"I tell you the man's dead, and all you care about is who's gonna square his debts. Wayne was right about you, lady. You're solid ice."

"Gimme a break, Kenny. I mean, who's cranking who? You hated the jerk as much as I did. He was a backstabbing, bottom-dealing bum. He cheated on me, and was always ripping you off."

"Yeah," said Kent, lowering his voice to a whisper. "But he was still my brother."

"Sit down. I want to hear exactly how it happened," Jeannette said as she began fussing around her coffee maker. "You mentioned cops earlier. If the police killed him, we might be able to sue the city.''

"It wasn't the cops," he mumbled.

"All right, so who killed him?"

Kent gazed down at his hands, unable to face her.

"Come on, Kenny. Spit it out. Who did him?"

"It was Spider-Man," said Kent. "Spider-Man."

Jeannette had a plan percolating long before the coffee finished brewing.

He was twenty feet in the air, his eyes growing wide beneath his mask, as the big burglar smashed into the smaller one, propelling him over the edge of the building, and down, down, down.

Peter's eyes shot open. He hadn't realized he'd been asleep. A quick glance at his clock confirmed that only a few minutes had passed since the last time he looked. His sleep had been a series of brief and violent snatches. His dreams kept returning him to the rainy rooftop, kept replaying the fight over and over like a movie caught in an endless loop.

If only he had leapt toward the larger burglar instead of away from him. If only he'd been concentrating on the fight instead of worrying about his pictures. If only he'd gone home when it had first begun to rain. If only—

"Peter? Are you awake?" Aunt May stood at the door to his room, a look of concern on her face.

"Just dozing," Peter said, realizing that he'd again drifted off. "I guess it's time to get ready for school."

"Do you really think that's wise? You don't look well this morning. You may have a fever."

"I'm fine, Aunt May," said Peter.

"I'll bet you were having nightmares, and I can guess the cause. You were dreaming about that horrible Spider-Man. I warned you about taking those photographs of him. A fragile and impressionable boy like you shouldn't be exposed to such a disgusting creature." She paused, taking a small breath before continuing, "Although I don't see how you can avoid him. He's all they're talking about on the radio this morning."

"Wh-what are they saying?"

"He killed someone last night, and the police are finally going to toss him in prison like any other criminal.'' Before he could learn more, the phone rang and May bustled off to answer it.

Bile rose in Peter's throat as his stomach embarked on its own gymnastic routine. Being wanted by the police was an unexpected complication. Sure, he felt guilty for the burglar's death. The man would still be alive if Peter had only acted a bit more responsibly. But Spider-Man was no murderer. What was he going to do? How could he possibly prove his innocence?

"Pick up the phone, Peter,'' Aunt May shouted from the kitchen. "It's that nice Mr. Jameson.''

Nice didn't belong in any sentence that described J. Jonah Jameson. The man was as cuddly as a rattlesnake and as warm as a glacier.

"Parker, my boy,'' he began. "How is my favorite freelance photographer this morning?''

"Uh, fine, sir.''

"You didn't happen to be out last night? In, say, the vicinity of Stockbridge Jewelers? There was an incident involving that slimebag Spider-Man, and I was wondering if you happened to catch any of it on film.''

"Yeah, shot a whole roll.'' As soon as the words escaped Peter's mouth, he regretted them.

"Really? Why don't you stop by the *Daily Bugle* on your way to school? If the pictures are any good, I might be able to take them off your hands.''

Peter didn't respond. He had no intention of selling these pictures. He would find another way to earn the money he needed for the mortgage and Aunt May's birthday.

"You still there, Parker? I'll take the whole roll so that I have an exclusive.'' Jameson mentioned a figure. It was a generous offer by his usual standards, almost half of what Peter could have gotten from the *Bugle*'s major competitor.

But Peter remained silent. A man was dead because he hadn't acted properly.

"Talk to me, Parker. I'm sure we can come to terms. You've practically been like a son to me, and I'll prove it to you.'' Jameson raised his figure.

Peter didn't want to continue this conversation, but his mind couldn't think of the words to end it. All he knew was that it would be wrong to profit from his mistakes.

"Have you been negotiating with my enemies behind my back? I'll bet you already heard from Barney Bushkin at the *Globe*. I can't believe you'd do this to me, Parker," Jameson said, his voice rising with each word. "I need those photos. They prove I've been right about that web-headed weirdo all along. I've got to have them no matter how much you're asking."

Jameson shouted another figure, an amount sufficient to cover the mortgage through the end of the year, with plenty left over for nonessentials like birthdays and holidays.

Peter was torn. A life had been lost. It would be wrong for him to capitalize on this tragedy. But he had responsibilities. He couldn't allow his personal feelings to affect his judgment, to keep him from acting in Aunt May's best interests.

So he accepted Jameson's offer.

"You're a thief, Parker. This is outright robbery, and you know it," Jameson said, his entire body twitching as he signed the ludicrously high-paying voucher. "You should be ashamed of yourself."

"I am, Jonah," said Peter. "More than you'll ever know."

For a moment, Jameson allowed himself to believe that Parker was actually considering a lower rate—a desperate hope that fizzled as the teenager snatched the voucher.

Jameson decided to take the high road, to forgive Parker for chiseling him out of a fair fee for the photos. The publisher could afford to be magnanimous, finding a small degree of comfort in the knowledge that he had already arranged to sell the pictures to the wire services for a tidy profit. A profit which could have been so much tidier if Parker had only accepted his usual pittance.

"As long as you're here, there's someone you should meet," he said.

"I really have to get to school, Jonah."

"This will only take a minute, my boy," Jameson said with a smile. "She's the wife of the man Spider-Man murdered."

"His name was Wayne. I'm not going to say he was a saint. He wasn't. I'm not even going to say he had any legitimate reason for being on that rooftop. He didn't. But burglary is not punishable by death in this state." Jeannette Weisinger paused. "And certainly not at the hands of some crazy costumed nut. This is America, after all. Everyone is entitled to a fair trial.''

''Isn't she great, Parker?'' Jameson could hardly contain his joy, which obviously was growing as fast as Peter's depression. ''I've already arranged to print up a special edition of the *Bugle* that will feature your photos, and go on sale right after she makes her big announcement on the early evening news.''

''Announcement?'' Peter asked, trying to appear calm.

Jeannette said, ''I've decided to institute a civil action against Spider-Man for causing the wrongful death of my husband. The way I figure it, anybody who can afford to spend his nights fighting crime has got to be loaded. So I'm going to sue the spandex off him.'' Jeannette was obviously pleased with her own cleverness. Under other circumstances, Peter might have laughed. *My net worth probably won't get her a pack of gum.*

She continued: ''I came to Mr. Jameson for advice because everyone knows that he's a humanitarian. He introduced me to a lawyer who is already preparing the necessary papers.''

Peter Parker felt like he was being smothered, like a spider who had become trapped in his own web.

Between a lack of sleep and an overabundance of personal adversities, Peter was hardly a model student at Midtown High School that day. His attention wandered in Geometry class, he broke two test tubes in Biology lab, doodled through Social Studies, and almost dozed off in English Lit.

No sooner did the last bell sound the end of classes than Peter streaked for the nearest exit. He had a deposit to make.

At the edge of the campus, he noticed Flash Thompson. Flash was Midtown's star athlete, a man in love with the sound of his own voice. Hanging with his usual band of sycophants, Flash seemed jumpy, agitated.

''I don't care what evidence they say they've got,'' said Flash vehemently. ''Spidey's no murderer.''

Peter couldn't help but smile, his only one of the day. Though Flash had little use for a bookworm like ''puny Parker,'' he had always been Spider-Man's biggest booster. But this time he was wrong. Spider-Man was responsible for the death of Wayne Weisinger, and no one knew that better than Peter.

''Maybe the wall-crawler didn't actually kill the man,'' said Peter. "But that doesn't mean he shouldn't be held accountable for what happened."

"What are you talking about, Parker? Either Spidey pitched this Wayne Whatever off the roof, or he didn't," said Flash, his finger stabbing toward Peter's chest. "The web-slinger I know doesn't play executioner. He's an honest-to-gosh hero."

To prove his point, Flash listed the many times Spider-Man had proven himself, recounting the web-head's victories over such foes as the Chameleon, the Vulture, Dr. Octopus, Dr. Doom, and Electro.

"That could be the trouble," Peter said as he slowly walked away. "Maybe he was too busy playing the big-shot hero and thinking of his press notices, when he should have been paying attention to the job at hand."

Reaching the bank before closing time, Peter paid the mortgage and the accumulated late fees, arranged for the next few months to be automatically deducted from his checking account, and still had sufficient cash to wow Aunt May on her birthday.

Though not much of a shopper, Peter could finally afford to buy his beloved guardian something special. He reasoned that a little mindless shopping might be in order. It could help soothe his jangled nerves and allow him to approach his problems with a fresh perspective.

After spending almost a full hour going from shop to shop, Peter finally admitted defeat. No matter what he looked at, his mind kept drifting back to thoughts of Wayne Weisinger's twisted body. To a lesser extent, he also worried over the widow's promised lawsuit, and the fact that the police were now hunting him. But his failure to save Wayne remained uppermost in his thoughts.

Near Carnegie Hall, he gave up, and was about to go down into the subway, planning to head home to Forest Hills, when he heard a woman scream.

A mugger had grabbed her purse and was racing away. Though the thief had a two-block head start on him, Peter realized that he could easily duck into an alley on Fifty-sixth Street, change into his costume, and attempt to catch up via his ever-reliable rooftop express.

But he hesitated. What if the very sight of Spider-Man caused

a streetwide panic? What if the mugger tried to avoid capture
and accidentally ran out into traffic? What if the police arrived
on the scene? What if . . . ?

Three blocks away, a slightly overweight gentleman responded
to the woman's cries, and tackled the thief to the applause of
everyone present. Everyone except Peter Parker. With many a
backward glance, he slowly descended the shadowed stairwell.

Jeannette wasn't happy. Not only had she returned to her apartment to discover Kent still sprawled across her sofa, but the
empty bottles on her coffee table attested to a successful raid on
her liquor cabinet.

"Wake up, you freeloading creep. This ain't no flophouse."

"Take it easy, Jeannie. And keep it down," Kent mumbled.
"Can't you see I'm in mourning?"

"All I want to see is you heading out that door."

"How'd things go at the *Bugle?*"

"Even better than expected," said Jeannette triumphantly.
"Old man Jameson is so hot to nail Spider-Man, he gobbled up
my act like a kid with a candy bar. He's handling everything. Says
nobody's gonna care about what Wayne was doing on that roof
when they get a load of those pictures of Spider-Man beating on
him. Jameson's even going to introduce me to a few book pub-
lishers. They say everybody gets their fifteen minutes of fame.
With a little luck, I could ride mine all the way to a movie of the
week. You're looking at a regular media darling."

"All this publicity may be great for your ego," said Kent as he
sat up on the couch. "When do we make any money off it?"

"*We* don't," said Jeannette. "*I* do."

She grabbed Kent by his right ear, twisting with all her
strength. "You see that door? Close it on your way out."

"But—but, Jeannie," Kent whined. "I thought we were a
team."

"You thought wrong. Wayne might have been a lazy, good-for-
nothing deadbeat," said Jeannette, "but *he* was the prize of the
litter."

A familiar scowl seared Kent's face as the door slammed shut
and numerous locks shot into place. Jeannette was headed for a
major score, and sharing wasn't a likely prospect.

At least when his brother cheated him, Wayne usually had the courtesy to do it behind Kent's back.

Peter Parker stood in the center of his bedroom in Forest Hills, but he was truly lost. He didn't know what to do or where to turn. Ever since he had gained his amazing powers, he resorted to web-swinging whenever his personal problems threatened to overwhelm him. That didn't work when web-swinging *was* the problem.

Peter closed his eyes, remembering a vow he had once made. Shortly after he first became Spider-Man, he had foolishly allowed a burglar to escape a pursuing security guard. The same burglar eventually murdered Peter's uncle. As a result, Peter had sworn that no innocent person would ever again be made to suffer because Spider-Man had failed to act.

It had never occurred to him that anyone would suffer because of Spider-Man's acts.

Wayne Weisinger didn't fit any known definition of innocent. He had suffered because Peter had acted irresponsibly, had padded a fight for a few lousy pictures.

Well, Peter had gotten his pictures. He also had the image of a broken and bloodied corpse branded on his soul.

Angry and disgusted with himself, Peter lashed out, accidentally hitting a large science text that caromed off the wall, and crashed to the floor.

"Are you all right, Peter?" Aunt May scurried into the room, curious and concerned. "Were you hurt?"

"I'm fine," said Peter, with more than a little shame. "I couldn't get a science problem to work out right, and I guess I just lost my temper."

"You'll never accomplish anything by getting frustrated with yourself, young man. Something's giving you a hard time, you face it and deal with it," Aunt May said as she thrust the heavy book back into her nephew's hands. "Problems are supposed to be difficult. That's how they got their name. Nobody likes them, but life would be pretty boring without them."

"Right now I'd settle for boring," said Peter. "It's gotta beat knowing that you really messed up."

A mischievous light twinkled in May's eyes, and she said, "Sounds like someone I know is shocked to learn he isn't perfect.

Everybody makes mistakes, Peter. You just try to learn from your
failures as best you can, and you move on. You'll always get another chance to do better as long as you keep at it.''

Peter lowered his head, trying to hide his embarrassment. He
knew better than to argue with Aunt May. Especially when she
was right.

Kent had spent the afternoon on a scenic tour of New York's
seedier locales. He eventually found himself at a diner that overlooked Stockbridge Jewelers. From his booth, he could view the
general area where Wayne had landed.

He was polishing off a really lousy cheeseburger when he saw
something disturbing. A news truck had pulled up, and was in-
terviewing passersby.

Kent dropped some bills on the table and made his way toward
the exit. He assumed, correctly, that the reporters were doing a
followup on Wayne.

*That's right, everyone's talking about Wayne and Spider-Man and
after that press conference they'll all be talking about Jeannie, too. They'll
all get on the news and on the front page, and Jeannie'll get her million
bucks.*

And I'm stuck spending my last five bucks on a crummy cheeseburger.

A large number of people had gathered around the news
truck, being asked if they saw the "incident," and what they
thought. *Wait'll they hear my answer,* Kent thought. Then he
smiled, and added to himself, *And wait'll my backstabbing sister-in-
law hears it.*

Eventually, the reporter asked Kent, "Did you see anything on
the morning of the murder?''

"I certainly did," said Kent. "In fact, you might say I had the
best view of all.''

Peter Parker had taken the subway into Manhattan to take another stab at finding Aunt May's present, and was climbing up
from the station when he first heard what sounded like gunshots.
Some people hear a gunshot and mistake it for a car backfiring.
Peter knew the difference.

He also knew what he had to do.

A quick jog took him to an alley. A twenty-foot standing leap
deposited him on a fire escape. He reached the roof barely ten

seconds later, and was soon kicking off his shoes, checking the cartridges in his web-shooters, pulling on a familiar web-covered mask, and webbing his civilian clothes into a handy backpack.

As he began traveling along the rooftops, he heard the shouts and accusations directed at him from the streets below. He did his best to ignore them, pushing them to the back of his mind where they joined his own doubts and insecurities. The casual arrogance that he had once possessed was gone, never to be recaptured.

But no one would suffer today because Spider-Man had failed to act.

The police car was parked at an angle in the center of the street. One officer was down, her face twisting as she pressed her hands tightly to her right thigh, desperately trying to staunch the blood that stained her fingers. The other shouted encouragement as he steadied his gun on the hood of the police car, aiming at a grocery store's shattered storefront.

A triple somersault planted the web-swinger beside the injured policewoman. Before either officer could react, Spider-Man had begun to bind her wound with a makeshift bandage composed of equal parts webbing and the shirt from his backpack.

"What's the story with the grocery store?" Spider-Man asked as he studied his handiwork. It would hold until the paramedics arrived.

"Three gunmen and maybe a dozen hostages," said the policeman. "They caught us by surprise, started shooting, and forced us to duck for cover before we could radio for backup."

"You know if that store has a drop ceiling?"

"I think so."

"In case you've forgotten, web-head," said the injured female cop, "there's a warrant for your arrest."

Spider-Man hesitated. He had forgotten that. He'd had problems with the cops before, but now they had an actual warrant.

Then the hesitation passed. It didn't matter what the police thought of him, anymore than it mattered what Jameson or Jeanette Weisinger thought. There were people in trouble. Spider-Man had the power to help, which meant he had the responsibility to help. That was all that mattered.

"You can arrest me after I free the hostages."

"Hold on," the policewoman said. "We don't want a replay of the other night."

"Trust me," he whispered. "Neither do I."

He sprang to the building directly across the street from the besieged grocery store, climbed up the the side of the wall, and began circling toward his true destination.

He just hoped the male officer was correct about the drop ceilings.

J. Jonah Jameson felt like a fool whenever he was forced to wear makeup. He did, however, accept it as a necessary evil. The lights in the television studio would make him appear pale and weak, and a crusading journalist needed to project strength and commitment. Jameson was very concerned with his public image, and would soon stage his greatest personal triumph.

He would introduce the world to Jeannette Weisinger, the grieving widow of the man Spider-Man had murdered in cold blood. She would shed the appropriate tears on this live television press conference, and announce her multimillion-dollar civil suit against the annoying web-spinner.

Whether or not the suit had any real merit was of no concern to Jameson. He only cared that it would generate sufficient publicity to make his special edition of the *Daily Bugle* an instant collector's item and hopefully spike his daily sales for the coming weeks.

Jameson had turned to study his introductory notes when a harried figure enter his dressing room.

"We got problems, Mr. Jameson," said a nervous individual with blond hair and a beard whom Jonah vaguely recognized as a new member of his editorial staff.

"Can't this wait until after the news conference?"

"I don't think you're going to want to hold this conference after you hear what just went down."

"I told you Spider-Man would be vindicated," said Flash Thompson. "I never lost faith in him."

He proudly held up the morning edition of the *Daily Globe* which detailed Kent Weisinger's confession. Kent had admitted in a televised interview that he deliberately pushed his elder brother off the roof of Stockbridge Jewelers because of numerous past frustrations that climaxed during their battle with Spider-Man. After the interview, Kent turned himself in to the police.

While the *Daily Bugle* made no mention of Kent's revelation, nor the fact that Jeannette had dropped her civil action, Jameson's newspaper did feature exclusive photos of the web-head's daring rescue of a number of hostages in a midtown grocery store. According to the accompanying article, Spider-Man had entered the store through the floor above, had crawled along its drop ceiling, and had managed to subdue the gunmen before they even realized he was among them. The officers on the scene had tried to arrest Spider-Man afterward, unaware of Kent Weisinger's confession, but the wall-crawler got away.

"Admit it, Parker. You were wrong about Spidey," Flash said sincerely. "He's the greatest hero of all."

"I'm still not convinced. A real hero would have found a way to save Wayne Weisinger. He would have acted smarter, reacted quicker, or behaved more responsibly," said Peter Parker. "And that's something Spider-Man will have to live with for the rest of his life."

With that, Peter turned away, not giving Flash a chance to respond. He still saw Wayne's battered face in his dreams, and he expected to be visited by these nightmares for the rest of his life, but he couldn't worry about that now. He was on the hunt for the most perfect birthday present of all.

He was crossing the street that bordered Midtown High, passing the midpoint of the intersection, when it began to rain. Peter Parker merely hunched his shoulders, and ambled on. He didn't expect any relief for a long time, but he wouldn't let that deter him.

CELEBRITY

Christopher Golden & José R. Nieto

Illustration by Darick Roberston & Jeff Albrecht

With ten dollars in his bank account, Peter Parker stepped off the elevator and into the *Daily Bugle* newsroom looking for work. A couple of people waved hello, a few even mouthed the word, but nobody took more than cursory notice of his presence. In high school, he was "puny Parker," thanks to people like Flash Thompson. At the *Bugle*, he had more of a chance to make friends, despite his age, and despite the *Bugle*'s tyrannical publisher, J. Jonah Jameson.

Jonah ran a tight ship. That meant that nobody on staff said or did anything without Jonah signing off on it. Most were frightened of the cigar-chomping tyrant, with his salt-and-pepper flat top and tiny swatch of mustache.

Peter, though, wasn't scared of Mr. Jameson, which made the job easier. Besides, he liked being a news photographer, and he was getting pretty good at it. And a few others weren't afraid of Mr. Jameson, either: Ben Urich for one, a great reporter who lived for the news; fellow freelance photographer Phil Sheldon for another.

And then there was Betty. The pair of them had actually started dating, a turn of events that Peter could never have predicted a few months before.

Peter walked between rows of desks where writers typed furiously or stared at their computer screens. Even if they weren't busy, they were trained to look busy just in case Jameson came out of his office, hollering for somebody's head. Which he did several times a day, even if there was nothing to scream about. Jonah liked to keep his people on their toes.

"Good afternoon, Peter," Betty said as he approached her desk.

"Hey, Betty," he replied. "Is Mr. Jameson here? I was hoping to pick up some assignments this weekend."

Betty smiled warmly at him, and Peter felt himself flush slightly. He wondered if he'd ever grow tired of that smile. He doubted it.

Betty Brant was just a little older than Peter, but she'd dropped out of school when her mother had fallen ill. After her mother, who had been Jonah's secretary, passed on, there wasn't anybody with the patience to take her place. Except Betty, who had spent so much time at the office that she knew how to run Mr. Jameson's life almost as well as her mother had.

"Of course he's here, Peter," she said. "Why would he go anywhere else when he has such a plentiful source of victims?"

"That kind of day, huh?" he asked, eyebrows raised in sympathy.

"Oh, yeah."

As if on cue, the door to Jonah's office burst open and Jameson himself came storming into the newsroom.

"Miss Brant! Get Parker in here on the double! I've got the perfect—" He stopped short when he saw Peter standing by Betty's desk. "Parker! Excellent timing for once!" Jonah put an arm around Peter's shoulder as he escorted him back toward the elevator.

"Johnny Storm is taking that teenage movie star Heather Fox to an early dinner at Angelique's before her big premiere tonight. Get down there and snap some splashy celebrity photos," Jameson ordered.

"Johnny Storm?" Peter asked.

"Yes, Johnny Storm!" Jonah repeated. "The Human Torch, of the Fantastic Four!"

"I know who he is, I just—"

"A fine upstanding young man out on a date with America's newest sweetheart-slash-flavor of the month. A *true* hero, unlike that vigilante menace Spider-Man! In fact, the whole article will compare the heroic Torch to the criminal insect! You'll do a great job, Parker. And I'll even give you half your usual rate," Jameson said magnanimously, and pushed the call button for the elevator.

"Half?" Peter asked. "Mr. Jameson, I don't know if—"

"Okay, two thirds, Parker, but only because I value you so highly," Jonah said as the elevator doors slid open. "You know these paparazzi things are a breeze. I can't pay you your regular rate for that! You're just lucky I'm feeling generous today!"

"Mr. Jameson, I—" Peter argued, but Jonah shuffled him into the elevator and interrupted him.

"No need to thank me, Parker, just get me those photos and get back here quick!"

Past Jonah, Peter could see Betty Brant on the other side of the newsroom, shaking her head and smiling sympathetically. He had been hoping to go out with her tonight, but that obviously wasn't going to happen.

Aunt May was barely able to provide for the two of them from her social security check. She hated that he had to work, that he took time away from his studies to earn money. He didn't have a choice, though. They needed every dollar Peter could bring in as a freelance photographer at the *Bugle*. Even from photos he sold at two thirds of his rate.

The elevator doors slid shut.

Angelique's was on Fifth Avenue, a pseudo-nouveau-French restaurant that charged too much money for too little food. But, as cuisine reviewers might say, you paid for the atmosphere.

There was a raised outdoor patio, one story up, right over the wide Fifth Avenue sidewalk. Patrons were kept from falling over the edge by a low iron fence. The beautiful people were always given preferential treatment for patio seating. After all, what better advertisement for Angelique's than to have supermodels, actors, and sports stars dining in full view of the public?

Peter stood on the sidewalk with about forty other photographers—paparazzi, Jameson called them. He wasn't even sure if they were all there for the same reason, or if some of them just trawled Angelique's as part of some kind of regular beat.

They seemed civilized enough, though.

That is, until the Torch and Heather Fox arrived.

"Johnny!" a woman with a camera screamed. "Johnny, over here! Heather, look this way!"

She practically climbed on top of Peter in her attempts to get him out of the way to get a picture. He was jostled from side to side. His feet were stepped on and nearly half a dozen people elbowed him in the back, the side, the head, the arm.

The Torch calmly went into the restaurant.

Peter could barely restrain himself. He wanted so badly to use his spider-strength to shove these obnoxious morons out of the way. But he didn't dare for fear of revealing his identity as Spider-Man.

When the Torch and Heather Fox sat on the patio, waving to the paparazzi, it was more of the same. Peter managed to snap a few decent shots, mainly by holding his camera above his head.

Other photographers would have messed up those pictures, but Peter was used to taking photos from odd angles.

Still, the way the press was treating Johnny Storm was beginning to annoy him. If Peter could simply have said, "Hey, Torch, over here! It's me, Spidey!" he would have gotten all the photos he needed. But he couldn't do that. For one thing, it would compromise his secret identity. For another, Johnny Storm was a celebrity, he was famous.

Spider-Man was infamous.

The city loved the Fantastic Four, and the Human Torch in particular. He'd even been on the cover of *Seventeen* magazine. Spider-Man's main source of press coverage were the vitriolic diatribes Jameson published on a regular basis.

Peter didn't want to be famous. He just wanted to be appreciated.

It was different when they were together as Spidey and the Torch. While they weren't the best of friends, they had fought side by side often enough to be comrades. Buddies. They traded barbs and watched each other's back whenever necessary.

But at the end of the day, Peter went back to high school as "puny Parker." And Johnny? Johnny Storm got to take Heather Fox, one of the most beautiful young women in Hollywood, out to dinner and to her movie premiere.

Life just wasn't fair.

And no matter how genuinely nice a guy Johnny Storm was, Peter knew he would never understand how great he had it. They were both heroes with extraordinary powers. But Johnny was eating in Angelique's and Peter was on the sidewalk getting trampled while trying to take his photo.

What is wrong with this picture? he asked himself.

He already knew the answer. He just didn't know if he would ever be able to do anything about it.

Will Baker stared at the menu in awe.

"William, is anything wrong?" Candace asked.

"No, no, I just can't decide what to order. It all looks so good," Will said.

Candace smiled and looked back at her own menu. Will still stared, but not at the entrees. He looked in horror at the prices. He'd known going into this that Angelique's was expensive. From the moment he'd bullied an old cellmate working in the kitchen into slipping his name onto the reservation sheet, Will had known he was looking at some serious cash outlay.

But this was incredible!

As inconspicuously as he could, Will slid his wallet from his back pocket and opened it below the table. He counted the cash—it wasn't easy for ex-cons to get credit cards—and realized that he had enough money for dinner and a cheap bottle of wine. As long as Candace didn't want dessert, he'd be okay. There wouldn't be much of a tip, but that was just too bad.

The money in his wallet was all Will had for four or five days. But it would be worth it, just to impress Candace.

He looked at her, sitting and reading her menu. She was gorgeous in a jade-green backless dress that matched her eyes. Her red hair was pulled back in a French braid, and her gold earrings sparkled. She was a hell of a woman, with more class in the tip of her nose than Will's whole family had.

Before his latest stint in jail, thanks to Spider-Man, as usual, Will had been casing a jewelry store where Candace worked. He never robbed the place, because that would have ruined his chances with her. For weeks, he tried to get up the courage to ask her out. But before he could, the web-swinger had taken him down.

Now he was back out on parole, lots of time off for lots of good behavior—the joys of the American legal system—and he finally had a date with Candace. He couldn't believe it when she said yes, and now that they were out together, he wasn't about to blow it.

"William," she said excitedly, "why are all those paparazzi outside?"

"Papa-who?" he asked, glancing out the window to the patio dining area. He'd actually wanted to sit out there, which would have impressed Candace even more, but there was only so much sneaking an ex-con sous-chef could do, even when Will threatened to rip his face off.

"Oh, my gawd!" Candace cried, letting Long Island slip into her voice. "That's the Human Torch!"

"Where?" Will growled, ready for a fight if that's what the Torch wanted.

But that wasn't it at all. In fact, the Torch was just eating dinner with some girl, just like Will was. And, truth to tell, as far as he was concerned, Candace was better looking than the Torch's bimbo, no matter how many people wanted to take her picture.

Will Baker smiled. *Imagine that,* he thought, *me having dinner in a fancy restaurant not ten yards from Johnny Storm. Talk about respectable.*

"Ooh," Candace crooned, "he's gorgeous!"

"He's just a guy, Candy," Will grumbled. "A kid, really. Probably still in high school, or something."

"My name is not Candy, William, it's Candace," she scolded.

"Look, let's just order," Will said.

Candace seemed miffed, but looked back at her menu. Will waved the waiter over. As they ordered, he thought about Candace letting her accent slip, and the way she had mooned over the Torch. She wasn't the sophisticate she pretended to be, that was for certain. She was just another girl from Long Island, who looked great and knew how to take advantage of it.

But she was still sensational. Spectacular. Amazing.

By the time the appetizers came, however, Will was seething. Candace kept glancing at Storm. Will looked over a few times and saw that the punk was sipping champagne and toasting the gathered photographers and his date. They held hands and whispered to each other, and Will wondered if it was all an act for the cameras.

Candace didn't hold his hand. But it was pretty clear whose hand she was aching for.

When Storm lifted his date's hand and kissed it, Candace actually sighed.

Which sent Will right over the edge. No woman had ever sighed for him.

"All right!" he roared, standing up and shattering the table with one massive blow of his fist. "That's enough of that! I'm right here, you stupid cow! I'm the guy who brought you to this way-too-expensive Lean Cuisine dive! Look at me for a while!"

"Oh, my God," Candace screamed. "What the hell are you?"

Will Baker stood over the cowering woman in the beautiful green dress. But he wasn't just Will Baker anymore. He was the Sandman, a man built of nothing more than grains of sand. Will was one of the most powerful criminals in all of Manhattan. He'd once taken out an entire SWAT team in fifteen seconds, and throughout his jail term, he never let anyone forget it.

He wasn't going to let this woman ignore him.

"You want to know what a real man is like?" he asked, his huge fists pounding together, showering sand onto the floor, where it was absorbed again at his legs. "I'll show you a real man, Candy."

The Sandman stomped across the restaurant, ignoring the screams of the other patrons, and crashed through the many-paned glass window that looked out on the patio. Johnny Storm was already up, shoving his date out of harm's way.

"Flame on!" Storm yelled, and his entire body burst into flames. They didn't call him the Human Torch for nothing.

"C'mere, pretty boy!" the Sandman snarled. "You're gonna be my visual aid for today's lesson!"

Even before the Torch could let off a blast of fire at him, the Sandman struck. His arm elongated, the sand hardened to almost the density of granite, and his punch sent the Torch up over the railing and down onto the street amid the gathered photographers.

Will was so angry he didn't give Storm time enough to recover. In seconds, the Torch was buried in sand, suffocating, and Will was calling out for Candace to come and watch.

"Will, no!" she cried, running out into the street. "Are you crazy? You'll hurt him!"

"No," Will replied with mock concern. "Really?"

Then the flames seared Will's face and upper body, burning off most of his jacket and tie, and scorching holes in his shirt.

"No," the Torch agreed, climbing to his feet. "Not really."

Johnny Storm prepared to attack again, and the Sandman met him head on. Candace was going to see a real man in action. Storm was just a punk kid who needed very badly to be taught some humility.

Peter unbuttoned his shirt as he shot through a pile of cardboard boxes into the alley that ran next to Angelique's. He should have left the paparazzi sooner and changed into his costume. But once the fight erupted, the photojournalist in him insisted on crouching and taking pictures of the melée. Old Jonah paid a premium for shots of "real heroes" in action—heck, with a couple of clicks he'd earned enough to fill Aunt May's larder. It wasn't until the Sandman knocked the Torch out over the crowd that Spider-Man—the new self within Peter—stirred into action.

The alley dead-ended abruptly at a dank garbage bin. Hurriedly, Peter stripped off his shirt and pants, revealing the red-and-blue fabric underneath. Too late he remembered to glance about for onlookers. Not that there could have been any: the alley was dark, the rear door to Angelique's closed, and the windows above looked caked with grease and dirt. All the same, Peter winced, embarrassed by his own carelessness. There was so much to being an outlaw hero: secrecy, setting priorities, thinking of others before yourself.

Then he remembered that his spider-sense would have warned him of any such danger. He had forgotten about that as well.

Power and responsibility. Someday he would get the hang of it. Soon, he hoped.

Right now, though, Johnny Storm needed a rescue. For all his flash, the Human Torch alone was no match for the Sandman. Peter grinned despite himself, and pulled on his mask. He webbed his street clothes behind the dumpster. With a single inhuman leap, he vaulted twenty feet in the air and grabbed on to a fire-escape balcony. He scrambled up and over, then crouched on the railing, the metal groaning under his weight.

A gust of wind pushed lightly against his mask. Even in the alley he could hear the crashing and twittering from the restaurant—the paparazzi couldn't have asked for a better show. Across the street, gawkers crowded the curb, shielding their eyes from the battle's fiery glare.

Time for my grand entrance, Spider-Man thought. Silently he calculated distance, angle of approach, web resilience . . .

Ah, the heck with it.

Exhilarated, he vaulted off the balcony, his legs and arms stretched, his back curved like a bow. Time slowed in the air. He flew over the garbage bin, and the strewn boxes, and the wide, glittering sidewalk, and a line of Checker cabs on Fifth Avenue. There was a tall lamppost right across the street from Angelique's and, as he darted past it, Spider-Man shot a stream of webbing directly at the steel tip. The strand caught—how he wished he could patent that compound, he'd make a fortune—and swung him toward the restaurant like a tethered ball.

He had but a second to assess the scene: Johnny Storm facing away from him, toward the ruined picture window, his flame licking in a thousand shards of glass; the Sandman readying himself for a granite punch, too intent to catch sight of the wall-crawler's approach.

Excellent. Spider-Man let go of the strand. He somersaulted in midair and thrust his legs forward, knees clenched, heels braced for impact.

He intended to take the Sandman by surprise, of course. If he could hit the Sandman hard enough to knock him unconscious while his head was still flesh and blood—rather than sand—the fight would be over. Surprise. That was his intention. It really was.

Spider-Man just couldn't help himself.

"Here I come to save the day. . . ." he sang in a false bass voice, doing his best Mighty Mouse impersonation.

The Sandman looked up. In an instant his face grew diffused, grainy, like a newsprint photograph. Spider-Man burst through him. With a terrible clatter his soles smacked against a patio chair, and he stumbled forward and over, onto a round wrought-iron table laid with plates of steak au poivre and asparagus.

The Sandman re-formed instantly, morphing so that his body switched direction without ever actually turning around. Now he faced Spider-Man, who, though unhurt, had paused to regain his bearings.

"This is too good!" the Sandman cried. "Oh, you really wanna see this, Candy! The two of 'em! I get to take out the two of 'em!"

Candace stepped back into the restaurant, away from the havoc Will—the Sandman—had created. She was mortified. This was, by far, her worst date ever—and she'd had some doozies in her day. Definitely she had to talk to someone about it. Despite the clamor, she heard a sigh behind her. She turned, and was stunned to see Heather Fox standing by the *maître d'* station, looking bored and exasperated.

Out on the sidewalk, Spider-Man watched as the Human Torch sprang toward his enemy, quick to take advantage of the distraction he'd provided with his arrival. Storm's body blazed like a meteor.

"Smooth move, web-head," he said with a laugh.

As usual, his voice was strange and annoyingly haughty, issuing as it did from living flame. His attack was far more earthbound: with joined fists he struck the Sandman in the middle of his back. The point of impact burst in a cloud of fire and dirt.

The Sandman cried out in pain. His right arm, which he'd held raised over Spider-Man and packed to cement density, suddenly turned pink and fleshy. Before Storm could hit him again, though, the Sandman swung his elbow—rock-hard, swollen to the size of an anvil—straight at the Torch's solar plexus. The impact made a sick thudding sound. Storm staggered backward, heaving, holding his palms flat against his blazing stomach.

"Now it's your turn, insect!" the Sandman screamed.

Blind with fury, his fist packed to a mallet, he struck down on the very spot where, seconds before, Spider-Man had been sprawled. But Spider-Man was gone. Will's hand slammed against the sidewalk. There was a loud, painful ring, and his forearm cracked lengthwise and shattered.

"Oh, I'm sorry, did you want me to stay put?" Spider-Man quipped, tipping his head in mock sympathy. He was now crouched against the brownstone wall, fifteen feet above Angelique's neon sign. Once again, his spider-sense had saved him. "That must've hurt," he added.

Below, the Sandman spun around and around, looking for Spider-Man, confused by the web-slinger's lightning-fast leap.

Johnny Storm stood a few yards away, dimmed. He held his head bowed, not moving, drawing long, hesitant breaths. The paparazzi gathered about him in a tight semicircle, as if to bask in his heat.

What fools, Spider-Man thought. *Can't they see . . . ?*

He felt like swinging down to street level and shoving them backward, screaming at them to take cover. Deep inside, though, he was glad for their attention—maybe for once the papers would print a true story about Spider-Man.

Last evening, while the city went about its nightly business, the mighty Spider-Man put an end to the notorious Sandman's long criminal career, at the same time saving the life of would-be/has-been hero Johnny Storm, aka the Human Barbecue. . . .

Right, he thought sarcastically. *Never happen.* Flicking his wrist, he released a thick stream of webbing, which found its mark in the Sandman's face, covering it like a shell. Soon he would begin to suffocate, lose his concentration, and solidify enough to be vulnerable. Then it would be a matter of throwing a quick hay-maker and rushing home to catch Johnny Carson.

Will Baker had learned a few tricks since his last encounter with Spider-Man. Rather than tear at the sticky veil, he willed his face to sand and shook his head over the sidewalk. The web came off in a single masklike clump, layered with grit.

"For my next trick . . ." he said, stretching upward, brandish-ing fists like wrecking balls. Not that he'd forgotten about the Torch—he would be taking care of Storm in due time.

By now Will's rage had all but subsided, replaced by something altogether different. The way he figured it, he'd already blown his parole to hell. He was a wanted man again, and the fact filled him with a strange, acid mixture of anger and glee. Jail had been terrible, no question, but what the goody-goody suits didn't know—what they would never find out in their miserable little lives—was that every second he'd spent in the hole, every arrogant smirk he'd suffered from the guards, every crumb of rotten food, was worth the freedom he now savored.

He'd felt so stupid in that monkey suit, trying to impress sweet Candy, pretending to be one of *them!* How could they stand it, the pretense, the frustration? Wanting something and not taking it. Hating someone and not hurting him.

And, idiot that he was, he'd even allowed himself to daydream about this well-lit world—about getting a girlfriend, a legit job, starting a family!

He should thank Spider-Man and the Torch for setting him straight.

And thank them he would.

"Did you see that?" Heather Fox chirped as Candace ap-proached her, pointing toward the fight and the ruined patio with a dainty index finger.

The restaurant was deserted; even the waitstaff had bolted through the rear access door. But Heather Fox was still here, and Candace would not allow such a golden opportunity to pass her by. Hey, if she ingratiated herself, maybe Heather would introduce her to her big-time Hollywood agent. Crazier things have happened.

Heather. Candace laughed to herself. Already she was thinking of the star on a first-name basis.

From inside the atrium, all she could see of the battle was Johnny Storm breathing—or, rather, trying to breathe.

"You're so lucky," she fawned. "Even flaming he's scrumptious. And he can fly too."

"No, no, no," Heather said, shaking the lovely blond curls that hung over her forehead, "did you see what the big guy did?"

Candace craned her neck to get a better look. And there he was, right outside the broken plate glass window: her ugly, stupid date. His legs, anyway. The rest of him had stretched grotesquely and disappeared behind the atrium wall, which rose twenty, thirty feet above the window.

Suddenly there came a sound like a pile driver. Here and there, the plaster walls bulged and cracked in concentric circles, as if the building were being struck from the outside by a wrecking ball. Fine dust sprinkled over the immaculate tablespreads.

"Oh, my God," Candace said, to herself mostly, her lower lip trembling, "I can't believe I actually went out with such a freak."

Heather's eyes opened round and wide. "You *know* him?"

"Well, I don't really *know* him as such," Candace answered, embarrassed. She hugged herself and scrunched her eyelids. "I mean, I didn't know that he could do . . . well, *that!*"

The ceiling groaned and a cracked. A track-light fixture came loose. For a moment it dangled, the wires sparking like camera flashes, and then the whole thing came crashing onto the marble floor. By then, Candace and Heather had taken cover behind the *maître d*'s heavy oak podium.

"He just stopped by a few times at the jewelry store," Candace continued, "and he was all sweet and nice, you know, funny. I thought he had a nice, honest face. Nothing like Johnny Storm, of course, but—"

"Johnny Storm is a bore," Heather interrupted. She looked at Candace. "The whole date thing was my agent's idea. He thought it would help 'solidify' my image. As if!"

"I didn't know they did that," Candace said, honestly surprised.

"You don't know the half of it, girl. I'm telling you, if it weren't for the money. . . ."

"But, but, it's Johnny Storm! I mean, from the Fantastic Four! They're honest-to-goodness heroes! They fought the Sub-Mariner and that creepy Doom guy and—"

"Oh, please," Heather said, laughing, "I'm as grateful as the next girl, but I prefer my men with a little bit of an edge, if you know what I mean. Not to mention older. Johnny Storm is a kid— all he can talk about is his toys and his little *Boy's Life* 'adventures.' Like, 'Did I tell you about the time the Thing and me clobbered the Mole Man? It was great!' And he knows nothing about art, or music, or literature!"

"That doesn't sound so bad," Candace said meekly.

"To tell you the truth," Heather added, "if I'd had my pick of the Fantastic Four—well, let's just say that Johnny Storm wouldn't have been first on my list. I mean, a girl *has* to be curious."

"You mean—?" Candace said, holding three fingers to her lips.

Heather answered with a shy grin.

"I hadn't thought of that," Candace muttered. She heard a racket outside and instinctively peeked around the podium. The Human Torch seemed to have regained his strength. With a flaming arm raised, he yelled at the photographers to seek cover.

"So," Heather said mischievously, leaning against Candace, "tell me more about this sandy hunk of yours. Does he have any tattoos?"

Spider-Man leapt aside, and the Sandman's fist missed and struck the wall, carving a deep navel on the brownstone.

"Stay put, you coward!" the Sandman growled, and his head turned to granite and shot toward Spider-Man like a battering ram.

"I'd rather not," he said and skipped—if you could call it a skip when the movement took place on a vertical surface—to avoid yet another bone-crunching blow. He was faster and more agile, and the jokes still came quick to mind, but with Torchy out of commission, and the paparazzi taking picture after picture, Spider-Man was feeling increasingly anxious. He'd done little but keep the Sandman distracted, away from Johnny Storm.

The restaurant was a wreck. The traffic jam on Fifth Avenue probably extended all the way to Harlem.

Jameson was going to have a field day with this one.

"Quit playin' around, ya bum!" one of the reporters cried suddenly from below, sounding for all the world like a cranky New York Yankees fan. "Ya can't expect real heroes like the Torch to keep bailing you out!"

Despite all the negative press, the fear, the attitude, he'd gotten from his fellow New Yorkers since his initial outing in costume, Spider-Man was furious. Couldn't they see that he was just doing his best to draw the conflict away from them?

"Okay," he said, scanning the crowd below. "Who's the moron?"

His spider-sense sent a dagger of pain into his skull. Intense. Agonizing.

Way, way too late.

The Sandman pummeled him, and Spider-Man fell twenty feet to the pavement. He could barely lift his head, but when he did, he saw two Sandmen approaching, ready to put him down for the count.

"Double your pleasure, double your fun," he mumbled, holding the sides of his head as if they might slide apart.

Wise remarks aside, though, he knew he was in serious trouble.

"The crowd goes wild, and the judges give Spidey a 9.5!" the Torch cried as he flew overhead.

Storm slammed into the Sandman at full speed and crushed him against a shiny new Corvette illegally double parked in front of the restaurant. Baker exploded in a shower of sand, pouring over the hood of the car and slowly coalescing on the other side.

"Quit daydreaming, buddy!" the Torch called back to him, as Spider-Man climbed unsteadily to his feet. "Maybe you should leave the crime-fighting to us full-time super heroes!"

It was an innocent jibe, typical of his relationship with the Torch. But for some reason, it bit deep. Rankled within him.

"Full-time super hero? Right!" Spider-Man said. "What was your mission at Angelique's today, Torchie? Battling the evil Asparagus Man? And like you didn't have a long enough time out, before? I think you need to do a few hours of aerobics, hothead! If that wouldn't take too much time away from your hard life of fame, fortune, and dating gorgeous starlets, of course! Full-time hero, my foot!''

Baker hadn't risen from beyond the Corvette, and the Torch took that moment to respond. He turned to Spider-Man, his grin as arrogant as always. Sometimes it was endearing. Not today.

''Do I detect a note of jealousy in your tone, *amigo?*'' Johnny asked.

Spider-Man didn't answer. He scratched his head as he watched the Sandman rise swiftly from beyond the car and seem to *flow* right over it toward the Torch.

''Well?'' Storm prodded, taunting him further.

Drawing back his fist, which grew in an instant into a massive concrete block, the Sandman bludgeoned the Human Torch across the back. Johnny shot forward, stumbled, and fell, his flames partially extinguished, at Spider-Man's feet. Spidey looked down at him and sighed.

''Jealous? Whatever gave you that idea?'' he asked.

''Your turn, now, chump,'' the Sandman called, and pointed a huge finger at Spider-Man.

''Whoops,'' he muttered, and immediately began to question the wisdom of not having warned the Torch in time.

Not that the guy didn't have it coming, of course. But he was handy to have around during a brawl.

''All right,'' Spider-Man said, resigned. ''Come to Poppa, you big beach bum.''

The Sandman started forward. It was always the same: no matter how many times he hit Spider-Man, the web-head kept coming back for more. *As it is,* he thought, *my date's gone completely to hell.*

''Jeez,'' Spidey sighed. ''There's never a lifeguard around when you need one.''

''You're not going to find too much funny when I'm—'' the Sandman began, then stopped.

My date's gone completely to hell. So why am I doing this? If he beat Spider-Man and the Torch, his evening would still be ruined. If he lost, he'd go back to jail.

Then he saw something out of the corner of his eye. Looking up, he saw the outline of some kind of doohickey flying through the air—with three familiar-looking passengers. *That,* he thought, *clinches it.*

"Another time, wall-crawler," Will Baker said. "You ain't worth it."

He turned into the alley next to Angelique's, willed his entire body to sand, and let himself flow down into the sewers. They'd never find him down there, and he'd wait until he was halfway across town before reforming. He'd smell lousy for a while, but it beat going back to prison.

Spider-Man considered going after the Sandman, but he was still somewhat disoriented. And if the Sandman truly meant to leave, he would have disappeared into a sewer drain or through cracks in a door or fence before Spidey could even round the corner.

"Wow," he said appreciatively. "Guess he's got arachnophobia. The costume must be more intimidating than I thought."

There was a sudden uproar among the crowd. Spider-Man turned toward them and executed a perfect bow. But when he stood, he was embarrassed to see that they weren't applauding and cheering for him. They weren't even looking at him.

He spun to see exactly what they *were* looking at.

A dozen stories up, the Fantasticar hovered in the air. He could see Ben Grimm, Reed Richards, and the Torch's sister, Susan.

The crowd began to close in, staring up at the Fantasticar. Some of them stood by the Torch, apparently wanting to help him up but unwilling to get near his flames.

"Flame off!" Johnny said, and stood up on his own. His fire doused, he walked over to where Spider-Man stood alone.

"Thanks for the heads-up there, pal," the Torch said angrily.

"Sorry," Spider-Man replied. "I guess I was overwhelmed by your wit."

"You need to relax, buddy," Johnny said, but already his anger seemed to have dissipated.

"Maybe you should get back to your date, Mr. Storm," Spider-Man said. "I'm sure she's really impressed by your feats of derring-do."

"Not particularly," a female voice commented behind them.

Spider-Man and the Torch turned to see Heather Fox and another woman, whom neither of them recognized, standing at her side.

"Heather!" Johnny said amiably. "I'm glad you're okay. What do you say we get out of here, go somewhere a little more intimate?"

The paparazzi bulled their way through the gathered crowd and began snapping photos.

"Actually, Johnny, I'm going to have *café au lait* with my new friend Candace here," Heather said, indicating the other woman. "You're not really my type anyway. I only came over here to ask Spider-Man if there was any way he could put me in touch with that Sandman guy."

As Spider-Man watched, Johnny Storm's face turned deep red. For once, the change in color wasn't brought on by fire.

"I guess that's my cue to leave," Spider-Man said.

As he swung up and away, Spider-Man grinned broadly beneath his mask.

A bit later, he began to whistle a happy tune.

BETTER LOOTING THROUGH MODERN CHEMISTRY

John Garcia & Pierce Askegren

Illustration by Alex Saviuk

Friday, 12:15 P.M., ChemCo chemical supply house

The man in the line ahead of Peter Parker seemed familiar. Something about the guy's stance, about his tone of voice, made Peter think he had encountered the other man before. Unfortunately, all Peter could see now was his back—and his hands, as he gestured angrily at the clerk.

"One isn't enough," the man said. "I ordered two helium cartridges, and I need them both!"

"Yeah, well, I need money for them both," the clerk said. He had beady eyes and buck teeth that gave him a ratlike look. "You think helium grows on trees?" he snickered.

The customer made an annoyed sound. "But the price has gone up," he said. "I don't have the cash with me, and I can't wait until Monday!"

The human rodent didn't say anything, but drew his thin lips back in an unpleasant smile.

"I can give you a check," the man said. Peter began to feel sympathy for him. A tight budget was his frequent companion too. Right now, however, he wished the other guy would make his purchase and move along. It was a good seven blocks back to Empire State University. He needed to complete his own business, then really hustle to make it back in time for his one o'clock history lecture.

"No personal checks," the clerk said. "Me and the banks, we have an arrangement. They don't sell chemicals, and I don't cash checks." He snickered at his own witticism, apparently thinking it was original.

"Can I put the balance on account, then?" The customer's voice took on a pleading note, and Peter's sympathy became embarrassment.

The clerk laughed.

"Fine, then! Fine! I'll take one cartridge!" The man ahead of Peter watched angrily as the clerk wrapped his purchase. "You'll regret this! I'm an important man!!"

"Yeah, yeah, yeah. That's what they all say."

The man turned to leave. Peter caught a brief glimpse of his features—aquiline nose, jutting jaw, stormy eyes. No doubt about it; this was someone he had seen before. He wondered where and when, but then put the questions out of his mind. He had a purchase of his own to make.

The clerk knew him. "Parker, right?" He set a bottle on the countertop. "Plastic polymer."

Peter nodded. ChemCo was the only local source of the compound that he used as the base of Spider-Man's webbing, and his web fluid supplies were perilously low. He anticipated spending a long night brewing another batch of the stuff, then filling the flat metal cartridges that lined his wristbands and belt. "That's me," he said. He opened his wallet and pulled out some money. "Twenty dollars should cover it, right?"

The clerk shook his head. "More like thirty, now," he said. "The price has gone up."

Peter looked at him, then looked in his wallet. It was empty. He looked at the clerk again, and tried to think of something to say.

He couldn't.

2:10 P.M., ESU campus

Peter reached the sidewalk almost before the bell stopped ringing. He was operating on autopilot, his mind considering and discarding financial options. He had no friends to loan him the cash, and no photography assignments were pending. He certainly couldn't ask his aunt May; he knew how tight *her* budget was. Besides, she had done too much for him already. Like it or not, he saw only one possibility. . . .

Still deep in thought, Peter abruptly collided with something soft and warm. Books flew, his and someone else's. Reflexively, he used his enhanced speed and agility to catch most of the volumes in midair.

"Nice save," Gwen Stacy said. Her tone was cold enough that icicles seemed to hang beneath each word. "But you should still watch where you're going."

"Oh, um, hi, Gwen," Peter said. He knelt and retrieved an errant text and handed it to the attractive blonde. "I'm sorry, really. I was thinking about—well, just thinking."

"About new carpeting for your ivory tower, I'll bet," Gwen said. She paused, and looked at Peter with a speculative expression that he had found puzzling. "You should really get your head out of those clouds once in a while," she continued.

Peter couldn't think of a response. Gwen often had this effect on him. Her eyes were somehow hypnotic, even when flashing angrily. "Uh, I'm really sorry," he said, all too aware how lame the words were.

Gwen sniffed disdainfully, then seemed to mellow. "Why are you in such a rush?" she asked. "Going to the basketball exhibition?"

"Basketball?"

"Of course, *you* wouldn't know," Gwen said. "Johnny Ramos is giving a demonstration. I bet you don't even know who he is."

She was wrong, of course. Even a nonsports fan had heard of ESU's most famous sports alumnus, the star of three championship teams. "The Ray is back in town?" Peter said, grinning. "Wow."

"There might be hope for you yet," Gwen said. "I'm going, and getting together with friends later." She paused. "Interested?"

"Wow," Peter said again. He had never expected to hear such an invitation from Gwen, of all people. "I'd really like to!" He suddenly remembered his nearly empty wallet, and the emptier web cartridges beneath his street clothes. "But I can't," he concluded weakly. "I have to run an errand."

Gwen looked at him, annoyed, disgusted, or both. Peter didn't dare think she was disappointed. "Your loss," she said. "See you around."

Peter watched her walk away, wondering yet again why his luck with girls was so bad. Since Betty Brant had left town, his social life had dwindled to a remarkably close approximation of zero. He didn't care about basketball, but would have enjoyed socializing with Gwen. Now, yet another opportunity had passed him by.

He shrugged, and put the thoughts from his mind. He still needed the polymer, and he knew that there was only one way he could get the funds to buy it.

Desperate circumstances called for drastic measures.

3:00 P.M., the *Daily Bugle* Building

J. Jonah Jameson smiled, which made him look remarkably

like a shark in human form. "Parker, Parker, Parker," he said. "We've had this little chat before. You take pictures, I give you money for them." He paused. "In that order, remember?"

Peter looked at the newspaper publisher glumly. It was true; this wasn't the first time he had endured this kind of chat, and it probably wouldn't be the last. Right now, however, Jameson was his only source of income. "I know," he said. "But this is an emergency. I need to buy some supplies." He was careful not to specify what kind of supplies; with luck, Jameson would think he needed film or developer for his photography work.

Jameson fixed him with one gimlet eye. "Oh? You're out?"

Peter didn't say anything. He hated these confrontations. They made him itch for a good tussle with a super criminal.

"That's not good," Jameson said, musing. "Can't have photographers, even freelance ones, working for this paper without supplies. Might keep them from being able to fulfill their assignments." He smiled again, looking even more sharkish. "Maybe I should reconsider our working relationship. Maybe I should give you that advance, after all."

Peter liked the words, but not Jameson's tone.

"Or maybe I shouldn't give you any more work, until you can learn to manage your affairs better," Jameson said. Then he was off, launching into another harangue about how things had been in his day, when a man had to know the value of a dollar.

Peter tried not to let his eyes glaze over as Jameson spoke. He had heard this spiel many times before. He had learned not to let himself get too angry about being lectured in economy by a man whose shirts cost more than Peter made in a month. The only solace he could take from the situation was that Jameson hated Spider-Man almost beyond belief, and had no inkling just how much money he had paid out to the super hero's civilian identity, mostly for pictures of Spidey's greatest triumphs. It was Peter's private joke, but only a small consolation.

"—banks and I have a working arrangement, too, Parker," Jameson continued, reaching some kind of crescendo. "They don't publish newspapers—"

"And the *Bugle* doesn't make loans," Peter finished the sentence for him.

"That's right," Jameson said, obviously annoyed at the interruption. He paused again, then continued. "Usually."

"Usually?" Peter tried not to let himself sound hopeful. Jameson hated it when people sounded hopeful.

Jameson smirked, demonstrating the smug confidence of a man who held all the cards. "Tell me, Parker," he said. "You know about the new *Bugle* section, right?"

Peter nodded. Jameson was launching a monthly section on emerging technologies, and how they might affect business opportunities. The subject matter sounded interesting, but Peter didn't hold much hope for it, mainly because Jameson's ideas on science and engineering seemed to have been firmly set sometime around the turn of the century. He knew that Jameson had scheduled an inaugural exhibit in connection with the launch.

"You're up on that Buck Rogers stuff, right?"

"That's one way of putting it," Peter said dryly. A full scholarship for scientific excellence in high school studies paid for his classes at ESU, and he knew that Jameson knew about it.

"Tell you what, Parker, I'm in a good mood. You attend the exhibit premiere tonight, you take some pictures of the gadgets and the celebrities, and I just might advance your fee."

"I thought Kuttner had that assignment. That's his kind of work."

Jameson stubbed out his cigar in a green glass ashtray. "Kuttner's goldbricking," he said. "He won't be able to attend."

That meant Kuttner was probably horribly ill, Peter realized. Jameson didn't have much patience with illness, and the *Bugle* didn't offer any sick leave to staff. "I can do it if you want," he said. "I'd like to see the exhibit, anyhow."

"I'm so glad you feel that way," Jameson said, his voice dripping with sarcasm. "Be here at eight-thirty, and be prepared." He tossed a leaflet at Peter. "Here's a list of the exhibits."

"I still need supplies."

Peter thought he could hear the wheels turning in the older man's head as he balanced options and expenses. This was an old game too; Jameson was fantastically tight with money, and surrendered as little of it as possible—which, in Peter's case, meant very little indeed. Finally, the older man named a figure so low that it made Peter gasp softly. "Lucky for you I'm such a big-hearted guy," Jameson said. "Take it or leave it."

"Okay." It wasn't as if he had any choice.

"Good," Jameson said. "You can pick up your check at four-thirty." He stood, and shrugged into his suit jacket. "Now take off," he said. "I've got to meet with the mayor." He grinned. "See you tonight."

"Lucky me," Peter said, and was surprised when Jameson seemed to believe the sentiment.

4:30 P.M., the Neville K. Trelayne Memorial Mineral Museum, the Upper East Side

Norton G. Fester strode though the doors just as the security guard started to close and lock them. Fester paused long enough to knock the elderly man unconscious with the handle of his hammer, then quickly made his way to the appropriate display. Once there, he inverted the tool and drove its metal head through the case, then reached inside and plucked his prize from among the glass fragments. One more swing of the hammer—this time using its pointed end—and the tennis-ball-sized meteorite split open neatly, to release a cloud of dense vapor. Fester leaned close and breathed the stuff in, doing his best to catch all of it in a single gasp.

The gas burned as it hit his lungs, and it burned even more when it reached his bloodstream. He could feel the fire surge through him, remaking muscle and bone and flesh as it swept though his body. The first time this had happened, the shock had rendered him unconscious; now, however, he was accustomed to the process, and felt only a brief moment of dizziness that passed swiftly. He dropped the remnants of the meteorite and left the museum, moving more quickly than when he had entered.

Much more quickly.

Someone had parked a motorcycle in front of the museum during his visit. Never one to pass up an opportunity, Fester grabbed the bike and threw it twenty yards or so into a convenient fuel truck. The tanker exploded, erupting into a cloud of orange flame and black smoke. Fester grinned. He glanced at his watch.

So far, so good.

4:45 P.M., Shutterbug Heaven, Third Avenue, near East Thirty-ninth Street

The camera shop's wares were impressive in their variety and frightening in their expense. Peter spent long minutes spellbound, staring in through the glass showcase at filters and lenses and flash accessories. He enjoyed looking at equipment like this, even though he couldn't afford to buy anything. Sometimes it helped him get his mind off his other problems—not the least of them, the fact that he had managed to fumble another opportunity to know Gwen better. It was only when the salesman offered to demonstrate an infrared sensor that Peter realized how much time had passed. Excusing himself, he made his way back to the *Daily Bugle* offices as fast as he reasonably could.

He was in time, but barely; the cashier, accustomed to the ways of hungry freelancers, issued his check and then cashed it, all in record time. Peter tucked the money—not nearly enough, really—in his wallet, and rushed toward the exit. ChemCo closed at five-thirty, which gave him just enough to time to make it there and buy the polymer.

"Parker!" The switchboard operator, an unhappy-looking woman with auburn hair, waved as he rocketed past. "Hold up! You've got a call!"

"Can't, really, I—"

"It's your aunt."

Peter stopped dead in his tracks. He had meant to call Aunt May after his history lecture, but had forgotten. He wondered what she wanted, and hoped with sudden apprehension that nothing was wrong. "Okay," he said. "Where can I take it?"

The operator gestured at a desk, and at the phone atop it. "I'll put it there," she said. "But make it fast; you know how The Master feels about personal calls."

J. Jonah Jameson's feelings were the farthest thing from Peter's mind as he snatched the receiver from its cradle. "Aunt May?" He tried to keep any anxiety from his voice.

"Hello, Peter." His aunt's words, frail and tentative, crackled through the earpiece. "How are you, dear?"

"I—I'm fine. How are you?"

"I'm fine, too, dear. But I was doing some baking, and I seem to have run out of eggs."

Peter sighed in relief. "I can pick up a dozen on the way home," he said. "But I'm going to be pretty late. Mr. Jameson has an assignment for me this evening. Do you need them tonight?"

"No, no, just as long as I have them in the morning." Aunt May sounded relieved and happy at Peter's words, and he wondered yet again at her ease in taking pleasure in little things. "I want to bake you a nice batch of your favorite cookies."

"That sounds great, Aunt May. I'll make sure I get them."

"Thank you, dear. Dress warmly, now, and I do hope you have your umbrella with you. The weatherman calls for rain."

"Yes, ma'am. I know." Peter looked up just in time to see Jameson glaring at him from an office doorway. "I have to go, Aunt May," he said hastily. "Don't wait up."

5:00 P.M., the Upper East Side

Fester took ten minutes to retrieve his work clothes and equipment from where he had cached them. Clad once more in the purple-and-white costume of the Looter, he strode along crowded sidewalks toward his first target. The tide of humanity parted before him as he marched along, and the few bystanders stupid enough to block his path discovered the hard way just how powerful the meteor had made him. It didn't take him long to reach his destination.

The electrical substation was a small one, but size wasn't everything. Fester had done his research. He knew that this site was crucial to local service, a switching center that handled the power for many blocks around. Effortlessly, the Looter leapt over the twelve-foot cyclone fence that surrounded the station, then dug his fingers deep in the heavy steel framework of the first tower. He yanked, hard.

"Hey, you! What are you—"

A worker or security guard had sighted him. It didn't matter. Fester ignored the man's angry words, and concentrated instead on the shrieking groan that the steel tower made as it broke loose from its foundation. Metal tore, then parted, and the concrete beneath his feet split as the support members came free. Heavy high-tension cables snapped and lashed about, spitting sparks and filling the air with ozone's sharp tang. The Looter pushed, toppling the tower so that it crashed into another. More cables broke, and more man-made lightning flew as the second tower collapsed. The Looter did not pause to take pleasure in his handiwork, but moved on instead to the next tower.

5:35 P.M., ChemCo chemical supply house

"Sorry, kid." The human rodent didn't sound sorry. He was smiling as he locked the door shut behind him. "Closed for the day. Closed for the weekend too. Heh."

"But—I—" Peter tried to shape his words into something the ratlike man would find believable. "I can't wait until then. I really need that polymer—"

"Monday." The clerk smirked, apparently enjoying his moment of authority. "You need it now, you'll still need it then." He walked away, whistling a happy tune.

Peter stared at the locked door. Spider-Man could rip it from its hinges in an instant, he knew, and take what he needed—but he couldn't let himself do that, no matter how tempting the prospect. He was going to have to make it through life until Monday with what limited webbing he still had. The prospect was not a pleasing one; the strength and agility that a radioactive spider's bite had given him were essential to his work as Spider-Man, but the webbing compound that Peter Parker's scientific genius had created was no less important. He sighed. Maybe the weekend would be uneventful—but he knew that wasn't very likely.

"Peter! Peter Parker!"

The words came from behind him. Lilting and feminine, the voice was familiar, but he wasn't sure who was speaking until he turned around to see. It was Sally Green, another ESU student. He had spoken to her only once or twice before, always casually. Their last encounter had been brief to the point of rudeness. He had no idea why she seemed so happy to see him now.

The attractive, dark-haired girl came closer, smiling cheerfully. "Fancy meeting you here," she said. "Buying supplies for the lab section on Monday?"

Peter shrugged, vaguely suspicious of any pretty girl who chose to speak to him. "Trying to," he lied. "But I got here late. I hope you don't need anything."

Sally shook her head, making the black mane of her hair glisten in the afternoon sun. "Nothing that place can supply," she said. "But I could use someone to walk me to Chesney's. I'm meeting some friends there. Interested?"

Two invitations in one day, Peter realized with surprise. Maybe things were looking up. Chesney's was a local soda fountain, where ESU students often met after class. Peter had been there a few times, usually by himself for a hasty lunch. He considered the offer, then looked at his watch. There was plenty of time before the *Bugle* exhibit. "Sounds good to me, Sally," he said. "But—"

"Good," she replied, and took his arm before he could offer it. "I've got some questions for you, Mr. Parker, and I've been waiting for a chance to ask them!"

6:00 P.M., Ninety-sixth Street and Lexington Avenue

As he reached the subway-station entrance, the Looter lashed out again with his left leg and smashed another fire hydrant. Water gushed up, then splashed back down to join the streams that flowed from the dozen others he had destroyed. That same water surged down the stairs, toward the subway station, but he moved faster than it did, and beat it to the main train platform. Like their fellows in the streets above, bystanders screamed and fled as he smashed his way though the turnstile and leapt down onto the tracks.

Fester clutched one rail of the tracks that carried the northbound 6 trains. This metal was tougher than the steel of the power station towers, but not tough enough to resist him. The spikes that held the rail to the ties broke easily, and spike heads ricocheted like bullets as he bent the metal back and up. The Looter gave a final tug and ripped a section free, then threw it aside. He stepped to the southbound tracks and repeated his actions.

He leapt from the tracks to the platform with casual ease and headed back to the surface. No one tried to stop him. By the time he was halfway up the first flight of stairs, the swirling hydrant-water was already inches deep around his feet.

6:30 P.M., Chesney's Soda Shoppe

"—won me the scholarship," Peter said. He took another sip from his milkshake. "Good thing too. I'm not sure I could hold down a full-time job and a full schedule of classes, and science means a lot to me."

Sally leaned closer. Her eyes flashed as she spoke. "I think that's so great," she said. "You haven't let anything stand in your way! I'm really glad we've finally had a chance to talk!"

Peter looked at her, confused. He didn't often sit across a table from a pretty girl who hung on his every word. Amazingly, her interest seemed sincere. The way she spoke fascinated him, a kind of breathy excitement that seemed both affected and effective. It had taken long minutes for him to relax in her presence, but now he was more than a little pleased he had accepted her invitation.

"Look, Sally," he said slowly, hesitantly. "I have an assignment tonight for the *Bugle*. It's a science exhibit. . . ." His words trailed off.

Sally looked at him, waiting. Her lips curved upward slightly as she Peter paused, and he could see a dimple form in her right cheek. He took a deep breath and continued. "If you'd like to—"

"Hey! Hey! Look who's here!" A broad hand slapped Peter's shoulder, just a little bit too hard to be friendly. Flash Thompson wedged himself into the booth, next to Peter. "Petey! Move over, buddy! Company's callin'!" The husky redhead gestured to his companions to join him. Harry Osborn, one of Flash's pack, pulled up a chair and stationed himself at the booth's open end. Peter's heart sank as Gwen slid into the seat beside Sally. These were the "friends" she had referred to earlier, he realized.

"Speaking of science," Peter said in a stage whisper to Sally, "here's proof that evolution isn't a one-way street." He gestured at Flash. "Behold, the throwback!" Though he tried to keep his tone light, he realized sadly that some kind of special moment had passed.

"Hello, Parker," Gwen said, her tone frigid again. She glanced at Sally, then back at Peter. "I thought you were *busy* this afternoon."

The next few minutes were unpleasant ones. Flash had been a high-school bully, and Peter's nemesis. Things weren't proving much better in college, but Peter had been able to hold his own against him so far. Gwen, on the other hand, was a more complex puzzle. She didn't seem to like Peter very much, but sometimes evidenced a baffling proprietary interest in him. Now, as Gwen and Sally exchanged slightly catty comments, Peter could feel the situation slipping away from him. He was trying to figure out how to salvage things when something else caught his attention.

It was a bulletin, crackling over the speaker of the soda jerk's radio. "This just in," the voice said. "The Upper East Side has been rocked by a series of disasters. Rescue and emergency efforts have been hampered by a blackout and disastrous traffic jams. Less than two hours ago, a major fire erupted along—"

Peter stood. His classmates looked at him. He looked at Sally. "I have to go," he said. The words did not come easily. "I have to run an errand for my aunt." He could tell by the look in Sally's eyes that she wasn't buying it, that she thought he was running from the encounter with Flash—but he couldn't think of anything else to say. "See you later?"

"Maybe," Sally said.

He knew she didn't mean it.

7:00 P.M., Thirty-fourth Street

In midswing, one hundred feet above street level, Spider-Man's spider-sense flared an angry warning. A second later, his left web-shooter failed. The right one had died a block or so before. Now, he was out of webbing completely. He dropped to a convenient rooftop, and pondered his next option. Hoofing it was out, if he wanted to get uptown in time and with enough energy to do any good. Cabs and subways were out of the question too; whatever was going on uptown had snarled traffic for many blocks around. He wondered what he was going to do.

A muffled, throbbing thunder answered his question, as a local television station's news helicopter came into view. Spider-Man waved to the pilot from his rooftop perch. A journalist himself, he knew just how cooperative a reporter could be, if promised a good story—and he could promise a dilly. Maybe he could cut a deal. He rehearsed his lines even as the chopper came closer.

Things were looking up.

7:15 P.M., the Upper East Side

The Looter, held aloft by his personal helium balloon, looked down on his work and saw that it was good. A smoky plume marked the site of the still-burning fuel truck. Horns honked and drivers yelled as they tried to make their way through streets snarled by dead signals and choked with emergency vehicles. Geysers of water still spewed from the fire hydrants he had ruptured, further hindering traffic. Hard work on his part had effectively paralyzed a large section of Manhattan, and given him the cover he needed to execute the rest of his plan.

Mere weeks before, he had discovered the meteor gases that gave him his power, and embarked on a crime spree. Spider-Man had put an end to those exploits, and turned him over to the authorities after a frenzied battle. What Spider-Man hadn't realized was New York's courts system was quite ready to grant bail to a depowered Norton G. Fester, and then release him to await trial.

The case against him was good. Fester knew that when he went to jail, he would stay there a long time. Now, suspended in mid-air, he relished his moment of freedom, and resolved again to extend it. That meant leaving New York for warmer climes, and that meant money—the kind of money he could raise easily enough under cover of the chaos he had created. Tonight, he would be a looter in fact as well as in name.

The Looter heard the sound of helicopter rotors, even over the wail of police and fire sirens. He spotted a news chopper skimming low above the rooftops and headed toward the fire. Clinging to the aircraft's hull was a familiar red-and-blue figure.

Spider-Man.

Behind the Looter's mask, Fester smiled. This was a bonus; his most hated enemy would doubtless be occupied for hours to come. He pulled a motorized propeller device from his backpack. The electrical motor spun to life, and the Looter's flight path, aimless drifting a moment before, became definite and specific.

It was time for Phase Two.

"This'll do, guys," Spider-Man said to the helicopter's occupants. He let himself drop. "Don't take any wooden press releases, okay? And stick around—I'll be right back." He yelled the words back to the pilot even as he fell. He grabbed a convenient flag-pole and spun once, twice, to expend some energy, then dropped the rest of the way to street level. Traveling without his webbing wasn't easy, and he didn't like doing it, but he knew the ropes. He touched down a half block from the construction site he had spotted from above. Behind him, he knew, the reporter and cameraman were watching his every move eagerly.

Right now, the fuel truck was the most pressing issue. It was burning like a torch, a column of orange flame spewing upward from its ruptured shell. Spider-Man had seen such fires before. There was no telling when the pyre's dynamic equilibrium would collapse and the truck would explode. Ordinarily, he might try to seal the breach with his webbing, but he couldn't do that now. He had to try something else.

A bulldozer was parked in front of the construction site's yawing excavation. Spider-Man had spotted it from his aerial perch. Now, he leapt easily into the driver's seat. No one tried to stop him; wisely, the workers had fled the scene. He took a quick look at the controls. They didn't seem very complex, at least not compared to some equipment he had operated, and he decided the vehicle was worth a try.

After all, it wasn't like he had much choice.

He punched the starter, and a diesel engine roared to life. Spider-Man steered the heavy earth-mover toward the truck. Hot wind washed over him, and he wished briefly he were somewhere else.

Anywhere else.

The pitch of the engines changed as its big blade met resistance. Spider-Man pushed the accelerator pedal and kept going. The ruined truck's undercarriage scraped sparks from the dirty asphalt, and rivulets of burning fuel trailed behind its sliding mass. He had to be very, very careful. Too much force, and the tanker would rupture completely, and release a flood of liquid fire that would incinerate anything it touched. Too little force, and the thing would stay where it was, burning out of control for hours to come. The object of the exercise was to keep the truck relatively intact, at least until he had it where he wanted it. Sweat trickled from his forehead, finding his eyes and stinging them, and the bulldozer's controls became hot enough to scorch his fingertips. His spider-sense screamed. He was too close to the fire, much too close to flaming death—

A new sound reached his ears, a thundering explosion that he felt rather than heard. Even as the blast erupted, he threw himself backward and away from the bulldozer, turning just in time to see the truck fall into the open construction pit, exploding again as it hit bottom. Spider-Man breathed a sigh of relief. The excavation had held the worst of the blast. As he watched, the pit's walls collapsed, smothering the remaining fire.

He looked at the still-hovering news chopper. Already, he knew, the reporter on board had nearly unprecedented close-up footage of Spider-Man in action. Behind his mask, Peter smiled grimly. He didn't mind giving the *Bugle*'s competition an exclusive, but he planned to make them earn it. He gestured at the helicopter.

It was time to move along.

7:45 P.M., Cassidy's Fine Jewels, the East Side

A concussion grenade split the safe door enough for the Looter to wedge his fingers inside; his enhanced strength did the rest. The heavy slab of metal tore free easily. Throwing it aside, he began scooping the safe's contents into his ditty bag. Diamonds, emeralds, rubies, sapphires—raw gems, rough and uncut, each worth much more than Fester could earn through long months of honest effort. They were his now, part of his retirement fund.

The Looter strode toward the shop's shattered front, stepping over the prone security guard who had been foolish enough to stand in his way. The coast was clear; the police were still too busy dealing with the effects of his rampage to bother looking for its cause. He looked at his watch. He had time for at least two more heists before Phase Three. Then, with any luck, he could gather more funds and finally leave this much-hated city.

His balloon was waiting for him, tethered to a fire hydrant. Fester donned its harness once more, and drifted up and away into the twilight.

8:00 P.M., the Upper East Side

High-tension cables lashed and spat electrical fire as Spider-Man approached the ruined power station. He looked at the gloomy tableau. This was the cause of the blackout, he knew, and the reason that traffic signals and streetlights were dead. He knew also that there was nothing he could do to fix it. All the spider-powers in the world weren't much help against electricity; he had learned that the hard way, more than once. This wasn't a job for Spider-Man; it was one for trained professionals. He silently thanked heaven that the site was deserted.

Or was it? One particularly bright spark briefly lent a frightening clarity to the scene. Spider-Man could see a human form slumped between the toppled towers. It was a security guard, injured or unconscious or worse. At the very least, the uniformed man was helpless. As Spider-Man watched, one of the broken cables danced dangerously close to the fallen man. The guy couldn't last much longer there, Spider-Man realized grimly. He had to help the fallen man, and fast. But how? Without his web, there was no way he could safely drag the cables or framework free.

A locked equipment cabinet caught his eye. A second later, it provided him with heavy rubberized gloves and boots. He donned them, pulling them on over his own costume. They would give him some protection, but not enough to make him safe. He rooted hastily through the rest of the locker's contents and found something else he would need—an insulated blanket. He looked back at the toppled towers, and at the man trapped between them.

He knew what to do, and he knew only a fool would try it.

Two seconds later, the fool known as Spider-Man jumped, twisting and spinning in midair to avoid the lashing cables and their charges of electrical death. His feet—made clumsy but insulated by the heavy boots—came down on a piece of fallen framework, then launched him upward once more. His spider-sense sang warning after warning as he bounced from point to point in a dangerous path that took him into the heart of the storm, deeper and deeper into the tangled array of broken steel and split concrete. Time and again, he bounced, twisted, and spun as supercharged cables lashed closely enough to him to make the hairs on his body stand on end. Each move he made changed the situation, by making the collapsed towers shift and twist as he struck them, but there was nothing he could do about that. Finally, one last, desperate leap brought him down inches from the injured man.

The man moved, and groaned, the sound barely audible above the hissing, crackling death that surrounded them both.

"Don't try to talk," Spider-Man said urgently. "Don't try to do anything. Just go limp and let me do the work." He wrapped the fallen man in the blanket and then lifted him in his arms. Still crouched in the space between two fallen towers, Spider-Man tensed the long muscles of his legs and waited for his chance. One second passed, two . . .

The chance came. Two of the heaviest cables collided in midair, attracted by opposing charges, then driven apart by the resulting flash of power. Both ricocheted outward, colliding again with other cables, creating a momentary clear space above the two men.

Spider-Man leapt, kicking against the dirty concrete as hard as he possibly could. He and his passenger flew upward in an acute trajectory that peaked eighteen or so feet above the ground. As they moved, one of the power lines bounced back to where they had been, searing and shattering the concrete where the security guard had lain an instant ago.

Coming out of the mess was even harder than going in had been. Spider-Man's burden made him clumsy, and made his footing unsure as he came down again, then bounced up. Still, progress became relatively easier as he moved outward. Two more leaps carried both of the men free of the tangled mess. Spider-Man set the guard down a safe distance from the sundered towers, and slumped beside him. For a long moment, he sat there, panting, desperately drawing cool air into his straining lungs.

The man spoke. "Crazy," he said. "Costumed lunatic."

Spider-Man looked at him, stunned at the ingratitude. "That's a heck of a thing to say," he said angrily. "I just risked my neck for you, buddy."

"Not you," the man said. "The guy who did this. Saw him. Knocked over the towers with his bare hands. . . ." His words trailed off into silence.

Interested now, Spider-Man leaned close. "Tell me who you saw," he said urgently. "Who did this?"

"Don't know. Some nut. Purple and white costume, had a backpack and a tool belt. Why would anyone want to do something like this?"

Purple and white costume. Backpack. Tool belt. They added up to one man, someone who should have been rotting away in a maximum security prison somewhere. Norton G. Fester, aka the Looter. With a sick feeling, Spider-Man realized just who had been in line ahead of Peter Parker earlier that day. The feeling worsened as he remembered something he had read only a few hours earlier. A dozen or so words, neatly typeset on a leaflet and casually tossed at him by J. Jonah Jameson.

He knew what Fester wanted.

9:00 P.M., the *Daily Bugle* Building

"The turnout's a little sparse, it seems to me," the mayor said. He gestured at the spotty crowd milling through the *Bugle*'s exhibit space. "Still, it looks like you've got the cream of the crop here. Should be plenty of good photo opportunities, eh?"

"There's been some kind of disturbance uptown," Jameson replied. "I've got some men covering it, but it's snarled traffic for most of the island. I'm surprised this many people turned out for the show." He sounded irritated. Around them, men and women in formal dress wandered among display cases, gazing reverently at complex exhibits they could not possibly understand. Jameson had pulled many strings to arrange for the display of some items, and it was frustrating to waste so much effort on such a small crowd. Attendance for the premiere was less than half what he had expected and he found one particular absence particularly rankling.

Where the devil was Peter Parker?

Jameson listened with one ear to the mayor's genial comments, but his thoughts were elsewhere. Right now, he would have loved dearly to see Peter Parker standing before him, not so that the younger man could complete his assignment, but so that Jameson could strangle him. Bad enough that he had to tolerate the kid's impertinence, but Parker had made things much worse by accepting his advance, then failing to uphold his end of the bargain. Without publicity photos, this evening's festivities were nearly useless.

Parker would pay for that, Jameson vowed silently. He would see to it that Parker spent years paying for this little *faux pas*. He would pay in lost assignments and missed opportunities. He would pay in reduced rates and casual indignities. He would pay by learning just what it meant to take advantage of J. Jonah Jameson's good nature and generosity. All of that would come later, though. Right now, he had to concentrate on the events at hand, and he didn't see any way things could get much worse.

Then the exhibition room's north floor-to-ceiling window shattered, and a man wearing a purple and white costume leapt through the breach.

•   •   •

The Looter released just enough gas from his balloon to start drifting lazily downward, and then let gravity do the rest. Once low enough, he anchored the flotation device to a streetlamp stanchion, then refilled it before unhooking himself and dropping the twelve or so feet to the sidewalk. Refilling the balloon used up his helium; not for the first time, he cursed the smug little man at ChemCo who had dared to suggest that Norton G. Fester could not be trusted for a few paltry dollars.

He drove his fist through a nearby window, then leapt inside. People screamed and ran as he entered. He kept moving, jumping and bounding from one exhibit case to another, throwing an occasional smoke grenade to add to the confusion. He moved quickly, not from fear of reprisal or apprehension, but because he had a schedule to keep. Just after a display of globe-shaped radiation generators and just before a full-sized mockup of the Fantastic Four's famous Pogo Plane, he found what he was looking for.

It was the Wakanda Find, dug from deep within the famous T'Kaing Crater, the largest single intact meteorite ever recovered. It was a chunk of space rock nearly the size of a telephone booth, only rarely put on display. Fester had read about it in scientific journals, seen photographs that plainly displayed its distinctive whorls and markings. He knew precisely what kind of meteorite it was, even if the fools who claimed it did not. He knew what treasures it held, the same exotic gases that he had harvested earlier in the day. The Wakanda Find was different, though, too big to move easily, and doubtless containing enough gases to empower him many, many times.

The Looter bounded to the top of the display case and plucked a specialized instrument from his backpack. It was a gas siphon of his own design, and having it fabricated had cost him much of his last cash reserves. One end came to a cruel point, and the other featured a compression cylinder similar to the helium cartridge he had used earlier. All he needed now was a minute alone with the ragged stone, time enough to find and steal the gases inside. Stored in the siphon's reservoir, this harvest would extend the Looter's career for many years to come.

"You! Get away from that!"

The angry words startled the Looter. He looked down from his perch atop the cabinet. An older man with wiry gray hair and a bristling mustache gestured furiously at him from the hall's floor. "I said to get away from that," the man repeated. "What's the meaning of this? This is a private party! What are you doing here?"

The Looter recognized him. He was J. Jonah Jameson, the *Bugle*'s publisher, and evidently too angry right now to think clearly. Fester inverted his gas extractor, and trained its sharp end at Jameson. "Go away, old man," he sneered. "This thing cuts through rock, but I'm sure it'll cut through you too."

Jameson paled and dropped the smoldering cigar from his lips, but he didn't say anything.

Someone else did, though.

Fester heard the beat of helicopter blades, but he did not notice it. He heard the sound of shattering glass, as a skylight broke, but he did not pay any attention. What he could not ignore was the hated voice that rang out through the exhibition hall.

"Your mother really should have taught you it's rude to point," Spider-Man said.

The Looter looked up just in time to see Spider-Man flying toward him, having launched himself from the skylight's frame. For some reason, he wasn't using his webbing to swing into the room. The super hero twisted and somersaulted in midair, so that his feet caught Fester squarely in the chest, knocking the wind from his lungs and driving him from his display-case perch. The gas siphon flew from his grasp, but the Looter barely noticed.

Jameson scrambled frantically to get out of the way of the two costumed men as they tumbled to the floor and began grappling. "I knew it," he yelled. "Spider-Man! You're behind this! You're working with this character!"

"Aw, put a sock in it, Jonah," Spider-Man said acidly. "Can't you see I'm busy here?"

The Looter didn't join in the repartee. He had his hands full warding off Spider-Man's increasingly effective blows. Even with the enhanced strength and durability that the meteor gases gave him, he could feel Spider-Man's punches. Worse, the other man was a more practiced fighter and Fester, until the accidental discovery that had given him powers, had been nothing but an anonymous research scientist with no combat experience. Besides, Spider-Man wasn't an easy target; he seemed able to predict Fester's blows and dodge them. Finally, one punch connected solidly with the super hero's stomach.

"That's it," Spider-Man said, grunting. "No more Mr. Nice Guy!"

Fester saw his chance and took it. His fist lashed out again and caught Spider-Man on the point of his jaw. The other man cried out in pain, his grip broken. The Looter scrambled out from beneath him and began running. Spider-Man gave chase, and Fester ran faster. The meteor had been his most important target tonight, but he could live without its bounty, if he had to. There were other meteors in the world, and there would be other opportunities. He couldn't let Spider-Man stop him again.

Fester leapt out through the broken window, with Spider-Man's hands closing on empty air an inch or so behind him. He hit the sidewalk and bounced, leaping frantically for the tethered balloon. Gripping the device's harness but not taking the time to don it, he snapped the anchor line that held the balloon to the lamppost, and sighed in relief as it pulled him upward.

He had made it. He was going to get away.

"Not so fast," Spider-Man snapped. Fester looked back and saw the super hero scramble up the *Bugle* Building's brick length, then launch himself into the air. Less than a second later, the Looter felt steel-hard fingers dig into the heavy fabric of his costume. Instantly, the balloon's ascent slowed and then stopped as its load increased.

"Get away! Let me go!" Fester screamed the words as Spider-Man shifted his grip.

"Sorry, you've got to say please." Spider-Man was clambering up the length of the Looter's body. Even as the two men sank to earth, he was reaching for the balloon itself, trying to wreck Fester's only possible means of escape. Thinking fast, the Looter looped one section of harness around his left arm, then laced the fingers of both hands together, making a double fist. He brought it down, hard, in a short, sharp arc that intersected Spider-Man's neck, midway between shoulder and chin.

Spider-Man didn't or couldn't dodge the blow. He gave another gasp of pain, and Fester felt his grip shift slightly. He punched Spider-Man again, and then a third time, and smiled in savage satisfaction as the super hero lost his grip and fell.

"That'll teach you," the Looter snarled. A wave of relief swept through Fester as the balloon began rising again—but then he heard the hissing noise. He looked up, knowing what he would see. It was a hole in the balloon's tough polyester fabric, a rent no longer than an inch.

But long enough.

The midair struggle had done it. With his weight and Spider-Man's weight combined, one of the harness cords had pulled just a bit too hard on a seam and split it open. The precious helium was seeping out now, and Fester could already feel himself falling. Desperately, he began shedding his load—the tools, the empty gas cartridge, all the instruments that had been essential mere minutes before were deadly ballast now. He kept the motorized propeller, and trained it in the appropriate direction even as his rate of descent slowed. He had only a few minutes before the asphalt came up to greet him, and he needed to be as far away as possible before that happened.

He had to get away.

J. Jonah Jameson, standing on the sidewalk, watched the struggle with interest and even amusement. Most of the other attendees had fled, but he had followed the conflict outdoors instead. Spider-Man had caused him much grief over the years, and it was always good to see the costumed adventurer get some for himself. Despite that, however, Jameson felt a twinge of concern when Spider-Man lost his grip and fell, and the Looter went drifting away. For some reason, Spider-Man didn't use webbing to catch himself, as Jameson had seen him do countless times before. Instead, the red-and-blue figure tumbled and twisted in midair, bouncing from wall to flagpole to lamppost, before landing only a few feet from Jameson.

"What's the matter?" Jameson asked the crouching super hero. "Your partner desert you?"

"Uh-huh, that's right, Jonah," Spider-Man said, with his typical, presumptuous familiarity. He stood and shook his head. "Me and the Looter, we're a regular Laurel and—hey! Watch out!"

Spider-Man's left arm moved with blinding speed, swinging out in a motion that Jameson thought was a punch, but that turned out to be an inelegant shove. His open hand struck Jameson in the chest, knocking the older man back, even as Spider-Man leapt aside. Less than a second later, a metal cylinder plummeted from the cloudy night sky and shattered the concrete where Jameson had stood. It bounced with a ringing sound, but Spider-Man caught it before it could hit the ground again.

"What the—!?"

"Helium cartridge," Spider-Man replied, after a glance at the thing. "His balloon must have sprung a leak. He's shedding ballast. This is empty, but it could still have done some damage." The blank white eyes of his mask turned in Jameson's direction. "You're welcome," Spider-Man said pointedly.

Jameson could barely hear him. Instead of replying, he looked up as the sound of a helicopter's rotors echoed in the nearly deserted street. He recognized the craft that hung low over his building. It was a local television station's news helicopter. Jameson groaned. Major news on *Bugle* premises, and someone else got the scoop!

Where the devil was Parker?

"Well, it's been fun, chuckles," Spider-Man said. He scuttled up and along the wall's brick surface again, moving fast. "Gotta run. My ride's here."

Ride?

"I knew it!" Jameson yelled the angry words, loud enough that he was certain Spider-Man could hear them. "I knew it! You're working for the competition!"

Spider-Man leapt from the rooftop and clung to the helicopter's hull. The pilot gestured for him to climb inside. Spider-Man shook his head, and shook it again as the reporter began barking eager questions about the evening's events. "Not now," he replied. "This isn't over yet! I know where the Looter is headed!"

The pilot looked at him, annoyed or concerned. He had ferried Spider-Man from site to site for most of the evening. "I can't keep this up all night," he said. "I'm running low on fuel!"

"Don't worry," Spider-Man said. "We're almost done."

11:00 P.M., the East Side

Fester pressed the accelerator pedal and snapped the steering wheel to the left, hard. The stolen police car's tires shrieked as he took the turn, then shrieked again as he swerved to avoid an angrily gesturing pedestrian. Traffic was bad, and he was still encountering some fringe effects from his earlier campaign of chaos. Fester cursed. He was running out of time. It had taken him too long to land his balloon and then patch it, and then to waylay the squad car's former occupants. He knew that the delay had given his enemies the time they needed to move against him. Spider-Man was out there, somewhere, no doubt in hot pursuit, and the conventional authorities were looking for him too.

He cursed again, the tone of his voice almost a sob. His plan had come so close to total fruition, before collapsing at the last moment. The Wakanda Find's craggy surface had been beneath his very fingertips when Spider-Man had interfered. Behind him, in the car's backseat, were jewels and bonds and other booty, enough to fund years of easy living on the run—but it was useless to him, unless he could get out of the city.

That wasn't going to be easy.

"—all points bulletin for Norton G. Fester, aka the Looter. Fester is not armed, but is extremely dangerous and possesses superhuman powers," the radio said. "Approach with extreme caution. Fester attempted to assassinate the mayor this evening."

Fester moaned. He had tried no such thing, but leave it to politicians to seek publicity from someone else's efforts. Now the authorities had sealed off the island, stationing guards at the airports, train stations, bridges, and ferries. His own efforts had nearly paralyzed the subway system, so that option was out too. He had only one chance that he could see, and it wasn't much of one.

Fester kept driving.

11:30 P.M., ChemCo chemical supply house

The Looter ripped the steel door from its frame. The lock's bolt and the door's hinges snapped instantly, and metal fragments flew in all directions. Fester ignored them, and bounded though the opening he had created. Another leap carried him over the sales counter and into the storeroom, palely lit by emergency lights. He began rummaging desperately among the shelves and pallets, searching for the familiar steel cylinders that he needed so badly.

"Looking for something?"

The voice. Fester knew that voice. Knew it, and hated it. He looked from side to side, but could not see the speaker. "How did you find me?" he asked angrily.

"It was easy. I just asked myself where I would go if I were you. What if I needed helium to fill *my* cockamamie little backpack balloon and escape from a sealed-off island? That much was easy." The voice paused. "The hard part was pretending I was an idiot."

Something heavy and metallic fell from above, and crashed into the floor. It was a helium cartridge. Fester looked down, then up, just in time to see Spider-Man drop from the ceiling.

"Victory through air power, Fester," the super hero said, just before smashing his fist into the Looter's nearly invulnerable jaw.

Fester fought back, with the furious desperation that came from the certain knowledge that his capture was imminent. He drove both fists into Spider-Man's abdomen, hard, and grunted in savage pleasure as the super hero doubled over in pain. Fester hit him again, but flinched as Spider-Man kicked him in retaliation. He punched Spider-Man again, and a third time, then dropped back as the super hero came for him again. He was doing better than he'd expected. Spider-Man seemed to be wearing down, perhaps tired out by the night's efforts, but the power in Fester's blood burned unabated. That, and adrenaline, seemed enough to turn the tide. For a moment, Fester thought he would win, thought that the would be able to smash his enemy and make his escape. Then—

Moving faster than any man could possibly move, contorting himself in stark defiance of the limitations of human anatomy, Spider-Man came at the Looter in a cartwheeling handstand. His hands pressed flat against the storeroom's concrete floor, and the big muscles of his arms flexed as Spider-Man drove his feet into the underside of Fester's chin. The Looter rocked back, staggered by the blow, and fell back farther as Spider-Man's fists pounded into him. The last blow sent him crashing into a shelving unit, and sent the unit crashing to the floor.

Wood and glass shattered as the Looter's nearly indestructible body smashed against shelving and bottles. Something slippery and clinging erupted from shattered carboys, and Fester recognized the chemical scent of a polymer compound as it filled the air. He lurched up from the broken containers, nearly losing his footing as the slimy stuff pooled beneath his feet.

"Hold that pose," Spider-Man said. "I want to remember you just like you were." The super hero had another bottle in his hands, a reagent jug with attached hose. Fester threw himself at Spider-Man, moving clumsily because of his unsure footing. The other man stepped nimbly aside, and squirted something at the Looter.

"I said to stay put," Spider-Man snapped, and Fester suddenly found that he had no choice but to obey. The second spray had done something to the polymer compound, made it harden and condense. Dozens of gray strands now stretched from Fester's body and anchored him to the surrounding walls and shelves. More of the stuff glued his feet to the floor.

"It's not webbing, but it'll have to do," Spider-Man said, apparently talking to himself.

Fester let out a howl of dismay and rage, and gathered his every last erg of energy for one final effort. For a split second, he thought he would succeed. He felt some of the still-gooey strands stretch and break, and the heavier globs at his feet peel loose. He brought his hands up, straining against the remaining strands, reaching desperately for Spider-Man's throat. If he could just get his hands around the super hero's neck—

"Some guys don't know when to call it quits," Spider-Man said. His fist came rushing toward Fester's face, and darkness fell.

So did the Looter.

Spider-Man clambered back to the ceiling. He had arrived at the scene with time to prepare for Fester's entrance, long enough in advance to wonder if he had been wrong in his theory as to the other man's destination. He had used part of that time to find a roll of duct tape and attach his automatic camera to a convenient joist. Now, he retrieved it and carefully returned it to the appropriate compartment on his belt. With even a little luck, the photos inside—exclusive shots of Spider-Man defeating the Looter— would go a long way toward buying his way back into Jameson's sort-of good graces.

Luck. He'd had plenty of that these days, and all of it bad. Between not recognizing Fester earlier, the Sally debacle, his problems with Gwen, and his ever-present money troubles, he was batting somewhat less than a thousand. Moreover, every bone, muscle, and joint in his body ached from tonight's efforts, and he knew that he still had a long night ahead of him. He needed to deliver his film to the *Bugle*, listen to Jameson rant for a while, and then head home and brew up a new batch of webbing. There was no way he dared let tonight's events repeat themselves.

Spider-Man picked through the wreckage behind the unconscious Looter, and found an intact bottle of liquid polymer. As he left ChemCo, he paused long enough to put the necessary money into the empty cash register. Then, he picked up a telephone and made a brief, anonymous phone call, telling the police where to find their quarry, courtesy of their friendly neighborhood Spider-Man

The helicopter had left, of course; the pilot had run dangerously low on fuel and returned to base before the Looter's arrival at ChemCo. Spider-Man would be gone long before a relief team could arrive, which suited him just fine. The news crew's reporter had proven entirely too good at his job, asking questions that Spider-Man didn't want to answer—even though the chopper's absence meant that he had a long walk ahead of him. Stiff and sore, wondering where he could buy eggs for Aunt May at this hour, Spider-Man stumbled into the darkness. As he did, he felt the first fat raindrop splash against his face.

Some days, it just didn't pay to get out of bed.

IDENTITY CRISIS

Michael Jan Friedman

Illustration by Rick Leonardi & Jeff Albrecht

J. Jonah Jameson—known as Jonah to his friends—sat back in his generously padded, black-leather lounge chair, puffed on his inexpensive domestic cigar, and considered the tendrils of blue-white smoke as they wafted in front of him.

From Jameson's point of view, Cuban cigars cost too much—and he was nothing if not a skinflint. In fact, he prided himself on his ability to squeeze a dollar until it bled.

Not that Jameson couldn't afford an imported smoke. He *did* belong to this club, one of the most upscale in New York City, didn't he? And he *did* run the *Daily Bugle*, one of the city's most profitable newspapers.

Beside him, curly-haired industrialist and inventor Norman Osborn sat back in a similar chair and puffed on a cigar of his own. But Osborn's cigar wasn't the least bit domestic. It was imported and more than a little bit illegal.

Osborn, by contrast, wasn't a skinflint at all. The way he told it, he'd made something of himself by dint of street smarts and hard work and he was determined to enjoy the fruits of his labor.

Not that the man was done climbing the ladder of success. He often said he had a way to go before he got to the top. But when he got there, when he was king of the hill . . . how sweet the fruits would be *then*.

So what if Osborn had suffered some business reverses recently? He'd get past them, he always insisted. He'd make his company—himself—stronger than ever. That was what life was about, wasn't it?

Strength. Wealth. Power.

"Say, Norman?"

Osborn turned to Jameson. "Mm?"

The newspaper publisher stroked his neatly trimmed moustache. "Have I ever told you about deep background?"

The other man looked at him. "Deep what?"

"Deep background," Jameson replied. "Information we don't normally put in our newspaper stories, for one reason or another—though we don't throw it away either. We keep it in our files, just in case."

"In case what?" Osborn asked casually, rounding his mouth to puff out smoke rings.

The newspaperman shrugged. "Let's say we find out Police

Commissioner Maneely has a girlfriend—one his wife wouldn't be too happy about. Well, juicy as it is, that's not the type of story we'd normally publish. But if the commissioner hands a big contract for bullet-proof vests to some company in Jersey, and the owner of the company just happens to be the brother of the aforementioned girlfriend . . ."

Osborn turned to him. Clearly, a light had gone on in that brain of his. "In other words," he said, leaning forward, "you've got information on any number of public figures. Puzzles just waiting for a few pieces to fall into place before they're complete."

Jameson grinned around his cigar. "Then you see the implications—"

"Of what you're saying?" Osborn finished for him. "Of course I do. You're going to expose the commissioner's love affair in the late edition. And if I move quickly, I can put in a call to Herb Irons, whose company came in second in the bidding for the bullet-proof-vest contract. Which can only endear me to Herb's pal Carlo Lucci, who runs the electrician's union and might be inclined to look the other way if I bring in cheap labor to rebuild my plant."

The editor winked. "I guess you *do* see the implications."

Osborn nodded. "Yes. And not just when it comes to Irons and Lucci." Apparently, he was thinking about something else as well. Maybe *someone* else.

That's what Jameson liked about his friend and fellow club-member. He saw all the angles. *All* of them.

"So," said Osborn after a while, "this girlfriend of the commissioner's . . . is she nice looking, at least?"

Jameson's grin widened. "Come on, Norman. You know I'm a man of principles. You'll have to read about that in the *Bugle* like everyone else."

Norman Osborn wasn't always himself lately—not since he'd been the victim of a chemical explosion that altered his outlook. Sometimes, he was someone else entirely.

Sometimes, he was the Green Goblin.

The Goblin was the bizarre embodiment of Osborn's hunger for power and recognition: the most grotesque and malicious elements of his personality given flesh-and-blood form.

And what a form it was. As the Goblin soared above New York City in the moonlight, he caught a glimpse of himself in the reflective surface of a brand-new skyscraper. A bony, angular figure with scaly green skin, he wore the long, tapered skullcap of a court jester and the pointed boots of an elf as he straddled a bat-winged, jet-powered glider.

But his most important feature, his trademark, was the mask he wore. A mask with pointed ears and a leering grin. And huge, arching eyes that seemed to covet everything in their purview.

The Goblin was a demon. An imp. A transplant from some ghastly fairy tale, wherein Rumpelstiltskin keeps the princess's baby and Snow White never ever wakes up.

In the past, he'd descended on the haunts of the criminal underworld, trying to become New York's kingpin by virtue of force and bluster. However, that turned out to be trickier than he'd guessed.

So he'd changed his strategy. He'd singled out the one objective that would gain him the respect of crooks everywhere. With that in mind, he approached the offices of a well-known metropolitan newspaper.

Noting the scarcity of lighted windows, it was easy for the Goblin to discern where people worked and where they didn't. Stopping to hover by one window in particular, he peered inside.

There was no one sitting by the window itself. But in the background, on the other side of the room, he saw several figures, a steaming cup of coffee, and a half-eaten burrito.

He could hear laughter, even through the glass. *Good*, he thought. If they liked a joke, they would die laughing at the sight of *him*.

With that, he hunkered down on his glider, kicked down on the accelerator, and burst into the room in a shower of glass. Once inside, he straightened to his full height and came to a halt in front of a clutch of startled faces.

There were five of them, to be exact. A heavy-set white-haired man who had to be nearing retirement, standing behind a desk with a freestanding metal plate that read NIGHT EDITOR. Another fellow, also middle aged and balding, in a rumpled suit with a pencil-thin moustache. A woman, middle aged, brunette, and not entirely unattractive. A frail-looking guy with a broom in a brown uniform—obviously the janitor.

And a teenager with a camera dangling from a shoulder strap. An overachiever, the Goblin decided. He'd have to be to work here at such a tender age.

These people knew who he was, too. He could tell by the look in their eyes. Not just surprise, not just a quick and shallow kind of fear. No, it was more an apprehension of what he'd done previously and what he was capable of.

He quirked his lip at them, his glider humming menacingly beneath him. "You must be the skeleton crew. How positively apropos."

"What are you doing here?" asked the woman over the howl of the wind through the newly broken window. "What do you want?"

The Goblin noticed some pictures in the boy's hand. He drifted in that direction and held his hand out.

"Let's see 'em," he demanded.

The teenager hesitated for a moment, then turned them over. The Goblin studied them. They were pictures of Spider-Man in whirling, looping battle with a bunch of armed gunmen in an alley somewhere.

Spider-Man. His nemesis. The reason he'd come here in the first place. Scowling inside his mask, he crumpled the photos in his gloved hand, much to the photographer's chagrin.

"Sorry," he snarled. "The morning edition will just have to do without them."

Out of the corner of his eye, he saw the janitor slinking toward the door. With practiced ease, he reached into his shoulder bag and produced a jack-o'-lantern the size of a grapefruit. Tossing it at a spot ahead of the janitor, he counted to two—then heard the concussion bomb in the jack-o'-lantern explode.

A moment later, the janitor had skittered back to where the others were standing, his uniform flecked with bits of pumpkin. He was scared out of his wits, as well he should have been.

"Don't run out on me," the Gobin warned, wagging a spindly finger at the man, "or I'll be tempted to expedite your exit, if you catch my meaning."

For emphasis, he activated the spark-shooter in the same finger, sending out a geyser of crackling energy. It made his hostages flinch—except the photographer, interestingly enough. But then, young people were often too brave for their own good.

"Now, then," said the Goblin. "Get me everything you've got on that wall-crawling interloper." He flung the crumpled photos at the city editor. "The one in these pictures."

"Everything we've got?" the balding man echoed.

The villain leaned forward. "Yes. You know, your *deep* background. The files you hang onto for a rainy day."

The editor's brow wrinkled, beads of perspiration collecting on his forehead. "Why? Whaddaya gonna do with it?"

The Goblin smiled a thin, dangerous smile. "Since you asked . . . I'm going to combine it with the information I have already, which is rather extensive. And then, when I have two and two to put together, I'm going to figure out who Spider-Man is beneath that mask of his."

He edged a little closer to the man. The editor swallowed rather hard. Not that the Goblin blamed him. Had he seen a gremlin out of a childhood nightmare approaching, he might have swallowed hard too.

"Won't that be fun?" he asked. "Unmasking Spider-Man?"

The editor nodded. "Yeah," he said flatly. "Fun."

Outside, the wind continued to howl. Papers ruffled on a dozen desks.

"And when I find out who he is," the Goblin continued, "I'm going to use the knowledge to frustrate him. To humiliate him. And finally to shatter his confidence. No, make that his *sanity.*"

He nodded, satisfied, as if it had all happened already. Then he emerged from his reverie and saw the heavyset man standing in front of him.

"Only then," he said, "will I destroy the web-slinger in the most literal sense. You see, in the colorful vernacular of the streets, I owe Spider-Man—big time."

The editor looked at the two reporters. The reporters looked back at him. They were all looking drained, hollow eyed with fear—but they weren't giving in. At least, not yet.

"What?" the Goblin blurted. "Don't tell me you're trying to protect that menace to society? That Halloween-costumed outlaw? Aren't these terms your own newspaper has applied to him?"

"That part's not a problem," said the male reporter, his voice trembling noticeably. "Me, I've always thought they oughtta lock up the guy and throw the key in the East River." He glanced at the other reporter, who was frowning through her anxiety. "Of course, not everybody agrees with me on that."

"Then what *is* the problem?" the Goblin hissed.

The balding man winced at the intruder's tone of voice. "Y'see," he said, his voice trembling a little harder, "a bunch of us worked pretty hard to accumulate what's in that file. Who knows? Maybe it'll win us all a Pulitzer someday."

The Goblin was mildly amused by the man's audacity. "If I don't get what I want, you won't live long enough to win a Pulitzer. You won't even live long enough to order breakfast."

"It's not just that," said the editor.

As the Goblin turned to him, the man blanched a little whiter. Taking a handkerchief out of his pocket, he used it to dab at his forehead.

"David," said the woman, "your heart—"

"Never mind that," the editor told her. He turned to the Goblin again. "There are contacts in that file. Names of people we've sworn not to expose, you understand? Some of them risked their jobs, even their marriages, to talk to—"

The Goblin moved closer to the editor, and spoke just above a whisper. "I want that file. And," he added, suddenly tripling his decibel level, *"I'm not leaving here without it!"*

Everyone recoiled at his outburst, but no one answered him. Least of all the janitor, who hadn't said a word since his arrival. Finally, someone spoke up, but it wasn't anyone he'd expected to hear from.

"I think we ought to give this person what he wants," the photographer advised, his voice amazingly clear and steady under the circumstances. "Can't you see how dangerous and determined he is? He's not going to leave the place without hurting someone."

"Easy for you to say," replied the balding man. His skin looked like wax, but he still held his ground. "You haven't spent the last six months pumpin' stoolies and street slime for anything they knew. You don't have anybody dependin' on you to keep them in the background. All you do is take your pictures and go home."

The photographer scowled at him. "Get a grip, all right? We're not just talking about your life, or David's or Rita's. We're talking about Smitty's too. And . . . and mine. I've seen people get hurt and I've lost people close to me. And I'd hate to have to lose anyone else."

"What about my contacts?" asked the reporter.

"Come on," said the photographer. His dark eyes blazed. "There's no one there with anything to hide except a little numbers running and some petty larceny. You know that as well as I do."

The Goblin stroked his chin. "Is that so? Have you been embellishing the truth a bit, my friend?"

The balding man shook his head with terrible intensity. "Don't listen to him. He's just a kid."

The Goblin leaned a little closer to the balding man. "It sounds to me like this 'kid' is the only one here with any common sense."

He reached into his shoulder bag and tossed a handful of narrow black cylinders into the air. Their onboard computers, responsive to any abrupt change of attitude, caused them to sprout bat wings and dive-bomb anything that moved—except for the Goblin himself, of course.

Scared that the bats were going to tear them limb from limb— or explode in their waxy, frightened faces—the five captives flinched as they approached.

There was a lot of shrieking and grunting and cursing. For a moment, one of the bats even got caught in the brunette's hair— until the photographer grabbed it and pulled it free.

Finally, the Goblin figured his hostages had had enough. He triggered the homing mechanism, and the bats returned to his shoulder bag, where they lay still and quiescent.

"Well?" he asked. "Where are those Spider-Man files?"

No one answered: the janitor, and possibly the teenager, because they didn't have the answer he wanted; the others because they chose not to.

This was getting tedious. The Goblin wondered if his captives were stalling him, hoping against hope that help would arrive. If he waited long enough, perhaps it would.

Obviously, he was going to have to speed things along. He would have to make an example of someone. But who?

The woman? The night editor with the weak heart? Or the janitor?

In the end, he fixed on the latter. First, the man seemed absolutely petrified. Second, the other four seemed to like him. They wouldn't relish the prospect of his getting killed on their account.

"Well," he said, "it's been a hoot, but I don't have all evening. It seems I'm going to have to show you I mean business. And for that trick, I'm going to need the assistance of my friend Smitty."

With a quick burst of speed from his glider, he crossed the room and homed in on the janitor. The man cried out and sank to the floor in desperation, his hands raised in front of his eyes— but the Goblin stopped mere inches away.

He shook his head. "No way, Smitty ol' pal. You think I'm going to make this quick and painless? Not a chance. I think your friends were looking forward to a real spectacle. A long, bloody—"

"That's enough!" someone shouted.

The Goblin looked back over his shoulder. It was the teenager, of all people.

"That's enough?" the Goblin echoed ominously. "Don't you know it's impolite to steal my lines? And here I thought you were such a bright young man."

"You want Spider-Man?" the boy said. He licked his lips. "All right. You've got him."

The villain peered at him from behind his mask. "I do?"

The teenager nodded. "It's me. *I'm* Spider-Man. Just let everybody go and you can do whatever you want with me."

The Goblin's first impulse was to laugh out loud. But he didn't. Something about the boy made him stop and consider the possibility he was telling the truth.

After all, he'd shown uncommon courage until now. And he'd said earlier that his family and friends had died violently. Certainly, that would be motivation enough to make a dedicated crime-fighter—and the web-slinger was nothing if not dedicated.

Of course, there was a simple enough way to find out.

The Goblin slid over to the boy on his glider and grabbed a fistful of his shirt. "If you're Spider-Man," he said, his face inches from the teenager's, "let's see what happens when I toss you out the window."

In an eyeblink, he dragged the boy toward the open window. The shards of glass still in the frame glinted like the teeth of some mythical beast and the night yawned like its maw.

"No!" cried the woman.

But the Goblin wasn't about to stop. Not for anything.

"The real Spider-Man would survive this," he said shrilly. "But anyone else would plummet to his death."

And before the teenager could respond, the Goblin sent him hurtling out the broken window.

He watched as the boy's figure diminished and dropped along the edge of a long, straight shadow. Unfortunately, he wasn't doing any of the things Spider-Man would have done to save himself. There were no webs, no acrobatic antics, no scintillating flagpole acts.

Too bad, the Goblin thought. If the boy *had* been the web-slinger, it would have been a simple matter of getting his name from the reporters and he would've had what he needed. As it was, he found himself back at square one.

Then his eyes popped out . . . as a slim, dark figure swooped down from across the street and scooped the boy up in his free hand, using the other to hang on to a length of webbing.

The Goblin bit his lip. Spider-Man. The *real* Spider-Man.

Unfortunately, he had been wasteful with his bag of tricks. He didn't have the firepower he needed for a head-to-head confrontation. There was only one option left open to him.

He zipped out of the *Daily Globe*'s window on his bat-wing glider and headed uptown for Norman Osborn's apartment. Maybe next time, he mused bitterly, he would try the *Bugle*.

I'm dead, thought the boy. *I'm dead I'm dead I'm dead—*

But before he could hit the pavement, he felt something slam into him from the side. He caught a glimpse of something blue and red and felt himself swinging dizzily through the air.

Then he heard a voice, close to his ear. "It's all right. I've got you and I won't let go."

As the boy got his bearings, he realized why he hadn't become a particulary sorry-looking lump of street pizza. He found himself looking up into the masked face of Spider-Man.

The Spider-Man. The same guy he'd been lucky enough to take some photos of the night before.

"My God," he said.

It was one thing to watch Spider-Man in action from afar—

but another to actually whip through the city's canyons with him. They came to a stop on a tar-covered rooftop.

"Are you okay?" asked the masked man.

Maybe it was the voice, or the choice of words, but the photographer had a feeling Spider-Man might be a teenager too.

"I am now," he said.

"What happened?" asked the web-slinger. "How did you fall?"

Suddenly, the boy remembered the others and looked up to find the window he'd fallen from. But before he could say anything, he saw a streak of fire emerge from the building and make its way across the sky. Spider-Man saw it too.

"The Goblin," he said. In the masked man's mouth, it was more like a curse.

"He broke into the newspaper office," the boy told him. "Terrorized us. Said he was going to kill one of us if we didn't give him what he wanted."

Spider-Man gazed at him, his eyes hidden behind opaque white plates. "And what was that?"

"The deep background files on *you*. So he could figure out who you are behind your mask."

The web-slinger grunted. "Gotcha." He glanced at the streak of fire a second time. "I'll never catch up with him. Too big a head start. Why don't I just deposit you down below?"

A moment later, he'd accomplished that. They stood in the shadows of a deserted street.

The boy considered him. "You're not a bad guy, are you?"

Spider-Man shook his head from side to side. "No."

"I didn't think so. You know, I saw you last night over by Thirteenth Street. You were mixing it up with some gunmen. I took some pictures."

"Pictures?"

"Uh-huh." The boy shrugged. "It inspired me, sort of. Made me want to do something heroic too."

The masked man looked at him askance. "Is that how you wound up flying out the window?"

The teenager nodded. "Yeah. I told the Goblin I was you. As if we had something in common." He chuckled.

"Hey," said Spider-Man, shooting a wad of thick, gray webbing at the building across the street, "you never know."

Then, as the photographer watched, he swung away into the windblown New York night.

THE DOCTOR'S DILEMMA

BAGS-96 & Albrecht

Danny Fingeroth

Illustration by Mark Bagley & Jeff Albrecht

*L*ove the power.

   Hate the responsibility.

   But it doesn't matter what I feel or what I like. It's beyond that now. Way beyond that. I've got the responsibility. And like it or not, I've got the power too.

   I've got to use that power to do the right thing.

   To take what I need.

   And to make anybody who gets in my way real sorry they got there.

Peter Parker thought about all that had led him to this moment. The spider's bite that gave him his powers. The flash of gunfire from the burglar's gun that left Uncle Ben dead and Aunt May a widow. The burglar—the murderer—whom he found and cornered. Whom he had let get away from a smaller, pettier, crime before. And didn't kill. And would always wonder why he hadn't.

But he scarcely had time to reflect on that. Like the opening gunshot in a race that never seemed to end, the need for a Spider-Man hardly ever let up. Just when he thought he'd fought his most dangerous foe, a new one would rise up to challenge him. And all the while, there was white-haired, devoted May, who'd always, no matter what, treated him right. Ben's absence now made it even more important that he take good care of her.

He had to take care of her. Peter Parker. The amazing Spider-Man. Man? He wasn't even eighteen yet. But the things of boyhood seemed far behind him. How could they not? In the short time he'd had the powers, he'd confronted so many dangerous criminals. Take Dr. Octopus—calling himself the "Master Planner" for some reason. Spider-Man had had to fight him and his forces to get hold of ISO-36, which he needed to save May's life (she took ill from a transfusion she'd received from her nephew with his irradiated blood). That was one of far too many times when his personal and "professional" lives had become just a little too intertwined, when the first of Aunt May's many illnesses had added another bit of pressure to his dual life. As if he needed more.

So it wasn't really surprising when Dr. Bromwell grabbed him by the arm that day in the kitchen and whispered that he had to speak to Peter about his "double life."

Okay, so maybe it *was* surprising. And yet, Peter felt a bit relieved. No more having to be duplicitous to the woman he loved most and owed the most to. He'd have to face up to what he'd been doing, take the responsibility. And even take pride in the good he'd done. Face up to the latter part of his taken heroic name, not cower in the shadows of anonymity like some little boy.

So some regret mixed in with the relief when Bromwell made it clear that he'd been talking about Peter's *other* dual life. (*Guess that'd make it a triple life, at least,* Peter thought.) Peter had taken the old camera he'd inherited from Uncle Ben and used it to snap pictures of himself as Spider-Man in action, then sold them to the New York *Daily Bugle*. It was a good way to make a few extra dollars to support him and May.

But as soon as he realized what Bromwell was talking about, he also knew what was coming next. Bromwell had always had a paternalistic streak in him, and with Ben gone, it was showing itself more and more, whether during Peter's office visits to take care of an ingrown toenail or Bromwell's increasingly frequent home visits to take care of May. And with Bromwell still charging 1950s-type rates to the family, he was a guy the Parkers couldn't afford to alienate.

"Peter," continued Bromwell, his breath smelling like a waiting room, "I've seen your photos in the *Bugle*. And while I have to say that they are newsworthy and some are even artistic . . . it's obvious that they're dangerous to take. Doesn't your aunt have problems enough without having to worry about you being out there at all times of the day and night, in all kinds of weather, risking your life to enrich Jonah Jameson and his cheap tabloid? You're a smart, capable boy. There must be a hundred other things you could do. Aside from the danger to yourself—and I understand that at your age you think you're going to live forever—think of your aunt. If something happened to you during one of these photo shoots, it would break May's heart. And I mean that literally *and* figuratively. I'm asking you, for her sake if not for your own, to give it up."

Peter had wondered when he'd hear this speech from somebody. May would bring it up once in a while, but he was usually able to sweet-talk her out of worrying, or she let him think he had, anyway. If he'd been rebellious like some other kids, May would have had real reason to worry. But here he was, the straightest and narrowest kid in the world. Okay, so he liked to crawl walls, beat up on super-creeps, and take pictures of himself doing it. Nobody's perfect. But he was always waiting for someone to give him "the speech." Heck, he'd given it to himself a hundred times, and he still couldn't figure out if he was the most selfish or most generous guy who ever lived for doing what he did. Yes, he'd thought about it a hundred times over, waiting to have to defend his life choices, and he was ready to give a reasoned, articulate defense of those choices.

So how come the words that came out of his mouth were, "I'd appreciate it if you'd mind your own business, Doctor"?

Peter regretted it as soon as he'd said it. But it was as if Bromwell's request had unleashed a torrent of confused and conflicting feelings in Peter, and they all came out and flung themselves at the doctor. Peter could see that Bromwell was somewhat taken aback by this outburst, but he just kept on going, building up steam as he went.

"It's easy for you to give advice, Doctor. But I'll tell you something. You sit all day in your fancy office—" (Bromwell had a tiny workspace in a nondescript walkup on Queens Boulevard) "—with your fancy patients—" (Bromwell made a point of helping people who didn't have a dime) "—and think you're some kind of a god who dispenses advice. With all due respect—" (right) "—I have to ask you, how else could Aunt May and I afford to live if I didn't do what I do? Could I make as much flipping burgers? Or should I see how the tips are over at the car wash? Uncle Ben was a good man, a great man, but he couldn't afford any insurance to tide May over in case anything happened to him. And medical insurance? There are forty million people in this country who don't have it. We're two of them. Aunt May is a great woman. And she deserves to have as much as I can legally make for her. So my buddy Spider-Man lets me get some shots of him in action. I've got to do what I've got to do. And that's just how it is."

Peter stopped to take a breath, and realized that Bromwell had backed against the kitchen table. Without another word, he handed Peter a prescription for May, mumbled something about the directions on the bottle, and made his way to the door.

Can't afford to alienate him—good work, Parker.

"Doc, wait!" Bromwell stopped halfway through the door and

turned around. "I—I'm sorry, Doc. You touched a nerve, but it wasn't right for me to go off on you that way. I know you have Aunt May's and my best interests at heart. I've gone through this a million times in my own head and what you've said isn't anything I haven't thought myself. But every time I weigh the pros and cons, I just keep coming back to the same conclusion: that what I'm doing is the best thing, despite the risks. I appreciate your thinking about us. I know you must have your own problems, as well as those of all your other patients."

Bromwell breathed what Peter hoped was a sigh of relief. "Peter, all I can ask is that you consider what I've said. Particularly the next time you weigh whether the risks of taking those photos is worth it. I mean, whatever Spider-Man may get out of the deal, he at least gets to be a star and some kind of hero—and, after getting that isotope to May that time, I'd say he's earned both terms. And if he gets killed doing what he does, he's the guy who'll get remembered in the history books, not you. Does anybody remember who took pictures of John F. Kennedy?"

Peter laughed inwardly at these unintnetional ironies of Bromwell. He extended his hand and the doctor took it. "Like I said, I appreciate all you've done—all you're doing—for us, Doctor, and I promise to give what you've said some real consideration. And I'll fill this prescription today."

Peter watched Bromwell as he got into his car and drove off. Then Peter went back into the house, crossed the living room in a single leap, and bounded up the stairs in another. He looked quickly in on May, who slept peacefully. Taking another effortless leap down the hall into his own room, Peter had his web-shooters loaded and his Spider-Man suit on in a matter of seconds. Two quick taps on his right web-shooter and a line sprang out of the window to the telephone pole down the street, and Spider-Man was off into the skies. (And, boy, was it handy he had that spider-sense to let him know that no one was watching him exit the Parker house.) Peter swung and leapt toward Queens Boulevard, then caught sight of Bromwell's car. Realizing he'd better kill some time before changing back to Peter and going to the drugstore, he headed for his alma mater, Midtown High.

As he watched a few kids play basketball in the yard, Peter wondered for the millionth time why a school in the far reaches of Queens should be named Midtown High. Then he wondered,

even though he'd never so much as been chosen in their basketball games, if they'd ever have a reason to call it Peter Parker
High—fantasizing that he'd win the Nobel one day and they'd
have no choice. He continued to let his mind wander, making
sure to keep the thoughts that Bromwell had triggered far at bay.
After waiting an appropriate time, Spider-Man crawled down the
wall and through the alley, changing back to his Peter clothes as
he went, and walked toward the pharmacy to fulfill a duty less
exciting than stopping a super-villain, but no less important.

Bromwell's mother had always wanted him to be a specialist. *The
days of the general practitioner are over,* she'd tell him. But, impossible as it seemed now, he wanted to be the doctor who could
be all things to all people. He was so idealistic in his youth, in
love with the old country-doctor image he'd seen in the movies.
So he wasn't blind to what Peter Parker was about. The kid
wanted to live up to some image of the crusading newspaper
photographer, and he wanted to be the good nephew to his dot-
ing aunt. He wanted to have it all. *Hell, that's what being a teenager's
all about.*
    Bromwell took May Parker's file out of his cabinet and made
some notes in it. Putting it back in, he saw Peter's right next to
it. He looked at it and looked at Peter's medical history from
birth through his most recent checkup, and his imagination
couldn't help but predict a DECEASED entry marked in with the
current year. He tried to stop the thoughts, but he couldn't. This
was the downside of being a general practitioner. Why couldn't
he be a celebrity specialist? Bromwell met those highfalutin types
at fundraisers all the time—they sat up front at the large tables
by the podium while Bromwell languished at the twenty-five-
dollar-a-plate tables in the back. These were men and women
with ice in their veins, totally detached, each patient a cipher, a
challenge to be met and then forgotten the second the very large
check cleared.
    But, like it or not, Bromwell couldn't be like that. And he
sensed a kindred spirit in Peter, too, sensed that this daredevil-
action-photographer role was a way to distance himself from the
good-little-boy role he had to play for his aunt. Bromwell had
known Peter from the time he was born, and knew that he was

truly good-hearted. Peter also had a great interest in the sciences. Bromwell hoped the kid wouldn't lose—

The sciences! That's it, he thought. Why hadn't he thought of it before? If he got Peter hooked up with some kind of scientific job, maybe it wouldn't be as glamorous as the picture-taking, but surely it would be tempting, especially if he could show Peter how it could open all these doors where he could make a very healthy salary and really do right by his aunt. Maybe he could even find some kind of work for Peter in his own lab.

The next morning, Bromwell got up even earlier than usual and headed over to Metro Hospital. There he searched out and spoke with the doctors who had helped May though her terrible ordeal.

"Dr. Gordon," he asked the serious, dark-haired fellow who opened the door for him, "do you remember May Parker?"

"How could I forget her? Spider-Man arrived with the medicine that finally brought her through. You don't forget a thing like that! Why? Has anything happened? Has she—?"

"No, she's getting along as well as can be expected. I'm just trying to help her with a family problem. It's her nephew."

"Peter? I'm surprised there would be any problem with him. He's so dedicated, so serious. I'd have figured him the last type to be in any trouble."

"It's not the sort of trouble you'd expect. He's so dedicated to May, though, that he may be inadvertently putting her at risk. I just wondered if he'd said anything to you while you were treating her."

"Not much I can remember—except that Peter did come in a couple of hours after Spider-Man and he was all beaten up, and on the verge of exhaustion. He wouldn't say what had happened to him. But I always felt that he was a straight arrow, a kid I'd like my own kids to be like, not a thrill-seeker like that Spider-Man. Still, spending his spare time taking pictures of people like Spider-Man, I'm not surprised that Parker must risk his life just keeping up."

"That's just the problem. Thank you, Dr. Gordon," sighed Bromwell as he turned to go.

In the crowded subway on the way home, Bromwell couldn't stop his thoughts from racing. None of it made a lot of sense. Okay, so Peter and Spider-Man had some kind of business relationship and maybe even a friendship. And, okay, an egomaniac like Spider-Man wouldn't care about letting a sweet kid like Peter risk his life. But what was in it for Spider-Man? Was Peter kicking cash back to the wall-crawler? It would make sense—Spider-Man had no visible means of income. He never collected rewards for bringing in criminals. Of course, no one knew who he was under the mask.

Well, Spider-Man's interest isn't my problem, he thought. *Let his own family worry about him. I've got to try to help May. Try to help Peter face up to his own problems.*

Spider-Man's face felt like it had been hit by a freight train. Underneath his silk-screened web-mask, Peter Parker could feel the welts rising already. *Good thing I've got my spider-sense,* he thought, *otherwise the cops would have to put a search party together to find my head.*

He'd gone out web-swinging for several reasons. The death of Uncle Ben had taught him that he had a responsibility to use his powers for good, which wouldn't happen if he just sat at home. He was hoping for some photo opportunities to make some extra cash to help pay Doc Bromwell's next bill. And, as much as anything, web-swinging was a blast.

Well, maybe not at this exact moment.

He'd been thinking about what Bromwell had said, thinking that maybe he was endangering May by endangering himself. So when he saw the eight-foot-tall, four-foot-wide gent in the green spandex suit smashing into the armored van and manhandling the trio of guards inside it, he was working more on automatic pilot than anything. Which, in this case, was obviously not enough. The giant landed his haymaker and Spidey was just beginning to recover from it.

"I don't wanna hurt anybody," the giant said. "I just want cash. And lots of it."

"Perhaps an aggressive mutual fund could be the solution to your problem, friend," suggested Spider-Man, sucking his strength up and leaping for the giant.

"You ain't funny, Spider-Man. And I ain't your friend." The giant pulled the truck toward him, then slammed Spider-Man with it. Spidey barely saw it coming. The guy was amazingly fast and as strong as the Hulk. Which meant Peter's spider-sense was nearly useless, even given his own superhuman speed. It would be like someone screaming "Look out for that bullet," after the gun fired.

Well, the job description includes the tough ones too.

Spidey pulled himself up from under the truck in time to see the big guy loading a huge sack with cash. "Hey, shorty, mind telling me why you're doing this?" It was less social work and more trying to slow the guy down so he could think of some way to stop him.

"I need money. And my name ain't shorty. It's—" and he stopped. It was clear he didn't want to give his real name and had never bothered to come up with an alias. Finally, he said, "Impact. My name is Impact. I need the money for my family. I volunteered for these science geeks to try some'a their radioactive steroids. They said it'd be okay. But I became a big freak. And their funding ran out—so they said—and I never even got paid. Trashed their lab real good, though."

"So now you're branching out into armored trucks, huh?" Spider-Man said as his fist *whooshed* through the air and landed full force on the back of Impact's head. The giant dropped the money.

He turned and grabbed Spider-Man by the foot as the wall-crawler was passing and slammed his head into a wall.

"Ow," muttered Impact, in a delayed reaction to Spider-Man's attack. He picked up the sack again, refilled it to the top.

He looked down at the semiconscious adventurer. "All I wanted was to make an honest buck. But no job ever worked out. My kids didn't stop needing to eat or stop being sick. I don't want to hurt anybody, including you. So just stay out of my way."

Spider-Man just lay there, the city spinning around him. Impact (*not bad for an on-the-spot name selection,* Peter mused through the haze) ran off at what must have been forty miles an hour. Sirens screamed. The arriving police wanted to question Spider-Man. He obligingly tossed off a few facts to the men in blue, made sure the guards were safe in the hands of the paramedics, then swung off. His pride was hurt as much as his head, and both pains were pretty extreme.

"Peter Parker, you come in here right now!" Peter was already halfway down the steps when he head May's call; he turned and dashed back up to her door.

She gasped. "All I was going to say was that I was surprised you'd leave for school without saying good-bye. But now I can see why."

Peter stood there. And even the Yankees cap pulled down low and the sunglasses couldn't disguise the bruises and cuts on his face.

May's mild anger quickly turned to intense concern. She got up as quickly as she could and gently put her hands on his face. "What on earth happened to you?" she whispered.

"Um . . . experiment in the lab at school . . . uh . . . was day-dreaming and mixed some of the wrong chemicals. All my fault, and nothing serious. Got to go. I love you." He kissed her and walked out of the room. *Got away with another one*, he congratulated himself.

At the front door, though, his luck gave out. Bromwell had arrived to check on May. Peter saw the rage flicker in the doctor's eyes as he surveyed the damage Peter had sustained. Then the physician calmed down, striving to speak calmly and reasonably.

"Peter, I've been thinking. I need someone to help me out in my own research and lab work. I've got a backlog of projects and patients' tests that I'll never finish in this lifetime. I couldn't pay you much, but we could start out at something low and, if it works out, go up from there.

"Look, I won't deny that part of the reason I'm making this offer is because I want you to stop taking those dangerous pictures. But I really do need someone to help me out. This could be the perfect solution to both our problems."

Peter thought for a very long few seconds, then put his hand out, and Bromwell took it in both of his. Peter covered his wince with a smile—the hand was still sore from colliding with Impact's hard head. "Okay, Doc," said Peter. "I'll give it a try. For Aunt May's sake."

"Thank you, Peter. You won't regret it. Now let me see about your face." Bromwell removed Peter's glasses and began daubing at the cuts with iodine.

On the floor above them, a frail figure was feeling pain neither of them could have imagined.

May Parker stood at the top of the steps. She had heard every word and was able to reconstruct the conversations she had not been privy to. Her stomach tied itself into knots. She had known all along that Peter was risking his life taking those photos, associating with a menace like that Spider-Man and the even worse creatures he fought. And she'd often expressed concern over what Peter was doing. But she'd never done anything about it, nothing really serious, anyway. Often, she just wasn't sure how to treat the boy. His parents were long gone. And when Ben died, she had to be mother *and* father to him, but truth to tell, she'd never had her own children and was never sure she was doing the right thing. She didn't want to overprotect him. *Boys need some adventure in their lives,* Ben had said once, *otherwise they'll never let go of the apron strings.* So she'd never put her foot down over the photography.

But the thought always plagued her: maybe it wasn't Peter she was concerned about. Maybe it was herself. Maybe she was just afraid that if Peter didn't bring in the money from taking those photos, she wouldn't have a way to live. Could it be? They'd always gotten by, but in large part because of that *Bugle* income. Would it have been so terrible for her to have convinced him to stop it? She could sell the house . . . even go on welfare, maybe even find some work she could do from home if her condition improved. Perhaps one of those alternatives would be better than letting Peter continue to risk his life on her behalf.

And what hurt most of all, was that it had taken a stranger, Bromwell, to find a way out of the danger for Peter.

May found herself short of breath. She trudged back to the bed and waited for the doctor to come see her.

The next day was Saturday. Peter got up bright and early and walked over to Bromwell's office. The doctor let him in and shoved a stack of papers at him. Even with his extensive knowledge of the sciences, this was a little much for Peter, but the doctor said to take his time and get familiar with the material. Then he went into the other room to see his first patient.

After about an hour, Peter's brain was still swimming in Bromwell's data, but something else preyed on his mind: Impact. He'd made another appearance since he battled Spider-Man. (*Battled? That's giving yourself too much credit, Parker. "Massacred" is more like it.*) He had to go find him and stop him. But he now had this commitment to Bromwell, and he couldn't give it up.

Then a thought occurred to him. *Since I am in a doctor's office, let's put it to good use. See if Impact's steroid story checks out.*

When Peter finished with one file, he decided to take a break and learn what he could about steroids from Bromwell's library. The floor-to-ceiling bookshelves that lined the office seemed to have every medical encyclopedia and journal known to the profession, so it didn't take Peter long to find several in-depth articles about steroids. He read them, mostly understood them, and found out that steroids can be helpful in certain medically mandated situations. But when used to enhance performance, mostly by athletes, they were definitely bad news. Potentially fatal news.

There was one article about "radioactive steroids." It said that they were considered especially dangerous, and that such medical value as they had was no greater than that of regular steroids; so the government had stopped funding the research being done on them. *Well, that jibes with what Impact said.*

Peter learned more about Impact from Jake Conover's column in the *Daily Bugle*, which he read over lunch. Conover had talked to Impact's family after they came forward to the police, and the *Bugle* ran the column alongside the news story on the robbery (complete with photos credited to one P. Parker). Apparently, according to "Conover's Corner," Walter Cobb had been a good husband and father, but the family had bills that, like the song says, no honest man could pay. Desperate, Walter had volunteered for "some kind of experiment," and then disaster struck. He became hugely powerful, couldn't get paid by the people he volunteered for, and then decided that crime was the quick, fast way to make money. But his wife couldn't live with knowing that their newfound riches were stolen. It was only a matter of time before he'd hurt someone seriously, but they couldn't convince him to go for help; his mind was too warped by the steroids. He was no longer the husband and father they loved.

Seems like every time you turn around, there's another hard luck story you're gonna hear, thought Peter.

But Impact's—Walter's—family situation didn't make what he did right. Power didn't give Walter Cobb the right to take what he wanted, no matter how tempting. It would just make things worse in the long run.

Maybe Spider-Man needed to save Impact from himself.
Right. And after that, I can start on poverty and injustice.

Peter spent long days and nights at Bromwell's. Impact kept busy too. A bank break-in here, a jewel heist there. One afternoon on his way out, Peter heard a news bulletin on the radio that piped into Bromwell's waiting room: Impact was stealing a huge gold display at the Metropolitan Museum of Art.

Changing in a flash, Peter was over at the Met in four minutes flat. Impact was gone, and so was the gold. Three guards were being tended to for injuries. One had a fractured skull. Spidey swung in to the jeers of bystanders. "Boy, that guy gave you a beating, and now you don't dare face him," razzed one kid. Spider-Man turned to the freckle-faced kid and took a menacing step forward. Then he stopped. Was the kid right? Was he losing his nerve?

Or was he just trying to look out for Aunt May and Impact?

Aunt May and Impact. Man, who ever thought I'd use those two proper nouns in the same sentence?

The routine went on like that for several more nights: Peter becoming more involved in the workday at Bromwell's, then barely missing a rendezvous with Impact. The other super-villains in town must have been taking a vacation that week, because Impact was all Spidey had to deal with. Or not deal with, as the case might be.

One morning—a Friday—Peter was working at Bromwell's. The phone rang. Bromwell answered, spoke tersely to the caller, then hung up and grabbed his medical bag with the other hand. "Trouble a few blocks away, Peter. I've got to go to the ER." Bromwell was on call at Parkway Hospital's Emergency Room on Mondays and Fridays.

"What kind of trouble? Maybe I can help."

Bromwell shook his head. "I don't think so. That Impact monster struck again, hurt a lot of people. We'll be fine at the hospital. You hold the fort here. And, Peter?"

"Yes?"

"Please don't try and get any photos. For me. For May."

The door slammed behind the doctor. Peter sat down. *Yeah. The Doc's right. Impact's gone. I can't undo the people he hurt. I have to think about Aunt May. How she'd want me to . . . want me to . . .*

. . . to do the right thing. I'm sorry, Doc. Love the power, hate the responsibility.

The trail was easy to follow, not Impact's usual MO. *The big man must have been really upset to be this careless,* Spidey thought. Crushed cars with size-twenty footprints in their hoods. Utility poles knocked over, their splintered stumps flaming from the crackling electric wires that touched them. Walls smashed like so much papier-maché.

Then the blare of sirens, the glare of police lights, and the bellowing of megaphones all indicated that something was going on. You didn't have to be Kraven the Hunter to find Impact. Not tonight, anyway. Peter thought how he could probably have found him any night if he'd really set his mind to it.

Stopping to assess the situation from a ninety-degree standing position on a shadowed wall, Peter absentmindedly took his camera from its hidden pouch on his belt. Okay, maybe his mind wasn't all that absent. Maybe he was doing it with more purpose than ever before. He'd show Bromwell, at least tonight. Maybe he *would* quit taking the pictures. Maybe he would quit being Spider-Man. But not tonight. Not while Impact was on the loose, having hurt innocent people.

Not while Impact had those two hostages.

"I told you cops not to try and stop me," the big man's voice boomed. "I just wanted the money. I didn't want to hurt anybody. But you wouldn't listen. You had to try and stop me. Well, now you've done it. I'll hurt these two if you don't all go away."

The young couple—a head in each of Impact's hands, looking like lemons compared to the size of those mitts—were frozen with panic. They'd had the bad luck to be on the wrong street at the wrong time. Peter felt for them. He even felt for Impact. Or maybe for himself. Because Impact was the dark mirror of Spider-Man; Walter Cobb's problems were much like Peter Parker's. But his response to them was so different, so . . . wrong. And now, seeing what the guy was willing to do to get money. . . .

Peter felt the old rage and indignation well up, the same rage he had felt when he looked into the eyes of the burglar who'd killed Uncle Ben. He had to act. But how could he and not endanger the hostages?

"Walter! Let them go! Please! The police have promised to go easy on you. You don't have to do anything like this for us. Please just let them go. Surrender."

All eyes looked over toward the voices. Marie Cobb and her children—eleven-year-old Gayle and six-year-old Philip—were there. Everybody knew who they were from the human-interest-angle stories on Cobb in the papers and on TV news programs, starting with Conover's column. Everybody knew about Philip's long weeks at a time in the hospital. About the special treatments and surgeries that were needed to correct the conditions he'd been born with. About how Walter had been swindled out of their life's savings. They were broke, desperate—and now their father and husband was a freakish super-criminal, on the verge of becoming a murderer.

The family was behind a police barricade. Not a bad plan on the cops' part, actually. In front of the barricade, a makeshift pit had been opened in the ground, a large tarp with some plywood thrown atop it. With his mind made careless by the steroids, Impact might well run toward the police and fall in, ripe to be shot full of tranquilizer darts.

Only, Impact wasn't taking the bait. Not yet, anyway. But Marie and the kids, bravely, were going to try to draw him out. Walter's face softened. He let his hands go from the heads of his hostages, who promptly ran for safety and within seconds were inside a police van. It seemed like things might be resolved peacefully.

Spidey started to relax. He set his back against the wall as he took the camera in hand and clicked off a few snaps. Marie was pouring it on. She loved him, that's why she didn't want him to do any more damage than he already had. Peter's own tough façade started to crumble. He thought of May, of Bromwell. In his mind's eye he saw Uncle Ben in a pool of blood, and then he saw Ben's face replaced with his own. And he saw Aunt May kneeling by him, holding his head in her hands, his blood staining her apron. And he saw her grasp her own chest and collapse atop Peter, the end of the Parker family.

Peter felt his heart open up. Maybe there was hope for Impact. Maybe for them all. Maybe someday he—*Dr. Peter Parker*—could use his skills as a scientist to go to the prison and cure Walter Cobb. He could walk proudly out of the prison gates with Cobb, and he could do more good, save more lives as Peter Parker, doctor, than he ever could as Spider-Man. One punch could only stop one criminal. One scientific discovery could change the course of human development.

Then the shot rang out and destroyed everything. Spider-Man snapped to attention. He affixed the camera to the wall with webbing from his left hand and, with his right-hand web-shooter, spun out a web-line on which he swung closer to the scene.

Spidey had no idea who the cop was who had fired the shot or why. Was it a cranky veteran who thought it was better to shoot first and ask questions later? Was it a nervous rookie who had panicked at the sight of Impact's huge self lumbering toward the police line?

Ultimately, it didn't matter. What mattered was the effect, which was negligible physically—the slugs barely creased his skin—but devastating psychologically.

Impact flung a nonstop barrage of cars, lampposts, dumpsters, and trees at the police, the crowd of bystanders, even his own family.

Working fast, Spider-Man let loose with a barrage of his own—webbing, and lots of it. In less than five seconds, a huge barrier of webbing stood between Impact and his intended victims.

And so did Spider-Man. If Peter *was* going to hang up the webs, this was the last loose end he had to take care of—unless, of course, that loose end took care of him first.

The hulking creature, snarling, teeth gritted, advanced with his usual speed. But Spider-Man was ready and deftly vaulted himself above Impact, using the brute's shoulder to lift off from. "Walter, why don't we try to have an honest-to-gosh talk? We have a lot in common, really. And the main thing is, we don't want anybody to get hurt any more than they already have. Right?"

"Not Walter. Not anymore. The doctors did it to me. With their interfering, with their help, with their smooth words. That cop—he showed me the true face of the world. They want to kill what they don't understand. Even turned my own family against me. And I did it all for them. But responsibility. Too much responsibility." The words were accompanied by a large slab of pavement flying very fast. Spider-Man sidestepped it—

—and stepped right into a flying Toyota that hit him square in the right side. It hurt like . . . well, like a Toyota.

Quickly turning a stagger into a backflip, Spider-Man shot out

THE DOCTOR'S DILEMMA
129

a dual blast of webbing, which he used as a lasso around Impact.
But before it could harden, Impact flexed his huge muscles and
the webbing stretched just enough to let him slip free of it. Impact pulled on it and whipsawed Spider-Man toward his head.
All Spidey saw was the huge head seeming to grow even huger
as he got up close and made painful contact with Impact's cra-
nium.

Through the pain, Spidey glanced over at the police barricade
covered with his webbing. Through the webbing's mesh, he saw
Impact's family. He also saw their fear and their worry and their
sheer panic over the fate of Walter Cobb.

Staggering to his feet, focusing all his energy, Spider-Man
charged Impact and caught him with a glancing blow, which
again hurt his fist more than it did Impact's face. But Marie let
out a wail that was no less anguished than if Spider-Man had
killed her husband, no doubt a wail similar to that which Aunt
May would make if she were to see Peter so treated.

He turned back toward Impact, pointing at Marie as he spoke.
"Can't you see what this is doing to them? Please, Walter, stop
this—I just want to help you and your family!"

Then Spider-Man looked, really *looked*, at the raging man-
beast, saw the hate and irrationality in his eyes, saw that the steroids had done their damage to his mind, that he was on a journey
he wasn't coming back from. And he knew two things: One, that
he was not going to get through to him with words. He was past
that. And two, that he wasn't going to raise his hand to this
creature, to this poor dumb beast, again. If there was any hope,
any slight chance to get through to him, he was going to take it.

Impact hit him again and again and again.

"I . . . only . . . want . . . to . . . help . . . you . . . and . . . your . . .
family," Spider-Man repeated in a whisper.

The pounding continued.

Finally . . . a glimmer of intelligence, a parting in the clouds
of rage and insanity showed through.

The blows stopped. And then Impact staggered forward. He
lurched toward the barricade and snapped through the webbing
as if it were bakery-box string. *He could have done it all the time,*
Spidey thought. *Had he just been too brain addled to do it, or did he,
too, need to bring this to some kind of conclusion?*

He would never know the answer, for as Impact reached toward his wife and children, he keeled forward onto his face. It was the last he would ever move under his own power. An ambulance was heard, and a doctor leapt out. Peter recognized the face through the cotton in his own head: Bromwell. He pronounced Impact dead at nine-thirty-two P.M.

The doctor made way for the police truck, which hauled Impact's corpse aboard with the winch they ordinarily used for double-parked Cadillacs. Walter's grief-numbed family got aboard as well. Spidey wanted to say something to them before they left but, in truth, he couldn't think of a thing *to* say. He let them be with their sorrow.

Bromwell came up to him. "You need any help, Spider-Man?" he asked, his voice tight with tension.

"I—I'm fine, Doctor," replied the masked young man. "But your concern is much appreciated." Spidey did his best to disguise his voice even more than usual—not that that was so hard, the way his lips were puffing up.

The tow truck carrying the corpse of Walter Cobb sped off. The crowd dispersed. An NYPD lieutenant helped Spider-Man up. "You saved us from a big mess, Spider-Man. We won't soon be forgetting it. Anything we can do for you?"

"Yeah," rasped Spidey. "Be good to your family."

"Something I can do," the cop pleaded with a laugh, "not the impossible."

Spider-Man spun out a web-line and swung off in a far from graceful manner. He was fine battling guys who wanted to take over the city or the country or the mobs. He was great with falling buildings and collapsing bleachers. *You want something heavy lifted, I'm there. You need someone to stop a madman with a set of mechanical arms, piece of cake. Just don't ask me to think too much about my own life. I do it too much already, and the bottom line is I do what I do because I believe it's the right thing to do. But then life throws this little lesson in my face. Bromwell tells me that I should think about my aunt— like I don't do that enough. Impact shows me that there's a right way and a wrong way to try to help those you love. All these lessons! But . . . what am I supposed to learn from them? Where's the curriculum? Where's the syllabus?*

Going on almost pure instinct, Peter made his pain-wracked way home. He crawled into his bedroom window and collapsed onto the bed, falling instantly asleep.

He dreamed of fists and guns and burglars and graveyards.

· · ·

The *Daily Bugle* felt unusually heavy in Peter Parker's hands as he picked it up from the newsstand on his way home from his class at Empire State University. There on the front page was a big, bold shot of Spidey getting slammed in the head by Impact. The headline read, IMPACT IMPACTS ON WEBBED MENACE. A caption promised more action photos of the battle in the center spread. The photo credit read P. PARKER—DAILY BUGLE.

Impact had died, and all he'd wanted was to help his family. The giant had made some key decisions, turned his back on some other choices, and doomed himself—and doomed his family to a legacy of heartbreak. *Sure,* Peter thought, *I stopped a menace. I made some money for Aunt May, too, like I've been doing all along. But if I don't want to end up like Impact . . . if I don't want Aunt May to end up like Impact's family . . . what choice do I have but to hang up my web-shooters?*

These thoughts went around and around in his mind the entire subway ride home. As his key turned the lock in the front door, he could hear the familiar clatter of dishes, pots, and pans, smell the welcoming odors of Aunt May's roast turkey and pumpkin pie. She was up on her feet, cooking. For him. Like everything else she did. For him.

They sat and ate. May was animated, more lively than he'd seen her for a while—almost too lively, as if she were sitting on something she needed to say. He knew she was upset over his new facial injuries. She'd seen them in the morning and tried not to show it, but she was worried. Peter sat and ate mechanically. He looked at her, thinking how he did what he did for her. So she could have as good a life as he could provide. So that he could have her to come home to. Like he never could with his parents. Or with Uncle Ben. But the thought of never again being Spider-Man . . . of never feeling the wind through his mask as he swung across the rooftops . . . somehow, the thought of losing that seemed too much to bear as well. Still, he had to be strong, he had to give it up. For her sake. Last night was the *last* night.

Then, through the fog of his thoughts, he finally heard what she was actually saying to him.

"I've never been one to tell you what to do. Anything I or your uncle ever suggested . . . well, we just were trying to think what your own parents would have said to you. And you were such a good boy, we never had to tell you much at all. Of course I worry about your risking body and soul to take those pictures for Mr. Jameson. But the point is, if you're happy doing it, then you should keep doing it. I just want you to be sure you're not doing it for me. There are other ways we can get money if we have to. We're Parkers, Peter. We'll always survive, and even thrive. We always have and we always will, even in the toughest times.

"You do what's right for you, Peter. You have some inner beacon that always leads you to do the right thing, just like your uncle did. Follow your heart, Peter. It won't lead you wrong. And I'll be proud of you no matter what you decide."

Peter wept a tear from the corner of his eye as he swallowed the last forkful of pumpkin pie. "I'm sorry that the whipped cream is store bought," May added with a smile, "but I'm not as young as I used to be."

Peter walked over to her and kissed her on the cheek. He wanted to get out of there before he broke down sobbing. "I've got some work to finish up at Doc Bromwell's," he croaked. "Don't wait up for me."

"You promised me, Peter. You promised. And then you let me down. For *this*!"

Bromwell shook the *Bugle* in Peter's face like he was some misbehaving dog. Peter took a step back and opened his mouth to apologize, but the doctor wasn't finished.

"Not only did you go out after photos when I'd begged you not to—but you left your work here unattended! Those tests you were running for me were important, and not just for me. For my patients! Luckily for you, no irreparable damage was done. Unless you count nervous patients having to wait an extra day for test results. But that's just because of sheer luck.

"I tried, Peter. I really did. I thought you cared about your aunt. I thought if I showed you another way to make some money in a field that you were really interested in that you'd be able to change. But I suppose you're just hooked on the excitement and adventure of what you're doing, and too young to see how dangerous it is, to realize that actions have consequences. You're just too selfish to change.

"That's the end for me, Peter. I've probably gone too far as it is. I care about my patients and their loved ones, but there's a limit. A man in my position could spend all his time worrying about other people's problems and end up ruining his own life. So I wish you well, Peter, and I hope you can keep living this charmed life of yours, for May's sake. But I've done as much as I can. Please pack up your things and go."

Peter was about to argue for another chance—sensed that Bromwell *wanted* him to—when he looked down at the newspaper Bromwell had dropped on the desk. In the background of the violent scene there were the battered, assaulted cops whom Impact had nearly killed. But he hadn't killed them.

Because of Spider-Man.

Yeah, Bromwell was more right than he knew. Peter was hooked. On action and adventure, sure. But he could give that up. If all he wanted was thrills and chills, he could spend his spare time on the Cyclone at Coney Island. He was hooked on something else, something good: helping people. Because, in the big picture, he was helping more than just Aunt May. In his own small way, he was helping the world. As May and Ben had always taught him, he was doing the right thing. To have such power and not use it would be betraying all they had tried to instill in him. If Uncle Ben could know what Peter was doing with his powers, he'd be proud as anything.

And, he was willing to bet that if she were to know his secret, Aunt May would be proud too.

Peter stuck his hand out to Bromwell. "I appreciate all you've done and tried to do, Doc. You've got the biggest heart in the world. Aunt May and I are lucky to know you. And I'm sorry I let you down, but it's probably for the best that I go back to doing what I was doing."

Bromwell looked at Peter, more than a little sadly. He had obviously been hoping that Peter would try to keep his job, to ask Bromwell for another chance. He took Peter's hand and grasped it warmly.

Peter turned to leave the office. Bromwell said, "Give my best to May, Peter."

"I will, Doc. I certainly will."

Peter walked down the stairs, exited onto 112th Street, and walked toward Queens Boulevard. The sights and sounds of his native borough greeted him like an old friend. He felt, for a rare moment, light and content.

Love the power, he thought. *Guess I'll just have to live with the responsibility.*

MOVING DAY

John S. Drew
Illustration by Pat Olliffe

May Parker sat alone in her bedroom amid a clutter of boxes filled with clothing and personal possessions. On any normal day, May would have been horrified at the sight of such disorder, but today was different and May's attention was fixed elsewhere.

She stared at a picture of herself, her nephew Peter, and her late husband, Ben. Even in the two-dimensional image, Ben seemed so alive, with his twinkling eyes and handsome smile. May placed the picture in an open crate, fighting back the tears that formed in her eyes.

May had known this day would eventually come, but had never expected it to hurt so much. Peter was moving into Manhattan to live with his college friend, Harry Osborn. Harry's father, Norman, offered to put the boys up in an apartment near the campus of Empire State University rent free. Peter could not refuse the offer.

At first, Peter had found it difficult to tell May. After Ben's death, they'd had only each other for comfort. Unbeknownst to him, May had recently arranged to move in with her next-door neighbor, Anna Watson. May's biggest problem then was trying to let Peter know what she planned. Peter's moving out had made the telling much easier.

Now May faced the heartache of separating from Peter. She often found Ben's gentle, smiling face a comfort in trying times; today, his image only deepened her sadness. The wound of his murder still festered in her heart. Despite the time that had passed, not a day went by that May did not find herself calling Ben's name or expecting to see him seated in his favorite armchair in the living room. The move made his absence all the more obvious and painful.

"Penny for them, pretty lady." Peter's voice drew May out of her thoughts. She glanced up and, for an instant, saw the image of a young Ben Parker in her nephew.

"Oh, Peter." May's voice cracked slightly. She stopped herself, promising she wasn't going to lose control. She needed to be brave, for herself and for Peter. Ben would want her to be strong and she couldn't let him down now. "I was just looking at this picture of you and your uncle Ben. Do you remember the day we took it?"

"Yes," Peter replied. "It was just after the holidays. Anna Watson gave us the portrait package from Sears as a Christmas gift."

"It was the last family picture we took. . . ." May's voice trailed off.

Peter took her hand. "It's time to go," he said gently.

May, lost in her thoughts again, looked at Peter oddly. "Go?"

"The truck's loaded up and the gang's all set."

May nodded numbly. "Go. Of course, it's time to go."

Peter led her from the room. Before they descended the staircase, Peter stopped and looked May in the eye. "You know, it's not too late to call this off."

May shook her head. "Nonsense. Ben and I knew there would come a day when you would have to move on. It just would have been much easier if Ben were still here."

"Are you sure you want to keep the house?"

May nodded. "It's all I have left. Losing your uncle Ben was a terrible shock and I have to admit to you, Peter, I never really got over it."

"Me neither," Peter said softly.

"Now I'm losing you."

"But you could—"

"No," May continued, "you have to move on with your life. You don't need this old woman weighing you down. I'll be fine. Anna's offer was so thoughtful and it makes perfect sense. Two old women living in two large houses by themselves is a waste. But I can't let this house go yet. The thought of somebody else living here bothers me."

Peter smiled. "Well, all right. But you know I'm going to be out here every weekend, looking for my wheatcakes and syrup."

"If you don't, Peter Parker," May teased, "I'll be breaking down your door with griddle and batter in hand."

Peter took her in his arms and embraced her warmly.

"I love you, Peter."

"I love you, too, Aunt May."

A truck horn blared from outside.

"Ready?" Peter asked.

May nodded. "Ready."

Peter took her hand and they walked downstairs.

Outside, Peter's friends Harry Osborn, Mary Jane Watson, and

Gwen Stacy waited beside a small moving truck. The vehicle's driver sat in the front cab, an impatient look on his face.

May and Peter stepped out of the house.

"Hey, Tiger!" Mary Jane bounded up to Peter. May smiled at the attractive redhead. You could always count on Anna Watson's niece to be a bundle of energy. "The truck's all packed and the gang's ready to split for your new digs."

"Great," Peter replied. "Thanks so much for helping me, guys. It's made all this a lot easier."

"I don't think I've ever seen one man own so much stuff. You'd think you were moving into a new house with an entire family," Harry joked. "What's with all the boxes?"

"Some scientific equipment, back issues of science journals, clothes," Peter explained.

"No record player?" Gwen asked. "What kind of parties are you going to throw without a record player?"

"I got that covered, Gwen," Harry responded. "A few months of living with Harry Osborn and the corners of this square cat will be smoothed over."

A look of concern crossed May's face. "I hope you're not going to be throwing a lot of parties, Harry," she said. "Peter needs at least eight hours of sleep each night."

"Don't you worry, Mrs. Parker. I'll make sure that Peter eats well, gets his rest, and keeps up with his studies. I gotta admit, that's one of the reasons I asked him to move in with me." Harry grinned. "Somebody's got to help me with my homework."

The horn blared again. The truck driver jumped down from the cab of the vehicle. His T-shirt, torn with holes, and his faded blue jeans barely held his wide girth in check.

"You think we could get a move on here? I've got another job this afternoon."

"We're coming, Joe." Peter turned to May. "Aunt May, you're going to ride with Joe in the cab while me and the gang take the subway into the city."

"All right, Peter. Be careful on the subway. Make sure you stand away from the platform until the train comes to a stop and—"

Peter kissed her on the forehead, cutting her off in midfret. "I will."

May and Peter looked toward their home of many years, giving it one final glance. May quickly turned away and walked toward the truck.

"Let's go, Joe," May said.

"You just sit back and relax, Mrs. Parker," Joe said with a flourish as he helped her onto the truck. "We'll be in the city in no time. I just got the shocks on this baby replaced, so you're in for a smooth ride."

Joe climbed into the truck and started it up. May waved to Peter as the truck pulled away. She could read the mix of emotions on her nephew's face as he stood there on the sidewalk. He was trying to be as strong as May. Ben would have been so proud of him. A moment later, Peter started off toward the subway station with his friends. May turned her view to what lay before her.

I can't look back now, she thought.

"So anyways, I says to the guy, 'If you're not going to pay me for my time, I should take my leave right now.' And with that, I walked out on Mr. Robert Moses hisself." Joe beamed proudly as he regaled May with yet another tale of his past. This had been going on for the past thirty minutes as the truck slowly made its way toward the Fifty-ninth Street bridge.

May nodded absentmindedly, a past image of Ben and herself signing the mortgage papers on the house foremost in her thoughts. May remembered how much she'd loved the kitchen when first she'd seen the place, and could not wait to prepare her first meal for her new husband. Ben had found the garage to be a nice size for a work space; he'd quickly gathered an impressive collection of tools. Their life together was almost complete.

The death of Peter's parents shortly after brought an addition to Ben and May's home. The first weeks were difficult as Peter adjusted to his new situation. There were many nights when Peter would just stare out into the night sky from his bedroom window, oblivious of his aunt's calls to dinner. It was almost as though he were looking for something among the stars. May never knew for sure what it was, but one thing was certain, Peter had an inquisitive nature.

Ben tried to make Peter's first Christmas with the Parkers special by surprising him with a new bike. Peter proceeded to examine it from handlebars to rear wheel spokes, as though he were planning on taking it apart and putting it back together. And that's exactly what he did, astonishing Ben several days later as the elder Parker entered the garage. There was Peter, kneeling on the ground, surrounded by the bike in its component parts. Ben's annoyance turned to amazement as Peter put the pieces together again. From that point on, Ben recognized Peter's intellect and nurtured his nephew's quest for knowledge by offering his total support and encouragement.

"Geez, what now?" Joe's attention turned to the traffic jam ahead. They were on the verge of getting on the overpass, but the flow of movement had ceased.

Joe shook his head. "How was I supposed to know this would happen? I thought I'd save us the toll by taking the Fifty-ninth Street bridge. I guess everybody else had the same idea."

May was barely listening, her recollections of Peter turning into a young adult keeping her occupied. He was quite the studious type, never one to go out with the boys or talk about girls. This never disturbed May, but Ben worried about Peter's lack of development in social skills.

May's happy contemplations shattered as a painful memory, one as fresh as the night it happened, surfaced.

The night Ben died.

It was a burglar. Ben had come downstairs for a midnight snack and surprised the thief. All it took was one bullet and Ben was gone. Living in the house proved difficult for quite some time. May never went near Ben's easy chair again, nor could she bring herself to open the window the burglar climbed through to gain access to the house.

"Wow!" Joe's exclamation cut through May's reverie.

May looked up in a panic. "What?"

"Look up there, Mrs. Parker!" Joe pointed toward the Manhattan skyline.

From May's point of view, everything seemed normal. "I don't understand. Is something wrong?"

"Over there! By the Chrysler Building!"

May focused her attention on the famous structure and gasped. "Oh, my!"

A number of bright flashes erupted from the top of the building. Two shadowy silhouettes stood out in the center of the brilliant kaleidoscope.

"What on earth?"

I'll bet it's one of those costumed super heroes, like Daredevil or something!" Joe guessed. "I like Daredevil!"

Joe turned on the radio, tuning it in to the all-news station, WINS. The voice of the anchorperson crackled slightly as Joe fiddled with the dial for better reception.

"An update on our news of the hour: The battle above the streets of Manhattan between Spider-Man and the notorious Mysterio continues. Mysterio, a former Hollywood stuntman turned criminal, attempted to frame the masked adventurer several months ago by committing crimes disguised as Spider-Man. He received financial backing from *Daily Bugle* owner-publisher J. Jonah Jameson in order to capture the real Spider-Man in his Mysterio persona."

The newsreader paused a moment. "We have word that Frank Meridith is in our traffic copter, surveying the battle from a safe distance. We switch to him now, live."

May spotted the chopper's circular motion around the Chrysler Building.

"Jim, the battle between Spider-Man and Mysterio has been raging for some time now. Police have cordoned off Forty-fifth to Sixtieth streets from Fifth Avenue to the East River.

"Mysterio appears to have the upper hand in the situation, deflecting Spider-Man's blows. Wait a minute, Spider-Man is stopping and looking about. It's hard to tell exactly what is going on with all the flashing lights around Mysterio."

The whine of the helicopter blades momentarily drowned out the reporter's voice.

May shook her head slowly. "I don't understand why something isn't being done about that awful Spider-Man person. The *Daily Bugle* is absolutely right that he should be put away. Criminals like this Mysterio or the Sandman are captured by the Avengers and the Fantastic Four. Why is Spider-Man so special?"

"I don't know, Mrs. Parker. I think Spidey's all right," Joe replied.

"Geez!" Meridith's voice cut through the interference. "Will you look at that? Spider-Man faked him out!"

"Oh, my!" May looked on in horror as Spider-Man and Mysterio toppled over the edge of the building in a cloud of thick smoke.

"Spider-Man and Mysterio appear to be falling, they . . . Wait a minute!"

Suddenly, a thin line shot out from the billowing fog, attaching itself to a nearby building. Spider-Man burst from the cloudbank, swinging to safety. The mist slowly dissipated, revealing . . .

"Spider-Man has stopped his descent, but it seems Mysterio has disappeared."

May leaned over and turned off the radio.

"Hey! Mrs. Parker!" Joe looked slightly annoyed and disappointed.

"I can't listen to this anymore. It's horrible! And to think that Peter is moving into all this! It's bad enough that he takes pictures of Spider-Man to make a living."

"Your nephew takes photos of Spider-Man? Wow! That must be exciting!"

"It's dangerous!" May's voice shook slightly. "Thank goodness Harry Osborn's father will be paying the rent. Peter won't need to worry about money as much. He won't have to chase after Spider-Man anymore."

"What if he wants to keep doing it?" Joe asked. "What if he enjoys it?"

"I know how proud he is earning his own money," May admitted. "Oh, when I think of all the nights I used to stay up late worrying about Peter out there chasing Spider-Man."

"You know, your nephew reminds me of my sister, Veronica. She wanted to be a truck driver. She always was a tomboy. The family thought that wasn't how a 'proper lady' acts."

"Proper lady! Poppycock!" May sat up, a tinge of anger in her expression. "If she's good at driving a truck and fancies it, what's to stop her?"

"Well, there are the long hours, the dangers of driving a rig on the lone highways, and how other men would look at her," Joe replied. "You see, it doesn't matter to her, though. She's saved enough to buy herself two rigs. I'm joining up with her in another month to haul as her second."

"But your sister needs to earn a living and this is what she enjoys doing. Peter doesn't need to worry about that now, as his needs will be taken care of," May retorted.

"Some people work just 'cause they *like* it. I know that if I ever won a lot of money, I'd still work, because I'd go crazy if I didn't."

"Peter's going to be a scientist. That's his career. Taking pictures for the *Bugle* was a way to make extra money, and he doesn't need to do that now. I'm glad Peter's in the subway. He'll never be able to get involved in what's going on up there." May looked toward the skyline. It was quiet now. Even the chopper was gone.

Joe looked disappointed. "Don't tell me it's all over." He turned the radio on again.

"There is still no sign of Mysterio, and Spider-Man has apparently left the scene. It appears the worst is over. WINS will continue to cover the skies with our chopper and let you know if any new developments occur. In other news . . ."

Joe turned down the volume. "Well, I guess traffic should start moving soon."

Suddenly, a burst of light directed May and Joe's attention ahead of them. The figure of Spider-Man careened over them in an arc. Mysterio floated several feet above the ground, laughing maniacally at the sight. The fishbowl-like glass covering on his head glowed with a pulse in time to his laughter.

Quickly, Spider-Man reached out, grabbed a cable of the bridge, and, swinging in a full circle, used the momentum to launch himself in the opposite direction toward his attacker. Mysterio, not anticipating this maneuver, fell to the ground with the force of the collision.

Mysterio rolled with the impact, jumping to his feet first.

"Joe, get us out of here!" May said, her voice quivering in fear.

"Where?" Joe asked. "There must be nearly a quarter mile of traffic backed up behind us."

"Then let's make a run for it!"

Joe took hold of May's hand. "Mrs. Parker, I know you're scared, but this is probably the safest place to be right now. Besides, if I know Spider-Man, he'll take the battle away from here. There's too many people."

May eyed the combatants warily. "I hope so."

Spider-Man jumped away from Mysterio as the villain tried to leap upon him. The wall-crawler landed on the hood of Joe's truck.

"Goodness!" May gasped.

"Go get him, Spidey!" Joe cheered.

Spider-Man looked into the cab. May sat frozen in fear. She felt as though he was looking directly at her. His body seemed to relax a moment as his head tilted slightly.

There was something almost familiar about him. The opaque coverings for his eyes were disconcerting to her. Ben often said you could always tell the character of a man from his eyes.

Suddenly, Spider-Man tensed and hopped from the truck toward his attacker.

"You all right, Mrs. Parker?" Joe asked.

May could only nod slowly. She watched in fascination as the battle raged.

Mysterio struck out with a left hook, staggering Spider-Man. He followed it with a strobe light, emitted from the palm of his right hand, blinding the masked adventurer, rendering him helpless.

Taking fast advantage of the situation, Mysterio grabbed Spider-Man and lifted him over his head.

"He's going to throw Spidey off the bridge!" Joe shouted, quickly getting out of the truck.

"No! Wait!" May yelled after him.

Joe, bent forward and, like a charging quarterback, rushed toward Mysterio.

Mysterio, obviously unaware of the impending attack, cackled in glee. "Our conflict is finally at an end, Spider-Man. It's just too bad there isn't a movie camera to capture the moment."

Joe struck Mysterio hard, bringing the criminal to his knees and making him lose his hold on Spider-Man. Joe fell backward, dazed with the impact.

"What?" Mysterio looked over the stunned individual who had knocked him down. "You didn't expect to meet such resistance, did you? I'm heavily padded." Mysterio stood up.

Joe took a deep breath, shaking his head. "I stopped you, didn't I?"

Mysterio grabbed Joe by his shirt and heaved him upward. Joe's feet dangled inches from the ground. "Indeed you did." Mysterio drew back a fist.

May closed her eyes and clenched her fists. "No!"

A web-line snagged Mysterio's balled-up hand. "Hey! What about me, Fishbowl Head? You know, I really hate it when people start something and don't finish it!" Spider-Man gave the web-line a hard tug, sending Mysterio flying over the edge of the bridge.

"No!"

Spider-Man quickly leapt to the railing, readying a web-line. But except for a few lingering wisps of smoke, there was no sign of Mysterio.

May got out of the truck and ran to Joe. She helped him to his feet.

"Are you all right?" May asked, brushing aside a lock of Joe's hair from his eyes.

"Yeah, thanks." Joe stepped over to Spider-Man. "Where'd he go?"

Spider-Man shook his head. "I don't know. I can't see any sign of him." Spider-Man paused as he gave the waters beyond a final glance and then said, "Thanks. I appreciate the help, but that was an awful big risk you took there. These jerks are difficult to deal with, even for us guys with the edge."

Joe extended a hand, which Spider-Man took. "I'll tell ya, if I could have avoided it, I would have. But even the guys with the edge need a hand sometimes."

Spider-Man leapt upward to one of the bridge's railings. "Well, thanks again." Spider-Man cast a web-line toward a nearby street-lamp and swung off.

Joe turned to May and smiled. "I'd better get you to your nephew, or he's going to be real worried."

May nodded. She didn't say a word as they climbed into the truck and waited for traffic to start moving. Joe was unusually quiet as well.

As the truck finally made its way downtown some twenty minutes later, May turned to Joe. "What possessed you to do such a foolish thing?"

Joe shrugged. "I don't know. It's just something in me, I guess. The guy was down and all."

"That was Spider-Man. He can well look after himself I imagine. You could have got yourself killed!"

"I could have died from the three fried eggs and bacon I had for breakfast this morning,'' Joe replied with a hint of sarcasm in his voice. He burped slightly, tapping his chest just over his heart. ''And if I keep eating that way, I just might.''

May didn't respond to his attempted levity. ''Look,'' Joe explained, ''we all have to do what we can to help in this world. Regardless of how you feel about Spider-Man, would you want to see him dead?''

May squirmed slightly in guilt. ''Well, no.''

''Then I think I did the right thing,'' Joe said, nodding his head. ''Let me ask you this: If your nephew were in the same situation, would you expect him to just stand by and take the picture?''

''No, of course not. Peter is just like his uncle. He would have done whatever he could to help Spider-Man. Which is another reason I worry about him taking those pictures. One of these days he may have to step in and help in some way and could get hurt.''

''Isn't that for Peter to decide, Mrs. Parker?'' Joe asked softly. ''I mean, he is moving out on his own and all. He's going to have to learn to make his own mistakes and earn his own wins in life.''

''That doesn't mean he's got to take risks, though!'' Tears welled up in May's eyes. ''He's all I've got left! I can't bear the thought of him . . . like Ben!''

Joe placed a hand on May's. ''My old man used to say, 'Life's like riding a bicycle. Once you get the hang of it, there ain't nothing you can't do.' ''

''I remember when Ben taught Peter how to ride his first bicycle.'' May wiped away the stray tear falling down her face. ''Peter walked into the kitchen, his ankles all torn up from the falls he had taken. Peter vowed to steer the bike straight if it killed him. I wanted the thing locked up in the garage and never mentioned again. It hurt me so to see Peter distressed and injured, but Ben would hear nothing of it. 'The boy's got to stand on his own. He's got to find his own way. We can guide him, but we can't do it for him.' ''

''He was right,'' May said softly. ''And so are you, Joe. I'm going to have to let go a little. It doesn't mean I love Peter any less.''

''Of course not. Why, I remember one time, when I was about

ten years old . . ." May smiled warmly as Joe began another tale of his past.

Peter ran to greet the moving-truck as it pulled up before the apartment building.

"I thought you guys would never get here," Peter said. He winked at May. "Were you trying to convince Joe here to take you to Atlantic City to do a little gambling again?"

"Oh, Peter, you're such a tease" May giggled as her nephew helped her down from the cab. "I do think I'm going to be a little stiff after sitting in that truck for so long." May looked about. "Where are your friends?"

As if on cue, Harry, Mary Jane, and Gwen called out from down the street.

"Here they come now," Peter said.

"Hey, roomie, where'd you split to?" Harry asked as they approached. "One minute we're all in a stalled subway car talking about the housewarming party, the next minute you're gone."

Peter looked at May. "The trains were stopped from coming into Manhattan while the fight was going on. I took advantage by slipping out to get a few pictures."

May frowned. "Peter! You could have been hurt! Are those pictures really—"

"Hey!" Joe called out. "Is somebody going to give me a hand here? The sooner I get this done, the sooner I'm out of here. Got a long drive ahead of me."

Joe gave May a quick wink and a nod. May closed her eyes a moment and then said to Peter, "You were careful, weren't you?"

"Always, Aunt May. Always."

May leaned forward and kissed him on the forehead. "Make sure you are. You know, you don't have to take as many risks anymore."

"I know."

Peter turned to his friends. "I'm sorry I cut out on you like that, guys. Look, with the money I make from these pics, I'll be able to take you out for a bite to eat in style."

"Burgers at the Coffee Bean!" Harry shouted.

"With milkshakes!" Mary Jane chimed in.

Gwen slid by Peter. Her long blonde hair brushed against his shoulder. "And after we're done eating we can hit the dance

floor. Maybe I can have the first dance with you, Mr. Parker?"
Gwen walked over to the truck. Peter could only blush.

Later that evening, May climbed the stairs of her home to the
upper floor. Her footsteps echoed in the emptiness. At this time,
May would usually have had the radio tuned in to *Saturday with
Sinatra* as she prepared dinner for Peter and herself.

She stopped before Peter's room and opened the door. Inside,
Peter's bed, bureau, and desk remained. The bed was bare of
sheets and blankets, Peter's many science awards were gone from
the top of the bureau, and the desk was cleared of any study
material. The walls, once adorned with posters, were now empty.

May turned and walked into her bedroom. She sat down on
her bed. She could see Anna Watson's house across the way from
her window.

She picked up the portrait from the box and ran a finger
along the picture of Ben. A single tear splashed upon the image,
blurring it.

"I'm trying, Ben, I'm really trying to let go and get on, but
it's so hard," May said quietly, pulling the picture close to her.

The front door downstairs opened.

"May, dear," Anna Watson's cheerful call rang out. "It's time
for dinner."

"Coming" May wiped away the trickling tears from her cheek.
"I'll be right over."

May put the picture back in the crate and turned to leave. She
stopped, turned back, and quickly picked it up, carrying it close
to her as she exited the room.

THE LIAR

Ann Nocenti

Illustration by James W. Fry

To her, it's simple survival. To others, it's an intricate lie.

A lace doily, a mandala, a death trap. She fixes the last strand, and waits. She sits unmoving for three hours until a hapless moth flutters her way. Stuck, it twitches powdery wings; a victim's panic, entangling it further. Still she waits, for the right moment. Till she is sure no one is watching, senses there is no danger, and only then does she reveal her true self.

Her dash is erratic, darting in a slight zigzag as if avoiding bullets, punctuated by a final leap. Poised, she grips the moth and executes a perfect poison jab. She holds her prey, almost tenderly, through its last death shudders. She tastes of the moth's lost vitality, and spins it in her silk.

Peter Parker sits in the window, watching and thinking. *How could I have anything in common with her?*

This is a rare mood for Peter; quiet and reflective. Usually he's running somewhere, late for something, too busy to think. But this morning he noticed her descent from the window lintel, this elegant queen of the web, and had watched as she spun her very first strand. Then, after breakfast, he saw that she had finished. The struts were evenly spaced, the concentric circling spiral of gradational circumference was stunning in its perfection. Peter stopped to admire her industrious perseverance, her stealth, her ability to wait.

Now home from school for lunch, Peter finds himself watching her again, this master of duplicity. *Twenty-four seven*, he thinks. She'd be adept at round-the-clock surveillance. Great at camouflage, and good for a fast kill. Peter shudders, remembering. *I am part spider.* The thought passes through his consciousness; strange, unreal, yet true.

Her beautifully constructed home is also a death trap. It conforms delicately to its surroundings, the window light glistens, creating an atmosphere that makes the web seem just an echo, an illusion of the cast light, an invisible veil.

The spider's elegantly poised web is a lie.

Peter Parker jumps up and, with a quick backhand scarring the weave, destroys it. He grabs his schoolbooks and runs out the door. Halfway down the steps, he feels the guilt.

Shouldn't have done that, he thinks. *She'll just spin another beautiful lie. She can't help it. Lie or die.*

"Peter!" He stops running. Aunt May's voice tugs at Peter like no other. He often feels an invisible connection, a leash, a cord; sometimes lax, sometimes taut, but always there between them. His one and only aunt May.

"I thought I might catch you home for lunch. I was just going to leave a note in your mailbox, Peter. I got a call from the university, worried about you missing three days of classes. What a ridiculous woman! I told her you hadn't missed a day."

Oh, yeah, Aunt May, I forgot to tell you I hitched a jet ride to Algiers, fought the Red Skull and a bunch of his thugs, 'cause I'd just found out my dead parents were spies and felt I wanted to know just a little more about it.

Peter looks down at sweet Aunt May. She seems so frail, clinging to the iron fence, waiting in earnest for him to dispel all her nagging fears. Peter's seen that concerned look on Aunt May's face his whole life. Well, technically, from when he was six years old on; before that, the look was on his own mother's face, but he doesn't think about that too much.

"You know, Aunt May, they've got computers in there now, doing the attendance. I bet it was some kind of error." Peter watches the network of worry lines in Aunt May's face make a near imperceptible shift from a web of worry to a web of relief. Her boy Peter doesn't miss school days.

"Geez, I'm in college now, you'd think they'd stop treating me like a kid."

There's that look again. It's a paranoid look, the look of someone who thinks her perceptions are failing her. It always reminds him of something. Déjà vu, but from an incident long ago. Aunt May knows something is always wrong but she's never sure what. It makes her distrust her own intuition. He knows that feeling too. But why? About what?

"Oh, Peter, were you washing something in my sink when you visited last night? Something red?"

Yes Aunt May, my mask. I was washing my secret life out in your sink, and the red dye bled all over. . . .

"Uh . . . no, Aunt May, I had a nose bleed."

"Oh, dear!"

"It's nothing . . . all gone now."

"Peter, can you help me grocery shop after school?"

"Sure. I'm not working after classes today, so I could help you for a while, and then I might see if Mary Jane wants to do something."

"Oh, how lovely, Peter. She's a wonderful girl! You know how often I've tried to match-make the two of you, from that first blind date on!"

"Yes, Aunt May, I sure do."

"I think she's just the girl for you! But you never listen to your aunt's intuition, do you? What a lively spirit that Mary Jane has!"

"Lively? She's *wild*, Aunt May!"

"Oh, Peter! Since when is a healthy zest for life a bad thing? That Mary Jane could teach you how to relax a bit!"

I'll bet she could.

It's moments like this, when May becomes almost coquettish, that Peter can see what a great beauty she is. And part of her beauty is her unrelenting ability to find something good in everybody. May does not judge, she has an unconditional acceptance of people, even the bad ones. Peter remembers many times, watching the news with May, there would be a story about an old gangster, a self-styled Jessie James or Clyde Barrow type, and May would lean back, eyes teary, and sigh: *"Poor man."* Sympathy for the villainous. It is a small comfort to Peter, this forgiving nature. She may need it for him someday . . .

"See you later, Aunt May. I'll meet you at the grocery store? About four?"

"That'd be fine Peter, thank you."

Peter waves good-bye, thinking about Mary Jane. *She's spirited, all right. So spirited she scares me.*

Mary Jane, besides being beautiful, has a glint in her curvaceous eyes that is so ornery, so mischievous; a kick-up-your-heels, pull-out-the-stops, let's-have-fun-till-we-burn-the-house-down kind of look. Sexy, intriguing, but scary. Her hair a wild red flame, one hand cocked on her hip like she's ready to shoot, she'll squint at him through long lashes, everything about her stance a beckoning challenge, as if to say: *Come play with me, if you dare.*

Gwendolyn, the other girl Peter has his eye on, is to Mary Jane as the moon is to the sun. Distant, cool, unapproachable as a queen. Peter often feels Gwen's pull, knows when she is near.

He'll be walking down the hall in school, and like a compass spinning north he'll turn, and there she'll be, true as the moonrise. They'll exchange more looks than words. They've moved toward romance many times, but something always ruins things. Her fair skin, snow-blonde hair, and green-eyed perfection make him tremble. Lately, she's been looking his way again and it is driving him crazy.

These thoughts take Peter as far as the newsstand, halfway to the university. He almost walks right by, when the phrase SPIDER-MAN MENACE stops him. The *Daily Bugle* is at it again.

Will J. Jonah Jameson ever stop hating Spider-Man? Peter gets some satisfaction working for the gruff publisher as a photographer—the old man would be mortified to know that when he hired Peter, he was also hiring Spider-Man. Jameson's editorial policy toward Spider-Man is all yellow. Sometimes Peter wonders if Jameson is just plain jealous.

He knows he shouldn't, but he throws down some change to pay for the rag. HE'S NO HERO is a two-page spread. They've dug up pictures from his first feeble attempts at deciding what to do with his powers. There he is, in his red-and-blue Spider-Man outfit, an early, badly sewn mess, on a national TV show, doing *spider tricks*, no less. And there he is again, in his first homemade suit, in the ring, rope-a-doping some ham-hock lug calling himself Crusher Hogan. All he did that time was put a fishnet mask over his head, leaving on his street clothes. He didn't even put on a pair of sneakers or jeans; there he is in his pressed slacks, knit socks, and Sunday shoes, leaping around like a clown. Oh, well, he earned a hundred bucks that night, which Aunt May needed to pay the bills that month.

PUBLICITY-SEEKING PHONY! That is the caption under another lovely shot of him hanging from a ceiling, a mock spider, like some sideshow freak. Underneath the editor has pasted a mock sign; MAN-SPIDER. There is another photo from his short stint on a variety show. Where'd they dig up these shots? HE'LL DO ANYTHING FOR A BUCK is the stupid headline, and they'd even gotten some bad artist to draw dollar bills raining down all over the page.

Those were confusing times—the surging new powers, his fingertips sticking to walls, the creepy reminders that it was a radioactive spider that had bit him—he felt so powerful and so lost at the same time.

Peter remembers diving into the study of radioactivity, and first asking, *Why isn't it killing me?* That soon switched to, *When will it kill me?* But he also felt stronger, healthier, than ever. At certain giddy moments, usually just before a fumbling fall, he even felt invincible.

A reluctant sense of responsibility had followed, born out of tragedy. His lazy indifference to stopping a thief had caused the death of his uncle Ben. Peter began to understand that great strength had to lead to heroism, or it led elsewhere: to dark, greedy, arrogant places.

To Peter, the *Bugle* editorial, in digging up these silly shots, was like getting caught with his pants down.

He crunches the paper up into a tight ball and throws a bank shot at a nearby garbage can. He hears the can crash over as he walks on. He didn't check his strength for the toss. Anger, it makes you slip up. *Good. Someday, I'll be angry enough to punch J. Jonah Jameson right in the nose.*

One minute before Chemistry Lab. Peter lopes into a jog, heads up the school drive, takes the steps three at a time, and slips in just as the warning bell rings. He hates being shoved around by bells. But that never used to bother him; is this another by-product of his powers? Feelings of anticonformity?

"Mmmm, don't break a sweat, Peter, it's only chemistry."

Mary Jane Watson leans in the doorway, waiting for him. Now he knows why she asked for his school schedule the other day.

"Hey, Mary Jane. I was just thinking how I hate those bells, hate how they make me break into a run. Pavlov's long dead, but we still act like his dogs."

"Speaking of which, whenever the sun's out for more than an hour, this little doggy starts craving a cool, delicious fudge twirl sundae to be melting in her mouth. Can't you just taste it?"

Peter pauses before answering. *Is it just my imagination or does everything she say suggest something else?*

"I'm game. I gotta help my aunt shop, but I'll be free around six."

"See you at the parlor. Now go beat the bell in there and learn all about chemical reactions, as if you didn't already know." She gives him that *look*, as if she knows the chemical reaction she is having on him right at that moment. *Geez*, thinks Peter, *does she know what she does to me?* The late bell rings.

"Break into four groups, and come up with your hypothesis—Peter, since you're late, you do the prep work—distribute the beakers, write out the scientific model on the board. . . ."

Leave it to Mr. Sebastion, he does it every time, thinks Peter. *Takes my favorite subject and pulverizes it to small particles of dullness.*

Fifty mind-numbing minutes of theory and formulae later, and Peter is gratefully released from Mr. Sebastion's chamber of boredom, only to see his advisor, Ms. O'Grady, approaching.

"Peter Parker!"

"Yes, ma'am?"

"I spoke with your aunt about your missing so many classes, and she doesn't seem to know about your being absent last week. . . ."

"Uh . . . her memory isn't what it used to be, I don't like to embarrass her. . . ."

"Oh, I'm sorry Peter. I didn't know. Well, that aside, I hate to see you waste good scholarship money by failing classes for poor attendance!"

"No, Ms. O'Grady, I won't do that. Thank you for your concern, ma'am." Peter walks off. A big one. The two this morning to Aunt May were little enough, but this lie is a big one. Aunt May can remember what he ate for breakfast three weeks ago, her memory is that stone-cold perfect.

The little fibs are like annoying black moths, fluttering at the edges of his consciousness; shadows that flit about and dog his heels, they haunt him when he least expects it. The big ones are like rocks tied to his feet, that he has to drag with him wherever he goes.

Peter forces these ominous thoughts away by thinking of Mary Jane and their promised chocolate fudge sundae. He is headed for his last class of the day, World History, when his thoughts go from fudge to vanilla; he sees Gwen Stacy coming in from gym class, a blonde vision in tennis whites. They're head-on in each others' paths, there is no avoiding it.

"Hi, Gwen. What's up?"

"Hello, Peter. Nothing much. I was just thinking about how

much fun it would be to go to the revival house tonight—they're playing *Casablanca,* my favorite film."

"That hill-a'-beans, here's-lookin'-at-you, of-all-the-gin-joints-she-hadda-walk-into-mine, play-it-again,-Sam flick?"

"Yes." Gwen laughs. "You like it, too, I take it."

"Never saw it. I can just round up the usual suspects."

"Never saw it!" She laughs again, her sweet little nose crinkling up. Gwendolyn. Her name is musical. "You have to see it, it's the best film ever made!"

"Well, I was thinking of going tonight."

"The five o'clock show? That's when I'll be there."

"Me too! Meet you in front of the theater?"

"Okay! See you then, Peter."

Peter goes off to history class. From fudge to vanilla. From gravy to mud, more like it. Aunt May at four, Gwen at five, Mary Jane at six? How will he pull this off?

"History is just the first draft of the truth. Written by the victors, it leaves out the side of the losers. Peter, you're late again."

"Sorry, Mr. Swenson. I got held up in Chemistry Lab."

"That's odd, I just saw Mr. Sebastion in the teachers' lounge."

"Uh, yeah. He left me alone to clean up the lab."

"Sit down, Peter. Well, class, Mr. Parker here has reminded me of another definition of history—by selective presentation of the facts, you can prove anything. Open your texts to page forty seven, let's begin to decipher the lies we call history. . . ."

Peter waits in aisle six, while Aunt May squeezes melons. Usually, he pushes the cart, waits in the line, and carries the bags home for her. He watches her check each melon before sniffing out the one she wants, and realizes this is going to take a while.

"One is his treasure, one is his treat . . ." The station that plays over the grocery store speakers is spinning a string of fifties songs. *"Livin' double, in a world of trouble . . ."* Peter is having one of those moments when every sappy tune seems to be written just for him. *"Can't give up either, they're both so sweet. . . ."*

His gaze wanders outside. A man is crossing the parking lot.

"Here, Peter. I want you to eat more bananas. Did you know that a banana is the perfect food?"

Peter isn't listening. Something is bugging him.

"Let's move on to meats. I haven't had a roast in ages, I think I'll make you a nice supper this Sunday."

Halfway to meats, it hits him. A warm sunny day, a man with a black wool cap, hands deep in his pockets.

"Aunt May? I just remembered I forgot to make a phone call. I'll be back in time to help you with checkout, okay?"

"But, Peter, you won't be able to tell me what you want for Sunday dinner. . . ."

"I might know what I want, Aunt May, but you know what I need. You do the picking."

"Okay, but hurry back."

Peter tosses his bookbag, now stuffed with his clothes, behind the furnace stack on the store's roof. Last week he'd sewn a secret pocket into his bookbag, after someone dumped it out in the library looking to borrow a pencil and almost discovered his red-and-blue spandex secret.

Right now he wears his secret over his skin. Peter pulls on his gloves, and yanks his mask down over his chin midjump. He activates his web-shooters, designed after hours of spider-watching and based on the spiders' spinnerets, and the web-fluid hardens on contact with the air, forming a nice-sized glob on the ledge and one loop around a pipe. He tests the line, and begins to rappel down.

Some eye I got, he thinks, watching the man, as predicted, yank his black skimask down over his chin to hide his face, and enter the store.

Spider-Man sees May reaching the head of the line, just as the man pulls out his gun.

"Nice and easy, put it all in a bag. Nobody moves, nobody gets hurt."

The checkout girl is surprisingly cool as she clanks open the register and begins taking out the stacks of bills. She shrugs her shoulders and gives the thief a look, as if to say, *Ain't my money, no skin off me.*

Her look changes fast enough.

"Omigod! Wow!" she squeals, and the robber spins around just in time to get his gun clogged with web-line.

"Spider-Man!" someone else yells. "I read about him but, gosh, I've never seen him!"

"Beat 'im up!" a little boy barks out. "Beat 'im up, Spider-Man!"

Spider-Man swings down from his perch over aisle four, and secures the thief in an armlock.

"Nobody's getting beaten up, but somebody's headed for a jail cell."

In a moment born of fear and relief, everyone in the store bursts into sudden applause, cheering Spider-Man. A woman steps closer and touches the cloth of his suit. Spider-Man is a hero. To those lucky enough to see him in action, he is a simple, irrefutable, do-good hero. There is no bitter resentment, no fear, no hatred toward this hero. A welcome change.

The store boss stumbles out from where he's been hiding behind a stack of soda pop bottles.

"Thank you, Spider-Man! Please, take a cart of food, on the house."

Spider-Man glances over at Aunt May, her little hands still clutched at her throat in nervousness.

"Hey, I just ate. But it looks like this poor woman got the worst fright. Maybe you could take care of her . . . ?"

"It's done, Spider-Man!"

"Well, I'll be . . . !" Aunt May glances shyly to the floor, then furtively looks toward him, but Spider-Man doesn't want to look in her eyes. He hustles the crook outside just as a cop car pulls up.

At the sight of the cops, the crook begins to squirm. *Just like a moth in a web, the more you resist, the more entangled you get.* With this thought, Spider-Man hands the thief over with relief.

"Oh, Peter! You missed all the excitement!" They're unloading the food at Aunt May's house, and she has already told Peter the story three times. He notices how truthfully she tells the tale; no embellishments, nothing exaggerated.

"One thing bothered me, though. That Spider-person, his manners were terrible."

"What? What do you mean?"

"Well, I was so grateful for the free groceries, I just wanted to thank him properly. But he just turned his back on me! Whoever his mother is, she sure didn't raise him right."

"I gotta go, Aunt May."

"I mean, that Spider-Man confuses me. Sometimes I think he's downright wicked, he even scares me sometimes. But bad manners? That's something I just can't tolerate."

"I gotta go. I'm meeting Gwen at the movies. I'll see you later."

"Gwen? I thought you said you were going out with Mary Jane!"

"Oh, yeah. Did I say Gwen? I meant Mary Jane."

Another little one. One more to nip at his heels. Aunt May watches Peter leave. Peter doesn't turn back. He doesn't want to see that look he knows is on her face. The one that says, *What's wrong with this picture?*

Five minutes into *Casablanca,* and Peter can feel the warmth of Gwen sitting beside him in the dark theater, and he likes it. He shudders, remembering. Remembering how much Gwen hates Spider-Man. How can he be serious about a girl who hates him and doesn't know it? Still . . . he feels so good with Gwen. She's like a warm bed you don't want to get out of in the morning. But he has to, Mary Jane wants her hot fudge sundae.

"I'm going to the bathroom, be right back," he whispers in Gwen's ear. Her eyes don't leave the screen, but in the dark he can just make out a wisp of a smile on her face.

Peter escorts Mary Jane to an outside table. He orders a strawberry sundae, and Mary Jane asks for the promised hot fudge triple.

"So anyway, this photographer really likes me and wants to do my modeling shots for free."

"That's great, Mary Jane."

"Modeling seems a little safer than my last gig, at the go-go club."

Peter tries to picture Gwen as a go-go girl. Never happen. Not only isn't she the type, but her retired-police-captain dad would never allow it. But Mary Jane, she always seems to do wild things. She is boy crazy to the bone.

"Only thing wrong with modeling is you have to get up early. It could put a crimp in my party calendar!"

"Mary Jane, don't you ever think about something besides having a good time?"

"Oh, Peter, don't be a drag. You sound like my father. He'd always say things like that right before . . ." Her voice trails off, but before Peter can question her she bounces back peppier than ever. "There is nothing else besides good times. When we die, the one who had the most fun wins."

"Wins what?"

"A big party in heaven."

Mary Jane laughs and laughs until their sundaes come. Peter is spooning in the first delicious mouthful, when he sees a huge bird swoop between the buildings in the distance. The bird twirls in a beautiful turn and disappears. The sun is warm on Peter's back, Mary Jane is gorgeous, and the ice cream tastes cool and perfect. Peter feels gleeful, almost giddy. Two dates at once, he is going to pull this off. Peter Parker is very pleased with himself.

Two scoops later, as Mary Jane is in the middle of a zany story about some wild motorcycle ride, Peter drops his spoon.

"Peter! What's wrong?"

There are no birds that big. Only vultures.

"Uh . . . I gotta go get . . . a bird."

"What?"

"I promised this guy, I'd help him move his birds."

"His birds?"

"Yeah, he's got a pet shop, and he's got a big delivery of birds, I promised I'd help, and I forgot. I'll be right back."

"What? Peter Parker, you better not leave me alone with all this ice cream. There's no telling what I'll do." Her voice is mock angry, but her look says, *Who cares?* Peter has to wonder; why is she being so agreeable to this? As if she expected it . . .

Peter jumps up.

"Twenty minutes, Mary Jane. Promise."

"Just get back before I eat yours, Tiger."

Spider-Man swings from roof to roof, eyes searching the sky. *"Just get back before I eat yours, Tiger." Wow. What a girl.*

He thinks he sees something perched in the distance. A vulture as big as a man. Over by the waterfront. What's over there? *The Marine Midland Bank, that's what.* Perfect target for Adrian Toomes, aka the Vulture.

The man who thinks he's a bird. Not only has Spider-Man fought this man many times, but he's humiliated the Vulture more than once. The first photos Peter ever sold to the *Bugle* were of the Vulture. The old man's electromagnetic harness allows him to fly like a bird, and Spider-Man has to be careful—the Vulture is always adding some deadly new gimmick to his wings.

Spider-Man zigzags from roof to roof, darting erratically as if avoiding bullets, just in case the Vulture has backup. His final leap lands him on the last building west, a tall tower with a long shadow that falls across the Hudson River.

He unhooks his Leica, and webs the camera to an aerial, pointing it toward the spot he imagines he'll end up, fighting the Vulture. He's fixed his camera with a new oscillating device that sweeps more of a wide range, and is anxious to see if he gets better shots that way.

Spider-Man peers across the roof. The Vulture. A mean old man with a pair of mechanical wings. Bitter, cynical, ornery as his shadow is long. The man is an electromagnetic genius, who seems to get a gleeful thrill out of robbery, as if he's fulfilling some complex revenge for a lifetime of wrongs committed against him.

Well, the dirty bird is no match for Spider-Man. He'll wrap this one up quick as this morning's thug, and be back before his ice cream melts.

Spider-Man swings in toward the Vulture's back, thinking at the same time that the old man must have been working out lately, his shoulders look wider than usual.

His spider-sense goes off, that strange buzzing intuition he has when there is some danger nearby. Spider-Man spins into a back flip just in time to miss most of the metal-tipped feathers, sharp as razors, but not all of them. The few that catch slice right through his costume, and three thin lines of blood form across his chest. Two Vultures!

"Always getting in my way! Always ruining things!" The Vulture's voice screeches like his namesake. "You're not going to mess with me again, Spider-Man! You're rotten to the bone, and somebody's got to stop you!" The Vulture circles above and tips into a dive.

The twisted logic of the villain, Spider-Man thinks. *It never ceases to give me a headache.*

"You're the one robbing a bank, but I'm the villain? How do you figure that?"

"You know. Don't pretend you don't!" His voice truly is an irritating caw.

"I know what?"

"What they did to me! How that money is mine!"

"Oh, right. The big conspiracy against you. Sorry, I forgot."

"Yes! See? You do know!"

Once again, Spider-Man is reminded of his cardinal rule: never argue with men who think they're birds. Or octopuses. Or fools who think they're scorpions. Or rhinos. The world is a pet store full of delusions.

"Give it up, Vulture. You know I always win." Spider-Man shoots two-fisted, a double stream of webbing, one to a chimney top to propel him into a somersault, the other aimed at the real Vulture's eyes. He comes out of his twirl just in time to slam both feet into the Vulture's chest, at the same time shooting his web-line backwards over his head at the second, phony Vulture. This black bird tumbles, as the real Vulture claws at his eyes to remove the sticky mess.

"My eyes! That was low, Spider-Man."

Sympathy for the villainous. Aunt May's little voice whispers in his skull. She would be furious at him, webbing shut an old man's eyes.

"Nice trick, adding razors to your feathers, Vulture. But all I have to do is avoid their touch and you're as outclassed as ever! As for the cheap clone job—next time train him better!" Spider-Man glances over to make sure the Vulture-clone is down.

Then he makes two mistakes. He waits till the Vulture gets the web-line goo off his eyes; after all, he doesn't want to blind the guy. He stands ready to bind the Vulture's wings to his sides, but that second of consideration is a second too long. His spider-sense warns him of danger, but he releases his line to bind up the Vulture, assuming that's where the danger is. Something hits him in the back and head.

He spins in time to see a third Vulture, and then a fourth. The old man is clever. Why stop at one clone? He's recruited three more just like him for this job. Built himself a whole flock of wings, attached to a gang of fine-feathered thugs.

Spider-Man's head spins. *Maybe there is only one Vulture, maybe I'm just seeing triple,* he thinks. He rolls and comes up punching. He enjoys a moment of foolish excitement when he thinks he has them, he feels so many solid hits connect, hears a few bones cracking, hears a score of painful cries. But then he's being lifted—they've each grabbed a limb and flown up and out over the river. Spider-Man kicks and claws and jackknifes his body so violently, he manages to get free of all four of them. And then he realizes it's the stupidest thing he could have done.

He is twenty-some stories up in the air, out over the water, and there's nothing within a thousand yards to shoot a line at.

"The righteous shall always prevail!" The Vulture's hideous screech echoes in Spider-Man's pounding skull.

No more sympathy. Never. Ever. Again. He realizes his fingers are instinctively flicking away at his web-shooters, spraying the fluid helplessly. No building to secure a web-line, no way to break the fall. He's already falling too fast to weave a web parachute. He's punch drunk from that first blow to his head, and the world that whizzes past keeps fading in and out of focus.

Oh, gosh. Mary Jane and ice cream. Gwen in the dark movie house. They'll find out. Aunt May. She'll know too. My face, my corpse, a front-page Bugle story. They'll all know what a liar I was. A lowlife fibster with a devil's tongue. A mendacious arachnid. A lousy deceitful cock-and-bull jerk. A two-faced stinker.

The words multiply and flutter about his head, stinging.

That's when he loses consciousness.

There is a time of fog, not pure blackness, but still very dark. So dark, he keeps falling through cobwebs he can't see but feels splitting apart on his face. *Why are there webs in the sky? Where am I falling to?*

"Mummy, could I have some grape soda?" Yes, darling. Of course. "Mummy, are you packing?" Yes, Peter. Your daddy and I are going to the Far East, on a trip. Aunt May and Uncle Ben will take care of you. "Oh."

Little Peter took his grape soda out of the kitchen and padded down the hall to see his daddy in the bedroom.

"Daddy? Are you packing too?" Yes, son. Mommy and I will be gone a few days. "Where are you going?" We're going to the West Coast. "Is the West Coast in the Far East?" No, silly. East and west are opposite directions.

New information. Daddy in the west, Mommy in the east. But somehow, together. Back to Mommy.

"Why are you going?" Your father and I are going on a vacation. "Are you going together?" Of course, Peter. "What will you do?" Oh, I don't know. Relax, swim, lie on the beach. "Will it be hot?" Oh, yes. Very hot where we're going.

Hot in the east that is also the west but isn't. Must ask Daddy about this.

Cold, son. We'll do a little skiing. "Oh. Can I go?" Not this time, Peter. Maybe next time. "Daddy? Can it be cold and hot at the same time?" No, Peter, that's impossible. "Oh. East isn't west and hot isn't cold?" No, little numbskull. And black will never be white and up will never be down. You sure are full of funny questions tonight, son. Give that little brain of yours a rest. "Okay, Daddy. I will."

They were spies. They led double lives. They weren't home much. I was three years old when I noticed the first little lies. By the time I was six, nothing quite added up. The world is a strange place when you're never sure of anything. You sense things are slightly off, so you ask questions. When you get funny answers, you think it's your own perceptions that are wrong. You never quite trust your own intuition again.

All those lies. I guess they thought they were protecting me. Benevolent lying. I know all about it. Which came first, that spider that turned me into Spider-Man, or my proclivity for leading a double life? Just like Mom and Dad. I'm my father's son. Momma's little boy. They were dead by the time I was six; did I then yearn to be just like them? Double agents. Genius liars. All for a cause, of course. Lie or die.

They may have been liars but they were heroes too.

"Aunt May? What's an orphan?" Oh, Peter, where did you hear such a big word? "At school." It's okay Peter. It's just a bad dream. Wake up, Peter.

Peter! Wake up!

Peter! Wake up!

He's glad Aunt May woke him up from the bad dream, until he sees what he's woken up to.

Spider-Man is seventeen feet above the water, falling fast. He sees a passing tugboat, and shoots both barrels hard—one web-line catches the stack. He uses the tension of the line to swing up, just skimming the rough tops of the hard-rolling river waves, braking his descent. The momentum of his fall dissipates further as he arcs up again, a violent pendulum. He swings back down safely and hits the river. The cold water brings his mind back full force. He sees the boat has come around for him, and a friendly red-faced man is waving at him. He climbs up the tires that hang off the boat's side.

"Welcome aboard, Spider-Man."

"Thanks. Can I hitch a ride ashore?"

"You bet! Be another good an' tall sea tale for me to tell! I saw you falling, so I swung around for you. I was trying to rig a sail like a trampoline to catch you, but it's a good thing you came to. I don't think I would have rigged it fast enough."

"Thanks for trying."

The old captain tosses him a blanket.

"You're drenched, son. Cover up. My name's Gallager. Come on up to the wheelhouse, I got something to warm your gut."

The captain notices Spider-Man looking at the sky.

"Fine day for a little sky-diving," he laughs.

"I was looking . . ."

"For what?"

"For birds."

The captain's eyes sweep the sky.

"That's odd. Rare's the day when there ain't a bird in the sky."

Spider-Man sits glumly on a huge roll of rope, watching Captain Gallager steer his boat to shore. He looks so capable in his stance, you can see he knows why he's alive, he's sure of why he's on the planet, and Spider-Man envies the man. As if reading his thoughts, Gallager turns back and winks.

"Mind if I ask what dark clouds are gathering in that noggin of yours, Spider-Man?"

"What do you think of liars?" Spider-Man responds impulsively.

"Depends. On what kind of lying. I've worked all kinds of boats, and on some of 'em, I gotta lie all day."

"You? Lie?"

"Sure. If I'm out on a rig with a crew and a storm hits, heck, even if it's clear sailing, I gotta order my men up and down the masts, make 'em hang off the gunnels, hoist this, rig that—I make 'em take all kinds of risks.

"Every time I give an order, it's to save the ship but risk the man. My voice and manner must have the confidence of a god. They trust me and I send them to risk death with every command. It's called keeping your eye on the ball. The higher purpose. Well then, a few lies along the way ain't really lies, are they? Not if you bring all your men home alive."

Spider-Man sits silently, watching as Captain Gallager swings his tug around portside, till he docks her so expertly that when the tires hit the pilings, it is gentle as a baby's kiss.

Peter Parker glances between Mary Jane's smirk and the melted pink puddle that was his strawberry sundae.

"Get those birds moved?" she asks.

"Uh, yeah. Sorry it took a little longer than I thought."

Mary Jane smiles.

"Did you have a nice swim?"

"What? What swim?"

"Never mind. Just a little daydream I had."

They talk awhile longer, and it's not till later, when Peter is reaching under the table, that he realizes his bookbag's made a little puddle on the floor around Mary Jane's feet. She's slipped off her sandals, and her red polished toes slap playfully at the puddle.

Peter sits back up.

"Rained while you were gone," she says, smiling.

Peter looks at Mary Jane gratefully, and for once tries not to think too hard.

He walks Mary Jane home, and runs to the theater, just as the show lets out. Gwen looks happy to see him.

"Where'd you disappear to, Peter?"

"After I went to the rest room, I couldn't find our seats in the dark. I watched the movie from the back."

"Didn't you just love that movie?"

"Oh, yeah."

"What a perfect ending."

"Yeah. I love happy endings."

"Happy . . . ?"

Gwen looks at him queerly, then smiles. They walk on silently for a while. Soon, it begins to rain.

DEADLY FORCE

Richard Lee Byers

Illustration by Louis Small Jr.

The multicolored lights of the theater district were beautiful from eight stories up, and the kiss of the evening breeze was cool and pleasant. But Spider-Man barely noticed, just as he only occasionally registered the ache in his stomach and the twinges that jabbed through his shoulders every time he transferred his weight to a new web-line. Even then, the pain didn't slow him down. His eyes burning, he scanned the darkness ahead.

And finally saw, after eight straight nights of doggedly combing Manhattan from dusk until dawn, a shadowy figure skittering up the side of an office building almost as quickly as he could have done it himself.

Spider-Man was all but certain he'd found the object of his search. Glaring through the one-way lenses of his scarlet mask, he landed on a ledge, and then, as he pressed the trigger hidden beneath his glove to release another strand of webbing, kicked off with all his superhuman strength, increasing the speed of his swooping progress down Forty-seventh Street. Perhaps the dark figure ahead heard the vigilante's feet thump against the concrete projection, or even the soft *thwip* of his web-shooter. At any rate, he glanced back and then started to climb more rapidly.

Oh, no, you don't, thought Spider-Man, pumping his legs to swing even faster. *You're not getting away from me now.*

Three weeks ago the criminal mastermind known as the Green Goblin had thrown Spider-Man's beloved Gwen Stacy off the Brooklyn Bridge; the crime-fighter had tried and failed to save her. And now, as if in grisly imitation of the tragedy, a super-powered serial killer was murdering lovely blonde girls just like her. Dubbed the Rooftop Ripper by the tabloids, his modus operandi was to snatch his victims off the street and carry them to the top of a nearby building, where he could torture them undisturbed. Ultimately he used his Herculean strength to tear them apart, then tossed the bodies back onto the pavement like so much litter. Evidently relishing his notoriety, he wanted to make sure his crimes would be discovered without delay.

And Spider-Man meant to put an end to the slaughter. Nothing had ever mattered more. In fact, with Gwen dead, it felt like nothing else mattered at all.

In his haste, he swung onto the façade of the office building a little clumsily, nearly bumping his knee against the stonework. Meanwhile, his quarry swarmed onto the roof and out of sight. Faster than an Olympic sprinter, Spider-Man raced upward, his hands and feet adhering to the vertical surface beneath them.

By the time he had scrambled onto the flat slate roof, the other man was standing casually near a ventilator. Built like a lineman, taller and huskier than his pursuer, the stranger wore high-top sneakers, chinos, a motorcycle jacket, and rubber gloves. A blue knit ski mask concealed his features.

"I knew I'd run into one of you sooner or later," the big man said in a pleasant baritone voice. "For some reason I thought it would be Daredevil, but I was actually hoping for you."

"Why is that?" Spider-Man asked, stalking forward. His arachnoid costume and crouching, sinuous glide had unnerved many a crook—and honest citizen for that matter—but to all appearances, the stranger was unimpressed.

"Well, he's not in your league, is he? He isn't strong enough to make it any fun."

"What kind of fun are you talking about? A fight?" Spider-Man continued his advance.

"Isn't that what you spandex rangers do?" the man in the ski mask asked. "Try to beat up bad guys? Well, you won't find a badder one than me. I'm the Rooftop Ripper . . . of course, I think you already had that figured out. Why else would you follow me up here in such a panic? Not that it's going to do you any good. I already snuffed one little blondie tonight, up by the Guggenheim. She had the pinkest, sexiest lips you ever saw. But I think that after our scuffle, I'll bag an extra one, and dedicate the kill to you."

The crime-fighter leapt into the air, his arm cocked to deliver a punch.

The Ripper sidestepped out of the vigilante's way. As Spider-Man hurtled by, the killer grabbed his arm and swung him, using his momentum against him as a martial artist might. Tumbling out of control, the crime-fighter crashed into the ventilator, snapping the pipe off at the base. A burst of pain jolted through his back. He started to spring to his feet. The murderer gave him an agonizing kick to the knee, dropping him back onto the slate.

"I'm disappointed," the Ripper said. "You're supposed to be hot stuff. You need motivation? You want me to describe how they beg for mercy, or splat like tomatoes when I dump them over the side?''

Ignoring the pain in his knee, supporting his weight on one hand, Spider-Man swept his legs in an arc, trying to catch his opponent's ankle and trip him. The Ripper hopped nimbly back, out of reach. The crime-fighter flipped to his feet and lunged at him.

The Ripper punched at his head. Spider-Man ducked and started to move in with attacks of his own, steadily increasing the force behind them as he'd learned to do early in his career. A man with the strength to press ten tons had to feel out an opponent with an undetermined level of super powers, discovering by trial and error just how hard to hit him. Otherwise he could literally knock his head off.

His first efforts knocked the Ripper back a step, nothing more. The murderer brushed aside a shot to the face, then jabbed in return. Spider-Man slipped that blow, and only his spider-sense allowed him to avoid what would have been an agonizing kick to the stomach.

But even his spider-sense and speed didn't help him avoid the Ripper's next punishing volley. A follow-up attack smashed down on the nape of the wall-crawler's neck and crumpled him onto the rooftop. He tried to jump back up but only managed to flounder around spastically.

"Don't tell me you've had enough already," the Ripper said. For a moment, Spider-Man, blinking away tears, could have sworn that the serial killer's woolen mask had somehow acquired the goggle eyes and pointed ears of the Goblin's false face. "It's up to you, but I should warn you, the next one is really going to suffer. I'm going to make the fun last a long, long time."

Spider-Man screamed, rolled to his feet, and lashed out with a haymaker, which missed his opponent's head by several inches. A return attack cracked against his temple. He reeled backward, and then the world went black.

Spider-Man awoke cradled in someone's arms. For a moment he thought it was Gwen, that they'd been cuddling and he'd dozed off. Then he smelled blood, felt tacky streaks of it drying on his costume.

His eyes popped open to meet the glassy gaze of a corpse.

Aghast, heedless of the throbbing pains aroused by movement, he tore himself out of the dead girl's embrace and backpedaled several feet across the roof, only to discover that viewing her from a distance was nearly as intolerable as touching her. Now he could see every ragged gash and mutilation. It looked as if the Ripper had carried away pieces of her as souvenirs.

Spider-Man's stomach heaved. Certain he was about to throw up, he yanked his mask off. The nausea abated. The anguish didn't.

The Ripper warned me he'd kill another girl tonight if I didn't stop him, the vigilante thought. *And here you are.*

For a while he simply stood and stared at her, incapable of registering anything else. Finally, however, he noticed the first tinge of gray in the eastern sky. The night was nearly over, and the Ripper long gone. There was nothing to do now but phone the police and limp home.

Suddenly unable to bear her blank, accusing eyes, he put his mask back on, dashed to the edge of the roof, and leapt out over the street. But no matter how fast he swung through the city, he couldn't leave the sight and feel of her behind, any more than he could forget the sight and feel of Gwen's inert body dangling in his arms.

His bruised and battered body aching, Peter Parker shuffled aimlessly across the campus of Empire State University. The morning sunlight stung his eyes, and almost made him wish he'd stayed in his apartment. But after lying in bed for an hour or so, staring at the ceiling, he'd felt the walls closing in on him.

Grinning, chattering students hurried past him on their way to class. One rangy guy in an ESU basketball sweatshirt was wolfing down a breakfast sandwich. The smell of the bacon made Peter queasy. He wondered without much caring if he was ever going to get his appetite back.

Maybe not. How could he enjoy food or anything else when everyone kept dying on him? His parents, Uncle Ben, and all the other people Spider-Man had failed to save. His whole miserable life amounted to nothing more than a parade of fatalities.

Well, that's over! he told himself with a sudden burst of fury. *It's all going to change, starting with the Ripper!*

Yet even as he made the vow, he wondered if he could make good on it. Even if he could locate the Ripper a second time, how was he supposed to take him down? The psychopath was stronger than he was, and had outfought him easily. He had every right to consider Spider-Man a joke.

Feeling useless, contemptible, Peter trudged on, trying to imagine how he could have changed the outcome. After a few more paces, an answer struck him, one so unexpected that it froze him in his tracks.

He'd fought the Ripper the way he fought everyone, taking care not to do any permanent damage. What if he'd gone all out? Used every iota of his strength from the first second, not caring if he pulped his adversary's head, broke his back, or drove his fist through his torso? What if he'd been willing to risk killing him?

"Are you all right?" said a husky alto voice. Startled, Peter whirled, his arms reflexively whipping up into a guard position. A plump, freckled coed in wire-rimmed glasses took a hasty step backward. "Hey, it's okay! I'm not trying to hassle you. I was just worried because you looked kind of freaked out."

Peter tried to dredge up a reassuring smile. "I'm fine. I was just thinking about an idea. A crazy idea." She eyed him dubiously, then shrugged and moved on.

Scowling, Peter wandered on in the opposite direction. A crazy idea was exactly what it was, one that violated everything he believed in. Spider-Man wasn't a killer.

No, not even after all these years, all these disasters, and maybe that showed what a slow learner he was. If he'd eliminated Dr. Octopus in one of their early encounters, the deranged scientist would never have gone on to cause the death of Gwen's dad. If he'd killed the Green Goblin, Gwen herself would still be alive.

And if Peter could make a case for slaying the kind of opponents he usually fought—ruthless megalomaniacs and brutal thugs, who killed for money, power, and revenge—how much easier it was to justify exterminating someone like the Ripper, who was viler than any of them. Who murdered purely for the evil sport of it. Who was going to keep doing it, night after night, until somebody stopped him.

Cops used deadly force when lives were at stake. Why shouldn't a super hero? Maybe Spider-Man didn't even have the *right* to hold back, not when people were in danger.

Yeah. Maybe. But Uncle Ben and Aunt May had raised him to

revere life. How would he ever be able to face his aunt again if he battered someone to death? What good were his spider powers, anyway, if they couldn't neutralize a threat with any more finesse than a hail of bullets?

On the other hand, what good were they if their possessor lacked the will to use them aggressively enough to protect the innocent?

Had his whole approach to crime-fighting been fatally flawed from the start? Was that why the atrocities never stopped? He walked for miles, mulling it over, but simply couldn't decide.

The dead girl lay sprawled in the gutter, her pale hair matted with blood and her limbs bent at unnatural angles. Her body really had burst like a piece of fruit, just as the Ripper had said.

A photographer circled her, taking one shot after another, his flash blinking. A stocky, balding detective wrote and sketched on a notepad, a uniformed officer stood ready to make sure no curiosity seekers passed the yellow tape, and a pair of EMTs lounged against their ambulance, waiting to take the corpse away. Twenty feet over their heads, Spider-Man hung in the shadowy corner where two grimy brick walls came together. Above him murmured the voices of the investigators examining the rooftop, where the murder had actually occurred.

The detective turned and trudged toward the entrance to the tenement, no doubt heading back upstairs. Spider-Man crawled along the wall until he was directly above him. "Hi," he said.

The detective's head snapped up, peered wildly about until he spotted the figure suspended upside down in the darkness. "You," he growled. "Aren't you still wanted for questioning in the murder of Norman Osborn?"

"Last I heard," Spider-Man said, creeping a little closer to the ground. "Do you feel like trying to arrest me?"

The cop snorted. "Nights like this, I feel like taking early retirement. I could go to Seattle, move in with my kid, and make *her* life miserable. I don't suppose you're here to tell me you caught the killer."

"Sorry, no. I arrived on the scene after you did."

"Too bad. I guess you know, this makes three victims so far this week. This dirtbag's worse than Berkowitz, the Boston Strangler, or any of them."

"Are you getting any closer to finding him?"

The detective shrugged. "You know the drill. You follow up on all your tips and bright ideas, and eventually, if you're lucky, something pans out. Theoretically, it could happen anytime. But frankly, right now, we've got nothing."

"I was hoping that with the description I phoned in—"

"Right. A husky white guy in a mask. That really narrowed the field." The detective grimaced. "I don't mean to bust your chops. I suppose you're doing your best, the same as us lowly normal people. I just wish you'd managed to drop this freak when you had him in your sights."

When Peter entered the office, Joe Robertson was studying the day's edition of the *Daily Bugle*. A handsome middle-aged African American, the one person who always seemed calm and unhurried amid the perpetual frenzy of the *Bugle*, Robbie looked around with the same pleasant, inquiring smile he gave all the people who were constantly barging in on him. But then his brow furrowed.

"Good Lord, son," he said. "When's the last time you shaved, or took a shower?"

Peter struggled to hold in a scowl. He didn't need Robbie nagging him. "There's no hot water in my apartment," he said. "The super's fixing it today."

"Ah," Robbie said. Peter got the feeling the older man suspected he was lying, but had decided not to make an issue of it. "Well, grubby or clean, it's good to see you. What's up?"

"I'm interested in the Ripper murders. Does the paper know anything it hasn't published, because the authorities asked us not to, or whatever? Do we have any special leads or theories we're following up ourselves?" The *Bugle* had a well-deserved reputation for investigative journalism, and once in a while its reporters even solved a crime in advance of the NYPD.

"No, not this time," Robbie said, and though it was the answer Peter had been expecting, he still felt a pang of disappointment. "To tell you the truth, I'm reluctant to put you on that story after what's happened in your own life lately."

Since acquiring his powers, Peter had supported himself and his aunt May by taking photos, frequently shots of his alter ego captured by an automatic camera. In better times, it had amused him to sell them to the publication that was Spider-Man's chief detractor. Even so, he didn't really intend to work on the Ripper story. The notion of profiting from the carnage seemed obscene. But he wanted to make sure he'd be privy to any information the paper uncovered.

"I'll be all right," he said. "I'm a crime photographer. I know how to keep my professional distance—"

The door banged open and an angry-looking older man stormed in. With his habitual glare and his head thrust forward, his gray crew-cut bristling, and a foul-smelling cigar jutting from his mouth, he radiated nervous energy and distemper. He was J. Jonah Jameson, publisher and editor-in-chief of the *Bugle*, and, for reasons Peter had never fully fathomed, the guiding spirit behind its anti–Spider-Man campaign.

"Parker!" he roared. "Where in blazes have you—" He faltered, no doubt belatedly remembering Gwen's death.

"Peter's ready to come back to work," said Robbie, filling the awkward silence. "He expressed some interest in the Ripper story, but I could really use him on the United Nations feature."

"Nonsense!" Jameson barked. Either he didn't have a clue why Robbie actually wanted to divert Peter to another assignment, or he didn't care. "Put him on the murders! *That's* what people want to read about, and I want Parker out there getting the best shots for the *Bugle*! Which reminds me, I've got page one." With a flourish, he placed a mockup on Robbie's desk.

Peter read the boldface title at the top of the page. The words hit him like a blow. IS SPIDER-MAN THE RIPPER? AN EDITORIAL BY J. JONAH JAMESON.

"Jonah," said Robbie, manifestly appalled. Unlike his boss, he had nothing against Spider-Man. "We can't print this."

Jameson scowled. "I'd like to know why not."

"Because there isn't a shred of evidence to support the allegation."

"Of course there is," Jameson said. "They're both strong, they both run around on top of buildings, and that wall-crawling freak has already shown he's capable of every heinous crime in the book. He's menaced this city for years, and it's the duty of this paper, *my* duty, to warn the citizens of New York about him. And in *my* editorial, I will speak *my* mind. I've got an amendment that guarantees *me* the right to."

"We have to maintain basic standards of fairness," Robbie interrupted. "We can't smear *anybody* with a charge like this, not without any justification at all, no matter how much you happen to dislike him, editorial, amendments, or whatever!"

His eyes glued to the headline, Peter stopped listening to the argument. Of all the outrageous lies Jameson had ever written about him, this was by far the worst. He ought to be furious, but the anger wouldn't come.

Because he couldn't shake the ghastly feeling that even though the accusation was completely false, on another level it was entirely valid. Spider-Man was to blame for at least the most recent murders, Peter thought, because he'd failed to stop the Ripper when given the opportunity.

At last he made up his mind. It seemed to happen in an instant, even though he sensed that in reality, a whole series of frustrations and reproaches, overt or implicit, had nudged him toward his decision. Jameson's diatribe had merely provided the final impetus.

"No more holding back," he muttered.

"Excuse me?" Robbie said.

No more holding back, Peter thought. If he only had another chance, he'd tear into the murderer like a wild animal. Use every vicious, potentially lethal fighting trick that any opponent had ever tried against him. And if he wound up killing the Ripper, well, fine. The world would be a cleaner place without him.

Spider-Man swooped along MacDougal Street, above cafés, music stores, craft shops, and boutiques. A light rain fell, making the pavement gleam and walls and ledges slippery, though the latter was nothing his clinging power and sticky webbing couldn't handle. Lightning flickered above the skyscrapers to the north.

He was desperate for a rematch. The need was like a fever, a seething inside him. Sometimes he felt that if his quarry didn't appear soon, he'd explode.

Thunder boomed, and at the same instant, a woman screamed.

Poised atop a parapet, about to shoot another web-line, Spider-Man peered about. Had he truly heard a cry beneath the thunderclap, or was his imagination playing tricks on him? And if he had heard it, where had it come from?

The woman wailed, "Help!" This time, with no thunder drowning out the sound, he could tell it had originated behind him. He whirled and ran, springing from one building to the next, splashing up water.

In seconds he reached a dark, narrow alley. At the bottom, a willowy young woman with long, pale hair wrestled desperately with a man in a leather jacket and ski mask.

Spider-Man leapt down to the pavement, his powerful legs absorbing the shock of impact, landing beside the Ripper and his prey. Instantly, before the killer even noticed his arrival, he punched with all his might at the other man's throat, a blow that might conceivably have felled even a behemoth like the Rhino.

Grappling with the blonde girl, the Ripper chanced to raise his arm, and Spider-Man's fist caught him on the shoulder instead of the neck. Bone shattered with an explosive crack. His grip on his victim broken, thrown into the air, the killer flew thirty feet before crashing down on a heap of soggy cardboard boxes, which collapsed beneath him. Off balance, the girl reeled.

Spider-Man felt a thrill of exultation, but didn't pause to savor it. Even with one arm out of commission, the Ripper was dangerous; best to finish him off without delay. He charged and leapt, drawing up his leg to smash a full-power stomp kick into his opponent's face.

His opponent's *naked* face, he suddenly perceived. The guy— just a scrawny teenager, with acne on his chin—was wearing a wool cap that had resembled the Ripper's ski mask from overhead. Frozen with terror, he stared up at his assailant.

Spider-Man frantically flipped forward into a somersault, landed behind the kid instead of on top of him. It was all he could do to look him in the eye.

"He was just trying to grab my purse," said the long-haired woman, sounding sick. "I wanted help, but did you have to be so . . . brutal?"

"I—I—" Spider-Man said, feeling profoundly ashamed. "I thought—" He looked down at the teenager's misshapen shoulder. "That should be immobilized. I can use my webbing—"

"No!" whimpered the boy, his face ashen. "Please, just stay away from me!"

"If you'll go call 911," said the blonde to Spider-Man, "I'll stay with him until the ambulance comes."

Without a word, the wall-crawler turned and scuttled up a concrete wall.

By the time the EMTs arrived, the rain was falling harder. Standing on a tiled, sloping roof, Spider-Man watched until the ambulance took the boy away. *Just a kid*, he thought miserably, *a thief, to be sure, but still just a kid. And it's just pure luck that I didn't kill him.*

He felt rather as if, somewhere along the way, he'd gone crazy, and the near-tragedy in the alley had shocked him back to his senses. What had given him the arrogance to assume he had the right to take *anyone's* life, in any situation whatsoever? It was the law's job to punish criminals, not his. He was only a self-appointed vigilante, with nothing to keep him from abusing his powers and becoming a menace in his own right except fidelity to a personal code of honor. And it now seemed obvious that an ironclad prohibition against killing should rank high among his principles. Otherwise, given his present mood, it was horribly easy to imagine reaching a point where he'd maim and slay as a matter of course, taking out his grief on any mugger or burglar unfortunate enough to cross his path.

So he *wouldn't* tear the bad guys apart, no matter how much he thought they deserved it. The problem with that was that it put him back exactly where he'd started. Helpless to stop the Ripper.

No. He couldn't accept that. There had to be a way. He squatted down on the wet tiles, put his head in his hands, and tried to think. And to his surprise, he found himself perceiving aspects of his clash with the killer which had hitherto escaped him.

When he'd caught up with his quarry, he'd been run down. Starving. Exhausted. Next time, it didn't have to be that way. Somehow he could make himself eat and even sleep.

He'd also been enraged to the point of hysteria, too berserk to use the tricks and tactics that had proven effective in countless other battles, some of them against opponents stronger than himself. He'd simply kept rushing in and slugging. It didn't have to be that way, either, provided he kept his head.

Lighting flared, the radiance flickering on the contours of a leering gargoyle across the street. As Spider-Man stood up, he realized his costume was soaked through. Hoping he wouldn't catch cold—that was all he needed—he swung toward home.

Elegant in a black velvet frock and white fringed shawl, the woman caught Spider-Man's eye from a block away, the instant she climbed out of the cab. It was her blonde hair, of course, short and tightly curled, shining in the streetlight's glow. The yellow sedan drove away down Central Park West, she turned toward the entrance to a luxury high-rise, and the Ripper pounced out of the darkness.

Unlike the girl in the alley, she never had a chance to scream, any more than Spider-Man had time to shout a warning. The Ripper grabbed her from behind and pressed down on her carotid arteries. In moments, she slumped, unconscious. He tossed her over his shoulder and swarmed up the façade of the apartment building. Her wrap slid loose and dropped away.

Spider-Man hurtled down the street, incipient panic clawing at his mind. There was no guarantee he could defeat the Ripper under any circumstances, and the presence of a hostage could only make the task more difficult.

He could still go all out. Fight as ruthlessly as human monsters like the Green Goblin. Try to end the fight fast, with one devastating, full-power shot to the eyes, or—

No! That wasn't the way. Scowling, he pushed the thought out of his mind.

By the time he reached the high-rise, the Ripper and his prisoner were most of the way to the top. Hoping to keep the murderer from spotting him, he swung around the corner of the building to scale the adjacent wall.

He tried to climb fast but silently. Even so, when he peered over the parapet, the Ripper was waiting for him. Perhaps the murderer had a sixth sense of his own.

One arm around his unconscious captive's waist, the psychopath stood near the center of a spacious terrace, beside an oval swimming pool. Lamps beneath the surface made the water glow blue-green. More lights shone from the penthouse behind him, but Spider-Man didn't see anyone inside. He hoped no one was home.

"How'd you like that hot date I fixed you up with?" the Ripper said. "Well, really, I guess she was probably cold by the time *you* woke up."

Spider-Man felt a surge of rage. Reminding himself that his adversary *wanted* him to lose his temper, he managed to suppress it. Without haste, he climbed onto the rooftop. "You can surrender," he said. "When you're facing a ticked-off Spider-Man, nine out of ten dentists recommend it."

Probably noting the difference in the vigilante's demeanor, the big man hesitated, then chuckled. "You can't take me. We already proved that, remember? And even if you could, how can you throw down on me while I've got a helpless little blondie in my clutches? Though it might be fun to toss her back to you, a piece at a time." He poised his hand over the blonde girl's face, the thumb and forefinger curling like pincers.

Spider-Man swept his left arm to the side, and the Ripper automatically followed the movement. Using his right hand, the vigilante sprayed webbing into the larger man's eyes.

Spider-Man charged. Scrabbling at the mesh adhering to his head, off balance, the Ripper backpedaled frantically. The crime-fighter then seized the captive, yanked her out of her attacker's now fumbling grasp, sprang to the far corner of the terrace, and hastily set her down.

As he spun back around, the Ripper tore off the webbing. The front of his ski mask came away with it, revealing a boyish face with apple cheeks and a snub nose, the face of a baseball player in a Norman Rockwell painting.

"A hostage can only save your keister if you hang on to her," Spider-Man said. "And it's really dumb to unmask yourself in front of the good guys. No offense, but you need to study your super-villain handbook."

The Ripper charged.

Spider-Man shot webbing at the killer's feet, trying to glue them to the concrete, but the other man leapt over the strands. In another instant he was close enough to attack.

He was as fast, skillful, and tricky as Spider-Man remembered. Only the vigilante's spider-sense, warning him of every punch, strike, and kick, enabled him to block or dodge them. Struggling against the temptation to go wild, to throw punches as fast and furiously as he could, Spider-Man kept his preternatural calm despite the evil that stood before him.

The Ripper swept his foot in a crescent kick. Spider-Man hopped backward and the attack missed his nose by half an inch. The murderer staggered, momentarily off balance.

Now was the moment to hit him, while he was most vulnerable. Spider-Man hooked a punch into the Ripper's ribs, hard enough to crumple armor plate. Even so, it wouldn't kill the other man. He knew that from their previous encounter. But it would certainly hurt him.

The Ripper blundered backward and tripped over a deck chair. Spider-Man followed up with a kick that tumbled the killer to the edge of the pool. As he started after him, the Ripper scrambled to his feet, his fists jerking up into a guard position.

Spider-Man yearned to charge the stronger man anyway. He dropped back into a defensive posture instead. "You can surrender," he said, "or I can finish cleaning the roof up with you. It's your choice."

His breath rasping in his throat, the Ripper stood and glared for a second, then ran at him. Once again, Spider-Man ducked and dodged the sociopath's attacks, waiting for him to leave himself open. When the moment came, he leapt into the air and stomped on the big man's shoulder. The kick smashed the killer to his knees. Spider-Man somersaulted over him, and then, as his adversary lurched up and around, sprang onto the sloping penthouse roof.

The Ripper clambered after him. Without looking, depending on his spider-sense to guide him, Spider-Man backed over the crest of the roof and down the other side. The murderer stalked after him more slowly than he'd been moving hitherto.

"What's the matter?" Spider-Man said. "Not as much fun going after someone who fights back? Someone who's going to see that you pay for each and every one of the innocent lives you took?"

The Ripper snarled and made a start for the web-slinger. As he did, Spider-Man sprayed webbing at the big man's face.

The Ripper jerked his head to the side, avoiding the strands, then came in jabbing. Attacking less aggressively than before, the murderer kept both feet planted and stopped kicking altogether. Spider-Man decided it was time to go on the offensive. Circling, trying to keep his opponent's back to the drop-off, he drove in one punch after another. The Ripper grunted, gasped, and finally began to stagger.

Despite his best intentions, the vigilante's anger boiled to the surface, making him careless. The Ripper swung and clipped him on the jaw.

Rolling with the punch, Spider-Man flipped backward and landed in a crouch, ready to defend himself. But the Ripper didn't press the attack. Instead he whirled, leapt back onto the terrace, and sprinted toward the girl in the velvet dress.

Terrified, Spider-Man gave chase. Saw that he wasn't going to make it. The Ripper picked up the hostage, swung her over his head, and threw her over the parapet. Apparently he'd decided to flee, and hoped that, one way or another, endangering the girl would hinder his foe from coming after him.

For a second Spider-Man had the sickening feeling that he was going to freeze and watch her plummet, tumbling over and over just like Gwen. Then he snapped out of it and started moving. He scrambled onto the outside of the parapet and leapt, his prodigiously strong legs propelling him outward and down like an arrow flying from a bow. It was the only way to catch up with an object that had begun to fall an instant before him.

His aim was perfect. He wrapped one arm around her waist and then they dropped together. He shot a web-line and swung onto the wall.

He'd kept Gwen from hitting the ground, too, but it hadn't saved her. The shock of the fall had still killed her. He studied the hostage's face, not daring to believe she'd survived until he saw her take a breath.

He set the woman down on the fire escape beneath him, then raced back up the building.

As he'd pretty much expected, the roof was empty, but he wasn't worried the Ripper would escape. Suddenly he was feeling something he hadn't felt since Gwen died, something he'd nearly forgotten he *could* feel. A calm certainty that he was going to nail the bad guy, that no criminal could escape Spider-Man.

He bounded onto the penthouse roof and peered out into the darkness. After a second he spotted the Ripper. His stride uneven, the psychopath was running along the top of the high-rise to the north, a structure slightly shorter than its neighbor.

Spider-Man leapt into space and shot a web-line at the east edge of the roof below. He swooped down and hurtled up, as high as his momentum would carry him. He released the web, twisted and flipped through the air, and landed in a crouch in front of the killer. The Ripper skidded to a halt. His features, now bruised and bloody, were an almost comical mask of dismay.

"What's your hurry?" Spider-Man said. "You didn't think I was going to let you get away this time, did you?"

The Ripper lunged, punching. Slipping the blow, Spider-Man landed three shots so quickly that the cracks of impact blurred together.

The killer reeled backward to the edge of the roof, and, his arms windmilling, began to topple over. Dazed and weak from the pounding he'd taken, he was no longer able to make his feet adhere to the slate beneath them.

Without hesitation, Spider-Man shot a web. The strands caught the center of the Ripper's chest. Jerking the line, the vigilante hauled him out of danger and into range for a final uppercut. The murderer collapsed, out cold.

The Ripper lay unconscious on the curb, wrapped in a cocoon of webbing. The cops snapped on the titanium restraints right over the mesh. From past experience, they knew the gossamer strands would compress, allowing the shackles to fasten tightly. Clutching a cup of coffee, a blanket around her shoulders, the woman in the black velvet dress sat in the rear of an ambulance, talking to the detective Spider-Man had approached earlier outside the tenement. A lanky young EMT hovered beside her, just in case she went into shock or developed a sudden urge to give him her phone number.

Spider-Man hung by his soles beneath a ledge, somberly watching the proceedings. He wished he could have caught the Ripper sooner, and saved the murderer's previous victims. Wished he could have saved Gwen, and all the other precious lives that had at one time or another slipped from his grasp.

But at least he'd tried. And he knew now that he would *always* strive to preserve life and never take it, even when facing an enemy as twisted and evil as the Ripper. That particular temptation was behind him. Spider-Man was one of the good guys, now and forever, and the knowledge eased his sorrow at least a bit.

The police loaded the Ripper into the reinforced paddywagon. Spider-Man shot a web and swung toward home.

THE BALLAD OF FANCY DAN

Ken Grobe & Steven A. Roman

Illustration by Neil Vokes

ven without his trusty spider-sense, Spider-Man would have been alerted to the presence of danger as he swung above the streets of the Manhattan neighborhood known as Hell's Kitchen. The burly man crashing out through the front window of Moe's Tavern was a dead giveaway.

Releasing his web-line, Spider-Man lightly dropped onto the top of a lamppost across the street from the bar and surveyed the scene. On the sidewalk, the hulky man was slowly rising to one knee, each movement creating a shower of window-glass fragments as slivers slid off his back. Gripping a severely dislocated left shoulder, the man staggered away.

The guy looks big enough to play for the Giants, thought Spider-Man. *Who could've tossed him that easily?*

The sounds of shattering furniture brought his attention back to the bar. A combination of people shouting, bodies slamming, and patrons stampeding made it sound like World War III was being fought in the middle of New York. Either that, or Daredevil was on one of his unique fact-finding tours of Manhattan dives.

Curious, Spidey leapt from his perch and flipped above the traffic flowing down Ninth Avenue, landing on the balls of his toes in front of the bar. Peering through the broken window, he could make out the dim outlines of bodies in motion, but the intentionally low-lit interior made it impossible to distinguish details.

His hearing worked just fine, though.

"All right, you mugs!" a nasal, slightly high-pitched voice yelled from the darkness. "I came here for some answers, and I'm not leaving until I get 'em!"

"Oh, brother," Spidey muttered. "Do I know *that* voice." He sighed. "I just finished dancing around with the Scorpion an hour ago. All I wanted was a shower and a couple of days' worth of sleep, but *noooo.*" Wearily, he shook his head. "My day's just getting better and better."

Jumping through the gaping hole, Spidey cleared the glass shards and landed in a crouching position atop the battered oak bar, pausing long enough to allow his eyes to adjust to the dark interior. Silence fell over the place as the remaining patrons realized just who had arrived.

"Can I help you, pal?" sighed the bartender. In his late fifties, his thinning gray hair swept straight across a pate as reflective as a cue ball, the bartender seemed undisturbed by this latest visitor.

"No," said Spidey. "Just looking." Now able to see clearly, he scanned the room.

The place lay in total ruin. Tables and chairs had been smashed to kindling. Shattered glassware covered the alcohol-stained wooden floor like confetti after a parade. A dartboard had been slammed down over the head of one man lying in a corner; it looked like his head had been cut off and placed on a checkerboard platter. Around the room were scattered a dozen more patrons, some moaning from injuries, others blissfully unconscious.

And standing in the midst of this chaos, like the calm eye of a storm, was "Fancy" Dan Brito.

Dan stood five feet three inches tall and was thin as a rail, cutting what he believed was a dashing figure in his customary mauve suit and yellow porkpie hat. Easily outsized by the bar's seamier clientele, he appeared to be the kind of man who'd have his head handed to him the moment he walked inside. But Dan was a master of jujitsu, the Japanese combat method that used leverage and a knowledge of anatomy and pressure points to overcome an enemy. With his formidable skills, Dan was more than capable of handling the overwhelming odds that had faced him.

"Well, if it ain't my good friend Spider-Man!" Dan yelled. He stepped over one semiconscious patron, digging his heel into the back of the man's outstretched hand. Dan smiled wickedly at the sound of knuckles popping under the pressure.

"You want to tell me what's going on here, Dan?" Spidey remained crouched on the bar, expecting the diminutive gangster to charge him at any moment.

Dan picked his way through the rubble and reached the bar. "I came here in the spirit of friendship in the hopes of procuring some much-needed information," he said. He gestured around the room. "My . . . associates were what you would call less than forthcoming with said information."

Spidey sighed. "You must really love prison food, Dan, 'cause Ryker's Island is your next stop."

"No, it ain't," growled Dan. "I got too much at stake, web-head, and I'm not goin' back into stir.'' His body flowed into a combat-ready pose. "Leastways, not yet.''

"Dan, Dan, Dan,'' scolded Spidey. "We go through this every time we meet. You threaten me in that charmingly Damon Runyonesque tone of yours, I knock you into the middle of next week, and you wake up in Ryker's with fewer teeth.'' He shrugged. "The thrill is gone, Danny.''

"Stop flappin' your lips, tough guy,'' Dan warned. "Let's make with the fisticuffs.''

"Hey, you wanna take yer business someplace else?'' the bartender interrupted. Frowning, he gestured to Spidey. "I gotta tell ya, all that squattin' on my bar is makin' me nervous.''

"Oh,'' said Spidey. "Sorry.''

Before Dan could move, Spidey wrapped him in strands of webbing, tucked him under one arm, and vaulted through the shattered window.

For a few moments, silence reigned in the saloon, the only audible sounds those of the Ninth Avenue traffic outside. Looking around at the remains of his establishment, the bartender pulled at his lower lip, then sighed. He reached under the bar, came up with a cellular phone, and dialed the special number he kept taped to his cash register.

"Hello?'' he asked hesitantly. "Damage Control . . . ?''

Swinging over the Port Authority Bus Terminal on Eighth Avenue, Spidey glanced down at his unwilling passenger. Normally full of bravado, Dan was unusually quiet this time; he sagged in Spidey's arm, all the fight gone out of him.

Maybe he only acts like a tough guy when he's got an audience, Spidey thought. *Or maybe it's finally sinking in that he's never going to get the upper hand on me.* Releasing his web-line, he came to rest on the side of a building and adjusted his grip on Dan. *Now, if only Doc Ock could get that message . . .*

"Uh, Spider-Man?''

Spidey looked down to meet Dan's gaze, expecting the gangster to launch another stream of invectives.

"Look, Dan, I'm not in the mood right now to trade insults with you, okay? So, do me a favor—keep your mouth shut, and when you get back to Ryker's, you can write me all the nasty letters you want.'' With his free hand, Spidey crossed his heart.

"I'll even respond to them personally if you toss in a self-addressed, stamped envelope."

"No, no," said Dan. "I just wanted to ask you something." He paused. "If that's okay with you." His voice was low, nothing like the voice of a man who had just single-handedly cleaned out a West Side bar. And there was something about its tone—something that Spidey would never have expected coming from "Fancy" Dan Brito.

Humility.

"I was gonna ask..." Dan's voice trailed off. Spidey loudly cleared his throat, a signal for him to continue. Dan swallowed, took a deep breath, then looked back at Spidey. "I was gonna ask for your help."

Spidey shook his head. "Exsqueeze me?" he said, turning his head to bring an ear closer to Dan. "You'll have to talk into my good ear."

Dan sneered at his old enemy.

"You heard me," Dan said. "Now lay off the snappy patter. I ain't got time for it."

"Ah," said Spidey. "Now, that's the Fancy Dan I know." He scratched the top of his masked head. "So, what is it that you need my help with? I don't validate parking tickets anymore, and I couldn't lend you any money, what with you being a risk and all—"

"*Knock it off!*" Dan bellowed. Veins pulsed along his neck, bright red against tanned flesh.

Surprised by Dan's outburst, Spidey fell silent.

Dan closed his eyes, took several more deep breaths, relaxed. He looked back to Spidey. "Sorry," he said.

Fancy Dan—apologizing? Spidey thought. *This* must *be serious.*

"So, what's the problem, Dan?" Spidey asked.

Dan grimaced, his face no longer that of a street-smart wise guy, but rather a kid on his way to the principal's office. He didn't like doing this, not one bit.

"My kid's in trouble," he said slowly, ignoring Spidey's double take. "I'm askin' you for help 'cause I've got nowhere else to go."

"So, let me get this straight," said Spidey a few minutes later. "Your son's been kidnapped, and you want me to help you rescue him?'' He crouched on the edge of a weathered brick chimney, having moved the discussion to a nearby rooftop.

Sitting on the tar papered roof, still wrapped in webbing, Dan nodded. "Yeah. His name's Rudy." He frowned, the heat of an old, obviously bad memory glowing in his eyes. "Leastways, it used to be. Now, his mom insists on calling him 'Rudolph.' I haven't been able to see the kid since he was born." White teeth ground together like pieces of sandpaper. "She was afraid I was gonna . . . taint the kid if he hung out with me. Make him a bad seed or something."

"You don't agree?" asked Spidey.

Dan shrugged. "I don't know. Maybe she's right. I ain't exactly role-model material, y'know." He glared into the distance. "It's not like I was gonna take him on heists. I just wanted to be a part of his life, to be his dad, y'understand?" Shoulders slumping, he stared forlornly at his feet. "Kinda hard to do that when you spend most of your time in the joint."

Dan fell silent. Spidey shifted on his perch, uncomfortable with the awkward silence.

"So," he said, "why ask me for help? What about your Enforcer buddies, Montana and the Ox?"

"I don't know where they are," Dan said. "After we got outta stir last month, we sorta drifted apart. Montana mentioned something about a big job comin' up, but he never got in touch with me after that. And the Ox . . ." He shrugged. "The Ox is just a big stiff. Probably got a job liftin' engine blocks or something."

"When did you hear about your son being kidnapped?"

"When I saw it on the news a couple days ago." Dan sneered at the web-slinger. "What, tough guy like you is so busy, you don't watch TV or read the papers?"

Spidey tilted his head to one side. "Wait a minute. Are you saying your son is Rudolph *Loyola*, that teenage piano virtuoso?" He shook his head. "Now I've heard everything."

"That's right, smart guy!" barked Dan. "His old man might be a stumblebum, but that kid's gonna be a big-time star. No two-bit dives for Rudy—he's goin' right to the top." His smile wavered, then faded completely. "Leastways, he is . . . if they don't hurt him." Lips thin and tight, he glared up at Spidey. "So? You gonna help me?"

"Help you? No," said Spidey, hopping down to stand beside

Dan. "Help your son? Yes. I'll do this my way, Dan, follow my own leads. You'd just be in the way." He pulled Dan to his feet.

"You're handin' me over to the cops, aren't you?" Dan said. He struggled against the webbing that encased him. "You don't get it, do you? My kid's in trouble, and I gotta find him!"

"I understand, Dan," assured Spidey. "But I work alone. I don't need a sidekick. Besides, that little tango of yours in the bar means you broke your parole, so it's back to the pokey you go." He patted Dan on the shoulder. "Trust me. I'll find your boy."

Dan leaned forward, his nose inches from the lifeless plastic lenses that stared back at him. "Yeah? And how're you gonna do that? Ask around all nice and polite and hope that someone will tell you something, pretty please?" He laughed, a short barking note. "You ain't got the stones to be another Daredevil, tough guy, but good luck to you, anyway. I'll tell ya this, though." His lips curled back, baring his teeth.

"If my boy gets whacked 'cause I wasn't there to help him, I'm gonna find the thing you love the most . . . and kill it."

After depositing Dan at a nearby police station, Spidey headed uptown to the offices of the *Daily Bugle* to learn if there were any leads on the kidnapping case.

On the roof of the *Bugle*, Spidey quickly changed into his street clothes and, minutes later, strode into the editorial offices as Peter Parker. Luck had been with him—the ever-volatile publisher, J. Jonah Jameson, was out of the office, but Ben Urich, the reporter Peter was looking for, was in, busily typing away on a story.

"Ben!" Peter called hopefully.

"No time, Parker," Urich answered without looking up from his computer terminal. "Spider-Man whipped the Scorpion over at the Chrysler Building this afternoon. Jameson wants a story for the morning edition—can't imagine why. Won't even make the front section without photos." He grimaced and continued typing.

Peter remained undaunted. "You got two minutes?"

"No. Go away."

"One! One minute!" Peter pleaded. "I'll make it worth your while."

Urich sighed, continued typing. "What is it?"

"What do you know about the Rudolph Loyola kidnapping?"

Urich grunted. "What's the matter, Parker—you too busy to read your own newspaper?"

"I try," Peter said drily, "but Jonah's editorials always wind up putting me to sleep." He sat down on the corner of Urich's desk. "So, what've you heard?"

Without breaking stride at the keys, Urich said, "Classic snatch-and-grab case. Piano wunderkind is being driven home after practice, sedan without plates comes out of nowhere, runs limo off the road. Goons jump out, make a grab for the kid. Kid's chauffeur tries to stop them, gets pounded for his troubles. Goons take off with the kid. Quick, clean, easy. No witnesses, unless you count the chauffeur, but he won't be identifying anyone for a while—guy's in a coma.

"The big difference, though," he continued without looking up, "is that the kid's stepfather is Joseph 'Baby Joe' Loyola."

"The big-time Atlantic City mobster," Peter said.

"*Alleged* mobster, Parker," Urich corrected. "The feds've never been able to pin anything on him. The guy's made of Teflon." Urich's hands flew across the computer keyboard, fingers appearing to move on autopilot. "I understand his wife's holed up in their brownstone apartment building over on Fifty-ninth Street and York Avenue, waiting for ransom demands."

Peter rose to leave. "Thanks, Ben. I owe you one."

"Pay it off by telling me how this interruption was worth my while."

With a slight smirk, Peter reached into the pocket of his jeans and pulled out a small plastic film container. He placed it on Urich's desk.

"Shots of the Spidey-Scorpion fight. Exclusives." He headed for the door. "Do me a favor and put in a voucher for me, okay?"

Ben Urich stopped typing.

Lightning slashed across the darkened skies as Spidey swung through the rain-slicked canyons of steel and glass. What had begun as a warm, sunny day had quickly degenerated into a howling torrential downpour, and the water was playing havoc with the effectiveness of Spidey's synthetic webbing.

It's times like this, he thought as he wiped his fogging lenses for the hundredth time, *that I start to consider having a new Spider-Mobile built. Sure, the original was ugly as sin, but who says the new model has to look the same? A nice, dry car, a roof over my head, maybe an ejector seat* . . . Spidey shook his head. *Nah. It's just not me.* He sighed. *The price we super heroes pay to look cool* . . .

Standing in the shadow of the Queensboro Bridge, the building owned by "Baby" Joe Loyola had all the personal touches that one would expect in the home of a suspected mobster: armed guards by the front door; thick, but ornate, metal bars on all the windows; security cameras on every cornice.

And a pair of federal agents sitting in a car across the street.

Keeping to the shadows, Spidey slipped through the security maze and huddled under a third-floor ledge, unsuccessfully seeking shelter from the pounding rain.

This kills me, he thought. *Dan's kicking back in a nice, cozy cell while I risk pneumonia watching his ex-wife.* Wall-crawling over to a window, he looked inside.

It was the Steinway, rather than the FBI agents, that caught Spidey's eye. Its case made of solid oak, the piano took up a sizable portion of one corner of the room. Carefully arranged on the top of the instrument were a number of photographs in gold-leaf picture frames. Sheet music had been set out—notes waiting to be played by sensitive fingers. The piano bench stood empty.

Spidey's eyes passed over each of the three FBI agents as they sat around the living room, smoking cigarettes and grinding them out in ornate brass ashtrays. Two of the agents—dressed in matching black suits and ties—sat by a wiretap setup, waiting for the phone to ring. The third agent sat in a big leather easy chair. His jacket casually tossed across a love seat, he lounged in rolled-up shirtsleeves and loosened tie, one leg hooked over an arm of the chair. He shot a look to the door leading to the hallway, then looked to the closed bedroom door. Seeing no movement from either, he dropped his cigarette on the Persian rug beneath his feet and ground it out with the toe of his wingtip shoe, allowing himself a self-satisfied smile.

"My tax dollars at work," muttered Spidey.

The bedroom door suddenly opened. The laid-back agent looked over, a wolfish grin coming to his lips as he leered hungrily at the woman approaching him.

Ginger Loyola stepped from the bedroom, her eyes reddened and misty, apparently from lack of sleep. In her early forties, Ginger was a stunning, sleek-limbed blonde with long dancer's legs and the kind of figure that demanded immediate attention from every man in a room. Spidey remembered hearing that, before meeting "Baby" Joe, she had been a cocktail waitress at Loyola's Diamond Casino and Hotel.

"Have you heard anything, Mr. Valentine?" she asked the agent draped over the easy chair.

Valentine stretched, grinned as he heard the vertebrae in his stiffened back pop into place, then settled back in his seat. "Nothing yet, hon, but we will." He grinned again, a condescending tone creeping into his voice. "You of all people should know how these mob guys work."

Ginger scowled at the agent, her eyes drifting down to the Persian rug . . . and the cigarette burn in it. She turned her gaze back to Valentine.

"Oops," he said, smiling.

Ginger's lips drew back in a wordless snarl. She turned on her heel and strode into the bedroom, slamming the door shut behind her.

Valentine chuckled. "No tip for you, sweetheart."

Inside the bedroom, Ginger sat in darkness, shoulders hitching with silenced sobs. There'd be no help from the FBI. With Rudolph kidnapped, law enforcement agents had been given the perfect opportunity to barge into Ginger's home and look for evidence to use against her husband. They'd wasted little time in carrying out their search, but had found nothing.

The FBI knew Joe Loyola only as one of the major players in organized crime, but there was more to Joe than that. The man the feds suspected of having engineered several murders was also the man who had wept openly when Ginger accepted his marriage proposal ten years ago; the man who, when Rudolph was three, would check under his stepson's bed for monsters; the man who encouraged Rudolph to hone his musical gift and ensured that he would never become involved with his father's "business." Joe had disappeared from his casino shortly after Rudolph had been snatched, presumably to look for the boy.

A soft tap on her window caused Ginger to start. She looked up to see the silhouette of a man clinging to the wall outside. A flash of lightning revealed the identity of her visitor. Ginger wiped her eyes quickly, drew in a deep breath, and crossed to the window.

"Hello, Spider-Man," she said as she opened the window. "Is there a reason for you being here, or do you often spend your free time peering into women's bedrooms?"

Spidey scrambled inside, his costume giving him the appearance of a soggy, red-and-blue sponge. "I hope I'm not intruding," he said.

"Of course not," Ginger said sarcastically. "With FBI agents in my home and the police constantly watching me from outside, why should I be inconvenienced by a super hero hanging around my bedroom window?"

"I'm here," he replied, not quite believing it himself, "because your ex asked for my help in getting your son back."

Ginger was nonplussed. "*Dan?* Dan Brito asked you for help?"

Spidey nodded. "Yeah. It was a shock for me too."

"Huh," Ginger said, shaking her head. "He never seemed that concerned about Rudolph when we were married."

"Well," said Spidey, "given the situation—"

"Don't!" Ginger cut in. "Don't try and stand up for him!" She poked a manicured nail into Spidey's chest. "Guys like *you* are part of the reason we broke up. If he hadn't kept running off with those idiots Ox and Montana—constantly trying to prove to me he was a tough guy—we might have had a chance at a normal life." Ginger dropped her hand to her side, the anger draining from her. "When he first started running around with those two, I warned him they'd be nothing but trouble. But Dan wanted to be a player in the syndicates—he was willing to take the risks. I wasn't.

"He had a family to support, but from the way he acted, you'd think Ox and Montana were his real family; Rudy and I were an afterthought. When he was busted during one of their 'enforcing' jobs—long before you ever ran into them—I finally decided enough was enough. I couldn't take it anymore. Rudolph was only eighteen months old, and I wasn't going to subject him to a life with a revolving-door felon as a father figure. Dan was still in jail when I told him I wanted a divorce. After the papers were signed, Rudolph and I moved to Atlantic City."

"Where you married a mobster," Spidey said.

"You shut up about my Joe!" Ginger growled, her face inches from Spidey's. She looked every bit the lioness protecting her brood. "He's a good man, a better man than—" she spat out the name "—'Fancy' Dan Brito will ever be!"

Spidey stepped back, holding up his hands in a gesture of surrender. "I'm sorry. I didn't mean to insult you." He dropped his hands, paused for a moment. "Look, I didn't come here to fight, Mrs. Loyola. I came to find out if you've heard from the kidnappers. Have they called?"

Ginger's head lowered, her eyes misting over. "No," she said, her voice laced with grief. "And the waiting is killing me." She wiped away tears with the back of a hand. "I don't even know if he's still alive."

Spider-Man shifted his weight from foot to foot, looked down at his own hands. Going ten rounds with a super-villain like the Scorpion was a breeze compared to uncomfortable moments like this. He cleared his throat, placed consoling hands on Ginger's shoulders.

"Don't worry, Mrs. Loyola," he said, trying to sound reassuring. "Busting kidnappers is a specialty of us friendly, neighborhood Spider-Men. I'll find your son, and bring him home safely."

The only problem, he thought, *is finding out where they*—

His spider-sense alerted him to danger a moment before the bedroom door burst open. Agent Valentine and his men rushed into the room, guns drawn. Spidey spun around quickly, placing himself between Ginger and the agents.

"Freeze, web-head!" yelled Valentine, his gun aimed dead center at Spidey's chest. "I knew I wasn't imagining hearing voices."

"Guess the medication must be working, eh?" replied Spidey.

Valentine growled, his complexion turning an unhealthy red. "I've heard all about you, wise guy—you think you're a regular funny man, don't you?"

"Well, I'm no Robin Williams, but I think I do pretty well with improvisation." Spidey spread his hands, palms up, and gestured toward the agents. "For instance, what do you call three FBI agents holding guns on a card-carrying super hero?" He looked around at the trio. "Give up? Well, the answer is—" he paused for dramatic effect "—a quick workout."

Before the agents could move, a thick layer of webbing erupted from the shooters on Spidey's wrists, clogging the gun barrels. As Valentine and his men tried to pull off the blockage, more webbing wrapped around them, pinning their arms and legs. In seconds, Spidey had three neat bundles lying on the plush carpeting.

Spidey walked over to Valentine, knelt down to be at eye-level with the agent. "Pretty funny, huh?" Spidey asked sweetly.

"Laugh it up, jerk," hissed Valentine. "The day'll come when I—*mmfff!*'

A glob of webbing shot out, covering Valentine's mouth. Spidey looked down at the web-shooter as though surprised, then back to Valentine.

"Oops," said Spidey.

Swinging away from the brownstone, Spidey headed up York Avenue to use the Queensboro Bridge as shelter from the rain while he planned his next move.

I could always go back to Dan, he thought. *See if he was withholding any information that might help—*

His spider-sense screamed a warning as he was about to alight on the bridge. Spidey twisted in midswing as a hail of bullets *spang*ed off one of the bridge's support girders, missing him by inches. Landing in the shadow of interlocking beams, Spidey looked down. There, on the street, stood the most ape-like man he'd ever seen, dressed in an ill-fitting gray suit and black tie. Short but solidly built, his arms hanging just slightly lower than his knees, the man didn't look like he had the level of intelligence needed to tie his own shoes.

But he certainly knew how to use a semiautomatic weapon.

"Spider-Man!" he bellowed, his voice coarse and bullish. A flock of pigeons near Spidey, frightened by the roar, took to the air. "I gotta talk t'ya!"

"About what?" Spidey called back. "Your terrible aim?"

The man laughed; it sounded like an animal dying. "Aw, if I wanted t'take you out, I could'a done it when you was peepin' in Loyola's bedroom winda."

I'm really getting tired of people thinking I'm some kind of pervert, thought Spidey. *I bet Captain America doesn't get this much disrespect.*

"I got some news fer ya 'bout that kid gettin' snatched," said the man. He paused, waiting for a reply.

Silence.

The man scratched his head; it sounded a lot like sandpaper being rubbed on an open wound. "Hey!" he yelled up at the shadows of the bridge. "Did'nya hear what I said? I said I got some—"

"Information about the kidnapping," said a voice behind him. The man turned quickly, raising his gun to shoulder level. A web-line clogged the barrel, and the gun was jerked from the man's paws.

Crouched on the roof of a car parked behind the man, Spidey reeled in the gun, bending its barrel out of shape with his bare hands. "You keep playing around with these, junior," he warned, "and you're liable to take somebody's eye out."

Instead of being angry, the man smiled, revealing nicotine-stained teeth. "Hey, you're good. I didn't even hear you land."

"It's a talent," said Spidey. "Now, about this information, Mister . . ."

"I'm Monk," the man said, poking a meaty thumb into his own chest.

"Of course you are," Spidey said, nodding in agreement. "You take up target shooting because things were too slow at the monastery?"

Monk stared at him, confused. Obviously, trying to use him as a straight man would be a waste of time.

"Never mind," Spidey sighed. "So, you were saying . . ."

"Yeah, 'bout the kid. My boss wants to see you, have a little sit-down."

"And your boss would be . . . ?"

"The Kingpin, o'course," replied Monk.

Spidey started. "Wait a minute," he said. "The Kingpin wants me to meet with him, and you thought the best way to get my attention was to *shoot* at me?"

Monk shrugged. "Well, he didn't say what kind'a *shape* you hadda be in for the meet."

From the top of his lofty tower in midtown Manhattan, Wilson Fisk looked down upon his kingdom and smiled. As the undisputed Kingpin of crime—New York's "boss of bosses"—Fisk certainly had a sizable domain: all five of New York's boroughs. This was his city, its inhabitants his subjects, to be used in his nefarious schemes as he saw fit.

At a first glance, Fisk looked less like a crime boss and more like a man inviting a heart attack. Just over six and a half feet tall, he tipped the scales at an unhealthy four hundred and fifty pounds. However, as his enemies had discovered—much to their horror—the Kingpin was not a fat man crammed into a white tailor-made suit; rather, he was an oversized engine of destruction, every inch of him solid muscle. And, when he wished, Fisk could move with incredible speed, as Spider-Man had often been reminded during their encounters over the years. These days, however, the Kingpin was less hands-on in his dealings with New York's super hero community—that's what his lieutenants were for—and more of a puppet master, pulling hundreds of strings throughout the city but never actually dirtying his hands. No law enforcement agency could touch him, no super hero could bring him to justice, though they had tried.

A soft knock on his office door brought the Kingpin's attention back to his immediate concerns.

"Enter," he rumbled in a voice that sounded like gravel wrapped in velvet.

The door opened, and Monk stuck his head inside the room. "I don't mean t'botha ya, boss," he said hesitantly, "but I brung ya Spider-Man."

"Excellent." The Kingpin smiled, dark eyes sparkling in the room's dim lighting. "Send him in."

Monk stepped aside and Spider-Man walked in, scanning the room for any hidden surprises. Just because he'd been invited, it didn't mean that Fisk wouldn't try to kill him.

"Welcome, Spider-Man," the Kingpin said. He looked at the web-slinger's drenched costume. "May I offer you a towel?"

"Just cut to the chase, Kingpin," snapped Spider-Man. "Your goon said you had information on the Loyola kidnapping."

"Ah, yes," replied the Kingpin. "A gifted boy, young Rudolph. He has quite a future ahead of him . . . should he survive this unfortunate incident."

With lightning speed, Spidey reached out and grasped the lapels of the Kingpin's jacket, pulling Fisk toward him with surprising ease.

"If you've had anything to do with this, Kingpin . . ." he warned.

"Release me," growled the Kingpin.

The two old enemies glared at one another, neither willing to give an inch. Then, slowly, the web-slinger relaxed his grip. The crime lord's heels settled back on the floor.

"This is pointless," Spidey said. "While I'm wasting time here, the kidnappers could be deciding that the kid is worth just as much to them dead as alive."

"True, arachnid." The Kingpin's lips turned up in a contemptuous smile. "You're not as ignorant as your choice of clothing would imply." He smoothed the lapels of his jacket, adjusted his ascot. "Now, if you're through trying to impress me with displays of your much-vaunted spider-strength, I suggest we get down to business."

Spidey followed the crime boss to an oversized mahogany desk, on which rested a walking stick roughly the size of a baseball bat. From his previous run-ins with the Kingpin, Spidey knew the object was more than a stylish cane; within the dark wood casing was a powerful laser-beam weapon.

With a creak of soft leather, the Kingpin settled into the high-backed chair behind the desk; there were no seats for guests. Elbows placed on the armrests, he steepled his thick fingers, studying his adversary for a moment.

"It has come to my attention," he said, "that young Rudolph is a guest of Martin Severino, a competitor of the child's stepfather."

"He owns the Best O' Times Casino," Spidey said.

"Precisely." Eyes narrowing, the Kingpin flashed a condescending smile. "I see you know how to read a newspaper." The smile quickly faded. "If you plan on tearing apart the casino to locate the child—the type of mindless action you costumed lunatics revel in—you'd only be wasting precious time. The child is constantly being moved."

"And you just happen to know where they're hiding him now."

"No," the Kingpin said. "The source of my information was unable to provide me with an address. He did, however, suggest keeping an eye on an establishment called 'Howie's Harmonies' in Atlantic City tomorrow morning for a lead." He smiled—a mirthless, shark's grin. "He was unable to say much else after that."

Behind his mask, Spider-Man's lips drew back in a snarl.

Someday, Fisk, he thought. *Someday I'll put you away once and for all.*

The Kingpin waved at Spidey, a dismissive gesture. "You may go."

Spidey folded his arms across his chest, stared hard at the crime boss. "Tell me something, Kingpin," he said. "Why are you doing this?"

The Kingpin glowered at the web-spinner, fingertips lightly resting on the deadly walking stick. "My reasons are none of your business, arachnid." The shark smile resurfaced as his hands slid away from the cane. "Let us just say that it's good for business."

A soft breeze wafted through the streets of Atlantic City, New Jersey, the wind tangy with the scent of brine. Just a few blocks from the neon lights and glittering sequins of the gambling halls lining the boardwalk, the world was a very different place. Here, the streets were not as well maintained, the housing far from opulent.

On a cracked, weather-beaten side street, in the shadow of Joe Loyola's Diamond Hotel and Casino, stood Howie's Harmonies, a music shop that had definitely seen better days. Its windows darkened by years of dirt and grime, its battered neon sign burned out long ago, Howie's Harmonies was the sole surviving business on the block. On both sides of the music shop stood darkened storefronts, boarded up and abandoned years before.

From his vantage point atop the roof of a run-down apartment building across the street, Spider-Man had watched the shop's owner—no doubt Howie himself—open for the day at eight A.M. The first ten minutes of the stakeout had been fairly interesting, as Spidey had scanned the rooftops around him for any sign of trouble, ready to spring into action at the merest tingle of his spider-sense.

By the second hour, it had become downright boring.

Spidey stretched, rubbing stiffened muscles to get his blood circulating. The rising sun had dried his soaked costume, but now he was faced with the problem of chilly ocean breezes cutting through the thin material.

If I don't come away from this with a case of pneumonia, Spidey thought, *I'll be one very surprised web-spin—*

The hairs on the back of his neck stood straight up as his

spider-sense tingled. It wasn't a strong sensation, warning of danger, but rather a soft buzz, signaling a potential threat.

Spidey looked down just as a lone figure turned the corner, heading in the direction of the music shop. Clad in an oversized trench coat, long blond hair flowing in the breeze, the figure—it was hard to tell whether it was a man or woman—strode quickly down the street, occasionally looking back over its shoulder.

"Ver-r-ry inconspicuous," said Spidey. Leaning forward, eyes narrowing behind the lenses of his mask, he studied the figure. There was something about this person's height . . .

"Aw, no," the wall-crawler muttered. His head dropped, a sigh escaping his lips. "Like my life isn't complicated enough."

Reaching the door of Howie's Harmonies, the figure paused, looking in all directions to make certain the street was deserted.

All directions but up, that is.

With a resounding *thwap!* a web-line adhered to the back of the trench coat.

"Hey!" a nasal voice cried. "What the—"

With a quick yank, the newcomer was pulled high into the air . . . and into the waiting arms of Spider-Man, who now perched atop a nearby streetlight.

"Why, if it isn't my old pal, 'Fancy' Dan!" exclaimed Spidey. "I haven't seen you in, oh, what—less than twenty-four hours?" His gaze drifted to the diminutive gangster's flowing tresses—a cheap nylon wig made more for a Halloween costume than a disguise. "I love what you've done with your hair, though."

"Shut yer piehole, smart guy," barked Dan, looking around quickly. "I'm supposed t'be incognizant."

"No argument there, Dan, but you mean incognito," corrected Spidey. "And doing a fine job of it too. Why, if it wasn't for the fact that you're an extremely short guy in a really bad disguise, standing outside a music shop that somehow ties in with the kidnapping of your son, I'd've never known it was you."

Once more tucking Dan under his arm, Spidey leapt from the streetlight to the store's roof, landing softly on the weathered tar paper. He set the gangster on his feet.

"What're you doing here, Dan?" he demanded. "The police wouldn't have just released you after breaking parole, so how did you get out?" He leaned forward, hands curling into fists. "You broke out, didn't you?"

Dan sneered, nonchalantly tossing away the wig. "That's all you costumed jamokes think about, isn't it? You put a guy in the joint, you figure he's outta the picture for good. But the minute he turns up again, you figger he must'a busted his way out." He chuckled softly, mustache twitching. "Wassamatta, tough guy—never heard of a lawyer before?"

"Where would you get a lawyer of your own, Dan?" asked Spidey. "A guy like you must have half the public defenders in the state on your speed dialer."

"For yer information, web-head," Dan said, "I happen to be what-ya-call 'connected.'" From a deep pocket in the voluminous coat he produced his porkpie hat. Batting it into shape, he placed the hat at a jaunty angle on his head. "One'a the Kingpin's mouthpieces sprung me and told me to case this joint for a lead."

The Kingpin again, thought Spidey. *I don't like where this is going. . . .*

A powerful chill ran down his spine; his spider-sense again, but stronger this time. Motioning to Dan to be quiet, Spidey looked over the edge of the roof.

"Curiouser and curiouser," he said softly. He waved over to Dan to join him. "What do you make of this, Dan?"

Following Spidey's gaze, Dan looked down at the familiar shape of a mountain-sized man as he entered Howie's Harmonies. Dan's lips curled back in anger.

"Ox," he growled. "Stabbed in the back by one'a my own buddies. You'd think the big dope would have more respect fer me, on account'a I used t'work with his twin brudder before *this* jamoke came along t'take his place." He rose, face reddening, fists clenching. "I'll show 'im what it means to mess with a man's family." He charged across the roof, heading for a door that led to the building's stairs.

With a leap that would have made an Olympic long-jumper envious, Spidey flipped over Dan, landing between the door and the gangster. Dan came to a quick stop and crouched low, ready to strike.

"Get outta my way, web-head!" he bellowed. "That big dope's got a world of hurt coming!"

"You're not thinking straight, Dan," cautioned Spidey. "Take a second and slow down." He paused, waiting for Dan to relax;

he didn't. "If you go after the Ox now, you'll blow our best chance of finding your son."

That did the trick. Dan slowly rose, anger draining from his face. "But—"

"Think about it, Dan," said Spidey. "Would the Ox be smart enough to kidnap Rudolph on his own? Of course not! So, if he's making a trip to a music shop, then *someone else must be watching the boy.*"

It took a moment for Dan to add it all up. Then his eyes widened with realization.

"Montana," he said softly. "*This* was the big job he was talkin' about."

"Exactly," said Spidey. "So if we just follow Mongo back to wherever he came from—"

"We find my kid!" Dan slammed a fist into the palm of his other hand, a wicked grin playing at his lips. "And then it's payback time."

Following the Ox back to his lair became a lengthy—and exasperating—process for Dan. After purchasing sheet music at Howie's Harmonies—Spidey could see the crumpled pages clutched tightly in one of the Ox's massive hands—the giant Enforcer went on a meandering tour of Atlantic City's streets: stopping at Dairy King for an ice cream cone; buying a newspaper at a corner smoke shop; window shopping at a jewelry store.

"He's certainly taking the long way home," Spidey observed.

"Big dope's probably lost," grumbled Dan.

Finally, after a few more stops that caused Dan's blood pressure to rise dangerously high, the Ox lumbered onto the boardwalk, heading for one building in particular. Twenty-five stories high, its walls designed to look like black marble slabs trimmed with gold, the edifice immediately brought to mind comparisons to the monolith in the film *2001: A Space Odyssey.* A gaudy neon sign in the form of a rocketship identified the building as the Star World Hotel and Casino.

Shouldering his way through a group of gawking tourists—and leaving behind a wake of sprawling, bruised bodies—the Ox stomped toward the large glass doors leading to the hotel lobby. A doorman, dressed in an oversized plastic-bubble helmet and a baggy, rhinestone-laden imitation spacesuit, moved hurriedly to open the door.

From the roof of a nearby concession stand, Spidey and Dan watched as the Ox pushed past the doorman, sending the man stumbling back into another group of hapless tourists.

Spidey whistled softly. "Talk about clearing a path," he said.

Dan nodded. "Ox ain't too acquainted with what ya call yer 'social graces.'" He pointed with his chin toward the casino. "So, what's our next move, genius?"

Spidey looked up at the towering monolith, rubbed his jaw. "Well, if this is where Montana and Ox are holding Rudolph, then it'd have to be someplace out of the way, someplace where the guests or staff wouldn't stumble across them." He looked at Dan.

"The penthouse," they said in unison.

At twenty floors above street level, the light ocean breezes had turned into fierce winds, making web-slinging an impossibility. So, with Dan hanging on to his shoulders, Spidey scaled the side of the building opposite the boardwalk, keeping to the shadows to avoid being seen.

"Slow down, tough guy!" yelled Dan as he readjusted his grip. "I can't fly like one'a you super-freaks!"

"Then you should've let me web you to my back like I suggested, Dan," said Spidey curtly.

"I don't play papoose for nobody, web-head," said Dan. "Leastways, not without a good reason." He made a quick grab for his hat as the wind threatened to snatch it away. "An' you ain't got the curves to be no Injun dame under that circus outfit."

"You'll never know how good it makes me feel to know that I don't appeal to you, Dan," said Spidey, sarcastically. "My girlfriend likes me just fine, though."

"Oh, yeah?" leered Dan. "She a looker?"

"Never mind," warned Spidey.

Dan grinned, happy to learn he'd hit a nerve. "She ever, y'know, put on the tights? Just fer fun?"

"Dan . . ." Spidey growled.

"Bet she fills 'em out better'n you, huh?"

Spidey sighed and concentrated on climbing.

Minutes later, they reached the uppermost floor of the casino, Spidey vaulting over the brass guardrail that ran across the penthouse's ivy-trimmed terrace. With solid ground under them once more, Dan released his hold on Spidey's neck and dropped to the floor. He shrugged out of his trench coat, ready to fight.

Motioning to Dan to be quiet, Spidey crept along the terrace, staying close to the wall, and stopped beside a large window. His mouth formed a thin line beneath his mask as he peered around the window frame to look inside the room.

The living area of the penthouse reminded Spidey of a Beverly Hills mansion he'd once seen on *Lifestyles of the Rich and Famous*—twenty-foot-high ceilings, hardwood floors, deep blue-and-red Persian rugs, expensive objets d'art arranged just so to catch the light for optimum visual impact. A heavy crystal chandelier hung from the ceiling above the center of the room.

"Whatever else Severino might be," Spidey murmured, "he's certainly a guy who knows how to decorate."

What ruined this picture of style and grace was the group of two dozen hard-looking men standing around with drinks in their hands. Of all races, heights, and body types, the two things they had in common with one another were their poor taste in clothing and their varying degrees of ugliness. It was clear they weren't gathered to admire Severino's art collection.

Crouching beside Spidey, Dan pressed his face to the glass. A low whistle escaped his lips. "It's like a leg-breaker convention in there," he commented.

Forming a loose semicircle, the thugs stood around the centerpiece of the room: a massive Steinway piano, strategically placed to make the most of the acoustics.

And seated at that piano, looking alone and afraid, sat thirteen-year-old Rudy Loyola. Wearing blue jeans, sneakers, and a black T-shirt emblazoned with a poor imitation of a numeral four from a Fantastic Four logo, he sat quietly on the piano bench.

A meaty paw dropped onto his shoulder. Rudy gasped and looked up to find the Ox looming over him. The man-mountain raised his other hand and placed the crumpled sheet music on the piano.

"Play," he rumbled.

Rudy selected a sheet, smoothed it out as best he could, and placed it on the music stand. Hesitantly, he looked up at the Ox, who nodded in approval. Slowly, Rudy began to play.

On the terrace, Spidey cocked his head to one side, listening. The tune was a familiar one, something he hadn't heard since his childhood, something his Aunt May had taught him. Then it hit him: "The Itsy-Bitsy Spider."

Dan's teeth ground together noisily. "Nursery rhymes," he growled. "I'm gonna kill that big ape." He walked back a few steps, stopped, lowered himself into a runner's starting position.

"Don't do it, Dan," warned Spidey. "You can't just go crashing in there."

Dan looked up, annoyed. "Why not? You super-mooks go crashin' through windows all'a time."

"Not without a plan," Spidey said. *Usually*, he thought. "If those jerks start shooting at you, your son might get hit by a stray bullet." His spider-sense tingled, and he looked back inside. "Wait a minute. Something's going on."

The room grew quiet as a door to an adjoining room opened, and Martin Severino entered. Just over six feet tall, clad in a black tailored suit, gold-plated jacket buttons glittering, Severino looked more like the chief executive officer of a major corporation than a suspected mob boss. The telltale bulge of a gun beneath his jacket, however, made it clear that his managerial skills hadn't been honed at Harvard.

Beside Severino, lariat in hand as always, stood the third Enforcer: Montana. As tall as Severino, Montana was lean and wiry and as deadly with a rope as the Ox or Fancy Dan were with their bare hands. He tugged at the brim of his white ten-gallon cowboy hat, glaring at the hoods around him. He wasn't impressed.

Severino scanned the room, eyes resting on Rudy, who had stopped playing when the mobster had walked in.

"Ah, Rudolph," he purred, "entertaining my employees, I see. Wonderful. They could use a bit of culture."

"When do I get to go home?" Rudy asked.

"Why, Rudolph, don't you enjoy being here? Haven't I provided you with everything—your favorite meals, the latest video games, eighty-nine channels of cable television?" He nodded toward the Ox. "I understand you've been beating your oversized playmate here quite handily at the new Super Mario game."

"That wasn't too hard," Rudy commented. "The guy's a moron."

The Ox growled.

On the terrace, Dan smiled at Spidey. "Still think he's not my kid?"

"I stand corrected," said the web-slinger. *Poor kid,* he thought.

"I'll tell you what," Severino said to Rudy. "What if, instead of taking you home, I bring a bit of home to you?"

Rudy's eyes narrowed. "What do you mean?"

Severino snapped his fingers. From the adjoining room came two more goons; between them they carried the battered, bloodied form of a man, his wrists and ankles bound in chains. The man offered no resistance, the fight already beaten out of him. The goons tossed him on the carpeted floor at Severino's feet. With a savage kick to the ribs, the dapper mobster rolled the man onto his back.

It was Joseph Loyola.

One eye swollen, blood seeping from a gash across his forehead, mouth covered with gray electrical tape, Loyola glared at Severino. Smiling wickedly at his helpless "guest," Severino wordlessly stepped aside to allow Loyola a view of his stepson, who stared back at him, horrified.

"Dad!" Rudy shrieked.

On the terrace, Spider-Man saw Dan stiffen momentarily.

Gleefully, Severino ripped the tape from Loyola's mouth. As Loyola struggled to his knees, Rudy dropped from the piano bench, racing over to hug his stepfather.

Severino sneered. "That's really quite touching." Sitting on the edge of the bench, he picked at a piece of lint on his pant cuff. "Well, now that we've had our little family reunion, it's time to get down to business." At a signal from the mob boss, Montana reached out, tearing Rudy away from Loyola. Rudy struggled to break free, but the lanky Enforcer was too strong.

"Now, Joseph, we've been at odds for quite a number of years," Severino said, "and I think it's admirable that you've been willing to give up most of your more . . . illegal interests. It's certainly made *my* life more profitable, allowing me to buy this establishment through one of my many dummy corporations. The FBI and the ATF are completely unaware that I own this casino." He patted Loyola on the shoulder. "But this stubborn refusal of yours to sell *your* casino to me—'' he dramatically waved his hand in the air ''—well, I just don't understand it. We both know there can only be one man pulling the strings in Atlantic City. You're already halfway to retiring from the business—why not go all the way?'' He gestured toward Rudy. ''It would certainly make your boy's life less . . . complicated.''

''You leave my son alone!'' Loyola bellowed. He strained at his bonds, but succeeded only in lacerating his wrists.

''Now you see, Joseph,'' said Severino, ''this is precisely why you should retire. I knew that, by abducting your boy, I'd goad you into doing something foolish.'' He smiled, capped teeth sparkling. ''Like looking for him on your own.'' Severino shook his head. ''You understand, Joseph? You're too vulnerable. So, please, do yourself a favor—sell the Diamond now, before something . . . unfortunate should happen.''

Suddenly, Severino unholstered his gun—a MAC-10 automatic pistol.

That's when all hell broke loose.

With an explosion of window glass, Dan burst into the room.

''Dan, stop!'' Spidey yelled as the diminutive Enforcer dropped down towards the floor. Spidey sighed. ''Oh, never mind,'' he muttered. He leapt after Dan.

Before Severino's thugs could unholster their guns, Spidey was in their midst, fists flashing out like lightning strikes. At his side, Dan was a martial arts whirlwind, his kicks and stiff-fingered blows connecting precisely with pressure points on his opponents' bodies. Unconscious thugs quickly began piling up.

Severino swiveled around, bringing his gun's muzzle to bear on Dan. Just as Severino pulled the trigger, Loyola pushed off the floor with his knees, slamming his shoulder into his enemy's gun hand. A dozen bullets tore through the plaster ceiling . . . and the supports for the chandelier. The weakened bolts groaned.

Pushing Loyola away, Severino turned back to Dan and pulled the trigger. Nothing happened.

The gun had jammed.

A sharp jangle from his spider-sense caused Spidey to leap straight up, narrowly avoiding the coils of Montana's lariat. With a graceful flip, the wall-crawler leapfrogged over a charging Ox, bounced off the heads of two unfortunate thugs, then cartwheeled forward, driving his feet into Montana's chest. The momentum carried both combatants through the penthouse's front door and into the hallway beyond. Spidey rebounded to his feet. Montana, having absorbed most of the impact, lay stunned on the floor. Using a thick layer of webbing, Spidey hogtied the Enforcer like a prize steer, then stepped back to admire his handiwork.

"Yippie-ki-yay, dirtbag," he said. Montana responded with a painful moan.

A jolt from his spider-sense cut off Spidey's next quip. Before he could move, a pair of tree-trunk-like arms swept around him, pinning his arms to his sides, holding him secure in a crushing bear hug.

"Now I get t'squash a bug," growled the Ox. He tightened his grip, driving the air from Spidey's lungs. Black spots danced before the web-slinger's eyes.

If he didn't break the Ox's hold soon, he would be a dead man.

Inside, Dan cut a swath through the few remaining hoodlums who stood between him and Severino. Unable to fix his gun in time, the crime boss backed away, trying to reach the next room. Two quick chops from Dan's steely hands, and the last two goons protecting Severino fell, their kneecaps shattered.

"Your turn now, tough guy!" Dan yelled at Severino. "Hope yer will's made out!"

Grinning, Dan took a step forward, only to be distracted by the shattering of the wall by the front door.

Spidey and the Ox tumbled back into the penthouse in a shower of plaster dust and splintered wood. Spidey had managed to drive the Ox headfirst through the wall in an effort to break free. Unfortunately, Ox's skull was too thick to be affected by the impact. The giant Enforcer's grip held.

Seeing that Dan was distracted by the intrusion, Severino took the opportunity to bolt from the room.

Spidey looked up, fighting the growing darkness that swirled before his eyes, and spotted Dan on the far side of the room.

"Uh, Dan . . ." Spidey gasped. "Could I . . . have a moment . . . of your . . . time?"

Dan moved to help the wall-crawler, then froze, his loyalties apparently divided.

Here was Spider-Man, the super hero responsible for ruining Dan's reputation as a tough guy, the thorn in his side all these years who had continually ruined Dan's chances of becoming a major player.

And the Ox was seconds away from finally removing this red-and-blue pain in the butt once and for all.

Then again, Spider-Man was the one person Dan had turned to for help. If it hadn't been for Spider-Man, Dan wouldn't be here now, wouldn't have been given the opportunity to save his son's life.

"Ah, nuts," Dan muttered. There was really no choice in the matter.

Dan charged across the room, leapt high into the air, one leg fully extended, and drove his heel into a pressure point just below the Ox's left elbow. With a bull-like roar, the man-mountain staggered back, his arm completely numb. Spider-Man slid from his grasp and collapsed to the floor, drawing in deep lungfuls of air.

"Whaddaya doin', Danny?" the Ox growled in a slow, irritating monotone. "How come yer workin' with Spida-Man? You workin' with the cops now, issat it? You come ta bust me an' Montana?" His lips drew back, exposing his yellowed teeth.

"Back off, ya big dope!" Dan ordered. "You ain't got no idea what's—"

The screech of tearing metal cut off further conversation. All three combatants looked up to see the chandelier snapping free of its supports. Beneath it, Rudy struggled to pull Loyola out of harm's way, but the boy wasn't strong enough to succeed.

"Rudy!" Dan cried. There was no way he could get to his son in time.

Summoning the last of his strength, Spidey leapt across the room and grabbed hold of both father and stepson, the web-spinner's momentum carrying all of them beneath the massive piano. With a loud *crash!* the chandelier slammed into the piano, burying the trio in twisted metal and shattered crystal.

Dan raced over, his vision obscured by thick clouds of plaster dust.

"Rudy!" he yelled. "Rudy! Are you okay?"

The dust settled, and Dan looked down to see white plastic lenses staring up at him. "Spider-Man! Is Rudy okay?"

Spidey moved his head a half-turn, looking into the debris. The sound of coughing echoed from within. "He's fine, Dan. We're all fine. We're just stuck." Spidey tried to pull himself out, but could find no leverage. He shook his head sadly. "I don't get paid enough for this."

A shadow fell over Dan, eclipsing the light in the room.

"Dan!" Spidey warned. "Look ou—"

As Dan turned, a massive fist connected with his jaw with all the force of a sledgehammer. The diminutive gangster crashed into an expensive mirror hanging on a wall. Slivers of glass sliced into Dan's suit, cutting his unprotected face and hands. Dan tumbled to the floor, rolled to his feet, and came up, disoriented, in an off-balance fighting stance. His jaw was swollen, the once-tan flesh now flecked with red. He coughed and spat bloody phlegm onto the carpet.

The Ox lumbered toward him, still favoring his numb arm.

"Y'shouldn'a done all'a this, Danny," Ox said. "Me an' Montana, we had a good thing goin'. There could'a been enough dough for all'a us." He gritted his teeth, eyes narrowing. "But you hadda go an' spoil it."

"You just don't get it, do ya?" Dan said. "If there was enough dough in it for all three of us, how come Severino didn't come to *me*?" The Ox looked at him quizzically, not quite sure where this was going. "All right, I'll tell ya how come. 'Cause the kid is my son, ya jerk!"

It took a few seconds for this news to sink in, but slowly the Ox realized what it meant. He nodded his head, as though confirming the information with himself.

"Oh." Ox shrugged. "Nothin' personal, Danny."

"The hell it ain't," Dan sneered. "*Nobody* makes my kid play nursery rhymes."

The battle that followed was brief. The Ox, though slow, had monstrous size and brute strength on his side. "Fancy" Dan was a martial arts master, a man accustomed to overpowering his opponents, no matter their perceived superiority in a scrap. Most of all, he was an angry parent, eager to mete out punishment to those responsible for kidnapping his son.

The Ox never had a chance.

•   •   •

For the FBI, mopping up was a simple task, given that most of the combatants were unconscious and webbed together in a large package. Alerted by local authorities, agents had flooded into the casino just as Severino was fleeing; he was detained before he could reach his car. After that, the agents had followed the sounds of battle to the penthouse to find Dan standing beside Spidey, who had finally managed to toss off the crushing weight of the piano and chandelier just as Dan defeated the Ox. The agents' first instinct had been to arrest Dan, but after Loyola and Rudy had explained the situation, they eventually backed off. Well aware of his poor relationship with all forms of law enforcement, Spider-Man stood off to one side and tried to look inconspicuous.

One hour later, Spidey and Dan sat in a corner, watching the agents pour over the room to gather evidence. At the front of the room, Loyola sat with Rudy; they were joined by Ginger, who had badgered Agent Valentine into bringing her to the casino. Spidey looked over at Dan, wondering what thoughts were running through the Enforcer's mind. The diminutive gangster sat quietly, watching the happy family reunion. A corner of his mouth twitched.

Dan gritted his teeth; it was obvious he was in a great deal of pain. His nose and mouth were crusted with dried blood, his expensive suit hung off him in tatters, and he was nursing his rib cage—something might have broken under the Ox's hammering blows, but Dan had refused to allow paramedics to examine him.

"Dan," Spidey urged for the twentieth time, "you've got to see a doctor."

"I'm fine, tough guy." Dan winced, glared at Spidey. "What, y'think I can't take a punch?"

"One punch? Sure. A few *dozen* from someone like the Ox? No."

Dan gnashed his teeth, drawing in a sharp breath. "Shows what *you* know." He fell silent, turning his attention back to the Loyolas.

Spidey softly cleared his throat. "Aren't you going to say anything to them?"

Dan shook his head. "What's to say? I was just doin' what I hadda do . . . as a father, y'know." He started, surprised by what he'd just said. He looked at Spidey. "Huh. Guess that's what people mean when they talk about actin' like a responsible parent." He smiled. "Maybe I ain't such a lost cause, y'know? Maybe it's time for me t'get a fresh start."

"I'm glad to hear that, Dan," said Spidey. He pointed past Dan. "And here comes your first step in that direction." He rose and walked away.

Dan turned. Rudy had wandered away from his parents and was heading straight for his natural father. Dan smiled as the boy approached.

"Mister . . . ?" Rudy began.

"Yeah . . . ?" Dan said slowly. Something wasn't right here.

"I just wanted to thank you for savin' me and my dad." Rudy looked over to Joe Loyola, smiled, turned back to Dan. "Are you a friend of his?"

A few feet away, Spidey heard Rudy's question and froze. "Aw, no," he said softly. He turned to look at Dan.

Dan's jaw slackened, his tanned skin turning a shade paler. It was obvious his thoughts were in turmoil. He looked past Rudy to see Ginger staring back, tears glazing her widened eyes. She shook her head slowly, saying nothing.

Rudy didn't know.

"You okay, mister?" Rudy tilted his head, confused by Dan's reaction.

Dan shook his head, turned back to Rudy. "Uh . . . sure, kid. I'm a . . . friend of your mom. . . ." His voice trailed off.

"Are you coming over to the house? I'm sure Mom and Dad would love for you to come."

Dan rose quickly; he had to leave. Now.

"Ah, n-no, kid," he stammered. "Some other time. I gotta be movin' on now." He reached down to retrieve his battered hat from the debris, unable to look his son in the eye. "I'm glad you're okay."

Rudy smiled. "Me too." He stuck out his hand. "Thanks."

Dan numbly shook it. "You're . . . welcome." Limping slightly, he headed for the front door. Ginger, watching silently, turned away as tears ran down her cheeks.

At the elevator, Spidey walked over to Dan, placing a consoling hand on his shoulder. "Dan . . . I'm sorry."

Dan shrugged him off. "Save it, tough guy. I don't need yer

pity." He stared straight ahead, drawing himself up to his full height. "Besides, what do I need with a family? Like Severino said, havin' a family just makes ya an easy target for every jamoke that hates yer guts." He looked over his shoulder to see Loyola hugging Ginger; Rudy's arms were wrapped around both of them. Dan gnashed his teeth. "I don't need that kinda hassle."

"What about that fresh start you were talking about?"

The elevator arrived, its doors opening. Dan stepped inside and punched the button for the lobby. "Fresh starts are fer chumps," he said bitterly. Leaning against the far wall of the car, the toughness slowly drained from his face. His shoulders sagged.

"Fer chumps . . ." he whispered hoarsely.

"Dan . . ." Spidey began.

The doors closed.

The Kingpin was pleased.

Looking over the front page of the *Daily Bugle*, he read of the Loyolas' rescue by the FBI and New Jersey police officers (making no mention of Spider-Man, naturally), of Joe Loyola's announcement that he was going to retire with his family to Florida, and of Martin Severino's expected indictment on racketeering charges. The Kingpin smiled.

It was a very good day.

"Feeling happy with yourself, Kingpin?" growled a voice from the surrounding darkness of the office. The crime lord continued scanning the headlines, not the least bit surprised by his unannounced visitor. The security guards outside, however, were in for hell the following morning.

"It's well past midnight, Spider-Man," the Kingpin said. "Is there some reason for this intrusion?"

Spider-Man stepped into the glow cast by the banker's lamp on the mahogany desk. He pointed an accusatory finger at the Kingpin.

"Your hand was in this from the beginning, wasn't it?" he demanded. "Severino couldn't have carried off the kidnapping without your awareness. You knew all about Loyola and Severino's rivalry, and you used an innocent boy to push them both to the edge. Then you used Dan Brito and me to bust up Severino's operation and, lo and behold, Loyola decides to retire, leaving a major gap in the balance of power in Atlantic City."

Spider-Man moved in closer, barely able to keep his anger in check. "Severino said there could only be one man pulling the strings out there. I guess that now means *you . . .* puppet master."

The Kingpin looked up from his paper, his expression revealing nothing.

"An interesting hypothesis, arachnid," he said. "However, were I you, I'd take care how you use my name in connection with acts committed by known criminals." His gaze hardened. "Slander often leads to messy court battles. I run a respectable import/export business, after all." The leather chair groaned as the Kingpin shifted his weight and sat back. He steepled his fingers.

"Let us suppose that there was a third party involved—based on your quaint conspiracy theory—and that he did as you described. What, exactly, is the problem? Look at the outcome." The Kingpin ticked off his points on his fingers. "An evil man is being punished, a good man has found peace, and a man somewhere between the two . . ." He chuckled softly. "Well, it's a pity Mr. Brito wasted all that time and energy on a boy who will always think of another man as his real father." The Kingpin looked at Spider-Man.

"As you might say, Spider-Man, the good guys won and the bad guys lost." He smirked at his costumed adversary. "At the end of the day—or night, in this case—can even *you* find fault in that?"

The question continued to haunt Spider-Man long into the night.

Dan Brito tossed fitfully in bed.

The motel room was dirty and smelled of grease and diesel fuel, scents carried through the open window from the truck stop across the road. Bandages and painkillers had relieved some of the aches of his battered body, but it wasn't the nagging pain that kept him awake.

Dan rolled onto his back and stared at the ceiling, seeing Rudy's face before him, eyes bright with happiness. His mother's eyes. Dan dragged a bruised arm over his own eyes, trying to block the vision. He didn't have time for sentimentality—that just made you soft.

And vulnerable.

In the morning, he'd hop a bus back to Manhattan, visit his tailor to pick up a new suit, then start the long process of looking for work. There was always some costumed freak out to take over the world who needed muscle to back him up, and Dan knew that his martial-arts skills made him a hot commodity; he'd have a job soon enough. After that, he'd look into getting Ox and Montana sprung. After all, they'd just been doing their jobs when they snatched Rudy. Nothing personal.

Next time around, the Enforcers would be at full strength—a force to be reckoned with—and no costumed hero would stand in their way.

Tomorrow would be a fresh start.

Dan buried his face in the lumpy pillow, waiting for the night to end.

The morning was long in coming.

POISON IN THE SOUL

Glenn Greenberg
Illustration by Joe St. Pierre

The burglar alarm blared into the night, disrupting the serene quiet that had settled onto Madison Avenue on the Upper East Side of New York City. In this part of town, antique shops, art galleries, and jewelry stores specializing in the finest in gold and diamonds were as plentiful as sand in the desert. It was well past midnight, and the streets were mostly empty. The stores and restaurants were long closed, having locked their gates at the end of business hours. Those looking for the New York City nightlife knew to head to Greenwich Village or the Upper West Side for the crowds, the food, and the music.

But Markie Macchio and Ralphie Bernardo weren't looking for the fabled Manhattan nightlife. They were looking for a big score, a stash of highly valuable goods that they could steal and sell off for the best possible price. They both wanted to retire from the crime business, after several hard years of break-ins, thefts, and varying sentences in prison. One big, final job would be enough to get them out of New York and down to Mexico, the Caribbean, or anywhere else they might want to go to live out their lives in peace. Once they were safely out of the country, Markie wanted to open a bar and Ralphie wanted to captain a charter fishing boat.

Robbing Adelman's Fine Jewelry Shop would give both men what they wanted.

They ignored the continued clanging of the burglar alarm as they swept through the inside of the store, smashing the locks to the cases storing the extravagant jewelry and stuffing as much of it as possible into their bags.

"Let's hustle," Markie said to his partner. "The cops'll be here any minute."

They had rehearsed this operation for days, calculating how much time they'd have before the police would arrive. They were right on schedule, but the slightest delay would mean their capture. "Almost done," Ralphie replied. "I just wanna get my hands on this engagement ring in the display case. Think I'll give it to my old lady."

Ralphie smashed the glass display case with a tire iron and grabbed both the diamond ring and the velvet-colored box that held it.

"I'm good to go," he said as he closed the box and tucked it into his pocket.

The two thieves collected their tools and loot, and made it back out onto the street, overjoyed and basking in the glow of their success. Bags slung over their shoulders, they headed off Madison Avenue and down a quiet residential block, smiling broadly but keeping their mouths shut, afraid of calling attention to themselves.

They'd done it. They were home free. They were going to get everything they had ever wanted out of life. They—

They were caught in a red spotlight with some kind of web pattern and two large white eyes.

And then they heard the voice. "Christmas isn't for another few months, and you two certainly don't look like Santa's helpers!"

Slowly, reluctantly, Markie and Ralphie looked up, and saw the very thing they prayed they wouldn't.

He looked just as creepy as they had always heard: the red-and-blue costume, the large black spider emblem on his chest, the large white buglike eyes. And he was somehow attached to the side of the building they had just passed, his feet sticking to the wall, and they saw that the bright spotlight originated from the buckle of his belt.

"S-Spider-Man!" Markie and Ralphie blurted out in unison.

He waved at them.

"Now, I'd like to think the best of you guys, and just assume that you're on your way to the police station to turn yourselves in," he said as he casually walked down the side of the building. "But I know I'd just be kidding myself, so what say I *escort* you there?"

Ralphie pulled out his tire iron and moved forward as Spider-Man nimbly jumped down to the sidewalk, shutting off the spider-signal on his belt buckle.

"You ain't takin' us in, wall-crawler," Ralphie yelled as he ran toward the costumed crime-fighter. He raised the tire iron and aimed for Spider-Man's head.

"Ralphie, are you crazy? We're through! Don't you know what he can do?" Markie yelled at his partner, but Ralphie ignored him. Nothing was going to come between Ralphie and his hard-earned loot.

A web-patterned gloved hand darted out, seemingly from no-where, and grabbed Ralphie's wrist in a viselike grip. His hand opened involuntarily, and he dropped the tire iron onto the ground, convinced that bones were broken.

Spider-Man bent down, still holding Ralphie's wrist in one hand, and picked up the tire iron with the other.

"Pay close attention, if you would," Spider-Man said as he let go of Ralphie's wrist and placed both of his hands on the tire iron.

Ralphie's jaw dropped as he watched his captor bend the iron bar as if it were licorice.

"Thank ya, ladies and gentlemen, thank ya verra much," Spi-der-Man said in a very bad Elvis Presley impersonation.

He then dropped the twisted metal to the ground, and leaned in close to Ralphie until they were almost nose-to-nose.

"My advice is to listen to your partner, Ralphie," Spider-Man told him. "He seems like the sensible one in this business rela-tionship."

Moments later, Ralphie and Markie were completely webbed up from neck to toe, hanging from a lamppost several feet above the ground. They could hear police sirens in the distance, grow-ing nearer and nearer.

Spider-Man had already confiscated all the loot—including the ring in Ralphie's pocket—and placed everything in a web-pack that hung from the lamppost beside the two thieves.

As two police cars rushed toward the scene, Spider-Man fired a web-line, which attached itself to a building on the other side of the street. The wall-crawler swung upward, and gave the two thieves a mock salute as he passed them by.

"Take care, fellas," Spider-Man shouted to them above the noise from the police sirens. "I'm about as popular as you are with the boys in blue, so I hope you don't mind if I make an early exit."

The two thieves remained silent as they watched their captor swing away into the night. Finally, Ralphie spoke up.

"So much for the charter fishing boat."

"And the bar," Markie responded.

Ralphie angrily glared at Markie as the police cars drove up and parked beneath them. "He called *you* the sensible one! You were the one who came up with this plan in the first place!"

. . .

As he swung over the city, gazing down upon the glorious Manhattan skyline and feeling the cool breeze caressing him, Spider-
Man's thoughts were focused on the robbery he had just foiled.
One particular object that he had recovered from the hapless
thieves burned in his memory.

That engagement ring in Ralphie's pocket, he thought. *It looks so
much like the one I gave to Mary Jane the other day when I asked her to
marry me. She still hasn't given me her answer yet, but there's no reason
I can think of that she'd say no. We've been getting along so great, we've
been so compatible—and here I was, thinking that no one could ever help
me get past the agony I felt when I lost Gwen.*

But Mary Jane Watson is one special kinda lady, Spider-Man
mused, smiling underneath his mask. *And I like the thought of
spending the rest of my life with her.*

As he continued his journey down to the Chelsea section of
Manhattan where he lived as Peter Parker, college student and
freelance photographer for the *Daily Bugle,* Spider-Man continued to reflect on his recent marriage proposal.

*I have to tell her that I'm Spider-Man, that much is certain. That's
scary. I haven't shared that secret with anyone! Question is, how and
when do I tell her? Should she know before she gives me her answer that
she'd be marrying Spider-Man, or do I wait until after she says yes? Gotta
figure this one out pretty soon.*

*All this on my mind, and I still have to prepare for college graduation
in a couple of months! Face it, Parker, the future is calling, and you
better be sure you're ready for it.*

Spider-Man arrived home and crawled into his top-floor apartment through the skylight that opened onto his bathroom. He
quickly peeled off his skintight Spider-Man costume and tossed
it into the bathtub, where he would wash it first thing in the
morning. He looked at himself in the mirror and frowned. "Petey, m'boy, you've been burning the candle at both ends, lately,"
he said aloud to his reflection, which revealed a haggard, weary-
looking young man with dark circles under his eyes. "You need
to get some sleep—and I do mean now!"

Peter jumped into his bed. His head hit the pillow at precisely
two-thirty-two A.M., and he immediately fell asleep.

. . .

Exactly seven hours and two minutes later, he was abruptly awakened by his telephone.

"Mmffnhhrna," Peter said into the receiver, feeling as if he had cotton in his mouth and Krazy Glue in his eyes.

It was Harry Osborn, Peter's best friend and former roommate. "Hey, Pete, sorry to wake you."

"Uh, that's okay Harry. What's up?" Peter replied. "Haven't seen much of you lately, pal. We've got to set aside some time to get together, like in the old days."

Harry chuckled and replied, "The 'old days,' Pete? We're way too young to be talking about the 'old days.'"

"Maybe," Peter replied, "but sometimes, what with all we've been through, it feels like we've been around forever."

There was an awkward pause. It seemed like Harry was trying to say something, but didn't know where to start.

"Okay, Har, what's going on? It's obvious you didn't call just to say hi."

"You're right. You remember Martin Schultz, right?"

Peter nodded. "Marty? Sure. I took a bunch of science classes with him freshman year at ESU, and we were lab partners in a couple of them. He's a really bright guy. Haven't seen much of him for a while, but he called me pretty recently."

Peter remembered the out-of-the-blue phone call from Martin Schultz. It had to have been two, three weeks ago or so. He hadn't seen or heard from his fellow Empire State University classmate for two whole semesters. They weren't exactly friends; Peter considered him more of a casual acquaintance, but they had always gotten along well. Perhaps a stronger bond of friendship could have formed between them, but in those days, Peter was involved with his own circle of friends at ESU, dating first Gwen Stacy and later Mary Jane Watson, plus freelancing for the *Bugle*, and spending much of his time as Spider-Man. There simply wasn't enough time to cultivate a friendship with someone as peripheral in Peter's life as Marty.

But when Marty called Peter several weeks ago, he had told Peter that he would like to get together to talk. And Peter, happy to hear from Marty again after so long, had gladly agreed to meet with him.

I ended up having to miss that appointment with Marty, though, Peter thought. *A residential building was on fire, and there were several families trapped inside.* Peter had to go there as Spider-Man and save them. By the time he got to the restaurant, Marty was already long gone. Peter figured that they'd just get in touch with each other again and reschedule. However, Peter hadn't heard from Marty since, and had been too busy to call back.

"Why, what's going on?" Peter asked.

Harry said simply, "He's dead."

"What?" Peter cried, shaking his head, not able to believe what he had just heard.

"Suicide," Harry continued. "They found his body yesterday, in his apartment. He left a note, saying that he couldn't get rid of the 'poison in his soul'—but nobody seems to know what that means. I've been making the rounds, telling everyone who knew Marty about what's happened, and when and where the funeral is going to be. I thought you'd like to know."

Peter sat in stunned silence. Harry told him the time and location of the funeral, and he mumbled an acknowledgment.

Harry sighed. "I'd better get going, Pete. There are a few more people I have to call. Try to make the funeral if you can," Harry said. "Marty didn't have much in the way of friends and family, so I don't think there's going to be a very big turnout."

Peter and Harry said their good-byes. Once Peter hung up the phone, he stood in the center of his apartment, silent, filled with regret and sorrow. His thoughts drifted back to several weeks ago, when he had gotten the unexpected call from Marty.

When he called me, Peter thought, *he must have been reaching out for help. Something was bothering him, enough to make him want to end his life. He was trying to reconnect with someone he considered a friend, someone he thought could help him through this bad period for him. And in the time of his greatest need, when I should have been there for him, I failed him. God only knows what he must have thought when I didn't show up. That's why I never heard from him again—he must've thought that he couldn't count on me! And in the weeks since then, things must've gotten so much worse for him that he . . .*

He broke off the thought, not wishing to continue. He stormed into the bathroom, and glared at the crumpled costume in the bathtub with bitterness and resentment.

It's because of Spider-Man that Marty Schultz is dead, he thought. *If I hadn't been off adventuring, I could've been there for Marty, I could have helped him through whatever was troubling him. He'd still be alive!*

But then a voice in his head responded. It sounded familiar, calm, gentle, understanding but firm. *And what about all the people in that burning building? If Spider-Man hadn't been there, they'd definitely be dead.*

The voice, Peter finally recognized, was his own.

No, not exactly his. It was Spider-Man's.

He closed his eyes, and slowly nodded his head. It was true. All the lives he saved that day would have been lost had he not been there to save them as Spider-Man.

But what about Marty? Couldn't he have been there for Marty, as well?

Peter sighed heavily, and set to work washing his costume.

The next morning at eleven o'clock, Peter stood across the street from the Brevoort Funeral Parlor, where Martin Schultz's funeral service was to be held. He could see a few familiar faces entering the building: there was Mary Jane Watson, whom he had just asked to marry him, arriving with Peter's high-school-nemesis-turned-college-buddy, Flash Thompson. There were some other people that Peter remembered seeing at school, but he couldn't remember their names. And finally, there was Harry Osborn.

Peter took a step toward the funeral parlor, then stopped. He couldn't bring himself to go any farther.

I can't help but feel that I'm part of the reason this funeral is happening in the first place, he thought. *How can I go in there, face those mourners, knowing that I could have prevented all of this?*

Peter turned away, stuffed his hands in his pockets, and sadly walked on in the opposite direction.

Inside the parlor, Harry stood outside the chapel with Mary Jane and Flash, watching as the mourners filed in and taking note of one particular absence.

"I thought Pete would be here by now," Harry said quietly.

"Aw, you know Parker, Har," Flash replied. "That guy'll be late to his *own* funeral."

"Not funny, Flash," Harry scolded. "He took the news of Marty's death pretty hard. I didn't think they were even that close, you know?"

"They weren't," Mary Jane chimed in, also wondering about the whereabouts of her would-be fiancé. "I know Petey liked him, but it's not like they ever really hung out. Peter's just a really sensitive guy. You two know what I mean. He's always walking around like he's got the weight of the world on his shoulders."

After wandering aimlessly through the city for a while, Peter ended up at the offices of the *Daily Bugle*. He needed some familiar surroundings, to see a few friendly faces, and the newspaper where he worked was the closest thing that fit the bill.

Peter was saying hello to his friend, Glory Grant, executive secretary to J. Jonah Jameson, the paper's publisher and editor-in-chief, when he heard that familiar, gruff, loud voice from behind him.

"Where's that blasted police corruption article?" yelled Jameson. "I wanted it on my desk half an hour ago! Somebody find Conover, and tell him if he doesn't finish that piece, I'll get Urich to do it for him! And then I'll fire his sorry butt quicker than you can say—"

Peter covered his face with his hand as Jameson headed in his direction. He hoped his longtime employer wouldn't notice him, that he'd be so caught up in his tirade that he would walk right past Peter and never even realize he was there.

No such luck.

"Parker!" Jameson bellowed.

Peter winced inwardly, and then tried to give his best smile, well aware that he was failing miserably.

"Uh, hi, Mr. Jameson. Just thought I'd stop by to—"

"To what? Loiter? This is a newspaper, Parker, not a soda shoppe, or wherever you lazy kids hang out these days!"

"Thanks for clearing that up for me, sir. I was just about to ask Glory for a vanilla egg cream," Peter replied, keeping a completely straight face. Beside him, Glory had to cover her mouth or she would have burst out laughing.

Jameson scowled at him. If looks could kill . . .

"Instead of distracting my staff with your nonsense, Parker, why don't you get your freelancing keyster out on the streets and get some photos of the Shocker?"

"The Shocker?" Peter replied, unable to conceal his surprise. Last he had heard, that old enemy of Spider-Man's was in jail.

"Yeah, Parker, the Shocker!" Jameson impatiently told him.

"He broke out last night. What, you don't even bother to read the paper you work for?"

"Go easy on him, Jonah," said a deep, gentle voice from behind Peter. He turned to see the paper's city editor, Joe "Robbie" Robertson, whose demeanor was as friendly as Jonah's was abrasive. There was no doubt that Jameson and Robertson were the yin and yang of the *Daily Bugle.*

"Peter's a busy college student," Robbie said, lighting his pipe. "Right now, the only news on his mind is what his midterm grades are going to be."

Peter smiled, grateful for Robbie's intervention.

But Jonah had an answer for that. Jonah had an answer for everything.

"Well, I don't pay him for getting straight A's, Robbie," he said. "I pay him for getting photos I can use for my front page!"

"You're right, Mr. Jameson," Peter quickly said, not wanting Robbie to have to defend him any more than he already had. "I'll get right on it, I promise."

As Peter said his good-byes and raced for the elevators, he could hear Jameson's voice behind him, calling out, "And don't come back until you've got something for me I can use!"

How about breath mints? Peter thought as he hopped into the elevator and the doors closed behind him.

Spider-Man glided over the city, totally enjoying the freefall that he was in. He then extended his arm, triggered his web-shooter, and fired a long web-line at a flagpole extending from the side of a tall skyscraper. The web-line caught the flagpole, and Spider-Man swung underneath it. He then let go of the line and was once again gliding, once again in freefall, until he fired out another web-line.

I never get tired of this, he thought. *No matter what, I absolutely love web-slinging!*

He was actually grateful to have the Shocker's escape from prison to keep him busy, to keep him distracted from the emotional turmoil he was experiencing over Marty's death.

And, thankfully, the Shocker was not exactly one of the big guns in Spider-Man's rogues' gallery. He was neither a murderous lunatic like the Green Goblin, nor a merciless genius like Dr. Octopus. No, the Shocker, comparatively speaking, was basically a very clever, technically proficient, low-level thief, who created very powerful vibration-generating wrist devices to help him commit his crimes, and wore a heavily insulated costume that rendered him immune to the effects of his so-called "vibro-blasts."

He would be fairly easy to apprehend, Spider-Man was confident, and Peter Parker would get the photos he needed to pay next month's rent. And judging from all the noise and commotion up ahead, it appeared that he was closing in on his quarry.

The Shocker stood in the center of Broadway and Nineteenth Street, blasting away at the police cars that surrounded him. Hundreds of people had gathered to witness this spectacle, despite the danger they were all in. The vibration waves generated by the Shocker's wrist devices were so powerful that they flipped the police cars completely over, sending dozens of those spectators running in fear and panic. Police officers raising their pistols and, aiming at the super-powered criminal, found themselves being thrown back and stunned into unconsciousness by his vibro-blasts.

"I told ya I didn't want any trouble!" the Shocker yelled at the police. "I wasn't even gonna put the suit on again! But ya hadda come after me, hound me! Well, I ain't goin' back to prison! I went through too much to get here, just to get captured and sent back again!"

"Yeah, how *dare* these cops try to do their jobs?" called a voice from above.

The Shocker looked up, and his eyes narrowed beneath his insulated mask. Spider-Man was swinging down on a web-line, right toward him.

The crime-fighter continued, "I mean, where do they get off, trying to send you back to jail so you can rightfully serve out your sentence?"

Spider-Man collided with the Shocker, landing a punch on the Shocker's jaw that sent the criminal sprawling to the ground.

"Everybody back off!" Spider-Man shouted to the crowd. "It's not safe to be around here!"

"Better heed your own advice, Spider-Man," the Shocker said as he rose to his feet. "I'm not looking for a fight. So just get lost and leave me alone, or I'll do to you what I did to these stupid cops."

He recovered quicker than I expected him to, Spider-Man thought. *The insulation in his mask must have absorbed the brunt of my punch.*

"No can do, Shockie," Spider-Man replied. "But if you surrender and come along quietly, I can see to it that you get a nice big lollipop."

The Shocker responded by firing an intense vibro-blast at the crime-fighter. A nearby fire hydrant was caught in the blast and fell over, sending a stream of water into the air that sprayed the crowd.

But Spider-Man, alerted by his spider-sense, an almost precognitive sixth sense that warned him of looming danger, managed to leap out of the way of the blast just in time. He sailed through the air, right over the Shocker's head, and gracefully landed behind his opponent.

The Shocker swiftly turned to blast Spider-Man again, but Spider-Man landed another punch, this time in the Shocker's stomach, once more sending the Shocker sprawling.

I pulled my punch before, because underneath that insulated suit, the Shocker's just a regular guy, Spider-Man told himself. *But if the suit is protecting him that much, I can cut loose.*

The Shocker got to his feet once again, and aimed his wrist devices in Spider-Man's direction. Spider-Man braced himself, prepared to leap up in order to evade the powerful vibro-blasts. Then, unexpectedly, the Shocker turned around and blasted an aging residential building on Nineteenth Street. The building, which already looked like it was about to fall apart, quaked under the onslaught of the Shocker's vibro-blasts, and large chunks of rubble and broken bricks began to fall onto the ground below.

Problem was, there were dozens of people standing there, about to be pummeled by the falling debris. While some of them would be able to get away in time, there was no way that all of them would.

Spider-Man leapt into action, landing directly in the path of danger, pushing people to safety as gently as he could. But his spider-sense began to buzz madly within his head, distracting him for a split second.

Must be warning me of the falling rubble, he told himself briefly. *But I'm already aware of that, so I can ignore it and just—*

He was caught completely off-guard as a vibro-blast from the

Shocker hit him square in the back and knocked him to the ground . . . just in time for all the debris to fall on top of him.

Half buried under several hundred pounds of rubble, Spider-Man struggled to maintain consciousness, to free himself and stop his enemy.

Stupid, real stupid, Spider-Man berated himself. *When are you gonna learn? You're always assuming you know better than your spider-sense!*

Through blurred vision, Spider-Man could make out the distinctive yellow and brown costume of the Shocker, and realized that the criminal was making his getaway.

What's this, he's not sticking around to kill me? Spider-Man wondered. *He must've been serious about not wanting a fight.*

Reaching out through the rubble, Spider-Man fired off a spider-tracer—a small electronic tracking device that was tuned to the same frequency as his spider-sense—and watched with hope and anticipation as it flew through the air, headed straight for the retreating Shocker—and landed right on the back section of the criminal's belt.

Spider-Man closed his eyes and breathed a heavy sigh of relief. Maybe the Shocker was getting away, but with a little luck—and a lot of perseverance—he would be able to catch up to the super-villain later on.

Sometime later—Spider-Man was not sure if it was a minute or an hour—the web-slinger's eyes snapped open as he felt a pair of big, strong hands pulling him out of the rubble, helping him to his feet. To his amazement, it was a police officer.

"You gonna take me in?" Spider-Man asked weakly.

"No way," the cop replied. "What'll we book you for, saving lives? I saw what you did for those people. You're a hero, fella."

Spider-Man smiled underneath his mask. "Thanks for the sentiments. It's nice to hear that not everyone's been swayed by Jameson's editorials."

The cop grimaced. "That crank? He's just a loudmouthed blowhard looking for attention."

Spider-Man patted the cop on the arm. "Officer, you just made my day."

"You want I should get you to the hospital?" the cop asked, concerned.

Spider-Man shook his head. "I'll be fine, thanks. Right now, I have to pick up the trail of the Shocker."

He lifted up his hand and fired off a web-line that caught on to the top of a lamppost. As he swung off, he could hear the cop call after him, "What does that nutcase want, anyway?"

"Good question," Spider-Man called back. "And I intend to learn the answer."

As he swung back up into the skies over Manhattan, Spider-Man's mind was filled with questions and observations about his quarry.

He seemed more desperate this time out, he thought. *He was looking to avoid a fight, that much is certain. He was anxious to get away from me and the cops. It's as if he's after something, and that's all he cares about. And it doesn't seem to be the usual thing, like robbing a bank or getting revenge on me. But what could it be, then?*

The sun had already set by the time Spider-Man picked up the signal transmitted by his spider-tracer. Like a homing beacon it summoned him, and he unerringly followed its call. He was surprised at the location at which he finally found his little device: the Forest Hills Cemetery.

Crouched on top of the main gate, Spider-Man looked into the graveyard, searching for any sign of movement or activity. A chill ran down his spine. He hated cemeteries—perhaps because he'd gone to so many funerals in his young life.

And if cemeteries gave him the creeps during the day, then at night they positively made him shudder. But he had a job to do, and the sooner he got it done, the sooner he could get out of there.

Spider-Man spotted a familiar-looking object lying on the ground by the gate, outside the cemetery. He leapt off the gate and bent down to examine it. Picking it up, he frowned.

It was the spider-tracer. The Shocker must have finally discovered it attached to his belt and discarded it. The web-slinger was back to square one, with no idea of where to begin searching for his old enemy.

He might still be here, though, Spider-Man thought. *It's worth checking out.*

Climbing over the fence and into the cemetery, he could not

help but think of those close to him, whom he had lost over the last several years.

The death of his uncle, Ben Parker, was the one that had weighed upon him the most. In a tragic twist of fate, Peter discovered that the same burglar who had killed Ben was also the thief that Peter had allowed to run past him days earlier. Peter had only recently gained his powers and become Spider-Man, but at that time, he was using those powers to become a television sensation. He planned to become an entertainer, and use his newfound abilities to make it big in show business. The thief had run past Spider-Man in a TV studio, shortly after the web-slinger's latest appearance. An elderly police officer was chasing the thief. Seeing the colorfully garbed youth standing nearby, the cop called out to Spider-Man, asking him to help stop this fleeing crook.

Spider-Man did nothing. The crook made it to the elevators and got away clean.

"All you hadda do was trip him, or hold him just for a minute," the angry cop said to him afterward.

"Sorry, pal, that's *your* job," Spider-Man had replied, flippantly waving off the old cop. "From now on, I just look out for number one! And that means—me!"

Those words would come back to haunt him when his uncle was murdered several days later. Peter put on his Spider-Man costume and hunted down the burglar, apprehending him in an old warehouse. But then he realized that this was the same thief from the television studio. If only he had done something then, if only he had used his powers *responsibly*. . . .

From that moment on, Spider-Man was a crime-fighter, a force dedicated to preventing this kind of tragedy from ever happening again. He had learned his lesson, but at a terrible price. And in the several years since then, he had not shaken the guilt he'd felt over Ben's death, and the sorrowful knowledge that he had failed his uncle, the kindest, gentlest man he had ever known.

Just like I failed Gwen, Spider-Man thought bitterly.

The Green Goblin, who had discovered that Spider-Man was really Peter Parker, had murdered Peter's girlfriend, Gwen Stacy, as a way of striking at the web-slinger through his loved ones. Spider-Man was on the scene at the time, battling the Goblin, but there was nothing he could do to prevent Gwen from dying.

Her only crime was that she had dared to love Peter Parker, and she had paid the price for it.

Am I crazy, asking Mary Jane to marry me? he wondered. *After Gwen, am I crazy to even be thinking of ever getting married? The Goblin may be gone, but what if one of my other enemies ever discovers my secret identity? How do I know I can protect Mary Jane? What if we have kids? Would I be able to protect them? Have I learned enough from what happened to Gwen to prevent it from ever happening again?*

Then a bitter thought entered his mind. *You can add Marty Schultz to the list of people you've failed, Parker. And that just happened within the last couple of days. Do you really want to saddle MJ with the burden of being part of Spider-Man's world? Because of Spider-Man, you couldn't give Marty Schultz even a moment of your time, and now he's—*

Then, the young crime-fighter stopped dead in his tracks as realization dawned on him. *Wait a minute! Forest Hills Cemetery . . . this is where Harry said Marty was going to be buried!*

Talk about irony, he mused. *The Shocker's trail has led me to the very place I've been trying to avoid.*

He thought for a long moment. *Maybe it's time I stop trying to avoid this, then, and confront it head-on. There's no trace of the Shocker here anyway, and I can continue the search later.*

Spider-Man began moving through the cemetery again, searching for one particular gravesite. After a while, he finally found it.

He stood by the grave of Martin Schultz, head lowered, feeling as if he was on trial, as if the grave was pointing an accusing finger at him.

He was wracked with overwhelming feelings of guilt and sorrow, not because he and Marty had been so close—they hadn't—but because someone in the world had counted on Peter Parker and he hadn't been there for that person, because Spider-Man was needed elsewhere. And now that person was dead.

I can't escape from the guilt and anguish I feel over your death, Marty, Spider-Man said silently to the grave. *I feel as if it's all seeped through me, right down to the core of my soul.*

Y'know, I think I understand now what you meant about having "poison" in your soul, and not being able to get rid of it. I'm sure feeling that way now. But whatever poison you had in your soul was too much for you to bear.

Then, suddenly, surprisingly, anger washed over Spider-Man.

But you took the coward's way out, Marty. The easy way out. Death is never a solution, no matter what problems have to be overcome. Life is too precious a gift, and you threw yours away. I've experienced a lot of tragedies in my life, but I never surrendered to depression. I fought my way back from it, because, for me, it was too important to go on living. Was death really your only option?

I refuse to believe that, Marty.

He took a deep breath, and struggled with his jumbled emotions. But suddenly, his spider-sense was triggered, and he crouched into a defensive posture. Then the Shocker burst out of the shadows.

The criminal's mask was gone, and his face was etched with unfettered rage. He roared as he flung himself at Spider-Man, pounding at the wall-crawler and trying to get his fingers around Spider-Man's throat.

"You followed me even here, huh?" the Shocker shouted angrily, landing blow after blow upon the crime-fighter. "Even here! You really have no sense of decency, do you, you wall-crawling freak? I told you I wasn't looking for a fight! That I wanted to be left alone!"

Spider-Man shoved the Shocker back, sustaining no serious injuries. They squared off among the gravestones, each waiting for the right moment to strike against the other.

"Sorry to get in your way, Shocker," Spider-Man replied sarcastically, "but let me point something out to you: you broke out of prison. You're an escaped convict. You're not the injured party here."

That seemed to enrage the Shocker even more. "I'm not the injured party?" he cried as he fired a vibro-blast at Spider-Man, who leapt out of its path.

"They wouldn't even let me attend his funeral," the Shocker continued. "They said I hadn't served enough time to get special treatment like that!"

"Whose funeral, Shocker? What are you talking about?"

The Shocker sneered. "Don't play stupid with me! You were just standing over his grave, looking for me!"

A cold chill ran down Spider-Man's back. The grave he was just standing over . . .

Exasperated, the Shocker continued, "Martin Schultz! My kid brother! He killed himself a few days ago!"

Of course. Spider-Man's mind raced. *The Shocker's real name is Herman Schultz! But I had no idea that he and Marty were related.*

"I . . . didn't make the connection," Spider-Man replied.

"Our parents died when Marty was a boy," the Shocker explained. "And I ended up away from home most of the time, and neglecting him for most of his life. I was in prison—thanks to you—when I learned about his suicide."

The Shocker's face softened, the anger replaced by sadness.

"I . . . couldn't help but feel guilty," he continued. "I'd never been there for him. We hadn't spoken in . . . I don't even know how long. But I always loved him, don't you dare think that I didn't!"

Spider-Man nodded silently.

"I don't even know why he killed himself! If only I had paid more attention to him while he was alive, maybe I could've helped him somehow, maybe . . . maybe . . ."

The Shocker rubbed his eyes, and went on, "Well, I told you they wouldn't let me come to his funeral. But I had to come here, you understand? The guilt, the grief . . ."

The poison in the soul, Spider-Man thought.

"If I couldn't be there for Marty during his life, I was at least gonna be there for his death. And no one—including you—is gonna stop me!"

The Shocker renewed his attack on Spider-Man, leaping toward the wall-crawler and firing off vibro-blasts in his direction. Of course, Spider-Man evaded them easily.

But Spider-Man could no longer bring himself to get tough with the Shocker. All he could feel for him was sympathy . . . and, in a way, empathy. Wanting to end this quickly, Spider-Man landed a punch directly on the Shocker's jaw that completely staggered the criminal, sending him to his knees on the grass. Not wanting to take any chances of further surprise attacks, however, Spider-Man completely covered the Shocker's wrist devices with webbing, so that Schultz could no longer reach their triggers with his thumbs to activate them.

"Listen to me, Shocker," Spider-Man said, pointing a finger directly into the Shocker's chest. "Your brother threw his life away . . . and it seems to me like you're heading down the same road. What do you have to show for yourself? A life of crime, in and out of prison. You designed those wrist devices yourself, right? Along with your costume? You obviously have talent, technological expertise. Couldn't you have used it more productively? Think of what you've done with all that talent, all that energy and potential, Schultz—you've wasted it! You've squandered it!''

"Shut up!" Schultz yelled, coming out of the daze that the slug to his jaw had put him in. "You don't know what you're talking about!"

Spider-Man grabbed the Shocker by his shoulders and shoved his face into Schultz's. "Oh, I think I do," he countered. "As the guy who seems to have cornered the market on sending you to prison, I have a pretty good idea of what you're about. And I'll tell you something else: it's not too late for you."

At that, the Shocker looked up and, for the first time, really looked at Spider-Man.

The web-slinger continued, "You have a chance to turn your life around. You're still a pretty young guy, plenty of years left in you, right? You can finish out your prison sentence, reform, and make something of yourself.

"You know, I've been thinking a lot about the future lately. How it offers no guarantees, how it's always uncertain and full of potential dangers and tragedies. But I choose to embrace it anyway, Schultz, because it's also full of hope and opportunity and joy."

The Shocker looked as if he was going to answer back, but then thought better of it. He remained silent.

"You have the chance to embrace the future," Spider-Man told him. "It's a chance your brother threw away. What's it going to be for you, Schultz, the future . . . or a dead end?"

Schultz looked down, closed his eyes, and took a deep breath. When he opened his eyes again, there seemed to be a serenity in them that had not been there before. Serenity, mixed with regret—and determination.

Spider-Man and the Shocker—Herman Schultz—stood at Martin Schultz's grave. Schultz had asked for a chance to pay his final respects to his brother before he was taken back to the authorities, and Spider-Man chose to grant him that chance. Schultz had decided that he was going to try to turn his life around, and had agreed to return to prison to finish out his sentence. He was looking ahead, to the future, and what he could make of himself for the rest of his life.

And as he stood at Schultz's side, Spider-Man silently said his own final farewell to Martin.

I'm sorry I wasn't there for you, Marty. I can't be everywhere at once . . . and God help me, I wish that weren't so. But the decision to end your life was yours and yours alone, and there was nothing I could have done to stop you if you were that intent on doing it. I realize that now, and I'm not going to torture myself over it anymore.

Schultz finally spoke up. "He wanted to be a scientist," he said.

I know, Spider-Man thought. *And having seen him in action in the labs at ESU, I could tell that he would have been a fine one.*

Spider-Man gently placed his hand on Schultz's shoulder.

"Time to go," he said softly, and he began to guide Schultz away.

As they walked toward the main gate of the cemetery, Spider-Man looked over his shoulder, to take one last look at Martin Schultz's grave.

I still don't know what the poison in your soul was, Marty, he said silently. *Probably no one knows, or ever will. But what I do know is that the guilt and anguish that I felt over your death—the poison in my own soul—is gone now.*

I'm not sure if your brother will really be able to reform. That's for the future to decide. But right now, at this very moment, all is right with the world, and the future looks bright.

And moments like this are so rare, so few and far between, that I can't help but cherish it.

Several days later, at sunset, Spider-Man stood on the top of one of the towers of the Brooklyn Bridge. It was not easy for him to be there; it was where Gwen Stacy had died. But at that moment, it seemed to him he could not be anyplace else.

"I've been thinking about you a lot lately, Gwen," he said, barely above a whisper. "Especially after all that's happened."

He swallowed hard. "Mary Jane turned down my proposal. Gave me back the ring. Said she was too much of a free spirit to be tied down. I guess that means she and I are through.

"Part of me feels I would've been better off not getting involved with her at all, that I should've built a wall around myself after I lost you, and never have let myself feel that strongly for anyone else ever again. That way, no one could've ever hurt me again. I would've been safe, reliving the times that you and I had together, reliving those memories over and over in my mind, so that you wouldn't really be dead.

"But then I remember how I chose to live for the future, rather than dwell on a past that I've lost and can never regain. And I'm making that choice again.

"I'll always love you, Gwen, and I'll always remember you. But the future is calling, and I have to go meet it head-on. I think that's what you would have wanted me to do."

Spider-Man turned, fired off a long web-line, and began to web-sling back into New York City. The sun was nearly gone, and night was approaching to embrace the city in its darkness.

But there would be a tomorrow. Spider-Man—Peter Parker—knew that. And with tomorrow, there was a chance for hope, for opportunity, and maybe, just maybe, for happiness.

LIVEWIRES

Steve Lyons

Illustration by Ed Hannigan & Al Milgrom

"**G**angway!"

Steve Hopkins shouted his warning too late. Halfway between his cubicle and the office door, he collided with Debra Whitman. Both hit the floor in a tangle of limbs and scattered papers.

"Oh, Steve!"

"Sorry, Deb, I really am." Steve was already scrabbling about for his belongings. "My chem lab session ran over and I'm late for a very important date."

Debra picked up a folder, then dropped it with a squeal. Steve flashed her an embarrassed grin and quickly whipped away the rubber spider that had fallen out. "One of your practical jokes!" she exclaimed. She was trying to sound stern, but couldn't conceal her relief.

"Er, yeah. Think Marcy'll like it?" No need to tell Deb that the spider had been bound for her desk drawer, Steve reasoned. It might still get there, eventually.

"She'll kill you!"

"Uh-uh. She can't do that twice—and being forty minutes late for her big moment is definitely a killing offense."

"Of course," recalled Debra, getting to her feet. "You're assisting on her research project, aren't you?" She shivered. "I don't know why Dr. Sloan has allowed it. I mean, to let such an evil, dangerous person loose on campus, after that business with Swarm—"

"Aw, Marcy's not so bad once you get to know her."

"Oh, no," protested Debra, "I didn't mean . . ." But Steve was already heading for the door. He glanced back to impart a knowing wink, and Debra realized, belatedly, that he'd been pulling her leg.

"See ya later," Steve promised as he left the Department of Graduate Studies and broke into a run.

That's right, Dillon, just hold that sneer for a few seconds longer, and—

"Parker!"

Peter almost yelped in surprise at the sharp voice, and at the hard green eyes that suddenly filled his viewfinder. He leapt back, lowered his camera, composed himself, and smiled winsomely at his fellow teaching assistant and postgraduate student.

"Marcy! I was, er, just getting a few pictures of your subject for the *Globe*. You don't mind, I hope?"

Marcy Kane did mind, and she said so with all her usual contempt. "I had to beg to get this project sanctioned. The last thing I need is some newspaper hack telling every would-be terrorist in New York that I've got Electro on campus!"

"I'm not stupid, Marcy. I won't file the story until Sparky here is safely back at Ryker's Island."

Marcy sighed. "You know, if you were half as interested in the possibilities of my research as in your grubby sideline . . ."

Peter didn't listen to the rest. Marcy's views on his supposed lack of commitment had been impressed upon him many times before. She had a point about Electro, though. Max Dillon was a dangerous man, and his presence at Empire State University made Peter Parker very nervous. In a sense, he was grateful that his new boss, Barney Bushkin, had given him the assignment—though it made sense, since Peter was the only *Globe* photographer who also attended ESU. And, unlike his former boss, J. Jonah Jameson of the *Daily Bugle*, Bushkin didn't try to use Peter's status as a student at the location of the story as an excuse to lower Peter's rates.

The assignment also meant that Peter could keep an eye on things. So far, however, there had been no problems. Electro had arrived in a security van, anesthetized, swathed from head to foot in nonconductive bandages, and accompanied by four armed guards. He had been carried into this remote laboratory building, wired up to Marcy's apparatus, and only then unwrapped. He had woken shortly thereafter, but was still groggy. He lay back on his semireclined pallet in the center of the room, not trying to move but staring hatefully at each guard in turn.

The arrival of another colleague diverted Marcy's attentions. "Here at last! Get yourself a lab coat, Philip. Hopkins hasn't turned up and Parker has 'better things' to do, so you're my new assistant."

Philip Chang was taken aback. "I didn't expect this, Marcy. I haven't read up on what you're doing."

"You don't need to," said Marcy brusquely. "Just follow orders and listen. Now, I'm hoping to find out what makes Electro's body such an efficient storage battery. My instruments will give us all the data we need as soon as he tries to use his powers."

"I take it something stops him from using his powers?"

"No problem. The equipment completes a circuit with Electro's biosystem. Any energy he builds up will be sapped and fed back into the generators. His actual discharges will be minimal, and I can cancel out each one with an equal and opposite current. I've run a cable to the main building, so we'll have all the spare power we need."

"I've got to hand it to you, Marcy," said Peter. "Using electricity against Electro—that's quite an insult, even by your standards."

"Still here, Parker?"

"I don't know, Marcy," said Philip doubtfully. "Is it right to use a human being like this?" Peter followed his gaze across the lab, to where Max Dillon had closed his eyes wearily. Bereft of his colorful costume, he hardly cut an imposing figure. He was just a helpless man, attached to contraptions that he probably didn't understand, about to become a most unwilling guinea pig.

"His DNA could hold the key to providing cheap, plentiful energy for the world," argued Marcy. "That makes it right!"

Peter didn't like the zeal in Marcy's voice, nor did he agree with her sentiments. "Not to mention," he said, "that your research might uncover a way of removing his powers, which would put an end to Electro as a criminal menace." Images of past battles flashed through his mind, and he shuddered as he recalled the occasions on which Electro's lethal voltage had almost killed him and others. It would be nice if Marcy found a way for Max Dillon to serve his time without the authorities worrying that Electro would escape again.

Marcy chivvied Philip across to the bank of output monitors, where she continued her briefing. Max Dillon's eyes opened again and he glared at Peter for a second. "I liked you better when you were doing your Boris Karloff impression," Pete muttered under his breath.

The photographer—Parker—wasn't afraid. Dillon felt a surge of rage at that realization. He *should* be afraid. He should know that Electro was a big man, a powerful man, and that the lives of his enemies were worth nothing. He should show respect. One day, he would. One day, when Electro's name was the biggest around; when people didn't dare to so much as sneeze without his permission.

For now, he was helpless. He could build up no more than a feeble voltage. He had tried letting out a feeler, just a tiny spark, but the machinery had anticipated and counteracted the move. It waited now for his next attempt. He could feel its current, trapped in the wires, inaccessible. He felt frustrated, like a thirsty man surrounded by water but unable to drink.

He closed his eyes and tried to control his burgeoning anger. He couldn't let it control him. It had been so long since he had felt cool air against his skin, free of the stifling bandages. He wanted complete freedom. He could have it, but only if he was careful and clever. He had to conserve his energy, to play dumb, to wait for an opening. It would come, if he was patient. Admittedly, that wasn't his greatest virtue.

". . . hear me, Dillon?"

He had settled into a light doze (blasted knockout gas, still clinging, making him sleepy). Dreams of vengeance played across the backs of his eyelids.

"I said, can you hear me?"

He surfaced, dragged into wakefulness by a cold voice. He didn't know how long he had been out. The photographer had left, but the guards remained. The female student—Marcy, they had called her—was standing before him, failing to hide her disdain.

"Come on, then, let's see this amazing power of yours!"

Oh, he'd show her the power. He would fry her, crisp her skin, blacken her bones. She would have just seconds of pain in which to regret her presumption. Then she would die.

No. Keep calm. Wait for your opening. Don't give them the satisfaction. Out loud, he said, "No way, lady. I ain't doing squat for you!"

"Of all the—!" Marcy, like Dillon, controlled herself with effort. "Can't you see we're doing this for your benefit?"

"All I can see is some would-be big-shot scientist trying to steal what makes me better'n you. And you expect me to roll over and help? What planet did you come down from?"

She glared at him venomously, then swung around in surprise as the door behind her opened. The guards had let in a handsome, athletic black man who was out of breath, sweat beading his forehead.

"Hopkins!" Marcy rounded on the newcomer and launched

into a tirade of recriminations. Dillon smiled to himself. He still felt an urge to cut loose, no matter how futile it would be—but his passive resistance had made his tormentor demonstrably furious, and that consoled him for now. He was winning.

He just had to keep his cool.

Peter was searching for a lost pen beneath his desk, when the voice came from behind him. "Excuse me, is this the amazing Spider-Man's cubicle? I have a delivery."

He started, banged his head, and cried out. He looked up, to see that Debra Whitman's face was a picture of contrition. "Oh, Peter! I'm sorry, I thought you were Steve. We had a, uhm, little joke about spiders before. I didn't mean to startle you."

"Don't worry," said Pete ruefully. "I did the same to you the first time we met, remember?" Debra giggled, and Pete turned his attention to the object she had wheeled in on a frame. "Now, I wonder what Steve wants with a full-size plastic skeleton?"

"It's a visual aid for a lecture he's taking," said Debra, "something about electrochemical reactions within the human body."

"Yeah, sure—only, knowing Steve, it'll be hanging from the doorframe by the end of the week."

"You're probably right," agreed Debra. "Well, I'm finished for today. I'll see you this evening, yes?"

"Oh." Pete's face fell. "I'm sorry, Debs, I can't make our date. I've . . . got an assignment from the *Globe*." It sounded lame, even to him—and Debra was clearly upset, although she tried to hide it.

"Another time, maybe?"

"Maybe. I mean, yes. Yes, *definitely* another time. Sorry, Debs, if I could get out of this—"

"You don't have to explain, Peter. I know you're a busy man. You must have better things to do than keep me company."

"I don't!" protested Pete, almost falling over his words.

"So it's just that you don't want to see me. I understand."

"No. I mean, yes. I mean—look, Debs, I'll make this up to you, I promise. It's just that the *Globe* wants photos and Marcy might need my help—with Electro, you know?"

"Don't worry about it, Peter. I could do with a night in. Really. On my own."

Pete felt like a heel as Debra left the office quietly. He would make it up to her, he swore to himself. He had let that poor woman down too often. His one consolation was that he hadn't had to lie to her this time.

Marcy might well need the type of help that only he could give.

"What are you talking about, 'replaced'?"

Marcy Kane folded her arms stubbornly. "Which syllable didn't you understand, Hopkins? You're late, so you're history."

Steve could feel his face burning from embarrassment, anger, and his recent sprint in equal measure. "I've put a lot of work into this," he reminded her, hefting his collection of notes and textbooks. "I thought you wanted my help."

"I wanted your mind," retorted Marcy. "I was forgetting how rarely you make use of it. Now, get out!"

"Not before we've discussed this!"

But Marcy had turned her back. Her fists were clenched and her shoulders trembled with pent-up frustration.

Philip moved in to play peacemaker. "Best leave it, Steve. She's wound up because Dillon won't cooperate."

"Yeah, I could see from her notes how that might be a problem." Steve glared at the back of Marcy's head. "I was working on it."

She turned at that, but ignored him and addressed Philip icily. "Do you think we could get on with it now?"

Phil shrugged apologetically and rejoined Marcy at the instrument bank. Steve watched them, face set into a scowl. When he looked away, he saw that Dillon had been observing him in turn, and smirking. He felt humiliated—but then a plan formed, and a smile tugged at his mouth. *What was it those reports said about Electro's ego?*

He glanced at the captive criminal and clicked his fingers in mock recognition. "Hey, you're that Living Battery guy, aren't you?"

"*Electro*, you jerk!"

"Of course. I almost didn't know you without the starfish mask—or without some super hero cleaning your clock."

Dillon seethed. "If I wasn't held down—"

"You'd do what? Come off it, Max, you've had more defeats than Dick Dastardly! How was it they caught you this time? No, don't tell me, I remember: Reed Richards tied you up with a rubber fire hose!''

"Just watch your step, wise guy!''

From the corner of his eye, Steve saw Marcy's frown of disapproval. She didn't move to stop him, though. A faint electrical corona was fizzing around Max Dillon's body. Steve's plan was working—and, more importantly, he was enjoying it.

"Remember that time when Spidey doused you with water and put your powers on the fritz? Or when he tied your hands and feet together and short-circuited you? You're a real class act, Electro. It takes a lot of effort to bring you down!''

"I'll find out where you live, punk! You'll get a thousand-volt surprise when you least expect it!''

Steve affected a carefree laugh. "Don't try it, Max. I've got a big jug of water at home, and I'm not afraid to use it.''

Electro screamed, and suddenly Steve was blinded by a flash of intense light. Something hit him and propelled him across the lab. He blinked stars out of his vision, frantic thoughts racing through his mind: *Electro's free, he's using his powers, he'll kill me!*

But Dillon was still confined to his pallet, sparks flying in all directions as he unleashed his incoherent fury. Phil was on the floor with Steve, having hurled him out of the imagined danger zone. He needn't have bothered. The equipment was performing handsomely, forestalling anything more than a harmless light show.

Steve was well satisfied. "So, Marcy? Got what you wanted?''

Marcy Kane's attention was reserved for her monitors, and for the precious data now displayed upon them. "One day, that sense of humor will land you in serious trouble,'' she grumbled. "But it did the job, I suppose.'' Steve grinned. From her, that was a high compliment.

"Philip,'' she called, "pick yourself up and get over here. I need you to take down some readings.''

Phil gave Steve a resigned look, then did as he was bade. Steve sighed. He shouldn't have expected Marcy to change her mind, of course. She wasn't like that. Still, he was proud of his day's work.

He left his colleagues to their research—and Max Dillon to his impotent tantrum—and headed across the campus to the main building, whistling cheerfully.

· · ·

The evening was drawing in, and Spider-Man shivered under his thin costume. *Typical,* he thought. *I could be out with Debra, catching up with my essays or looking for a photo opportunity—so where am I instead? I'm hanging upside down in a wet tree, staring at the outside of a laboratory building in case a supercharged criminal gets past his guards and spoils for a fight. Boy, Donahue could get a whole series out of my psychoses!*

Flexing his weary muscles, he dropped to the ground with an impressive somersault, scaring the daylights out of a late-working preppie who happened to be passing. *Oh, great! "SPIDER-MENACE STALKS CAMPUS." Why don't I just phone Jameson and give him the headline myself?* He gazed up at the shuttered windows of the lab again, but there was no sign of anything untoward. Presumably, Marcy's precautions were still working as planned. There was no need for him to have put on his rubber gloves and stood guard.

No point in prowling around here like a caged animal, waiting for the worst to happen.

He would go back to his cubicle, that's what he would do. He would get on with some work, knowing that in the unlikely event of a disaster, he'd still be nearby. *Yeah, that's the ticket. Catch up with your studies and do the hero thing at the same time. I might even get some pictures for Bushkin, if Marcy's in a better mood when she finally finishes up. So that's three problems solved. Now all I have to do is find some way of dating Debra and visiting Aunt May, too, and I might just start to get my head above water.*

Still lost in thought, he slipped into the bushes and retrieved his clothing from a web-pack. *What I need,* he considered as he began to change, *is a clone or two. That'd make things a lot simpler.*

Peter was still pondering the tribulations of his life as he pushed open the office door and his spider-sense rang out. A figure dropped from above and he sprang aside, instinctively. He crouched, alert for a second attack—then sighed as he registered the presence of Steve's skeleton, lying in a heap where he had just been.

"Oh, classy joke, Steve! Like there's a single person within three states of here who wouldn't have guessed you were gonna try that!"

"Is that you, Pete?"

The voice was muffled and more distant than it should have been. It took Pete a moment to locate its owner. Steve was in Phil Chang's cubicle, lying beneath his desk, and it didn't take a genius to deduce that another prank was in the offing. *I don't want to know,* he decided. He sat at his desk and pulled over a stack of papers.

Steve's voice drifted relentlessly from beyond the partition. "Don't you want to hear what I'm doing?"

"Not especially."

"This'll give Teacher's Pet something to think about," Steve chuckled, ignoring that expression of disinterest.

Peter had heard about the altercation at the lab. "That's not fair, Steve. It isn't Phil's fault that Marcy froze you out."

"Come off it, Pete. I'm well aware that Ms. Kane needs no help in the freezer department."

"So what's with the revenge kick?"

"Who mentioned revenge? I had some unexpected free time and I've thought of a new way of driving a good friend stark raving bonkers, that's all."

Peter shook his head, but felt a smile forming despite his best efforts. Steve's jokes were an accepted consequence of working in the department, although sometimes they went too far. "And what's your latest big idea, then? Drawing pins under the table? Sticky tape on his chair? Whoopee cushion?"

"Much bigger."

"Two whoopee cushions? No, let me guess, something even more sophisticated: fake doodoo on the carpet! Am I warm?"

"By the time I've finished, he won't know if he's coming or going."

"You've swapped the refills in his black and red pens again?"

"Nope." Steve's beaming face appeared at the top of the divide. "I've crosswired everything in his cubicle."

"You've what?"

"When he turns on his desk lamp, he'll activate the radio. When he tries to use the fan, he'll operate the heating instead. And, while he's still trying to work out why his printer won't come on—" he waved two slices of bread triumphantly. "—he'll get toast!"

Peter opened his mouth to say something, but Steve had disappeared again. "Stand by for testing. You coming over to watch this?"

The realization crashed into Peter's mind with devastating force. He recalled that Steve had not been present during Marcy's briefing; he didn't know that she was drawing electricity from outside the laboratory. The main building's power supply was already being taxed, and if Steve was putting more strain on it, the results could be unthinkable.

He was out of his seat and yelling in a second. He skidded into Phil's cubicle and reached out to prevent a tragedy. The penny hadn't dropped yet, and Steve was grinning at him in triumph. His finger was on the master switch for the power points to which the sabotaged appliances were connected.

"Steve, no!" The moment seemed to freeze. Not long enough. The warning came just fractionally too late. Pete hurled himself across the room. But Steve had thrown the switch.

The lights went out.

Max Dillon breathed deeply and clenched his fists until his fingernails made his palms bleed. He tried to ignore the hollow pain that gnawed at his insides. Every few minutes, he let out a cathartic scream and released what little power he had been able to build up. He knew that he was sating Marcy Kane's scientific thirst, but he no longer cared. All he could think of was revenge, but with each passing moment, his hopes of escape grew slimmer.

He closed his eyes and felt hot tears welling onto his cheeks. He was hurt and humiliated and somebody was going to pay!

The opportunity, when it came, lasted for but a second. It was long enough. The fluorescent tube above him clicked off, and Dillon was suddenly, shockingly aware that the unattainable reservoir of power that confined him had gone. Free to act, but still exhausted and drained, he reached out with his mind. He sensed the charges of static electricity that clung to the particles in the air, and he drew them into himself. With practised ease, he converted the accumulated voltage into a usable form and released it, melting the wires that bound him.

He felt the lab's emergency generators kicking in; the lighting was restored. The student woman and her assistant had only just begun to panic, and the guards were still bringing up their weapons. Dillon's first thought was to fake them out, to make them think he was still their prisoner until he had had time to replenish his energy levels. But the uncontrollable lunatic grin stretched across his face precluded any such deception. They knew the truth, but their sublime expressions of horror convinced him that that was not such a bad thing after all.

Why hide the fact? Electro was free—and, soon enough, the whole world was going to know about it.

"Peter?"

Steve stumbled through the darkness and cursed as he hit his knee on Philip's desk. He still couldn't believe what had happened. He had checked and rechecked his wiring. He hadn't been putting *that* much demand on the system, had he? Certainly not enough to trip the fuses.

"Pete? You there, pal? I don't know what's happened, but— look, stay still. I'll try and get some light in here."

There was no response, and the silence made Steve feel lonely. His eyes were beginning to adjust to the darkness, and he picked his way across the office without further incident. He pulled back the blinds and allowed the early moonlight to illuminate the room.

The blackout couldn't have been his doing. Its timing had to be a coincidence. He only needed to convince himself of that fact.

He turned from the window, hoping to beg some moral support from his best friend at ESU. But, somehow, Peter had vanished.

Cold air rushed into Spider-Man's face and numbed his senses. His heart ached with the familiar misery of a disastrous stroke of luck; one that would more than likely catapult him into a desperate situation. He gritted his teeth and prayed that his worries were unfounded. He shot out another web-line and launched himself into a graceful arc, shrugging his shirt—the final remnant of his hastily discarded civilian clothing—into a convenient bush below.

The lab's power supply would only have been interrupted momentarily. Emergency backup generators would have kicked in almost instantly. But *almost* wasn't good enough; not where Electro was concerned.

As Spider-Man dropped to the ground, his worst fears were realized. An alarm bell was ringing and his nose wrinkled at the smell of burnt ozone. He paused, suspecting an ambush, but his spider-sense was silent. He entered the building at a run, his eyes adjusting quickly to the gloom inside. He was greeted by a gut-wrenching scene of devastation. The pallet on which Max Dillon had lain was distorted and blackened. A circular hole had been burnt through it. A wisp of smoke curled upward from Marcy Kane's monitoring equipment, betraying the fatal overload that had destroyed it.

Worst of all, six bodies were strewn about the floor, unmoving, twisted in pain.

Spidey stifled a heartfelt cry of despair. His powerful leg muscles propelled him across the room, to where Marcy and Philip lay entangled with each other. To his relief, they were still breathing. Even as he checked Phil's pulse, Marcy groaned and began to stir.

"That's it, Ma—er, miss," he urged her, gently rolling Phil's body aside and helping Marcy into a sitting position. "You've had a shock, that's all. How are you feeling?"

She blinked, and tried to focus upon him. Her face was pale and her blonde hair singed, but her breathing was steady enough and she didn't seem to be in pain. "H-how's Philip?"

"He's out, but he'll be fine."

"It happened so fast," recalled Marcy, her voice faint. "Dillon broke free. He went berserk, hurling bolts everywhere. I thought we were dead. Philip got between me and him, and took the brunt of it." She smiled weakly. "Thank heavens you're here."

It occurred to Spidey, not for the first time, that Marcy's hard front and barbed comments disguised a very attractive woman. At times like this, when the front had disintegrated, her beauty was hard to ignore. Of course, she didn't have the time of day for Peter Parker. It was an unusual turnaround for Peter to find somebody who thought more of his costumed self than of him. *It's probably too much to ask that someone should like both of us!* he thought wryly.

"Listen," he said, "did Electro say anything? Any clues about where he might be headed?"

Marcy shook her head. "He just ranted about being noticed, about being a big man."

Spidey scowled. "That's par for the course with Dillon. But if he only stunned you, it's probably because he's not up to full strength yet. That gives us time. Look, miss, I know you're shaken, but I need your help. Can you get to a phone and call an ambulance for your friend and the guards?"

She nodded spiritedly, already climbing to her feet. "No problem. Just give me a minute, I'm feeling a bit wobbly."

Spidey gave her an encouraging smile, although she couldn't see it through his mask. He knew that Marcy was more than capable of handling things here until campus security arrived. He had more pressing business.

"I'm going to find Electro," he muttered as he headed for the door, "before he really does kill somebody."

Max Dillon flung himself against the wall as a patrol of booted security men stomped by. He fingered the gun he had taken from one of the guards at the lab. He was itching to use it, but he couldn't afford to attract attention. He was tired and weak, and it would be some time before his body could fully recharge. He was shaking and drenched in sweat, which didn't help much.

He picked his moment, then dashed out of the shadows and across to the front of the university's main building. To his dismay, somebody saw him. A gruff voice yelled out, "Hey!" and he could hear footsteps again. He didn't bother to stop and look. He barreled through the entrance doors and pelted down darkened corridors, negotiating junctions at random. It galled him to flee like this, but he had no choice for now. He needed time.

He came up short as he rounded the next corner, heart sinking as he made out the silhouetted figure of a man, dead ahead. He brought up the gun, his finger poised on the trigger.

"Hello?" said the silhouette nervously. "Is somebody there?"

It wasn't a guard, Dillon realized. Just somebody lost in the darkness: a student, maybe, or a lecturer working late.

"Hey, pal, say something," the stranger called. "You're not helping my nerves with the silent act, you know." He stepped forward into a pool of moonlight, cast from a window.

And, to his surprise, Max Dillon recognized him.

"You! The Hopkins boy!" The student jerked to a halt. He

knew that he was in trouble, if not the reason why yet. Dillon smiled grimly and moved closer, the gun trained on his head. "I told you I'd come looking for you, didn't I? I told you that nobody mocks Electro and lives!" Hopkins knew the worst of it now, and he reacted with appropriate horror. He raised his hands, as if that could help him.

Dillon began to squeeze the trigger, slowly. This was to be his first act of vengeance: the first humiliation wiped out, the first tormentor punished, the first example made. The first of many.

He was going to enjoy this.

Then a booming voice interrupted his moment of pleasure. It came from outside, and he recognized the distorting and amplifying effect of a police megaphone. "We know where you are, Dillon. You were seen entering the building. All exits are covered by armed officers. Come out with your hands up. Make no attempt to use your powers."

Spider-Man had guessed wrong. He had wasted time searching nearby streets in the hope of spotting Electro as he fled. Instead, as the wailing sirens of arriving police cars told him, the villain had gone to ground on campus. Spidey set a new record for web-slinging as he dashed back to the main building, noting as he passed that medics had arrived to take care of those injured during the escape. Philip and the guards were entering the ambulance under their own steam, which was good news. Of Marcy, there was no sign. He might have guessed where she would be.

The police had cordoned off the area around the main building, but Marcy was among the spectators who had congregated beyond the yellow tape barrier. Spidey also recognized his old friend Curt Connors, who had no doubt been burning the midnight oil when chaos struck. He nodded an acknowledgment to him, then set about finding the police lieutenant in charge of the operation, a bald black man named Billinghurst.

"I take it from the reception that Electro's in there?" he said.

"One of the guards saw him going in," Billinghurst confirmed, "and we got the place surrounded as soon as we could."

"Any hostages?"

"Not that we know of, but it's possible. A few people were working late."

Spidey nodded. It felt weird to be working with the authorities, so soon after his acquittal of long-standing murder charges. "I'm going in there," he announced. Billinghurst opened his mouth to protest, but Spidey cut him off. "Electro's weak right now—but the longer we wait, the more power he'll have. He's gone into hiding because he can't afford a confrontation. Our best bet is to hit him hard and fast, and the best person to do that is me."

The lieutenant thought about that for a few seconds before reluctantly assenting. "You've got ten minutes."

Spidey pulled on his rubber gloves again and clambered over the tape. As he did so, a familiar voice distracted him. He turned to see Debra Whitman, approaching Marcy with a worried expression. "Oh, thank goodness I've found you. Where's Peter? I can't find him. Has something happened?"

Marcy calmed her with an effort. "I haven't seen Peter all evening. I thought he went home hours ago."

"But—but he said he was staying on campus with you. That's why I came here. I thought I could . . ." Debra tailed off, her face betraying her dawning disillusionment.

Oh, wonderful, thought Spidey bitterly. *That's just the morale booster I needed right now.* He leapt up the steps to the main entrance doors and threw them open. "Okay, Electro," he growled out loud, "you've just succeeded in ruining my whole day. Now I get to return the favor!"

"Hey, man," Steve bleated as he was hurled to the floor of the Department of Graduate Studies, "I didn't mean anything by what I said before. I was just upset, you know?"

"Can it, punk," snarled Dillon, "before you start to upset me!" He moved to the window and cautiously checked the situation outside. "You might be useful as a hostage—but one more word and I'll take my chances without you!"

Steve believed him—just as he believed that, once his usefulness was over, Dillon would kill him anyway. He was lucky to have survived thus far; it was only the well-timed police ultimatum that had given Electro a reason to spare him.

He eyed the door longingly, but didn't imagine for a second that he would be able to reach it. He couldn't hope to outrun a bullet. Anyway, Electro's attention was back upon him. His tone was resentful, and his words seemed to be for his own benefit more than Steve's.

"All my life, I've been put down by jerks like you. Well, that's gonna change. I've had a few bad breaks, but I've got power and that's what matters. Insulting me just became a capital offense—and you'll be the first to die for it!"

"Hey, Dillon!" came a voice from the doorway. "I've seen prettier faces than yours on the back ends of horses!" Then, with mock regret: "Oh, you just said not to do that, right?"

"Spider-Man!" Electro spat the name before Steve could even identify the speaker through the darkness. His gun arm snapped up and he let three bullets loose. The newcomer avoided them as if he had somehow predicted their flight paths. It took Steve an instant too long to realize what the villain's next move would be.

Spider-Man sprang across the room, but came up short as Electro slipped an arm around Steve's throat and hauled him to his feet. The cold round muzzle of the gun imprinted its shape upon his temple, and Steve could feel himself sweating.

"One step closer, bug, and I'll put a bullet through Smart-Mouth's brain!"

"You must be feeling pretty weak if you can't muster the voltage to hurt a defenseless student," Spidey taunted. "If you're not careful, you'll get yourself drummed out of the super-villains' union. I mean, even the Shocker doesn't carry a gun!"

Steve felt Electro bridle at this latest assault upon his fragile ego. With a low hiss, he turned the revolver on Spidey once more—and as soon as Steve was out of immediate danger, two silky strands of webbing shot across the room. The weapon was yanked from Dillon's hand and Steve was pulled to safety, and into an undignified sprawl on the floor.

Spider-Man followed through with a leap, but Electro reacted faster than he had anticipated. He brought up both hands and unleashed a shower of sparks that caught his attacker in midair. Spidey yelled in pain and crash-dived.

"I'm more charged up than you thought!" Electro boasted. He stood astride his fallen enemy and clenched his fists, knuckles pointed downward, as he prepared to deliver the killing blow. Steve wanted to do something, but fear kept him paralyzed. "You're no match for even half my powers!"

Steve blinked involuntarily as the blast illuminated the office. He offered up a desperate prayer—and then, his vision cleared and he saw that Spider-Man had leapt out of harm's way, performed an amazing handspring, and even managed to aim an upward kick at Electro's jaw. The villain pulled back, but took a glancing blow that left him stunned. "Guess again," said Spidey. "I've had bigger shocks from static-charged door handles!" Despite his jocular manner, he had clearly been shaken and was in no shape to press his advantage. Both combatants retrenched and locked glares, each waiting for the other to make his next move.

Electro acted first. He released a series of bolts, like indoor lightning, which Spider-Man was hard pressed to avoid for all his agility. Feeling suddenly exposed, Steve found the strength to drag himself behind a nearby filing cabinet for shelter.

"You can't keep this up all day!" Electro threatened.

"Who needs to? You're no strongman, Dillon. You'll run out of sparks soon, and then all it'll take is one good punch to lay you out. Why not save yourself the broken jaw and give up?"

A renewed barrage of lightning was Electro's immediate answer. "I'm drawing power from all around me, insect. You'll fry before I run out of juice!"

"How many times do I have to say it?" groaned Spidey. "It's *arachnid*, not *insect*. Boy, it makes me so mad when you guys won't even listen."

And, at that, he leapt into Philip Chang's cubicle and didn't emerge again. Steve held his breath. Had the web-slinger been hit? In the confusion, he couldn't be sure.

Electro wasn't sure either, and he was taking no chances. He powered down and leaned against the wall for support, breathing heavily. But Steve could see the glint of alertness in his eyes, as he watched for the first sign of a trick. Several tense minutes passed before he slowly, carefully, made his way toward the cubicle.

And something flew at his face.

Electro reacted instantly, subjecting the flying object to a critical blast. Steve barely had time to recognize that the melted, misshapen lump that fell to the ground had once been a harmless pen—for, suddenly, Spider-Man was taking advantage of his foe's distraction and tackling him around the midriff. They flew across the room together and hit the cabinet behind which Steve hid. He was hammered back into the wall, and he suppressed a squeal at this latest mistreatment.

For a second, he thought that Spidey's ploy had ended the battle. He was wrong. Electro had gained the upper hand again: he had managed to seize the web-slinger's wrists, beneath his rubber gloves, and he was channelling power into Spider-Man's defenseless, grounded body.

Spidey resisted valiantly. He dragged Electro across the room, but the villain wasn't about to release his grip. They circled together for a long minute, locked into a macabre death dance, until Spidey's knees buckled at last and he sagged to the floor, his pain-wracked body writhing and his costume charring. Electro kept up the lethal punishment.

"I've waited years for this, bug! I might need a recharge, but I've still got enough voltage to microwave your insides!"

That horrific image galvanized Steve into action. One part of his mind was still screaming that he could do nothing, but another, stronger instinct was insisting that he had to try. He couldn't simply watch as Spider-Man died.

"One good punch," Spidey said—and Steve's research had told him that Max Dillon had only normal human strength and stamina. Right now, he also had his back to Steve. If ever there was a cast-iron opportunity, this was it.

He only needed to throw one good punch.

He was out of hiding and standing behind Electro before he could even think his course of action through. Belated doubts assailed him and froze him into position. *What if one punch isn't good enough? If I screw this up, I'll be dead before I get a second chance! And, anyway, I can't touch him without getting a shock. Surely Spider-Man can handle this. He's always won before. He'll break free and he'll wipe the floor with Dillon. I don't have to risk my stupid life!*

Time seemed to stretch forever, but in truth, the decision was made in a second and without much conscious thought. When Steve thought back to it later, he remembered only a vague imperative to find something nonconductive; something he could use as a cudgel. And he remembered finding it, and lifting the awkward shape as high above his head as he could manage.

Steve Hopkins brought the makeshift weapon down hard against the base of Electro's neck. And, just like that, it was all over.

•   •   •

Forty minutes later, Peter Parker stood in the cold moonlight, feeling like a potboiled lobster and hoping that no one would notice the red coloration of his skin. The police were still present, although Electro had been rewrapped and carted off to Ryker's Island. The crowd of spectators had grown and several news teams had now arrived, including—to Pete's chagrin—the *Daily Globe*'s own April Maye. She had expressed surprise at finding him here, and had made it clear that she had brought her own photographer. "You may as well leave that camera in its case," she had said.

So, Pete thought, *I got no college work done, no pictures taken, and Debra isn't talking to me. Again. Apart from that, the day went fine!*

He had company in his misery. "I'm sorry it went sour for you," he sympathized with a down-mouthed Marcy Kane, as she appeared at his side.

She shrugged and tried to pretend it didn't matter. "I got some good results before Dillon escaped. Enough to finish my paper, anyway."

"That's something."

"At least somebody's happy," said Marcy. Pete followed her gaze to where Steve Hopkins was being interviewed by an eager pack of media hounds. He glowed with exuberant pride as he posed for photographs with a not unfamiliar plastic skeleton, now back on its frame.

"Electro's not so tough as people think," he boasted. "Last time out, he was defeated by a fire hose. I just thought, well, nobody could top that. So that's what I used against him: 'no body'!" He grinned inanely at his own dreadful pun, and planted an affectionate arm around the skeleton's shoulders. A dozen flashbulbs ignited.

Marcy scowled. "He had a lucky escape today," she said. "His clowning around could have gotten him killed. I did hope he might have learned a lesson from it."

"He did," said Pete, "but you know Steve. I think he just unlearned it." He found himself smiling at the thought, although he wasn't quite sure why.

The funny thing was that, when he later recalled the scene,

he could have sworn that Marcy Kane had smiled along with him. But then, he told himself, it had been dark and he had been exhausted, distracted, and hurt.

Perhaps he had imagined it.

ARMS AND THE MAN

Keith R.A. DeCandido

Illustration by Grant Miehm & Jeff Albrecht

As I look back on my life, I have to say that the dumbest thing I ever did was tell my editor that I wanted my next book to be on Dr. Otto Octavius, aka the super-villain Dr. Octopus.

Said editor, a charming British woman named Kathryn Elisabeth Huck, stared at me from across the table in the nice midtown Manhattan restaurant and said calmly, "It's happened, hasn't it? You've lost your bloody mind."

I smiled as I sipped my mineral water. "C'mon, Kath, you know I lost my mind years ago, otherwise I wouldn't have tried to make a living as a writer."

I had just turned in my biography of Tony Stark, the fifth in a series of celebrity life stories I'd written in the past few years. The contract called for six books, and Kathryn and I were discussing the subject of the final bio over lunch.

"Yes, but—why him?"

"Why not?"

She glared at me for a moment, took a bite of her steak (probably as a cover while collecting her thoughts), then said, "Because he's a thief, a cop-killer, and a bloody lunatic. Why would anyone want to do a biography of that?"

Grinning, I said, "Because he's a thief, a cop-killer, and a bloody lunatic."

"Who just tried to murder five million people."

"And was captured by Spider-Man," I added. "Which means he's in Ryker's Island prison, which is why this is the ideal time. He's easy to track down for an interview. If he were at large, I'd never consider it."

Kathryn glowered at me. "Don't be ridiculous, of course you would. I've seen that look on your face before—once you've got a stupid idea in your head, you can't get it out with a crowbar." She took another bite of steak. "You realize that I have to run it by Blake first, yes?"

"Yes. And I also realize that if you're behind it, then Blake will sign off on it. He trusts your judgment."

She muttered, "Right now, I'm having trouble understanding why." She sighed. "All right, then. I've a meeting with Blake tomorrow morning. I'll tell him that you want your final bio to be of Dr. Octopus."

"No no no," I said, "not just Dr. Octopus. Otto Octavius. He was a respected scientist before he got his extra arms and went cuckoo. People talk about Doc Ock all the time. I want to let everyone know who Otto Octavius is.''

The next day, Kathryn called me with the official okay, and also with the welcome news that my payment for turning in the Stark book was being processed. This meant two things: I could pay off my hemorrhaging credit-card bill, and I could start to work on *Requiem for an Octopus: The Life of Dr. Otto Octavius.*

Okay, so I stole the title from Rod Serling. It's not like they'll use it. Kathryn didn't use my titles on any of the other five, why would she here?

Randall Andros's Guide to Writing a Biography Step #1: Research. I spent a week in the New York Public Library digging up everything I could. I had two piles: copies of articles and monographs on Otto Octavius and copies of same on Dr. Octopus. The first pile mostly came from material in the library's Science and Technology Division. The second pile was a lot bigger.

Octavius came to public prominence when he worked at the United States Atomic Research Center, specifically for his development of a set of robotic arms. Four titanium-alloy tentacles with pincers at the end, able to extend from six feet to twenty-four feet, connected to a harness worn around the waist. The harness contained the controls for the arms as well. The tentacles' original purpose was to allow him to manipulate radioactive material from a safe distance.

After an explosion during one of his experiments, the arms were fused to Octavius, both physically and mentally. He didn't need the manual controls anymore, and the arms were now permanently attached to his waist—or so everyone thought. During one of his prison stays, the arms were separated from his body (the details of the procedure were never revealed to the public, which meant I'd have to do some digging). Even so, he retained mental control of the tentacles, even if they were as far as several hundred miles away from him.

In the explosion he apparently suffered some kind of brain damage as well, presumably the root of his subsequent actions: he turned to what old radio dramas used to call ''a life of crime,'' which included robbery, extortion, and murder—most notably of retired NYPD Captain George Stacy.

Most recently, Octavius had obtained some kind of poison and planned to put it in the ink that the New York *Daily Bugle* was printed with, thus killing five million New Yorkers. Spider-Man stopped him, as usual, and he was arrested and sent to Ryker's Island, where he was now awaiting trial.

I didn't read every single thing; I didn't need to yet. This was just to get me started.

Randall Andros's Guide to Writing a Biography Step #2: Talk to family and friends.

This proved more of a challenge. Both of Octavius's parents were dead, and the only other family I could find were a paternal uncle named Karl Octavius, living in Detroit, Michigan, and a maternal cousin named Thomas Hargrove. Karl wasn't listed in the phone book. Given his nephew's notoriety, this hardly came as a surprise. I'd try to track him down later. Hargrove had worked with Octavius at USARC.

As for friends: well, the closest he'd had to friends since becoming "Doc Ock" would be the other criminals he'd formed the "Sinister Six" with. Only one of them was not at large: Adrian Toomes, aka the Vulture. I made an appointment to see him at Ryker's the following week.

That left USARC—source of both the one easily findable family member, and whatever friends he might have made while he worked there. Unfortunately, as I soon discovered by reading through various articles in the library's aforementioned Science and Technology Division, USARC had been shut down by the Department of Energy.

However, tracking down its former employees proved easier than I'd thought; most had landed on their feet in private companies. Sadly, Hargrove was not among those I could find immediately, so that would take a bit more work.

As it happened, two of the people I needed to talk to worked at Cross Technological Enterprises. Brian Huss, who headed up one of USARC's government contracts, now performed a similar function for CTE, and he had brought his assistant, Dinah Dunn, with him to the new job.

"A pleasure to meet you, Mr. Andros," he said as I entered. "I enjoyed your book on Rip Chord."

I blinked in surprise as I shook his hand. He didn't look like the type who listened to heavy metal music. The man stood immensely tall, with short receding black hair, and wore an immaculately tailored suit.

"Thank you very much, Dr. Huss."

"Not at all. Please, have a seat. I understand your next book is on Tony Stark."

As I had a seat, I replied, "Yes, it should be out within six months or so."

"I look forward to it. Always good to read the dirt on your competitors," Huss said with a smile. He sat back down behind his enormous oak desk and said, "But I believe you're here to talk about Otto."

"Yes, he's the subject of the book after Stark. Do you mind if I record the conversation?" I asked, producing a small tape recorder.

"Not at all."

I pressed the PLAY and RECORD buttons, set the recorder on the table, and asked, "How well did you know Dr. Octavius?"

"Not very well. I had my own projects to deal with, so I didn't cross paths with him very often. Mary Alice was the only one who really came close to knowing Otto—and she didn't know him as well as she thought."

This was a new name. "Mary Alice?"

"I'm sorry. Dr. Mary Alice Anders—Burke now, she got married a few months ago. I believe she and Otto dated for a bit, but he broke it off. Rumor has it that he got her fired, actually."

That explained why I didn't recognize the name: her termination had predated the place's being shut down.

"Rumor, Doctor? Surely as a fellow employee . . . ?"

Huss smiled. "As I said, Mr. Andros, Otto and I didn't cross paths much. And if you weren't directly involved with his projects, he didn't acknowledge your existence. Which is too bad—a bit more communication might have prevented the accident that, ah, *damaged* Otto."

Damaged. What a wonderful word for it.

Huss continued: "I can assure you, by the way, that such an accident would never have occurred in *my* section. The Center's safety standards were embarrassing. It's no wonder the place was shut down."

The last thing I wanted to hear was Huss's attempts to distance himself from the company norm. "Can you tell me anything about their relationship?" I asked.

"Not really. I'm afraid that I just didn't know either of them very well. You'd probably be better off talking to some of the other staff members."

"I understand his cousin worked there as well, a Thomas Hargrove?" Huss nodded. "You wouldn't know where I could find him, would you?"

"I'm afraid not. Mr. Hargrove left about a year after the accident. Last I heard he was living in San Francisco, but I have no idea if he's still there." He sighed. "I wish I could be of more help, but most of what I know about Otto I've gotten from news reports on him since he became, ah, more famous—or infamous, I suppose."

I talked to Dunn next. First thing she said when I closed the door to Huss's office behind me was, "Pretentious, isn't he?" Before I could reply, she added, "Lemme guess—he went into the whole such-an-accident-would-never-happen-on-*my*-watch routine, right?"

"Uh, well, he did say something along those lines."

"Figures. Always overcompensating. It's probably 'cause he's so tall."

Not wanting to pursue that line of thought, I prompted, "Did you know Octavius, Ms. Dunn?"

"Call me Dinah. And, yeah, I knew him. In fact, I was the one who started callin' him 'Dr. Octopus.'"

I frowned. "I thought the newspapers came up with that."

"Nah, we were callin' him that long before the accident—right after he made those goofy arms. And lemme tell you somethin' else: The guy was a fruitcake. Always had been."

I took the tape recorder out of my pocket. "Mind saying that for the record?"

"No problem." She waited for me to push PLAY and RECORD, then repeated, "The guy was a fruitcake. The accident just made him a little fruitier. The only one who even liked him was Mary Alice."

"That would be Dr. Mary Alice Burke, née Anders?"

"Uh, yeah. She saw *somethin'* in him. Can't imagine what. Anyhow, he broke up with her and got her canned, and that was it. Nobody else liked him, and he didn't like nobody. Didn't surprise me when he went crazy."

Four days later, I sat in my Upper West Side apartment, going over the three tapes' worth of material I'd recorded at CTE, Stark International, and a few other places where former USARC employees had settled down. I had been hoping to get a clear picture of Otto Octavius before the accident. No such luck.

"He was a good man. Quiet, but, boy, did he know his stuff. The man was on his way to revolutionizing the field of nuclear research before the accident. A tragic waste, that. I keep hoping that they find some way to cure him of that awful insanity. It really changed him—made him into something totally different."

"God, what a scumbucket. I'm sorry, but all the accident did was save him a little manual labor with those stupid arms of his. He was arrogant, condescending, egotistical. He treated everyone like dirt—especially Mary Alice. And she kept coming back for more. It was revolting."

"He had a bit of trouble relating to people, really. You know he lived with his mother up until she died? He dated that Anders woman for a bit, but that was the closest he came to a social life. He had absolutely no clue about interpersonal relationships. To be honest, I think that's why he built the arms—they helped him keep his distance even more."

"People keep saying that the explosion turned him into a criminal, but I'm not sure I buy that. I mean, I've seen footage of him, and he sounds like the same Otto Octavius I had the misfortune to be lab assistant to. And I was one of many—we couldn't stand him. I think he went through five or six lab assistants a year."

"I met his mother once. It was the one time Octavius came to the company picnic, and his mother was his date. Pathetic, huh? Anyhow, she had him wrapped around her little finger. I tell you, with that kind of home life, it's no wonder he turned into a nutcase."

"I never had a problem with the guy. I mean, sure, he was a little arrogant, but look at what he accomplished—I'd say he earned his arrogance."

And on and on. No two people had the same impression of him. None of the articles I'd photocopied about Octavius prior to the accident said anything about his personality either.

Obviously I needed to talk to Mary Alice Burke.

• • •

The next day, I went back to the library and checked all the local phone books. Plenty of Burkes, none of them named Mary Alice, though I found a couple listed as "M. Burke" or "Mary Burke." I didn't know her husband's first name—stupid oversight on my part—so looking for him was out. Realizing I was going about this backward, I checked the periodicals and newspaper indexes for references to her under both her birth name and her married name.

I turned up something faster than expected: Dr. Mary Alice Burke and her husband, Ronald Burke, had been among the victims in a nasty car accident on the West Side Highway a month previous. Mary Alice had survived; Ronald hadn't. She had been taken to St. Luke's near Columbia University. I headed up there, to learn that she'd been admitted for a week, then gone home. I spoke to her doctor, who couldn't give out her number, but who did agree to call her and give her my number.

Since I had to wait for her to call—if she called at all—and since I didn't feel like trying to track down Hargrove or the uncle in Michigan just yet, I decided to jump ahead to Randall Andros's Guide to Writing a Biography Step #3: Talk to the people who saw him last. Spider-Man would be a bit hard to get at, but Octavius's last escapade had been an attack on the *Daily Bugle*. And I got more articles on "the renowned super-criminal Dr. Octopus" from the *Bugle* than from any of the other New York papers. Calls there got me appointments with Editor-in-Chief/ Publisher J. Jonah Jameson, City Editor Joseph Robertson, and several reporters for the following day. I also called my research assistant and had her start tracking down Thomas Hargrove and Karl Octavius. That's what research assistants are *for*, after all.

The reporters I talked to included the paper's two best crime reporters, Ben Urich and Charley Snow, and Jake Conover, who is, in my humble opinion, the *Bugle*'s best columnist. Actually, it was the "Conover's Corner" column that got me reading the *Bugle* in the first place years ago. They all had some interesting insights into Octopus's criminal career, most of which repeated what was already in their articles. Conover, it turned out, did a piece on USARC shortly after Dr. Octopus's first big crime spree that I'd managed to miss in my research. I promised to look it up as I went in for my noon appointment with Jameson.

I had wanted Jameson to be the subject of my third bio. Unfortunately, somebody published an unauthorized bio of him that tanked. Only sold about fifteen percent of its print run, and almost put the publisher out of business. Kathryn told me that there was no way in hell she could convince her sales force to sell a book with subject matter similar to one with eighty-five percent returns. So we scrapped that and did musician Rip Chord instead.

Jameson's office stank of cigar smoke. Given that the man had a lit one in his hand, this wasn't too surprising. He stood behind his desk, holding a mockup of a page from the paper to the light with the hand that didn't hold the cigar. He wore a simple white shirt, dark blue tie, charcoal-gray slacks. A matching gray jacket hung loosely on his chair. His assistant—an understandably harried-looking woman named Glory Grant—indicated the guest chair and bolted.

"Who the hell're you?" he asked me without looking away from the mockup.

"Randall Andros, Mr. Jameson, I had an appointm—"

"Oh, right, right, you're writing a biography of Dr. Octopus."

"Yes, I was wondering—"

Jameson put the mockup down and started pacing. "Nutty as a fruitcake, that one. As big a menace as Spider-Man."

"Do you mind if I record this conversation?"

"Not at all," Jameson said with a dismissive gesture—though he had yet to actually look at me. "My entire life is on the record."

As he paused to suck on his cigar, I got the recorder going. "Spider-Man did just stop Octopus from sabotaging your paper. How does that make Spider-Man as great a—"

"What was Spider-Man doing there in the first place, hm?" Jameson interrupted, still pacing, still not looking at me. "Obviously Octopus beat him to whatever act of sabotage that webbed menace had planned."

"One of the crimes Octopus has been charged with is the murder of George Stacy. Now, you accused Spider-Man of that murder, and—"

"And printed a retraction when evidence came to light that Octopus was responsible. According to the reports of eyewitnesses and the evidence that had been made available to the press *at the time*, Spider-Man looked guilty. Of course, if not for Spider-Man, Stacy wouldn't have been in any danger in the first place. And that's the main problem: Spider-Man.''

"I beg your par—''

"Every time Octopus is around, there's Spider-Man. And whatever crazy thing they've got going is personal—but it's always innocents who get hurt. Innocents like George Stacy and Peter Parker.''

"Peter Parker?'' I prompted, not recognizing the name.

"One of my photographers. He dressed up like Spider-Man one time to try to stop Octopus. Nearly got himself killed. Octopus kidnapped my secretary at the time, Betty Brant, and said to get a message to Spider-Man to come rescue her—and I could bring one photographer to record it. I sent Parker, and he went in a Spider-Man suit. He and Miss Brant were apparently dating at the time. Teenagers.''

I quickly made a note to track down this Parker person, then said, "I'm curious what you think of Octavius himself. He—''

"I told you, nutty as a fruitcake. That explosion did something to his head—the doctors said so right afterward. Besides, only a lunatic would do what he did.'' Finally, he turned to look at me. "Do you know that he had no ransom demands when he threatened the *Bugle*? No 'or else'? He told the mayor that he'd kill five million people—and then *after that*, he'd request some ridiculous amount of money. No matter what happened, he intended to murder all those people. That falls into my definition of the word *lunatic*. Of course, Spider-Man doesn't even have *that* excuse. Why . . .''

Jameson went on another spider-rant, which I ignored. Something had clicked in my head when he mentioned the doctors.

He was interrupted by someone coming in with a question about the evening edition. I'd gotten everything I was likely to get out of him on the subject, so I let him continue with the business of running the *Bugle*. I needed to check something. I still had an hour and a half before my meeting with Robertson—not enough time to schlep back home from midtown, but I was in the building with the *Daily Bugle* morgue.

Sucking up to Conover turned out to be useful. Mind you, I was sincere in my sucking up, but that didn't mean I wouldn't take advantage of it. The columnist vouched for me to the guy who ran the morgue, and I dug up the articles on Octavius from right after the accident.

He'd been treated at the Bliss Private Hospital near USARC by a brain specialist named Kevin Hunt, who gave a press conference while Octavius was still in a coma following the explosion. He stated in no uncertain terms that Octavius had suffered brain damage. Dr. Hunt and some other members of the hospital staff were subsequently kidnapped by Octavius, who had them gather various materials for him to work with. Spider-Man stopped him—the first time the pair of them met, but by no means the last—and Octavius went to jail—his first sentence, but by no means *his* last. Hunt had been quite sure of himself then.

But only three weeks ago, Hunt was interviewed on a local news program right after Octavius's most recent capture, and he hedged a good deal more about the apparent brain damage.

Okay, the next step: Find Dr. Kevin Hunt.

Well, not quite the next step. First I had my appointment with Joe Robertson. The *Bugle*'s city editor made for a more pleasant interview than his boss—for one thing, he actually let me finish my sentences. He didn't have much to say about Octavius, but he had been very close friends with George Stacy. Robertson's memories of that friendship would provide useful background on Octavius's most famous murder.

As I was leaving Robertson's office, Ben Urich called me over and introduced me to Phil Sheldon. I recognized the name and face as belonging to the one-eyed photographer responsible for the coffee-table book of super hero photographs *Marvels*. He freelanced for both the *Bugle* and their chief competitor, the *Daily Globe*. He looked older in person than he did in his author's photo, though of course I didn't say so, remembering how misleading my own author's photo was.

Sheldon, as it turned out, had interviewed Octavius shortly after Stacy's death. "It was pretty frightening," he said to me. "Everyone always blithely talks about how nuts he is, but the man I talked to was almost frighteningly sane. Cruel, certainly, and unpleasant, but he was fully aware of his surroundings and had all his wits about him. I've seen crazy people up close—Dr. Octopus doesn't fit the bill in my book."

•   •   •

Dr. Kevin Hunt worked at the Empire State University Medical Center these days. A pleasant-looking man with brown hair and a moustache, he gladly agreed to an interview. The first thing I asked him about was the seeming discrepency between his initial press conference after the accident and his statements of three weeks previous.

"Yes, I guess that would seem odd to someone who compared them. The fact is, Mr. Andros, that we know a good deal more about the effects of radiation now than we did then. Dr. Octopus had his, ah, accident when the field of paranormal research was at its embryonic stages. The work that Reed Richards and Henry Pym have done in this field has been invaluable, as well as the genetics work of Charles Xavier and Bolivar Trask."

Great. A name-dropper. "So if what you saw wasn't brain damage, what was it?"

"I'm not saying it wasn't brain damage, simply that I can't be one hundred percent sure of my diagnosis." Hunt hesitated. "The human nervous system isn't accustomed to dealing with a body part like Dr. Octopus's tentacles. We tend to move around with muscles and joints. The tongue is the only real body part that doesn't follow that rule—except for Dr. Octopus, who also manipulates four metal tentacles with as much dexterity as he does the arms he was born with, if not more. I think that, while it could have been brain damage, it could also have simply been his cranial chemistry rewriting itself to accomodate these four new limbs."

I frowned. "This puts a different spin on his subsequent actions."

"It might. I spoke dismissively a moment ago, observing how, back then, the study of radiation's paranormal effects was only in its embryonic stages. But I'm afraid it's not all that much better now. So many of what we believed to be hard-and-fast natural laws have been thrown out the window in the past few years, it's difficult to be sure of anything."

I didn't like the way this was all going, so I decided to get back to Step #2 and talk to family. My assistant had found both Thomas Hargrove and Karl Octavius.

Hargrove had indeed moved to San Francisco after leaving USARC, as Huss indicated, but now lived in Washington, working as a consultant to the Department of Energy. He proved less useful than I'd have hoped, because he had been advised not to speak of the United States Atomic Research Center due to several outstanding lawsuits related to the Center, the DOE shutdown, Octavius, and the explosion.

However, Hargrove was able to talk about Octavius as a child: shy, bookish, overweight, often the target of bullies. Hargrove claimed to be the only member of the family who even tried to get along with Otto, the one who tried to get Otto involved in various activities at family functions. Unfortunately, Otto's mother, Mary, was something of an outcast for having married a construction worker (the Hargroves being prototypical upper-class New England WASPs for the most part), which didn't help Otto any. Neither did Mary's "ridiculous overprotectiveness," as Hargrove put it, which only got worse when her husband died during Otto's first year in college.

While Hargrove wasn't as forthcoming as I would've liked—his inability to speak of his time at USARC meant I couldn't ask him about Mary Alice—he was Deep Throat compared to Karl Octavius. It took three phone calls for the man to even admit he was related to "that scuzzwad." And then, his insights on his brother Torbert, his sister-in-law Mary, and his nephew Otto were limited to the following: "My brother was a fat slob who married a fatter slob and they had a fat slob of a kid who grew up to be a psycho chicken."

Two days before I was to go to Ryker's to talk with both Octavius and the Vulture, I got a phone call from Peter Parker. I had given both Urich and Conover my number, and asked them to pass it on to Parker when he came in next. After setting up my answering machine to record the conversation, I asked him about the incident Jameson had referred to.

Parker laughed. "Yeah, that was one of the more boneheaded stunts I pulled. He'd kidnapped Betty, and I was pretty sweet on her at the time. So I put on a Spidey suit and went after her. Octopus wiped the floor with me. I was never particularly athletic, and on top of that, I was coming down with a flu bug at the time. What can I say, I was young and stupid," he finished with another laugh.

"You've taken a lot of photos of Octavius over the years."

"Yeah, well, you could say I've got the Spider-Man beat, which means I've got a good number of pix of Ock too."

I smiled. "You may be hearing from my publisher about using some of those in the book. What's your impression of Octavius from all these years of taking his picture?"

"Oh, my impressions of him are a bit more personal—y'see, he lived with my aunt for a bit."

I nearly dropped the phone. "I beg your pardon?"

Perhaps realizing how that sounded, Parker amended his comment. "It's not what you think—my aunt took him in as a boarder, thinking him to be just a kindly gentleman looking for a place to stay. He just needed somewhere to lie low for a bit. Poor Aunt May had no idea who he was, but I recognized him right off and put the kibosh on that little scheme of his. I tell you, Mr. Andros, to this day it gives me the creeps to think of what that guy would've done to my aunt if I hadn't ratted him out."

I talked with Parker a bit more, then looked over my notes.

The more I learned, the less I knew. Was he insane or not? What kind of person had he been before the accident? What kind of person had he become afterward? Had he "become" anything, or had he not changed? About the only consistent character attributes from one story to the next were his brains and his arrogance.

Then I noticed something that I hadn't connected up to this point: Mary Octavius had died of a heart attack only three weeks before the accident. In fact, that was a factor in the trial that followed his first little crime spree after the explosion.

Both Hargrove and several of Octavius's coworkers said that Mary had kept a very tight leash on him. Of course, it could simply serve to explain why the accident happened in the first place: grief might have blinded him to a mistake that led to the explosion.

Still, nobody seemed to have a handle on him. The only people who had any chance of knowing him at all well, I hadn't spoken to yet, and except for the Vulture, I wasn't likely to either: the other members of the Sinister Six and Spider-Man. I particularly wanted to talk to Spider-Man—after all, who knows you better than your greatest enemy? But one could hardly look him up in the yellow pages. Unlike the Avengers or the Fantastic Four, he didn't make himself easy to find.

The day before I was to go to Ryker's was the twenty-eighth of June. I remember that because that date has become enshrined in the Andros Annals as "Lawyer Day."

I woke up at my usual time—around noon—and went into my office to see the message light on my answering machine blinking. (I kept the phone and answering machine in the office, located on the other side of the apartment from my bedroom, to avoid being awakened up by calls from people who keep more "traditional" hours than I.)

"This is a message for Randall Athos." A woman's voice, and she said my name like she was misreading it off a piece of paper. *"My name is Clarice Levin, I represent Mary Alice Burke. Could you please give me a call?"* She gave her number.

I had a cup of coffee—I didn't fancy the idea of facing a lawyer without caffeine—then returned the call. After correcting her misreading of my last name, we got down to business.

"May I ask, Mr. Andros, why you wish to speak to my client?"

"I'm writing a biography of Dr. Otto Octavius. I understand the two of them had a relationship, and I'd like to discuss it with her. You can verify this with my editor, Kathryn Huck." I gave her the name of my publisher, Kathryn's number, and the titles of the four extant bios I'd already written as proof.

"Very well. I will verify this information, and then, assuming it's genuine, I'll pass it on to Ms. Burke. I should warn you, though, that I intend to advise her not to speak to you."

I frowned. "May I ask why?" I said, unable to keep the annoyance out of my voice.

Levin obviously picked up on this. "It has nothing to do with you or your work, Mr. Andros. I just fear that her speaking to you for the record would jeopardize the pending lawsuit we have against Dr. Octavius, Mr. Thomas Hargrove, and the U.S. Atomic Research Center for wrongful termination."

"Wait a minute, the Center's been shut down."

"The corporate entity still exists, even if the site is now closed," Levin explained, which was true. "The lawsuit predates their shutdown in any case."

I sighed. "Might it help if I promise only to ask questions

about their personal relationship? The employment practices of the Center aren't really my major concern here—I'm trying to get a handle on Otto Octavius as a human being.''

"Unfortunately, Mr. Andros, the relationship Ms. Burke had with Dr. Octavius is very much germane to our lawsuit. I'm sorry.''

Great. Hargrove's lawyers wouldn't let him talk, and now neither would Mary Alice Burke's.

The next phone call was from a woman named Ruth Ashby, who represented Adrian Toomes. "I'm afraid that I cannot allow you to speak to my client regarding this subject.''

"May I ask why?''

"My client is attempting to rehabilitate himself. He does not wish to speak of his time as the Vulture, nor of the people he associated with during that time. Talking to you could damage his attempts to once again become a member of society.''

What a crock of crud. But there wasn't a helluva lot I could do.

At three, Kathryn called from her office. Without preamble, she said, "Randall, you will drop whatever you are doing, get into a cab, and get yourself into my office immediately.'' Her British accent was even more clipped than usual—she sounded very tense. And she only calls me "Randall" when she's unhappy.

"What's going on, Kath?''

"There is a young man named Alan Schechter cooling his heels in the conference room. He is Otto Octavius's lawyer. He wishes to discuss your book. I said I wanted you present, and said you'd be here in twenty minutes. So kindly stop asking stupid questions and *get down here*.''

I got down there. Schechter looked about like you'd expect a lawyer to look: short hair, glasses, expensive suit, pickle up his butt.

"Mr. Andros, as I explained to Ms. Huck before you arrived, I intend to get a court order that will prevent you from working on this biography until after Dr. Octavius's trial.''

"What!?'' An inadequate response, I know, but it was the best I could do. This was just too much.

"This trial will be a lengthy process. You've probably already spoken to several potential witnesses, and your questions may prejudice their testimony. I wish to limit the damage to my client."

I couldn't believe this. "The man has been charged with crimes that start with property damage, move on to dozens of counts each of kidnapping, breaking and entering, robbery, assault, aiding and abetting known felons, attempted murder, and any number of other things, culminating with the murder-one charge for killing George Stacy."

Schechter looked at me coolly. "Those crimes have yet to be proven. That's what the trial is for. I have a responsibility to my client to protect him from prejudice, which means that your attempts to slander him cannot go unchallenged."

"I'm not trying to slander him!" Realizing that my voice was rising, I took a breath, then went on in a quieter tone. "I'm trying to get to the truth of who he is."

"And a court of law is trying to establish the truth of what he's done," Schechter said without missing a beat. "In this case, the court of law wins, Mr. Andros." He stood up. "The judge will be rendering his decision regarding my motion to suppress your research tomorrow morning. In the meantime, you can consider your appointment to meet with Dr. Octavius tomorrow to be indefinitely postponed."

And with that, he left.

I turned to Kathryn. "And thank you *so* much for your support, Kath."

"What was I supposed to say? He's right."

"C'mon, the book won't even be published for another year at the earliest."

"Which is completely irrelevant. His complaints are with your research, which might affect his client when he goes to trial."

I rolled my eyes. "Right, like that's gonna happen."

She frowned. "What do you mean?"

"Otto Octavius has been arrested dozens of times, yet in his entire life, he's only seen a trial through to completion three times. And that's only if you count when he served on jury duty when he was twenty-three. He was tried right after Spider-Man fought him the first time, and the judge let him off easy—he had been a respected scientist, it was his first offense, and everyone assumed the accident, so soon after the death of his mother, had unhinged him. He served one other prison sentence about a year ago, but broke out long before his sentence was up. *That's it,* Kath. Most of the time, if he doesn't break out before the trial, he breaks out during it, and five'll get you ten he'll do it again now.''

Kathryn spent my entire diatribe staring at me with the same cool gaze Schechter had used. "Are you finished?"

I blew out a breath and slumped my shoulders, my anger burned to ashes, replaced with frustration. "Well, that kinda depends on what that judge says tomorrow morning, doesn't it?"

The judge said I had to cease and desist with my research on this biography until after the completion of Octavius's trial. Somehow, this didn't surprise me.

What did surprise me was the phone call I got later that day from Kathryn.

"You're not going to believe this."

"Believe what?"

She sighed. "Really, you're not going to believe this."

"Well, Kath," I said patiently, "I certainly won't believe it if you never tell me what 'this' is."

"Sorry, I'm just amazed. Schechter called. Apparently Octavius wants to talk to you. No tape recorders, no lawyers, no notes, just a conversation. If you're still interested, that is. I mean, this trial could take ages, and Blake won't want to wait around for it. You'll need to pick another subject for number six."

I thought a moment. "Yeah, maybe, but I've been trying to get a handle on this guy for weeks. I can't pass this up."

So I took a trip to the dank little island nestled between the Bronx and Queens that served as New York City's largest prison.

The room they took me to could've been used to illustrate the definition of *drab.* Beige walls, broken only by the door, an air-conditioning vent about the size of my hand, and a security camera that didn't record sound (conversations with lawyers went on in here, after all). No windows, except for the one on the door. Octavius was brought in five minutes after my arrival, sans tentacles. He looked completely unbothered by his present location. Indeed, he walked like he owned the place.

"So," he said after the guard had left us alone, "you're the biographer."

I stammered. "R-Randall Andros." It didn't hit me until just then: *I was locked in a room with Dr. Octopus.* I'd been training myself to think of him as "Octavius," just another person whose life I was trying to understand, so it wasn't until I sat face to face with him that I realized that this was *not* a comfortable place to be sitting.

Then rational thought took over. We were in a prison, his tentacles had been removed, and there were guards right outside and at wherever that camera fed to. I was in no danger.

After an uncomfortable silence, I said, "I'm surprised you asked to see me after your lawyer moved to have me stop researching you."

"I was curious. Why, exactly, do you feel the need to pick apart my life, biographer?"

I shrugged. It wasn't the first time I'd been asked that, though his phraseology was more obnoxious than the others'. "It's what I do."

"Yes, I'm *aware* of that," he snapped, in a tone that one would use with a five-year-old. "I meant why *my* life in particular?"

"Curiosity. I just finished a biography of Tony Stark, which gave me the chance to interview Iron Man. That led me to thinking about all the paranormals that have been populating the world lately, and I wondered what would lead someone to that type of life. And then you made your attempt on the *Daily Bugle* presses, and I realized that no one really knew you that well." I sat back and smiled. "I like a challenge."

"Interesting." He regarded me like a lab experiment that wasn't going right. "I expected some kind of puerile desire to feed off my fame."

"Well, that entered into it, though honestly my editor didn't want to go for this. I'm sure they would've preferred someone like Captain America or Reed Richards. But your life seemed more interesting. That's certainly proven to be the case."

Octavius looked at me with the bad-lab-experiment gaze some more. Then: "Very well. You may pose whatever questions you wish to ask of me for as long as I remain interested in hearing them. I cannot guarantee I will answer them, but you may ask."

How magnanimous. But, hey, it *was* what I wanted.

"Okay, then, same question you asked me: Why? Why did you, to coin a cliché, turn to a life of crime?"

He actually chuckled at that. "Laws are merely an impediment to such as I, biographer. Radiation is perhaps the greatest force that the human race has encountered. It has changed the course of human evolution, altered the destinies of countless individuals—and I am its master. I more than anyone on this pathetic world understand the intricacies of radiation, what it can and cannot do. What more reason do I need?"

The accounts of his coworkers, particularly his beleaguered ex–lab assistants, didn't do this man's ego justice. "But why did you start when you did, after the accident?"

"Accident?" Then Octavius laughed—a mirthless, highly unpleasant sound. "Weren't you listening, biographer? *I am the master of radiation.* Everything under my control goes exactly as I plan it."

Unable to resist, I responded, "Then why are you in here?"

He frowned. "Spider-Man cannot be numbered among the things under my control. But that will change. He emulates the creature he names himself after in some respects: he is purely reactive. A spider will often not bother to seek prey, preferring to weave a web and wait for the prey to come to it; then it acts. Spider-Man is the same. He cannot anticipate my actions—he cannot ever hope to. He can but react when I make my move. Thus far, he has been lucky. But I rely on skill and genius, not luck. I am a scientist. When an experiment fails, you collect the data and move on to the next one until you achieve success. That will happen someday. I can afford to be patient."

I jumped back to the previous comment. "So you're saying that the explosion was no accident."

He simply stared at me in reply.

I continued, "If that's so, why then? Was it because your mother died?"

His only reply to that was to smile. The kind of smile that makes you want to cover your neck.

Then he leaned back and said, "I grow tired of your questions, biographer. This interview is at an end."

I spent the entire trip back home in a daze. More and more, I started to believe that Phil Sheldon was right: the man I had talked to was many things, but crazy just was not one of them. And I thought about all the other people whose lives had been affected by radiation, from the Fantastic Four to the coming of mutants—*homo sapiens superior*, the next evolutionary step. Radiation had given them strange powers and abilities, but had it truly affected their mental health? Or had it just enhanced what was already there?

I shook my head as I got out of the cab in front of my building. I just couldn't grasp him. Maybe it wasn't possible. Maybe you had to be like him to understand him.

And I did not want to be like him. The very idea made my flesh crawl.

When I entered my apartment, I found a strange man sitting on my couch, reading one of my magazines.

"Who—?"

Upon my entrance, he put the magazine down and unholstered a gun equipped with a silencer. "My name's Niner. We got a mutual acquaintance in common, Mr. Andros. Name of Otto. He wanted to send a message to people who mess around with his life."

Then he squeezed the trigger.

A moment of pain, both in my chest and in the back of my head—the latter from when it crashed onto the hardwood floor as I fell.

I lay there for . . . well, for a while. I bled all over the floor, knowing that no one would find me. I lived alone, I didn't even know my neighbors. I'd probably rot for days before someone noticed the stench.

Then I heard a tapping on the window. And again. Then I heard the window being opened.

"Holy—!" said a voice.

And then Spider-Man stood over me. I couldn't believe it.

"You must be Randy Andros. Where's your phone, I'll call an ambulance."

"Study—through that door." I managed to point to the door to my office.

Spider-Man disappeared. Then I heard him calling for an ambulance to this address. Then he came back to my side.

"What're you—you doin' 'ere?" I croaked.

"Don't try to talk. My old buddy Parker said you were writing a bio of Doc Ock. I came by to chat about it—and tell you to pick another subject. Looks like I'm too late."

"Doesn't matter—Octavius—got restraining order—can't write book."

"Then who did this?"

"Octavius—one'a his guys—shot me."

"Just take it easy. The ambulance will be here in a minute."

There was an uncomfortable silence. Then I asked Spider-Man the same question Octavius asked me and I had asked him. "Why?"

I couldn't read his expression, what with his full face mask. It was disorienting to say the least. Made for a pretty effective disguise, though. "Why what?" he asked.

"Why—you always—fight Octavius?"

"It's funny, I've been thinking about that since Parker told me about you. Part of it's just dumb luck. But part of it's a kind of there-but-for-the-grace-of-God thing. I got my powers from radiation just like he did, but it didn't make me nuts."

"Didn't—for him—either."

"Huh?"

"Listen—" I started, then I coughed blood. It had a salty taste, which surprised me for some reason.

"Lie down," Spider-Man said, "and sit still. You have to—"

I grabbed him by the chest—where his lapels would've been if he hadn't been wearing a bodysuit. *Listen!* I said. "Ock's—not—nuts. I—talked—t'him, I—*listened*—t'him. Not insane. He's—aware of—actions—" I coughed some more blood for good measure, then continued: "—he just—doesn't—care."

My energy, already fairly low, dimmed to almost nothing, and I started to black out. The last thing I remember wanting to say was, "Not nuts, just *evil*" but I have no idea if the words ever came out before I lapsed into a coma.

I woke up in a hospital, being stood over by a pretty black woman. I felt giddy in my head, and my body felt all fuzzy below my neck, like someone had hit my funny bone, but the effect went all the way to my toes. The woman, who identified herself as Nurse Miller, told me that Spider-Man had saved my life—another few minutes, and I probably wouldn't have made it.

I spent the next three weeks in the hospital. During that time, I received flowers and sympathy cards from friends, family, and colleagues. Most were of the basic hope-you-feel-better-soon variety, but one stood out from the crowd. A small bunch of roses with a card that read, To: *Randy Andros.* From: *Your Friendly Neighborhood Spider-Man. Best wishes for a speedy recovery. I hope you're wrong.*

Every time I closed my eyes, I saw Octavius's face laughing at me in a drab beige room. Then I saw Spider-Man's unreadable mask hovering over me in my apartment. Still do, sometimes.

I never did finish that sixth biography. Started writing fiction instead. Reality didn't hold as much interest for me as it used to.

And when I think back over my life—a frequent occurrence since almost losing it—I come to the same conclusion: the dumbest thing I ever did was tell my editor that I wanted my next book to be on Dr. Otto Octavius, aka the super-villain Dr. Octopus.

MY ENEMY, MY SAVIOR

Eric Fein

Illustration by John Romita Sr.

J. Jonah Jameson stood at his office window and marveled at the city spread out before him. His trademark cigar sat tightly clenched in the corner of his mouth.

He spoke into a handheld tape recorder. "I am flattered that the citizens of New York City have chosen to honor me with the title of Humanitarian of the Year. The thought that my work as the publisher of the *Daily Bugle* would qualify me for the afore-mentioned award never once crossed my mind. Not when there is so much yet to do in my battle to rid our fair city of the menace of Spider-Man and his ilk—"

Before Jameson could finish, he was interrupted by a tentative knock at the door. He snapped off the tape recorder and stalked over to the door, yanking it open.

"What is it?!" he barked.

"Sorry to disturb you, Mr. Jameson, but I've got to clean up your office," said a short, heavyset night porter, whose name Jameson couldn't remember.

"Why you stu—"

"By the way, congrats on the humanitarian award thing," the porter said as he shuffled past Jameson pushing a small cart that held all the necessary cleaning equipment.

Jameson caught himself and finished, "—pendous fellow. How nice of you to mention it."

"Oh, it was nothing. Someone circulated a memo to remind everyone to compliment you," the porter said as he started to empty the trash can into the proper compartment in his push cart.

"Er, yes, well, I should be going," Jameson said.

"Good night, Mr. Jameson," the porter said as he started to sweep up the office.

Jameson pulled on his overcoat, picked up his briefcase and tape recorder, and left. He'd finish the speech at home.

A moment or so later, Jameson exited the *Bugle*'s lobby. The night watchman nodded to Jameson as he brushed by him.

It was a cold December night. Jameson let out an involuntary shiver, pulled his coat collar tight around his throat, and ducked into the sleek black limo that waited for him at the curb.

As the car pulled away from the curb and made its way into

the flow of traffic, Jameson decided to get back to work on his speech.

Suddenly, the limo shot through the intersection like a bullet. It clipped a taxi that had just passed in front of it.

"What the—? Are you insane?" bellowed Jameson at the chauffeur. Jameson couldn't remember *his* name either.

"It's not me, honest!" the driver said as he fought to gain control over the car. "I can't get my foot off the gas. Something is tied to it— Oh, God!"

The car swerved out of control. It ran up onto the sidewalk, careening into a garbage can as it plowed forward. Several pedestrians dived out of the way. The driver tried to pull the steering wheel straight, but it wouldn't respond.

"I demand you stop this car at once!" Jameson bellowed.

"I can't. Something freaky is happening," the driver said.

"Try switching off the motor, you oaf," Jameson said.

"Yeah, that could wor— Aargh!"

The driver convulsed and then slumped over sideways across the front seat.

"Oh, no," Jameson said. He reached forward and shook the driver. The man's mouth was open and he was groaning. *At least he's still breathing*, Jonah thought.

Suddenly, the limo swerved right. The momentum tossed Jameson out of his seat.

He got himself up on his knees in time to see that the limo was headed down a dead-end alley. It hit the wall with enough impact to crumple its front like an accordion. The force of the collision slammed Jameson into the back of the front seat.

Moments passed. The rear door of the limo opened. Jameson managed to crawl out of the car. Off in the distance, he could hear the wail of sirens. But, this being New York, he couldn't tell if they were responding to his plight or to one of the numerous other emergencies taking place at that moment.

He fell to the street. A trickle of blood ran from a gash on his forehead, near his hairline. His vision had gone blurry. He tried to get to his feet, but was overcome by dizziness. He crashed to the street. Before he lost consciousness, he could make out the form of a large man approaching him.

• • •

"Come on, Jameson, stop stalling and get into the vehicle," said the man who sat at a control console in a dimly lit lab. The console had a bank of video monitors that displayed various angles of the block that the *Daily Bugle* stood on.

"Ah, there we are," the man said as he watched J. Jonah Jameson exit the *Bugle* building and enter the waiting limousine. The man pressed a button and the spiderlike droid that had been perched outside of Jameson's office window shot down the side of the building. It hit the ground running and attached itself to the rear bumper of the limo as it pulled away from the curb.

"It's time to give you a ride you won't forget, Jameson." With that, the man pressed another button. The spider-droid responded to the signal by popping a panel on its back and shooting out a bundle of fiber-optic tendrils that made their way under the moving car.

One set of tendrils attached themselves to the steering column. A second set silently bored their way through the floorboard and very carefully encircled the driver's right foot, attaching it to the gas pedal.

On the video screen, the man could see the limo slow down for a red light. It was at that moment that he triggered the spider-droid's final action. The tendril that had wrapped itself around the driver's foot contracted, slamming the foot down onto the accelerator with great force.

The man laughed out loud as he watched the limo careen through traffic. *I wish I could see the look on Jameson's face now,* he thought.

Once the limo had crashed in the alley, the man spoke into a commlink, "Mr. Gargan, our prey has been subdued. Please, take the necessary action."

"My pleasure," said a harsh voice.

Spider-Man enjoyed the cool breeze that hit him as he made his way across town. He extended one hand, palm up, squeezed the trigger at the center of his palm, and a stream of webbing shot out of the nozzle attached to his wrist. He grabbed on to it, the other hand automatically coming forward as the other went back. Another web-line was shot.

Spider-Man went on like this building by building, block by block.

There's nothing like a good web-swing through the city to get the kinks out after a night of beating bad guys and cramming for finals, Spider-Man thought. *Yup, no crowded subways or buses stuck in traffic for this webbed wonder.*

When he was a block from his destination, Spider-Man set down in a deserted alley behind a dumpster, so he could change into his street clothes, which he carried in a backpack made of webbing. He had changed in less than a minute. That kind of speed was to be expected from a man who had been bitten by a radioactive spider and gained the proportionate strength, speed, and agility of said spider.

Peter Parker had put his clothes on over his costume. He stuffed his mask and gloves into his jacket pocket as he neared the mouth of the alley that led to the street. His spider-sense "told" him the coast was clear and he entered the flow of street traffic and made his way down the block to the building that took up most of the street and towered over the other buildings in the area—the *Daily Bugle.*

What a great day, he thought. *I bet the pix I got of myself as Spidey battling the Rhino last night get me a nice, big, juicy freelance check.*

A few moments later, Peter entered the city room of the *Daily Bugle* to find it a frantic hub of activity—more than usual.

"I want Urich and Conover in here on the double! I don't care where they are or what they're working on! And get Joy Mercado, too!" screamed Kate Cushing, the *Bugle*'s city editor. She was a tall, willowy blonde with hard eyes that missed nothing.

Behind her stood Joe "Robbie" Robertson, the editor-in-chief. His arms were crossed over his chest and his face was grim. The lines on his forehead and around his eyes were deep furrows. His hair was a tight-cropped afro that had gone silver-gray years ago.

"Hi, Kate, Robbie. What's all the excitement about?"

They looked at him with amazement.

"Excitement? Parker what have you been doing for the last several hours? Meditating? Don't you watch the news?" Kate shot the questions at him in quick succession.

Before he could answer, Robbie cut in. "Jonah's missing. He never got home last night. The police found his car a few blocks away from here. They think he was kidnapped—or worse."

Kate added, "Yeah, and since Jonah is the *Bugle*'s publisher, we thought we might assign a couple of reporters and maybe a photographer or two to look into the matter. You know, not look like total imbeciles while the competition already has front-page coverage,'' Kate said.

"Sorry, Kate,'' Peter responded.

"Forget it. I didn't mean to snap at you. I'm just stressed out over this whole thing. Why don't you head over to the crime scene and get some shots now that the police are done with it?'' She handed him a slip of paper with the address written on it.

"Okay, I'll see what I can dig up.'' Peter started to leave, then paused. He turned to them and said, "I'm sure Jonah will be all right. He's a tough old goat.''

"Wake up, Mr. Jameson,'' said a harsh voice, amplified by some kind of loudspeaker.

Jameson's eyes snapped open with a start. He tried to get up but couldn't. He was chained down to a hospital gurney. The room was dark except for a bright bare bulb that glared into Jameson's eyes, making him squint.

"Much better,'' said the voice.

"What the hell is going on? I demand to be released at once!'' said Jameson.

"You're literally in no position to demand anything, Jonah.''

"I don't know who you are, but I'll see you in jail for the rest of your life. I mean it! I—''

Laughter came from every direction, cutting him off—loud, harsh, and distorted. "A fighter to the very end, eh, Jameson?'' the disembodied voice asked mockingly.

"Why don't you show yourself, you coward?'' said Jameson.

"As you wish.''

Suddenly, the room was flooded with bright light revealing it as a high-tech lab. Next to his gurney was a large mechanical construct twenty feet tall and ten feet wide, surrounded by scaffolding and held up by suspension cables. It looked like a large spider. Last-minute touches were being administered to it by several smaller robots that made their way up and down the construct. They reminded Jameson of the Spider-Slayer robots that he'd commissioned years ago—an action that he would later deeply regret.

"What is this?'' Jonah croaked.

"Why, this is nothing more than your funeral,'' said the voice.

"What did I do to you to deserve this?" Jameson asked.

"Oh, quite a lot, Jonah."

The voice was closer now. Jameson could hear the footsteps approach him from behind. He twisted his head to look as far back as he could and was rewarded with the sight of Alistair Smythe. *My God*, Jameson realized, *those* are *Spider-Slayers!*

"It's been too long, Jonah," said Smythe.

"I thought you were locked up," said Jonah.

"Tsk, tsk, Jonah. How can anybody keep a genius like me locked up for long? Especially since I've spent a lot of hard work to better myself."

Smythe stepped around to stand before Jameson.

"What happened to you?" asked Jameson.

Smythe leaned in close to Jameson, "It's really not as bad as it looks, Jonah. I've simply encased my body in a biorganic carapace, which I designed to boost my strength to superhuman level. The carapace also allows me the mobility I lost when Spider-Man shattered my spine years ago."

"What is all this about, Smythe?" asked Jameson.

"My father," said Smythe.

"I can't believe you still hold me responsible for what happened to your father."

"Shut up! It was because of you that he died a criminal. He created the Spider-Slayers for you. And when the first Slayers failed, you pushed him to build newer ones, over and over. And each time Spider-Man defeated the Slayers, my father lost more and more of his sanity.

"He was humiliated. Eventually he was killed by the radiation he exposed himself to every time he built a new Slayer. He died a common criminal in the eyes of the world. While *you*—you used your rag to trumpet your vendetta against the wall-crawler, making yourself out as a man among men.

"I have inherited my father's journals and his lab equipment. And I have inherited his crusade. My father's enemies became my enemies."

"Your father wanted to *kill* Spider-Man," Jameson said. "I just wanted to unmask him—expose him for the coward he is—"

"Silence! Your rationalizations do not move me. Only your death will balance the scales."

"Yeah, you tell him, Smythe," said a gruff voice that accompanied heavy footsteps. "How ya doin', Jameson?"

"Scorpion?" said Jameson.

"I hope you didn't forget about me, 'cause I sure didn't forget about you," said the Scorpion.

"You see, Jameson, Mr. Gargan and I recently crossed paths and he explained to me how he was another victim of your crusade. How you hired Gargan when he was a private investigator. How you had him follow one of your photographers to find out how he got action shots of Spider-Man in the hopes of being led to the man himself.

"When that failed to supply you with a way to Spider-Man's downfall, you took advantage of Gargan's hard times and gave him a paltry ten thousand dollars so he would be willingly transformed into a superhuman killer. Then you set him loose after Spider-Man.

"You gave no thought to the psychological damage the treatments had done to Gargan. And though the Scorpion did his best, he, like my father, was defeated by Spider-Man and then humiliated in your paper.

"And like my father and myself, he, too, has been left an outsider with no hope for a normal life—while you turned our every defeat into the subject of one of your scathing editorials—boosting your standing in the community and the sales of your paper.

"Even when you confessed to your complicity in both the creation of the Spider-Slayers and the Scorpion, all you got was a slap on the wrist and the loss of your position as *Bugle* editor-in-chief. While we were sentenced to rot in jail.

"But the final indignity was this," said Smythe as he held up a week-old edition of the *Bugle*. " 'Publisher J. Jonah Jameson to be honored as city's Humanitarian of the Year,' " Smythe read aloud. "The hypocrisy is too much for me to swallow."

"You're insane," said Jameson.

"Perhaps, but that's beside the point. You must be punished for your crimes against my family and Gargan."

"Okay, I'll admit, way back when, I was misguided. But I didn't force either of you to continue to break the law. I had nothing but the best intentions for this city, to rid it of the menace of irresponsible superpowered beings," Jameson shot back.

Smythe, a remote control device in his hand said, "I understand, Jonah. I'm going to arrange for you to finally be the hero you've spent years saying you are, by letting you destroy your favorite public enemy, Spider-Man. Of course, there is the chance that Spider-Man will finish you off first."

"What are you talking about?" asked Jameson.

"The Spider-Slayer you see before you has been constructed to carry a passenger—you. It is equipped with audio and video so that you can see and hear what is going on around you. But, you won't be able to do anything about it. I will be the one to control it."

"I refuse to play your sick game, Smythe," Jameson said.

The Scorpion burst out in laughter. "You hear that, Smythe? Flat-top is giving you orders. Just like he gave your old man orders. Like he gave me orders." The Scorpion leaned over Jameson so he was nose-to-nose with the publisher. "Well, *we're* givin' the orders now, Jonah."

Scorpion laughed with childlike glee as he unchained Jameson and ripped him off the gurney and dragged him over to the Spider-Slayer.

The robot drones had completed their tasks and scurried off the Slayer and into the dark corners of the lab.

The compartment resembled the interior of a space capsule. The chair had several restraining belts to keep Jameson immobile.

"There you go, Jonah, snug as a bug in a rug," said Scorpion. "How does it feel to know that you're going to die?"

"A lot better knowing I didn't spend my life like the bumbling idiot I know you were," said Jameson.

"Nice try, Jameson. But you're not gonna goad me into losing my cool now."

Smythe stood by his side and smiled. He patted Scorpion's shoulder and said, "That's right, my friend. Don't let Jameson distract you from what's important—his ruination and that of Spider-Man as well."

Smythe glanced at the wall clock. "You should be going, Scorpion. You need to be in position to see that everything runs as planned."

As the Scorpion left, Smythe looked at Jameson and said, "Let the games begin."

•   •   •

Something doesn't feel right about this, Spider-Man thought. He was on the roof of the *Bugle* Building, perched atop the B in the DAILY BUGLE sign. He thought again about the tip that had brought him here. One of his street sources had told him that something big was going to happen at the *Daily Bugle* today. And the guy behind it was the Scorpion.

Spider-Man knew the Scorpion had a grudge against Jameson. But the Scorpion wouldn't go around making sure every lowlife on the street knew something was going down. That involved planning, and the Scorpion wasn't one for planning anything.

Everything was quiet. Spider-Man had set up his minicamera, webbed in place on top of the D. He had tilted it downward, so that it would capture the action as it unfolded. If it unfolded.

I'm beginning to think this is a wild goose chase. Then, suddenly, a buzzing sound screamed in his head. *Whoa! Spider-sense just went off the Richter scale.*

He looked up into the sky and saw a large object arcing down toward him. He hit the camera's timer that would allow it to snap a photograph every twenty seconds and leapt off the sign just as the object, which looked like a Corvette with eight tentacles attached, crashed into it.

The impact took out several letters so that the DAILY BUGLE was now the DA   UGLE. The object suffered no damage from the impact. Its segmented body and arms shuffled around as its scanners pinpointed Spider-Man's location.

Although the design had been upgraded, Spidey recognized his attacker with little effort. *That's a spiffy new Spider-Slayer—which means Smythe's back. I knew Scorpion wasn't in this alone. Then again, I haven't even seen Scorpy. For all I know, he could be home polishing his tail.*

The Spider-Slayer shot twin laser beams from its eyes. Spider-Man flipped out of the way. The beams cut into the concrete ledge of the building. There was a small *crack* as parts of the ledge broke off and fell to the street below.

Spider-Man leapt over the ledge and shot a web-line. It engulfed the wreckage, wrapping it up into a bundle. Spider-Man pulled it up and swung it over his head like a lasso, then let it fly into the oncoming Spider-Slayer.

The Spider-Slayer shook off the blow and continued to move toward Spider-Man. He shot a series of web-lines to the still-standing remnants of the *Bugle* sign. He forced himself to stand still and wait till the Slayer was in position. When it was, he tugged on the web-lines. The letters toppled over and landed on the Slayer.

The Slayer didn't move. Spider-Man edged closer to it. "This was too easy," he said.

His spider-sense blared a warning. The four limbs on the side of the Slayer facing him came to life. They shot out, each one splitting into two separate tendrils.

Spider-Man back-flipped out of the way, crouched, then leapt forward. He managed to dodge all of them except one. It wrapped itself around his leg just above his knee.

He pulled at it, but it wouldn't budge. It emitted an electrical shock that forced him down to one knee. He went to touch it again and received another jolt. It ran up his leg as well as his hands.

"This isn't going the way I planned," he muttered to himself.

Meanwhile, the Slayer began sprouting new limbs in place of the ones it had jettisoned.

"That can't be good," Spider-Man said. "Come on, Spidey, move faster."

He shot a small amount of webbing onto the tendril and touched the webbing. There was no shock. Encouraged by that small victory, he applied more webbing to the band.

When it was completely covered, he gripped it with both hands and pulled with all his might.

He knew he was taking a risk. If he pulled too hard, he'd wind up breaking his own leg. And if he didn't pull hard enough, he wouldn't get rid of the tendril.

As he pulled, the tendril sent out another series of shocks. Spider-Man grunted in pain but didn't give up. The webbing started to melt from the heat. In another couple of seconds, Spider-Man wouldn't be able to grasp the tendril.

Okay, web-head, it's now or never. He tugged one last time. The tendril came free of his leg. Spider-Man screamed in pain. The tendril had taken a piece of his costume as well as some skin. He covered his wound with some webbing.

"Just call me Dr. Spider-Man."

The Spider-Slayer reared up from under the wreckage and

shot a laser blast at Spider-Man. He leapt out of the way just in time.

"Sheesh, I thought it was a funny line," he said to the Slayer.

The Spider-Slayer then blasted a hole in the roof. Spidey did a triple back-flip to avoid the blast.

Inside the Slayer, Jameson moaned in pain as if he had been blasted rather than the roof. He could see via the video monitor mounted before him what the Slayer had done to the *Bugle* building.

"No! Not the *Bugle*! It's my life's work!"

The commlink inside the Slayer crackled to life and Smythe's voice came over it. "Is that agony I hear in your voice, Jonah? Don't worry. If all goes according to my plans, Spider-Man will stop the Slayer before it can destroy the entire building."

"I hope you wind up in hell for this, Smythe," snapped Jonah.

"I'll go if you will, Jonah. And since it looks like you'll be getting there first, you can save me a seat next to you."

Jonah looked at the video monitor. It showed the Slayer's progress. It was smashing its way through one of the *Bugle*'s editorial conference rooms. There had been a meeting going on, but the participants had scattered as the Slayer advanced toward them.

The Spider-Slayer moved its head from left to right and back again. Each time, it let loose a series of laser blasts that sent people and furniture flying. Screams of terror and pain filled the halls.

As the Slayer progressed, Jonah heard something land on its back.

"Please, let that thud be Spider-Man," said Jonah. "Stop this thing. Even if you have to kill me to do it."

"What a revelation," said Smythe over the radio, "Rooting for your greatest enemy to succeed. What would your adoring public say?"

"If it means saving lives, I don't care what anyone would say," said Jameson. "I just want this to end."

"Oh, it will. Very soon."

"Whoa, Nellie," said Spider-Man. He sat astride the Spider-Slayer's back. He had fashioned a harness out of his webbing. The Slayer veered left and right as it tried to shake Spider-Man off.

Spider-Man held on tight. He slid forward so he could reach down to the joint that connected the head to the body. It was made of a flexible material. Spider-Man braced himself and then punched into the joint. He could feel a nest of wiring and circuitry surround his hand.

He grabbed as much of it as he could, then yanked with all his strength. Sparks shot out from the Slayer's "wound." It emitted a high-pitched noise that, if Spider-Man hadn't known any better, would have sounded like a pain-filled scream.

The Slayer stopped dead in its tracks. Its red eyes dimmed.

"Whew. That was close," said Spider-Man.

People started to emerge from their offices. When they saw that the danger was over they started to cheer, swarming around Spider-Man to express their gratitude.

Inside the Slayer, Jameson allowed himself a smile. He said, "You blew it, Smythe. Spider-Man beat you."

"Ah, Jonah, you forget that nothing has happened that I didn't plan on. Spider-Man may have defeated the Slayer but I counted on that. Now, it's time for the wrap-up. Or, in this case, the blow-up."

Spider-Man had extricated himself from the crowd, and gone over to the Spider-Slayer to try to figure out how to dispose of the thing, when an ominous voice came from the mechanical monstrosity: *"This mechanism will self-destruct in sixty seconds."*

"You have *got* to be kidding me," Spider-Man said. "Didn't self-destruct mechanisms go out with fringe vests?"

People began to panic again.

Spider-Man sprang into action. He lifted the Slayer up and made his way to the hole the Slayer had blasted in the ceiling earlier.

With the Slayer in tow, he jumped up onto the roof. He then moved to the side of the building that faced the East River and threw the Slayer toward it. As soon as he did, his spider-sense, which had been tingling continuously through the battle, kicked into overdrive.

Unfortunately, having just finished fighting a Spider-Slayer and then having to heave it into the river, Spider-Man was in no condition to dodge the blast his spider-sense warned him of.

Blinking to clear his head, Spider-Man looked up from his prone position on the roof to see the Scorpion standing over him. "Not bad for a day's work, huh, webs? First you knock off Jameson for me, then I kick your butt."

Spider-Man looked from him to the Slayer that was headed toward the river, and realized that this Slayer had a passenger.

"Thanks for the tip, Scorpy," said Spider-Man. He shot a glob of webbing into Scorpion's face. At the same time, he shot a spider-tracer onto Scorpion's upraised elbow. Then, Spider-Man swung off after the Slayer.

I can't have more than fifteen or twenty seconds to get Jonah out of that tin can. If he's even in there to begin with, Spider-Man thought.

Spider-Man used the buildings before him to gain speed, pushing off them with tremendous force. He managed to shoot a web-line that caught the tail end of the Spider-Slayer. He pulled himself to it and climbed onto its back.

Inside, Jonah watched the Slayer getting closer to the water.

"I guess this really is it. I didn't even get a chance to say good-bye to Marla or make peace with my son."

"Is the great Humanitarian of the Year about to cry?"

"Why don't you shut up and let me die in peace, Smythe?"

"Because I want you to suffer for every remaining second of your miserable life, Jameson. Which, according to my count-down, won't be much longer."

At that moment, the sound of metal being rent could be heard from above. Jameson looked up to see Spider-Man peeling off the Slayer's roof.

"Hey, Jonah, didn't your mother teach you not to play with mad scientists?" the wall-crawler said.

"Get me out of here! This thing's about to explode!" Jameson screamed.

Spider-Man ripped the restraining belts off of Jameson.

"Uh-oh," he said suddenly.

"What's wrong?" Jameson asked.

His response was the sudden impact of the Slayer hitting the water. Then everything went dark.

Spider-Man broke the surface of the water with a gasp. He had an arm wrapped around Jameson, who was unconscious and very pale.

He headed for shore. He was only about a hundred yards away, but in his current condition, it felt like a mile.

"Hang on, Jonah. I didn't go through all this to have you die on me. Besides, with my luck, I'd get the blame."

When Spider-Man made land, he immediately tried to rouse Jameson, slapping the publisher's face a few times.

"Under different circumstances, this would be kind of fun," Spider-Man said. "But we're not doing too well. I guess I'm going to have to do mouth-to-mouth. There's a photo I never want taken."

Spider-Man had just raised his mask to expose his mouth when Jameson's eyes opened.

"Y-you," he coughed.

"Me," said Spider-Man as he quickly pulled the lower part of his mask back into place.

"You saved my life," said Jameson.

"Yeah. Everyone is entitled to a few mistakes. I guess this is one of mine."

Jameson tried to stand up but couldn't. Spider-Man helped him.

"Easy, you've had quite an adventure. Wait here, I'll go get help."

Jameson just nodded.

Spider-Man extended an arm, brought his finger to the palm trigger mechanism that fired his web-lines, and pressed it. A stream of river muck came spurting out. Spider-Man tried his other web-shooter. He got the same results.

He turned to Jameson and said, "You wouldn't happen to have a spare token on you, would you?"

Scorpion burst into Smythe's lab carrying two bottles of champagne that he had stolen from a liquor store. He broke off the top of one of the bottles with his thumb. The liquid shot out, making a puddle on the floor.

"Hey, Smythe, you around? It's time to celebrate. You should've seen it. It was amazing."

Smythe stepped out of the shadows. He was not amused.

"You forget, Gargan, I had a video feed. I saw everything that transpired. I saw you disobey my direct orders by making yourself known to Spider-Man *before* Jameson was dead. As a matter of fact, because of your big mouth they're both alive. Would you like to see?"

Smythe didn't wait for an answer. He pointed a remote control at a bank of television monitors. They all flashed on. Each was tuned to a different station. The various newscasts reported Jameson's dramatic rescue from the river.

Then all the stations carried the same feed. Jameson, still dripping from his time in the water, was giving an impromptu press conference.

"I want to thank the men and women of this fair city who put aside their own troubles to help resolve my situation. As for those responsible, I can't wait to face those cowards in a court of law. Then we'll see just how tough the Scorpion and Alistair Smythe really—"

Smythe clicked off the televisions. "You've ruined everything, you thickheaded lout! I should kill you, but I have more important things to do. So just get out."

"Hey! No one treats me like this. All my life people have treated me like I was garbage. I won't stand for it anymore!" The Scorpion was seething with rage. He hurled the champagne bottles to the ground.

Hoping Smythe would be distracted by the shattering bottles, Scorpion blasted the scientist with his stinger-blast. Unfortunately, it didn't work. Smythe dodged the blast and retaliated with a spin kick to the chest.

"You think a stupid little kick can stop me?"

"No, I think it can maneuver you into position for this."

Suddenly, Scorpion found himself attacked by dozens of miniature Spider-Slayers. They tore at his armor. Scorpion swatted away as many as he could with his tail and arms. But they kept on coming.

He charged forward. The Slayers stayed with him as he did so. Smythe sidestepped him and took the opportunity to trip him up. Scorpion crashed to the floor. Smythe towered over him.

"Now it's time to put you out of your misery."

"Hey, that's real generous of you, Smythe, old boy, but let me take it from here."

Smythe swung around in the direction of the voice. He got two red-clad feet in the face for his trouble. Spider-Man landed in a crouch and then sprang up at Smythe, who was still off balance from the previous attack.

"How did you find me?" asked Smythe.

"I placed one of my handy-dandy spider-tracers on Scorpion when we fought earlier, and here I am."

"It's because of you and Jameson that my father is dead and my family's reputation is destroyed. But I'm going to rectify that," said Smythe.

"Oh, here we go again, another chorus of 'My life stinks and it's all your fault,' " said Spider-Man. "Well, let me tell you something, bug-boy, I've had it with you idiots. Neither one of you can admit to the fact that you're both responsible for the shambles that your lives have become. Yeah, Jameson helped by making the offer or funding the projects. But you dopes embraced his cause all the way."

And then Spider-Man pummeled Smythe. He kept him on the defensive. But he was interrupted by a sting-blast. He turned to see the Scorpion, the worse for wear from his battle with the mini Spider-Slayers, stagger toward him.

"Thanks for softening Smythe up for me," the Scorpion said. "I'll be sure to take advantage of his condition as soon as I kill you."

"Listen to me, you green-tailed doofus, I've had it with you and Erector Set Lad over there. This ends now."

The Scorpion had raised his tail, ready to strike, but Spider-Man reached up and grabbed it, flipping Scorpion over his shoulder. He landed with a loud thud that shook the whole lab. Before Scorpion could get his bearings, Spider-Man once again grabbed him by the tail, twirled him over his head like a bola, and let him go.

Scorpion went soaring through the air. He crashed into the scaffolding that had previously been used for the Spider-Slayer. The scaffolding collapsed on top of him, pinning him down. Scorpion let out a low groan and then passed out.

Spider-Man walked over to the unconscious Smythe and webbed him up thoroughly. *That ought to hold you until I can contact the cops and they can send Code Blue to take you away. I'm glad my spare cartridges of webbing weren't water damaged.*

Speaking of damaged, I've got to stop off at the Bugle *and dig my camera out of the rubble.*

He looked around the lab. He shook his head. *All this technology. All this intelligence. And what's it used for? Petty revenge. That really stinks.*

The next night, at the Humanitarian of the Year Award dinner, Jameson sat at the center of a large dais flanked by his family and friends. The room was filled with city officials, including the mayor, local and national celebrities, and a select group of *Bugle* employees.

Peter Parker moved through the crowd, totally ignored. He didn't mind. He wasn't there to mingle; he had been assigned to photograph the event. *Well, this is one way to get invited to a ritzy shindig,* he said to himself.

Jameson got up to speak.

"As you are all aware, I've recently gone through a rough time. But I want to let you know that my commitment to my work and this fair city is stronger now than it has ever been before. That said, I must turn down your most generous award. It would at this point strike me as hypocritical to accept it—having just come face to face with two villains whose origins in a small part can be traced to me. Though I had the best intentions when I took part in the projects that spawned them, that does not excuse the destruction and terror they have wrought on our city over the last several years. It is because of these facts that I must humbly and graciously turn down your honor.

"But make no mistake, I will strive to meet the high expectations the public has set for me. And, I can promise you that I will continue to crusade against the costumed vigilantes and other superpowered crazies that they attract. Especially that menace Spider-Man, who I can assure you exacerbated the problem with Smythe and the Scorpion—provoking them to even higher extremes of violence than had they been left to their own devices. Thank you."

The crowd gave Jonah a standing ovation. And he milked it for all it was worth. It would have made a great front page, had it been photographed.

But Peter wasn't around. His spider-sense had alerted him to danger in the area. Sure enough, after a quick change in a

nearby stairwell, the amazing Spider-Man encountered and subdued a band of heavily armed men about to break into the ban-
quet.

The funny thing was, that *did* make the front page.

THE STALKING OF JOHN DOE

Adam-Troy Castro

Illustration by Alexander Maleev

In Manhattan, stormy nights are crazy nights.

The clouds roll in like conquering armies laying claim to all the buildings and people below; they block the few stars bright enough to shine through the glare and the pollution, and they turn every alley into a hostile landscape from another world. On stormy nights, the rainswept streets turn into streaky reflections of headlights and brake lights and neon; the subway stations turn into puddled caves filled with the shivering forms of those who could find no other shelter for the night; and all the darkest secrets of a city already known for its violence and corruption seem to come out all at once, mutated into something worse under the pressures of the storm. There are lots of impulse murders on stormy nights, lots of people living on the edge of violence who crack beneath the sound of the thunder rattling their tiny apartment windows.

Stormy nights are crazy nights. And for Dr. Gwendolyn Harris, crazy nights were busy nights.

She was working the second half of a fifteen-hour shift at the Emergency Psychiatric Unit of the Midtown Hospital, and she'd seen more business in the past three hours than she'd expected to see all day. The cops brought them in, one after the other: the off-duty taxi driver who'd decided that his thirteen-year-old daughter was a demon and attempted an emergency exorcism with a .45; the homeless man who'd run into the middle of traffic screaming of the transmissions attempting to control him from space; the thirteen-year-old girl high on the latest designer drug who'd hated her own face so much that she tried to remove it with her fingernails; and the ranting little man who'd attempted to smuggle a gun into a Rick Jones concert, in what was an apparent attempt to become the next Mark David Chapman.

They kept coming, one after another: all lost, all wounded, all crazed, and as much a danger to themselves as they were to the world around them.

The main examination room was one big puddle from the rain they and the cops brought in with them. Gwendolyn had promised herself several times that she'd call somebody from maintenance to mop it up, but it had been hours since she'd even had five minutes to sit down.

It wasn't even nine o'clock when she squared away the Chapman wannabe and Bill The Security Guard waved her over to his desk. Of course, busy as she was, it wouldn't have occurred to Bill to go over to her; he was a retiree desk potato, whose nights, unlike hers, were stress-free exercises in crossword puzzles and sitcoms. The laugh track on the little portable TV behind him tittered uncontrollably as he said, "Hey, beautiful. What do you want first, the good news or the bad news?"

Dr. Harris sighed, brushed an errant strand of long blonde hair away from her eyes, and slapped her clipboard against the counter with perhaps a little more force than was strictly necessary. "Just mix it up together and tell me, Bill. I'm a little too busy for punch lines tonight."

He was visibly disappointed. "Cops just called. They're bringing in another John Doe. One they say they don't recommend placing in the general ward."

"Dammit." She was fast running out of isolation rooms. "What's this one's story? Did they say?"

"Not really." Bill took a deep breath, and reported the rest of it with the self-satisfied relish of the kind of man who thinks reporting a story makes him part of it. "Only that he's totally out of his head, strong as a moose, and that it took more than a dozen cops working tag-teams to wrestle him into a pair of straitjackets. A pair, mind you. One over the other. Woulda liked to see that, beautiful. Bet you a weekend in the country he's built like a refrigerator."

Dr. Harris hoped not; the last refrigerator-sized patient she'd had to deal with, about six months ago, was a psychotic fat lady named Rose who'd ended up going berserk and putting one of her orderlies in the emergency room. Rose had killed her husband by sitting on him. She'd attacked the orderly by physically picking him up and throwing him against the wall. Dr. Harris wasn't looking forward to a repeat of that. She said, "When did they say they'd be here?"

"They already got his prints and pictures. They oughtta be here anytime."

She said a word that her mother had taught her. "All right. Call up a couple of big ones from Security. And let me know the instant Admitting calls—I want to be here to greet Mr. Doe when they drag him in."

"Sure thing, beautiful." He turned back to his *Daily Bugle*, which—as it seemed to one day out of five—featured a front-page photograph of its publisher. "You want to take me up on that bet?"

She wanted to snap at him, but that wasn't the way to handle people like Bill. "Absolutely. You're my dream man, you know that."

Dr. Harris spent the next five minutes in the washroom, splashing water on her face. It was necessary on nights like tonight; it didn't do to ride the edge of exhaustion while the rest of the world rode the edge of insanity. She washed her face and hands, brushed the hair from her eyes again—she kept it longer than was strictly practical, but figured she was entitled to a little impracticality—then replaced her clear window-pane eyeglasses, and practiced a moment's worth of Serious Professionalism in the mirror. She had to do this often because she didn't possess the kind of face people take seriously. It was a little too smooth, a little too soft, and a little too wide eyed; it may have been a beautiful face, even a model's face, but it wasn't one that easily communicated her intelligence and her dedication toward her work. She'd seen movies get bad reviews purely because actresses who looked like her seemed miscast as doctors. Hence the glasses, which were a purely cosmetic sop to the necessities of public relations; hence the necessity to consciously practice the compensatory Serious Professional look. As always, it felt stupid. She said the hell with it and returned to Admitting to see if the promised John Doe had arrived yet.

He hadn't, but that was okay: he arrived just in time to stop Bill from hitting on her again.

She should have taken him up on his bet, because this John Doe was no human refrigerator. To the contrary: he was a wiry Caucasian male in his twenties, with short-cropped brown hair and eyes that could have been inviting were they not crazed, disoriented, and filled with fear. He was double-straitjacketed, and beneath that wearing nothing but a sodden pair of blue tights; his legs were so powerfully muscular that she almost suspected jailhouse bodybuilding before taking a closer look and deciding that they looked a lot more like the attributes of a professional gymnast. That and whatever was wrong with him seemed to have made him impossibly strong. As the five cops dragged him in, two of them held each arm and one had only a marginally effective chokehold around his neck. They needed all their strength to control him despite the straitjackets and the short link of chain that connected one ankle to the other. His face was pale and feverish as he screamed, "You can't do this! He's coming to get me! He'll be here before you know it! He'll kill all of you to get at me, don't you know that?"

One of the cops slipped on a slick spot on the floor. It was a small lapse, so brief that it was practically subliminal—but John Doe took advantage of it at once, with a move that should have been impossible. To wit: he leapt. His ankles were bound together, and his arms were held tight by cops, but he leapt anyway, with an effortless flick of his feet that nevertheless propelled him straight up, all the way to shoulder height. The cop with the chokehold fell back; the four holding John Doe's arms were almost lifted off the ground with him. Through sheer force of will they managed to drag him back down, preventing another leap only by sweeping his legs right out from under him. As he immediately struggled to rise again, all five cops piled on, desperate to regain control of him, but clearly fighting a losing battle. And throughout it all, their urgent shouts of *Get his arm, dammit Joe, get his arm, Jeez I can't hold him, I can't hold him!* were matched shout for shout by John Doe's own anguished ranting: "He's after me, he'll track me down, it's what he does, it's what he knows, he'll find my trail and *get me.* . . ."

There was no time to slip him a trank or call Security for reinforcements. Instead, Dr. Harris moved as close to the fight as she dared and faced John Doe head-on. She spoke softly, but firmly, with a quiet confidence that easily rose over all the shouting voices: "It's all right. He's not here yet. You don't have to be afraid."

John Doe's eyes widened just enough for Dr. Harris to note just how dilated they were. All at once, he froze—not calmed, like she'd hoped, but shattered to the core by the shock of imagined recognition. His mouth opened twice before he managed to speak. "G-Gwendy?"

Behind his desk, where he'd been intently following the proceedings without any apparent ambitions of getting involved himself, Bill The Guard whistled. "Holy—! You know this guy, beautiful?"

Dr. Harris hated the nickname Gwendy almost as much as she hated Bill The Guard calling her beautiful. And she'd never laid eyes on this John Doe in her life. But she didn't have time for denials. She faced the John Doe. "My name's Dr. Gwendolyn Harris, of the Midtown Hospital Emergency Psychiatric Unit. I know you're afraid and I know you're not in control of yourself and I need you to calm down so we can help you. Will you do that for me? Please?"

John Doe's eyes were frantic with terror. "You can't be Gwendy. The Goblin killed Gwendy. I saw him kill Gwendy . . . unless . . . ohmigod . . . maybe I'm imagining that too. . . ."

"You're not imagining anything," Dr. Harris said. "This is the Psychiatric Unit, like I said. I don't know the Gwendy you're talking about, but I'm not her; it just happens to be my name. If you trust me, this goblin you're talking about won't be able to get you in here. Will you trust me?"

And then, with the suddenness of a cold wind blowing out a candle, John Doe's terror vanished, replaced by anguished weeping. Tears ran down his face as he pleaded. "Help me, Gwendy . . . you know I'm not like this . . . it's him . . . not the Goblin . . . the Hunter . . . that dart he shot me with . . . it's some kind of rare psychoactive snake venom derivative . . . making all the nightmares come back . . . I'm f-fighting it but . . . my thoughts . . . my thoughts . . . I can't seem to focus my thoughts. . . ." His eyes unfocused and went somewhere far away. "Is it really you, Gwendy? Please tell me it's really you. . . ."

On an impulse she reached out, placed a palm against his cheek, and lied through her teeth. "It's me," she whispered.

His lips curled in the kind of tentative smile native only to men daring themselves to believe in a miracle. He turned his head just enough to kiss her wrist, then began to cry again; but whatever his private sorrow was, he kept it to himself and fought no more.

The two behemoths from Security were old friends of Dr. Gwendolyn Harris; when you dealt with dangerous psychotic episodes on an almost daily basis, it was prudent to be nice to the fellows paid to protect you from your patients. They were a salt-and-pepper team named Gordy and Flack, with physiques capable of intimidating even the occasional refrigerator-sized patient. She'd dated Gordy a total of twice, in the distant past. Flack was a nice guy, but the wrong persuasion. Together with Dr. Harris and the five hyperventilating cops they led the trembling John Doe down the hallway and into a padded isolation cell, where they strapped him to the posts of his bed. He kept murmuring about Gwendy and the goblin and Mary Jane even as his captors locked him in.

There were any number of things that needed to be done— blood workup, physical examination, even neurological tests— but they would keep for a few minutes; right now, a little back-ground would be more helpful than any of them. She faced the five cops, and saw a group of young, strong, brave men who were all trembling from exhaustion and relief. The apparent leader of the bunch, a man older than the others whose shield identified him as a Sergeant Monaghan, exhaled with palpable relief as he licked the blood from his freshly swollen lower lip. "Good Lord, what a psycho."

Dr. Harris let the nomenclature pass, but not the sentiment: "You don't believe him? About being drugged against his will?"

Monaghan rolled his eyes. "By who? The goblin? The hunter? Or any of those other zoo animals he went on and on about— lizards, vultures, tarantulas, pumas, cobras, rhinos, black cats, oc-topuses—"

"Octopi," said a younger cop, whose shield identified him as a Patrolman Ditmeyer.

Monaghan did a double take. "Say what?"

"It's not *octopuses*," Ditmeyer said, in the manner of a man who wished he'd kept his mania for accuracy to himself. "It's octopi. Octopi being the proper plural of octopus."

As the three other cops ostentateously looked away, Monaghan assumed the look of the eternally suffering martyr condemned to an eternity of tolerating the follies of those not nearly as wise. "You got to forgive Stanley, ma'am. He goes to this writing group on Thursdays, trying to make himself the next Joe Wambaugh. But the point is that yon psycho came out of that alley stripped to the waist, wired like all the crackheads you ever saw, screaming about the monsters. Attacked a whole bunch of folks lined up at the Cineplex, calling 'em murderers and villains, tossing 'em side to side like it was bowling night or something. Even jumped a poor fat guy, calling him the Kingpin. When Stanley and I showed up, he almost tore us to pieces. We had to pump half a

dozen trank darts into him just to slow him down. Gotta tell you,
I ain't never seen a reaction that wild, not even with junkie con-
noisseurs on crack-and-PCP cocktails. He's definitely on something, but that's still some serious psycho strength that nut-job's
got there.''

It was obviously meant to be the last word, but Ditmeyer broke
in. "I don't agree, sir. He's hallucinating, sure, and from the way
he goes on he sees enemies everywhere he looks, but even with
his strength, even in a state of panic, he's managed to resist doing anybody any serious harm. That shows a core of sanity still
struggling to pull the strings. As for the junkie theory, well, I'm
sure the doctor's more qualified to diagnose that than I am, but
he has no obvious track marks, no jaundice, no pallor, no de-
generative septum, no physical evidence of chronic drug use. If
anything, his physical condition is phenomenal. I've been on
Nautilus and off donuts for five years now and I'm miles away
from having definition like that. For what it's worth, I think he's
telling the truth. I think he was dosed with something.''

Monaghan glared at him for daring to have a different opinion, then shrugged in a manner that rendered the entire con-
troversy moot. "Whatever. We took prints and pictures and we
got a couple of detectives cross-referencing with both known of-
fenders and missing persons. I promise you, ma'am . . . if there's
a name on this guy, we'll have it for you before you waste too
much time changing his diapers.'' He gestured to Ditmeyer and
the others. "Come on, guys. I gotta get back to the precinct and
see if I can talk myself into taking an early night.''

As the cops walked away, arguing among themselves—with Ditmeyer taking the brunt of the abuse—Dr. Harris turned and saw
both Gordy and Flack grinning at her. They shared the same
stance: a rueful grin and a pair of burly arms folded across great
pickle-barrel chests. As she stared back at them, they both raised
their eyebrows in unison, and she had to look down to stifle a
grin.

"Gee, Doc," Gordy drawled, "you really do get all the interesting patients in here, don't you?''

"I want to watch," said Flack. "See how a true professional
delves into the innards of a tortured soul's psyche.''

"Psyche? Isn't that what Tonto was, to the Lone Ranger?''

"No," said Flack. "That was sidekick.''

"Ohhhhhhh. . . ."

All of which came at the right psychological moment: Dr. Harris had to cover her mouth to hide just how close to an explosion of nervous laughter she really was. It was the difference between their corny humor and Bill The Security Guard's; she genuinely liked them. It was several seconds before she managed to slip the No-Nonsense Professional face back over the face she considered her own. "If you gentlemen don't mind," she said, "I'd like you to stick around for a couple of seconds while I get the blood work."

"No problem," said Gordy. "After what we just saw and heard, I insist on it."

Dr. Gwendolyn Harris should have been used to the smell of fear. In her line of work, she sensed it every day. It came from children whose parents had become their torturers; from drug addicts unable to escape the nightmares they'd invited inside their heads; from schizophrenics who knew their fears were formed from nothing but couldn't deny the way this nothing made their hearts pound like engines. In her line of work, she knew that inappropriate fear was usually a simple physiological reaction to chemical changes inside the brain. But every once in a while she encountered a patient who exuded enough sheer terror to get past her defenses—who was so tormented by his own personal demons that she was almost able to feel them gathering around herself as well.

When she returned to the dimly lit padded room that now belonged to John Doe, she began to see that he was one of those patients.

He lay on the bed, twitching and grunting beneath his straps, speaking to phantoms that only he could see. "Mary Jane . . ." he whispered. "I need you, Mary Jane . . . the monsters . . . they keep coming . . . I fight them every day and they keep coming . . . I beat them back and they keep coming . . . I put them away and they keep coming. . . . I take them two or three or six at a time and they keep coming . . . and they're tougher, Mary Jane . . . darker . . . and I'm so tired . . . and I can't fight them anymore . . . and now it's the Hunter and he wants to kill me and he never gives up and I don't even know what's real and I don't know how I'm going to stop him. . . . Felicia? Mary Jane? What's he going to do when he gets me? . . . What kind of trophy am I going to make?"

Dr. Harris made eye contact with Gordy and Flack. She saw at once that it wasn't just her. It may have been just another penny-ante paranoid delusion, but there was something about the way John Doe presented it, something about the conviction behind his words, that hit all three of them at the base of the spine.

Part of her wanted to go right back out the door, leaving John Doe to his miseries. But she had a job to do, and she had to do it even when it wasn't pleasant. She took a single step closer to John Doe—

—and he screamed. *"Oh my God, Gwendy!"*

She quickly moved to his side. "It's all right. I'm here."

"I thought I dreamed you! I knew you couldn't be here, you're gone . . . but you looked so real . . . it's impossible, I lost you at the bridge, I tried to catch you but heard that awful awful snap. . . ." He arched his back so violently that the entire bed lifted off the floor, then landed with a room-rattling thump. "What's real, Gwendy? I'll never live through this if I don't know what's real. . . ."

Dr. Harris placed a hand on his wrist. The contact was electric for both of them. In his case, because it was something tactile, to anchor him to the world of flesh and stone; in her case because in his corded flesh she sensed a strength even greater than what she'd seen him use on the cops. Gordy moved to yank her away—she gestured for him to stay at a distance, and turned her attention back to her patient. "I'm real," she said. "I'm Gwendolyn, but not the one you know. I'm just your doctor and your friend and I need to take some of your blood so I can find out what's wrong with you. I promise you it won't hurt. Will you let me take some of your blood?"

Astonishingly, he started laughing. "My blood, my blood—I wouldn't even be in this mess if not for my blood! That spider, messing up my life—take it all, why don't you? Every drop! Go ahead, Gwendy! Call Morbius and have yourselves a kegger!"

She moved quickly, then, managing to free his arm, find the proper blood vessel, and draw his blood before his increasingly brittle attention span took him to the next series of delusions. During the few seconds she needed, he calmed down and stared at her—not exactly with the rapt gaze of a man in love, but with the baffled, desperate look of one who didn't want to grasp the lifeline he saw before him. Aware of the look, she ached to know who he was, what unknown traumas had led him to this time and place. But she didn't ask him; instead she just used this brief window of cooperation to take his temperature (which was high but not in the danger range) and his pulse (which was dangerously fast—racing in the manner that bursts blood vessels and shreds heart tissue). She would have prescribed something to put him to sleep, but didn't dare until she got a bead on the precise mix of the pharmacological cocktail that he must have already tasted tonight.

Just as she was done he swallowed and came out with: "M-my name's . . . P-p . . ."

She turned toward him. "Take your time. I'm listening."

"P-p . . . P-p . . ." He closed his eyes.

"Are you having trouble remembering?"

"It's n-not that. You're Gwendy. . . . I want to tell you. But something inside me says I shouldn't tell you. Th-that if I tell you . . . everything I care about ends." He lifted his head as much as the restraints allowed, and with deep frustration pounded it back against the pillow. "If only I could remember . . . the Hunter . . . how to stop him before he shows up and kills us all. . . ."

Unexpectedly, Flack spoke: "Chill out, mister. We won't let him get you."

John Doe laughed again, but it was a hollow laugh, the kind of sound that sounds like it should come from graveyards on cold autumn nights. "You don't know him. You don't know what he is. He's coming. And you won't even slow him down. . . ."

He was still laughing when Dr. Harris and the two guards closed the door to his room behind them. All three let out their breaths at the moment the door clicked. They looked at each other, and Gordy said, "Well, we know one thing about him. He's a lady's man. He started off talking about Felicia and Mary Jane and now he's on and on about Gwendy. Betcha we hear about all the rest of his conquests before he's through."

Flack said, "Unless . . . well, I admit it's stupid, but Mary Jane may be a reference to marijuana."

Gordy gave that the disgusted snort it deserved.

Dr. Harris smiled. "Watching *Dragnet* reruns, are we?"

·   ·   ·

Normally, given her current caseload, she would have corralled an orderly to act as courier for her, but she was hyped, and she had a few minutes, so she personally ran down to the lab to get a priority order on John Doe's blood. The unusual urgency must have shown on her face, since the tech—a skinny guy named Willie, whom she knew slightly—goggled impressively throughout her briefing.

"Unknown white male," she said. "Late twenties, suffering severe dissociative psychosis, possibly as a reaction to an involuntary drug overdose. Whatever it is has him running on overdrive: the cops tranked him six times and he *still* has the kind of pulse that would make me worry about a foreign car. I want this tested for alcohol, crack, PCP, all the other usual psychoactive agents—and one other thing. Snake venom."

Willie sucked on his double-thick strawberry malted. "What kind of snake venom?"

"I don't know. Something exotic and intensely hallucinogenic. The patient claims he was given a dose."

Willie emptied the malted, licked the rim, and placed it back on the desk. "Gwen . . . I don't know how to tell you this . . . but we're in midtown Manhattan. The only snakes out there are lawyers. I'm not set up to test for exotic venom derivatives, let alone identify them."

"Can you test for something generic? Like rattlesnake?"

"If this was Texas, sure. Here? I don't know. Maybe. I'll have to ask around."

"I don't need any specifics," said Dr. Harris. "At least, not right now. Right now, I just want to know if it's possible he's telling the truth."

Outside, the rain intensified, becoming the kind of downpour that is less a storm than an assault. The wind blew in angry gusts, turning hats, umbrellas, and paper into so much airborn debris. On Second Avenue, an awning that had lasted for twenty years whipped itself to shreds; in Central Park, a derelict wandering across the sodden expanse of the Great Lawn was fried by a well-aimed bolt of lightning; on the East Side, an entire section of the FDR Drive flooded out and became a soup of trapped commuters forced to flee their cars. And in midtown, the cops were besieged by screwball reports of a half-man, half-lion spotted on the rooftops.

Stormy nights are crazy nights.

The emergency room sent up an elderly man in striped pajamas who couldn't remember who he was or where he'd come from, or for that matter, where he got the knife or why he was covered with blood; another teenage girl, this one wasted by anorexia, who came in ranting about the space aliens who had kidnapped her to Arcturus; and a homeless schizophrenic man who had not been well served by the state budget cuts that had sent him untreated and unmedicated into a world that to him looked like random nonsensical horrors glimpsed through the distorting glass at the bottom of a fishbowl. Dr. Harris did what she could for them, which was to say get them out of their wet clothes and into hospital-issued gowns, and not much else. There wasn't time for anything else. They came in one after the other, each one needing personal treatment, each one getting little more than a few words of comfort, some medication, and a quiet place to sleep while awaiting a somewhat less overworked staff to arrive first thing tomorrow morning.

It must have been a couple of hours before Dr. Harris retreated to her little office—a cube that would have been a closet had somebody not discovered it was possible to jam a desk into it—and plopped down on her chair, exhausted. It had been a long day, and she was looking forward to that moment now only a couple of hours away when she could herself run screaming into the night. Of course, it was pouring outside, and it would take her the better part of an hour to get home, and it would probably be wisest to just make a bed in the on-call room, but there were nights when practicality was the most impractical thing, and she wanted nothing more than her own bed, her own down comforter, her own ticking alarm clock, and her own cat, Buster Kitten, purring by her side . . .

. . . but tired as she was, that kind of image was the last thing she needed right now. Right now was a good time to fill out the new patient evaluations she hadn't had a chance to get to all night. She sighed, angled the desk lamp, selected a favorite pen, and pulled the first of the forms toward her.

It wasn't a form. It was the lab's report on John Doe.

Indicators normal on cholesterol, blood sugar, blood alcohol levels. Negative on cocaine, PCP, and all the popular name-brand hallucinogens. Negative on HIV, too, which ruled out dementia—

not that Dr. Harris had ever even considered it, given the man's impressive physical condition. And, bless Willie, positive on snake venom—it wasn't the rattlesnake venom he'd tested for, but it did share several of its indicators. Willie had also appended a personal observation on a yellow stick-it note: that the blood was *also* positive for another factor, that had screwed up all the tests until he compensated for it: a factor that was like nothing else he'd ever seen. NOT ONLY THAT, Willie wrote, BUT HE'S ALSO SO SUPEROXYGENATED THAT I'M TEMPTED TO ASK IF YOU GOT THIS FROM HIS FEMORAL ARTERY. Dr. Harris didn't have the slightest idea what to make of that.

For a moment she pictured a dark, shadowy hunter, somewhere out in the night, drawing closer and closer while she diddled about making tests. . . .

The usual comeback to a thought like that was a dismissive, *Naaah.* Dr. Harris invited the *Naaah* to come. It didn't. The Hunter of her imagination merely took another step closer, and smiled at her.

The evaluations sat where she'd left them, waiting.

Right now, nothing seemed so irrelevant and pointless.

It had never been like her to neglect such paperwork, which she knew to be a vital part of the job, but her bone-weariness had suddenly been replaced by a restlessness that made sitting still an impossibility. She got up, left her office, and went straight to the door of the padded room where she'd left Mr. Doe.

When she looked through the window, she saw him sitting on the side of his bed. It should have been impossible; he'd been left strapped to the railings. He shouldn't have been able to lift his head, let alone sit up. But the leather straps were lying on the floor by his feet. He looked disoriented, but considerably calmer than he'd been the last time she saw him: there was a certain native intelligence beginning to shine through his fog.

She should have called Gordy and Flack. It was proper procedure, not to mention common sense. But without knowing why, she found herself unlocking the door and walking in alone.

He didn't jump up and stop her from locking the door behind her. Indeed, he didn't even seem to notice her until she was almost by his side. At which point he looked up, with dry eyes and a grim mouth.

"The Hunter's coming," he whispered. "I can feel it."

"Nobody's coming," she said.

"He is. He's closer than you think. He probably already knows where I am. He's probably already watching the building now. There's a—a tingling. . . ." His eyes lost focus, seeing something far away, beyond this room, beyond this ward, beyond everything she'd ever known. Then he shook his head and tried again. "You can't understand. You can't know. But I know danger. I can feel it. I can tell when it's coming."

"There's no danger," she told him. "We're in a big hospital. With police, security, and locked doors. Nobody can get to you in here."

"He can," he said, bleakly. "You don't know him. You don't know what he can do. He's hunted everything that walks or crawls or flies. He's made trophies of everything that lives. Nothing's ever gotten away from him but me, and you don't want to know what he'll do to get me once and for all." He looked past her again, at something hidden within his clouded memory. "He was the Chameleon's friend . . . funny how I forgot that . . . it's so hard to remember that his kind can have friends too. . . ."

Then he fell into brooding silence, leaving her to reflect on the sheer width and breadth of his delusions. The Hunter was at the center of it, of course . . . but he'd named a dozen others, from the goblin and the octopus to this new addition called the chameleon. Was his fevered brain just keeping up with the pace of the babble? Or was there some core of truth behind the delirium? Was he simply handling a life filled with terror the best way he knew how?

She was still considering that when she realized he was staring at her, with a depth of understanding that belied all his delirium so far. It was a stare that frightened her, a stare that linked awe and accusation: a stare that seemed to notice her presence for the very first time. "You're *not* Gwendy," he whispered. He said it like a man who couldn't decide whether he should be horrified or relieved. "I thought you were . . . but you're not. You just look a little bit like her, that's all. Your hair . . . and your eyes . . . you could almost be her, in the right light . . . but you're not. If I wasn't so confused . . . if I could keep the same thought in my head for more than thirty seconds at a time . . . I would have known . . . I would have been able to tell . . . I wouldn't have made the mistake. . . ."

It was a breakthrough, of sorts. "You're not yourself," Dr. Harris assured him. "Who was she?"

It was a long time before he answered. "I loved her. I would have done anything for her. But the Spider came between us, and the Goblin came, and he—he . . ." Then he stopped, closed his eyes, and formed both his hands into fists. "No. Can't do this. Can't get sidetracked by the Goblin. I have to remember . . . it's not the Goblin. It's the Hunter. He's the one who jumped me in SoHo, who dosed me with the stuff that made all the monsters come back. All around me: the burglar . . . the Jackal . . . Mysterio . . . the Scorpion . . . even Jonah, if you believe that. They all came back. Surrounding me. Jabbing at me. And the Hunter stood there laughing . . . that terrible laugh, like a jungle drum . . . and he said I was helpless . . . that he could take his time and track me down whenever he wanted. I had to run . . . get as far uptown as I could . . . find an alley . . . didn't even care if anybody saw me . . . just couldn't let *him* see me . . . couldn't afford to go ballistic in the suit . . . had to get away . . . gain some time . . . strip down . . . ditch the mask. . . ."

At the word *mask*, he went silent. His eyes went wide and his mouth contracted to the size of a dot. Then he howled. "Oh, my God! My face! My face! You can see my face!" The realization terrified him. He bent over, covering his features with both hands, burying them, hiding the invisible scars that only he could see. Dr. Harris immediately reached out and grabbed him by both wrists. She intended to pull his hands away—but though she was far from gentle, John Doe moved not at all. He was too solid to move. He was a granite sculpture, held in place by a physical strength greater than any she'd ever known. She remembered the five cops trying and failing to hold him still, and for a moment felt an uneasy chill of panic. It was stupid to wrestle with him, she'd never be able to defend herself if he went berserk again. But she didn't need to match his strength to show more will, and when she refused to release her grip he meekly permitted her to pull his hands away from his face, revealing an expression that was at once forlorn and terrified.

"I don't care who you are," she said. "I don't care what you look like. I just want to help you, so you can face this thing that scares you so much."

He took her by the wrists. "I wish I could, Gwendy. But I tried to save you last time. I even thought I did. I caught you . . . I heard the snap . . . and I pulled you back and I held you in my arms and I thought I'd saved you and I was so happy I had . . . and you were still warm, Gwendy, so much like you were still alive . . . but you weren't moving, Gwendy, you weren't moving . . . you were just—just there, Gwendy . . . your head hanging at the wrong angle . . . your mouth slightly open, and no breath coming out . . . and I kept saying you can't be dead, you can't be dead . . . but you were . . . and the Goblin flew around in circles, laughing at us. . . .''

She tried to free herself from his grip and found she couldn't. "Listen to me. Remember what you said just a few seconds ago. I'm not your Gwendy. I'm just somebody who looks like her. You have to concentrate and focus on where you are now and what you have to do to get well."

She expected an argument. Most patients this obsessed would have held on to her indefinitely. This one released her at once, with a shocked and apologetic look that made her doubly certain he posed no threat. He would have died rather than hurt her.

He said, "You're right. The Hunter's coming. He'll track me down. He's a hunter. It's what he does. I can't be around you when he shows up. I have to go. . . .''

And with that, he got up, walked right past her, and opened the door.

The locked door.

The door with the thick iron deadbolt designed to stand up to men reduced to little more than beasts; the door that had remained closed even as hysterics burning with their own adrenaline charged it again and again and again. The door that had been kicked and cursed and fought and attacked by literally hundreds of patients. The door that supposedly made this room as secure as any jail, that supposedly would stand up to anything this side of a battering ram. The door that resisted John Doe for less than a heartbeat before he yanked it open with one annoyed tug. A fairly large piece of wall came with it.

It happened so quickly that Dr. Harris didn't have any time to react. Later, thinking about it, she'd remember the way John Doe looked as he crossed the room and realize precisely what he had reminded her of. He'd reminded her of a movie filmed at normal speed and played at fast motion. It was the look of a man moving in what for him was no particular hurry, but was for the rest of the world the velocity of a horse at full gallop.

By the time she was able to get to the doorway herself, the shouting had already started in the corridor.

It was Gordy and Flack, of course; they'd promised to keep checking in on John Doe for her, and it was just their luck to synchronize this particular visit with his attempt at escape. They were each twice his size and weight, they were each (by weight comparison, anyway) high-school bullies to his science-club nerd—and though they each hung on to an arm with the will of men determined to give this fight everything they had, they were both whipped around like yo-yos at the end of strings. As John Doe fought to shake them off, they peppered his stomach and ribs with blows that should have sent him to his knees. He didn't even seem to notice. Instead, he just twisted his back in a manner that should have made cracked poker chips of his spine, slipped free of their grasp, and ran like hell.

His run was as crazily sped up as his walking inside the padded room. And it was more: the strangest-looking dash that Dr. Harris had ever seen. It was a strange, skittering, hunched-over kind of run, that should have been unbearably awkward—but was instead so preternaturally graceful that she had trouble believing that his feet touched the floor.

Neither Gordy nor Flack should have ever been able to catch up with him—but halfway down the corridor he turned around and faced them both, his teeth spread in a wide mischievous grin. As they ran toward him, he made an odd gesture with both hands: hands out, middle two fingers of each curled inward to tap the palm. The way John Doe did it, it seemed confident, practiced, and terribly significant. He seemed genuinely astonished when nothing happened—and was taken utterly by surprise as the two burly men both tackled him at once. All three of them hit the ground in a frenetic tumble of flailing arms and legs.

Dr. Harris ran after them. It took her a heartbeat to catch up; by that point Gordy was flung four feet straight up; Flack was whipped from side to side like a flag waved by an overzealous patriot. As Dr. Harris circled the fray, desperate to catch John Doe's attention, momentarily unsure how, a pair of orderlies galloped around the corner and piled on. One got batted aside by Flack's out-of-control form; one managed to get enmeshed in the clumsy tangle of guards and patient and orderly before landing a solid blow to John Doe's solar plexus. That kind of blow usually left the victim paralyzed by pain; it didn't even slow John Doe down. Nor did it slow him down when a third orderly appeared out of nowhere to add his own weight to the whole; instead, the entire living sculpture first bucked and heaved from the struggling of the man at its bottom . . . then all at once rose, subject to that man's impossible determination to defy them all and stand up.

She thought of running to the supply room for a hypo filled with Thorazine. She thought of going to call more security. She even thought of joining the fight herself—but though she'd had to do it before, with other patients, she honestly didn't see how much her own weight would accomplish when five men who probably weighed half a ton among them weren't enough to stop John Doe from standing on his own two feet.

Instead, she simply cried out, "Stop!"

And he stopped. Just like that.

Because his Gwendy had said so.

He stared at her from the center of a knot of desperate men, with a face as pale and sweaty as their own, once again seeing her as if for the very first time.

"The Hunter's coming," he whispered. "I'm not imagining it. He's coming."

Dr. Gwendolyn Harris answered in his own terms: "You're in no shape to worry about him."

His eyes glazed. "Maybe. . . . I'm still so weak, Gwendy. . . . I should be able to take these guys . . . I should be way past them already . . . I'm used to being able to take dozens like them at a time . . . what happens when he shows up? What happens when he comes after me for real?"

She gripped him by the hand. "Look inside yourself. Whatever he is, whoever you are, there's a part of you he can't touch. Hold on to that."

He smiled. Pathetically. Gratefully.

And then he fainted.

They took no chances with John Doe after that. They secured him with every restraint in their arsenal. That included another straitjacket, leather straps binding wrists and ankles to the guardrails of his bed, a secure canvas apron tied tight over both, another padded room, and Gordy and Flack on vigilant guard duty outside the securely locked door. It didn't feel like enough. It wasn't all that much more than what had so unsuccessfully caged him before. Dr. Harris could only hope that the snake venom would have flushed itself from his system by the time he woke up again.

But even worse than that was the catchphrase that kept running through her mind, again and again, with all the tenacity of a commercial jingle:

JUST BECAUSE YOU'RE PARANOID DOESN'T MEAN PEOPLE AREN'T REALLY OUT TO GET YOU.

It was one of the biggest pitfalls of dealing with diseased minds for a living—they didn't always sound delusional. Far from it—they could sometimes be more persuasive and articulate than the so-called sane. Some were capable of describing their twisted worldviews in the most reasonable terms, offering logic, intelligent persuasion, even evidence. Indeed, Dr. Harris had read of one incident where a school principal suffering from paranoid fantasies had talked three otherwise intelligent teachers into guarding her house night and day, to protect her from an assassination plot on the part of her students; she'd offered no explanation of how she'd learned of this plot but had still gotten half her department heads involved in the fight to save her life. And such cases weren't even all that unusual—if it weren't possible to get reasonable people to believe the rantings of the insane, then a fair percentage of cult leaders and politicians would have been out of work.

Dr. Harris knew that intellectually; she knew it with every ounce of professional experience at her disposal.

But she couldn't stop thinking about the Hunter.

John Doe hadn't described him, but she'd already developed a vivid mental image of the man. In her mind, he looked a little like Stewart Granger did in the fifties, when he played the African explorer Allan Quatermain: clad in bush jacket, jodhpurs, and pith helmet, toting a rifle capable of bringing down charging rhinos with a single shot, and facing the world with narrowed eyes that remained calm and collected despite any crisis. (Come to think of it, she was probably mixing that up with elements of *The Most Dangerous Game*.) But her nightmare Hunter had features Granger couldn't have matched without the aid of modern day special effects: namely, a grin wider than his mouth and eyes that glowed red when seen in the wrong light. This Hunter killed for the sheer savage joy of it, and would track his chosen prey across rivers, over mountains, and through the darkest jungles, just so he could escape the onus of admitting to himself that he'd given up.

It didn't matter to her that there was no such man; myths and archetypes possess a power far out of proportion to their accuracy. What mattered was that John Doe obviously believed in him. And though Dr. Gwendolyn Harris could not, that didn't stop her from feeling him draw close, somewhere out there in the night. . . .

When Willie the lab guy caught up with her, she was standing in a little alcove just outside the Emergency Psych Unit, staring out the window at the sheets of rain that whipped against the concrete and bricks of the garbage-ridden alley below. It was much too dark outside to see anything, except for those fleeting moments when lightning lit up the sky; without realizing it, Dr. Harris had been spending those moments searching for the Hunter.

When Willie coughed to get her attention, she almost leapt out of her skin. "*Jeez*—oh, it's you. Damn. Don't do that."

He was holding two cups of coffee, both steaming, both decorated in the faux-Greek mosaic favored by so many Manhattan all-night diners. "Wow, you're jumpy tonight. Maybe caffeine's the *last* thing you need."

"No," she said, as she took hers, "actually, I was just thinking how much one of these would hit the spot right about now. Thanks."

"Isn't it time you started home? Or at least got some sleep?"

She sipped daintily. "I was thinking that, actually. But you know how it is when you want to leave somewhere, and you can't because part of you keeps waiting for something to happen? That's what I'm feeling now. It's like there's this big balloon that's been inflating all night long, and I can't leave now because if I do I won't get to be here when it pops."

"It's the storm," Willie said knowledgeably. "The way Hollywood's trained us to see thunder and lightning as ominous."

"I suppose so." Dr. Harris sighed. She drank another mouthful of coffee, found it bitter, and as she frowned finally identified one of the things that had been nagging at her all night long. "Willie? That sample I sent down earlier tonight? The patient who got dosed with snake venom?"

"Yes? What about him?"

"Was there anything in your analysis that would lead you to believe he could have been—" she hesitated, knowing that if she opened this door she might not be able to close it "—a paranormal?"

Willie didn't laugh. "You mean like the Thing? Or Captain America? Or one of those guys?"

"It's possible. There must be a couple thousand of them in this town, good, bad, and indifferent. What are the signifiers for something like that?"

"If he was a mutant," Willie said, "and you couldn't tell from his visible phenotype, you'd need DNA tests for a definitive diagnosis. If he was paranormal in some other nonphysical way, there's usually not much you can do to tell—at least, unless he starts flying and shooting ray beams from his pinkies. This guy has some blood factors I couldn't account for, but then I didn't have two or three days to run every possible test I could conceive of. Translated, that means I wouldn't say no, but I don't see any particular reason to assume it either. Why? Do you think he might be?"

"Well . . ." Dr. Harris began.

And then she heard several sets of running footsteps, pounding down the corridor. She turned to see what it was, and saw two cops and three of the larger specimens from Security, making a beeline for the stairwell at the end of the corridor. The cop in the lead shouted something into his walkie-talkie, which excitedly squawked back; the security guys bringing up the rear ran in what Dr. Harris could only interpret as formation, their batons out and their helmets on. The last time she'd seen an alert of this size, it was last year, when a pair of street gangs who'd just torn each other to ribbons in a battle over turf decided to fight round two downstairs in the emergency room. There'd been a nurse shot, that time. Now?

As the five men barreled into the stairwell, Bill The Guard emerged from the Emergency Psychiatric Unit. "You better get in here, Doctor. You, too, son. We have a serious security problem, and we shouldn't be loitering about while the trained folks take care of it.''

Dr. Harris felt a chill. "What's wrong?''

"Some crazy off the street. Tall, muscular guy, Russian accent, wearing leopard-skin tights and a skinned lion's head for a vest, if you can believe that. Walked right past Admitting and didn't stop when the guy there asked him where the hell he thought he was going. He said he was the hunter and said he'd go wherever he chose to go. The cops who tried to detain him for questioning are now being worked on in the emergency room. So's some poor guy in the elevator who gave him a lecture about the evils of wearing fur. The cops have sent some extra squad cars, and Security's searching every floor trying to track him down, but until they do he's loose in the hospital somewhere.''

The more he spoke, the more Dr. Harris felt the entire universe tilt at a forty-five degree angle: a sensation that comes naturally whenever somebody else's paranoid fantasies decide to leave the world of nightmares and enter the world of real life.

The Hunter.

As she and Willie followed Bill back into the Emergency Psychiatric Unit, she heard a thin bansheelike screaming from the isolation rooms. "Bill, I want that door locked and chained—even blocked with furniture, if you have time. I also want you to call Security and pry loose any extra help you can get. Tell them that until we hear otherwise, we're operating on the assumption that this intruder is headed directly for this unit, for the specific purpose of murdering one of our patients. I want you to do that and I want you to break out any weapons you might have been issued and I want you prepared to shoot any unauthorized person who comes through that door without their hands up. Is that clear?''

Bill, who had probably never experienced a genuine crisis in all his years of riding a desk, could only repeat, "Shoot?''

Dr. Harris directed Willie to stay and help him, then hurried through the swinging doors to the isolation section, where Gordy and Flack were positioned at the door of the room caging John Doe. She was not surprised to note that the wailing she'd heard before was clearly emanating from inside the room. Now that she was close enough, she could even hear that the wails manifested themselves as words, mostly pleas to be let out before the Hunter came and got him.

Flack saw the urgency in her eyes and said, "What's wrong?"

She faced both of them. "Did either of you say anything to him? Anything to give him any idea that something was up?"

"Hell, no," said Flack. "I thought he'd gone down for the night."

Gordy said, "He was quiet as a church mouse until about five minutes ago. Then he went nuts."

Dr. Harris bit the tip of her fingernail, trying to hold back her suspicions, aware that sharing them would constitute her last surrender to the paranoid ravings of a disordered mind. Crossing that threshhold had been easy with an obnoxious, do-nothing security guard for whom she harbored zero respect; doing the same with Gordy and Flack was considerably harder. But it didn't take her any more than two seconds to make up her mind. She whispered the words to keep John Doe from hearing them. "We got trouble. The Hunter's here."

The two men glanced at each other, clearly wondering whether the pretty doc had lost it, before they broke down and responded in unison. "Wha-a-a-at?"

"Some beefcake in a Frederick's of Hollywood Tarzan suit, identifying himself as the Hunter, just busted up a bunch of people in Admitting. He's violent, loose in this hospital, and pretty clearly what our John Doe's been trying to warn us about all night. It won't be long before he shows up here. Meanwhile, I'll need both you guys by the front desk to help Bill."

"Jeez," said Gordy. "The dude's real?"

"Apparently," Dr. Harris said. "And he's on his way."

All three of them jumped when the steel door beside them thumped loudly: a sound that could only be a human body slamming itself against a barrier. The impact was paired with another sound: that of a man screaming in terror and anguish. Another slam followed. And another. Dr. Harris couldn't help realizing that the same arms that had easily forced open an identical door not two hours before, were now pounding against this door in vain. *We've weakened him,* she thought in horror. All the trank darts and all the confinement and all her good intentions—not to mention the exhaustion that came with fighting his demons for hours on end—had finally taken their toll; he was losing his will to fight, just at the point when he most desperately needed it.

Then came a thud so loud that the entire corridor seemed to shake from the power behind it, and Gordy said, "Great. That's all we need. A two-front war."

"Never mind him," said Dr. Harris. "Get yourselves up front. And be ready for a fight: any guy capable of giving this particular patient a hard time has to be stronger than anybody has the right to be."

There was another thud, and another cry of frustration.

Flack hesitated. "You sure you don't want one of us to stay here with you? If he gets out—"

"He's not the danger!" she snapped. "Go!"

Gordy and Flack glanced at each other again, and a silent understanding passed between them. They nodded, at each other and at her, and then they barreled through the double doors that separated the isolation section from the front desk. Dr. Harris watched the way the doors swung wide to accommodate them, then swung back, and back again, providing her glimpses of them as they took up positions at either side of the locked front door. Somewhere out there, Bill The Guard was shouting into his telephone: the target of his rant being the morons who insisted on not understanding his demands for help, more help.

She heard a tearing noise from John Doe's room.

It took her a second to identify the sound as being caused by the rubber padding being ripped off the door in sheets.

It was impossible, of course. The padding was the same combination of rubber and reinforced plastic used on heavy-duty raincoats. It wasn't supposed to rip beneath an assault by human hands, no matter how powerful. But John Doe was tearing it to shreds. Another second passed before she realized why. The last time he'd tested his strength against a door like this he'd grabbed the door handle and *pulled.* This door was newer: it had no internal handle. There hadn't been anything for John Doe to grip, so he'd been limited to trying to batter the door down. Only, that was a bit more difficult, since the layers of heavy padding had muffled the force of his kicks and punches and distributed most of their power throughout the entire width of the wall.

But once the padding was gone, the door would have to bear the brunt of his attack unprotected.

The door resounded with a loud *clang*. One patch at about eye-level bulged outward, in a bubble approximately the size and shape of a human foot.

Dr. Harris could have shouted for him to stop, to leave the door alone, because she was about to let him out. But she didn't. There are some things simply too big to be absorbed all at once, and the sight of that steel door warping and buckling beneath John Doe's blows happened to be one of them. How strong was he, exactly? And what did this little performance have to say about what she could expect from the Hunter?

The door *clanged* again; a crescent-shaped section by the door frame bent outward, tearing free of the wall. A pale, sweaty hand emerged from the crack, closed around the edge of the door, and pushed. The door shuddered, creaked, then broke away entirely, with a violence that tore jagged lightning-shaped cracks in the surrounding wall. John Doe forced his way out through the slit. He was flushed, once again wearing nothing but the blue tights he'd had on when the cops dragged him in, and covered head to waist with a cold sweat. The effort of busting out seemed to have taken all the strength he had; as soon as he saw Dr. Harris, he gasped and collapsed against the wall. "I swear to you, Gwendy . . . every time I see you . . . it's like the past slapping me in the face. . . ."

"I'm not the past," she told him. "I'm not Gwendy. I'm Dr. Gwendolyn Harris, and we never met before tonight."

He fell on her, then, but it was not an assault; it was just the act of an exhausted, feverish man who for the moment needed the support she could provide. "Forgive me," he said, as his legs turned to jelly beneath him, and only her strength kept him from sagging all the way to the floor. "I'm still . . . not a hundred percent. I'm feverish, and I'm weak, and I'm tired, and I'm still seeing things . . . like right now it's Mary Jane, and what she'd say if she saw what I was doing . . ."

"You'll get better."

"I don't have the time to get better. I need gauze."

"Why?"

"Because . . . if he sees my face when he gets here . . . then my life is over. Can you trust me on that, Doctor? It doesn't matter

... what else happens tonight ... if I hide or get away or find some way to beat him ... if he sees my face tonight, I'm history. He'll be here in a couple of minutes. I need you to wrap my face in gauze ... now.''

His eyes were wide, pleading ... and sane.

She responded at once, drawing his arm around her shoulders and half walking, half carrying him down the corridor to the supply room. There was an uncomfortable moment when, struggling under his weight, she fumbled inside her pocket for the keys and didn't immediately find them among a jumble of quarters; he relieved her of the time and trouble by simply reaching out with his free hand and breaking the door open with a nudge. By this point she was beyond shock at such things. She just lugged him inside, sat him down on a big cardboard box by the far wall, and rushed over to the cabinet where the unit stored its first aid needs. After a second she came back with a roll of gauze and began to wrap his head: first under the chin, then over the top of the head, and then around and around the face, until she'd covered everything but a narrow slit for the eyes.

She was still securing the loose end when she heard the explosion from up front—a terrible all-encompassing burst of noise followed by the clatter of falling debris. Both Gordy and Flack started yelling, Bill The Guard—predictably—screaming. Their voices were soon lost behind a cacophony of others': the terrified reactions of the other patients in the isolation rooms and elsewhere in the ward. Dr. Harris almost dropped what she was doing and ran up front to see if anybody needed her help: but John Doe stood up first and she surprised herself by shoving him back into a seated position long enough for her to pin the loose end in place.

Somewhere, a baritone voice as deep as a bass drum thundered, "Arachnid! Show yourself!"

"The Hunter," she whispered, scarcely daring to believe it.

John Doe stood up and went straight for the door, pausing just long enough to turn back to Dr. Harris. "Hide," he said. "It doesn't matter where. In a cabinet or a closet or under a desk. Just curl up in a ball and don't come out until this is over. You can't help me and you might get in my way."

Muffled by the bandages, his voice sounded deeper. Stronger. More confident. Almost like it came from a different person. Too

much so, in fact. She didn't have time to reflect on that before
he sped back out the door in a blur.

Dr. Harris considered his advice for all of one second. Certainly she was terrified: her heart thumped in her chest like a
wild beast clawing at the walls of its cage. Certainly she wanted
nothing more than to find some dark and quiet place where the
madness wouldn't touch her. But she'd be damned if she'd cower
in the shadows while her staff and one of her patients fought for
their lives.

She snatched a fire extinguisher off the wall and ran down the
corridor, toward the double doors that were even now swinging
open, swinging shut, granting her moment-by-moment glimpses
of human bodies hurtling back and forth across the room on the
other side. She saw a lion's face, a blur of motion, Gordy flying
backward against the far wall, Willie in the corner trying to make
himself very very small.

And then she was through the doors herself, and she got her
very first look at the Hunter.

She understood at once why even a man as powerful as John
Doe would be afraid of him.

Her first impression was size. The Hunter was huge. Not just
in terms of height (though he had that) and not just in terms
of his musculature (though he had that too). Far more terrible
than both, there was his presence: a confident, pitiless arrogance
capable of filling up worlds. It was an aura reeking of death, of
jungles, of countless wild things reduced to carrion beneath his
knife. The lion's-head vest he wore, which would have looked
absurdly pretentious on anybody else, was no more and no less
than a promise that nothing that lived could escape him, even if
it was the most dangerous thing that walked. Dr. Harris believed
that promise. She had to. It would have been impossible for any
living thing to look at this man and not consider itself his natural
prey.

Only after she realized that did she pick up on the others: the
battered, moaning forms of Gordy and Flack, who were lying on
opposite sides of the room and struggling to get up without success; the bleeding form of Bill The Guard, who was curled in a
fetal position by the desk that had always been his safest haven;
the frozen, terrified face of Willie, huddled in the corner. And

John Doe: facing the Hunter in a position midway between a crouch and the confrontational stance of a boxer.

Based on size alone, John Doe seemed pathetically over-matched.

The Hunter's smile seemed to bear that out. It was a broad, hateful smile, perfectly framed by his moustache and goatee: the kind of smile practiced by bullies who want their victims to know they've already lost. When the growl formed in his throat, Dr. Harris saw that it was even more than that: it was the snarl of a beast, instinctively showing its teeth. As if to stress the point, he jabbed at the air with the curved jaguar tusks he held in each hand; they were both dripping with something black and foul. Sparing but the briefest glance at Dr. Harris—barely seeing her; letting her know with a look that she was beneath his notice—he turned his attention back to John Doe and spoke, with the lightest trace of a Russian accent: "You have recovered more than I would have guessed. But you are still just the most insubstantial shadow of yourself."

John Doe didn't take the bait. "That's still ten times as good as you ever were."

"You are an accident. A mistake. A freak of nature."

"One that's beaten your sorry butt more times than either one of us can count."

"For the last time," said the Hunter.

What happened next occurred so quickly that Dr. Harris's eyes refused to register it all. The Hunter lunged forward, swinging both those razor-sharp tusks in great hungry arcs that seemed capable of slicing the entire room to ribbons. John Doe leapt, too, passing through that arc without seeming to be touched by it, while aiming a kick directly at the Hunter's jaw. Of the two, it was John Doe who connected. He knocked the Hunter flat on his back, and landed in a roll ten feet beyond him.

The impact looked and sounded like it should have taken the Hunter's head off. But by the time John Doe rose to his feet, the Hunter was already up and slashing with those jaguar teeth again. John Doe grabbed the Hunter's wrists as they came down, stopping the points before they found skin; the Hunter roared and kneed John Doe in the belly with a force that should have paralyzed him. Instead, John Doe merely let go of the Hunter's wrists and high-jumped straight up, somersaulting over the Hunter's head to land in a perfect crouch directly behind him.

All of this happened in less than two seconds.

Then they *sped up*, moving with such superhuman speed that Dr. Harris found herself unable to follow it all: a frenzied explosion of kicks and punches and impossible somersaulting leaps, a kung fu fight played on fast forward. Her mind processed only the most transitory images from the whole: first John Doe slapped the jaguar tusks out of the Hunter's hands. Then, with a blur of movement, the Hunter grabbed John Doe from behind, linking his fingers behind Doe's head and exerting all his strength in a deadly struggle to break Doe's neck. Next, another blur of movement, and the Hunter smashed headfirst against the wall, while John Doe leapt forward to press his advantage. Then another blur, and the Hunter held Bill's desk high above his head while a dazed and staggering John Doe waited for the furniture to fly. Then another blur, and John Doe *ran across the surface* of the flung desk during the fraction of a second that it was still in the air.

As John Doe leapt off the desk, he shouted a word, but Dr. Harris couldn't entirely make it out over the sound of the desk smashing to pieces on—and through—the wall. To her ears it sounded like "craving."

Then he landed on his feet in front of the Hunter, and the two men eschewed the fancy leaping and dodging just to stand face to face and hurl punches at each other. John Doe erupted in a blur of movement, and blood appeared on the Hunter's lips; the Hunter did something too fast to see, and John Doe staggered back, a reddish stain spreading across the gauze that masked his face. Another dozen blows sped by in rapid succession; there was no way to tell which ones were blocked, which ones connected, and who landed more. But then they finished, John Doe staggered backward, clutching his bandaged face in both hands, and the Hunter raised his fists high above his head for a killing blow.

Dr. Harris had been waiting for an opening, a moment when it would have been possible to get past the fighters, to summon help or, if nothing else, to drag Willie and the others from the room. But there hadn't been an opening. This wasn't two bruisers in a bar, clumsily pummeling each other until one collapsed in a pool of blood—this was two forces of nature, battling with a speed and a power that no human being had ever been meant to possess. Entering that space would have been like embracing an explosion. She saw no opening, no moment when any action on her part would have accomplished anything but getting herself hurt or killed.

Which is why it was so remarkable that Gordy, who'd used up most of his strength in the last few seconds just trying to stand, chose that moment to tackle the Hunter from behind. He lowered his head and charged across the room and piled into the Hunter with every ounce of his three hundred pound musculature. Gordy had been a star quarterback in college. He'd almost made it to the pros. He didn't even budge the Hunter; he might just as usefully have tackled a pillar, or a flagpole. But the Hunter's reaction was immediate; he just swung his arm downward and elbowed Gordy with a force that sent the security man flying like a scrap of paper caught in a high wind. Gordy hit the wall almost as hard as the desk had. The Hunter spared him only the most contemptuous glance. He didn't devote any real attention to making sure Gordy was finished. The Hunter knew he was finished. John Doe was his prey now.

Except that John Doe was gone.

Dr. Harris didn't see him, and neither did the Hunter. He'd vanished, in the instant that Gordy had distracted them; and as Dr. Harris stood helplessly against the swinging doors, thinking both *He's gone, he's run away, the Hunter can't get him,* and *Oh, my God, he's abandoned us, he's left us here with this monster,* the tall man with the lion's-head vest merely scanned the room . . . looked at the ceiling . . . and then at her.

The feeling she got when the Hunter met her eyes was precisely the feeling that a deer gets when it's blinded by the glare of onrushing headlights. And when he started toward her, she knew she was dead. She dropped the fire extinguisher numbly, knowing that she'd never have time to use it.

Then something lifted her off the ground, up near the ceiling, in fact, and she found herself flying back down the corridor, with the Hunter in close pursuit. She was so lost by the savagery of his gaze—and the understanding that the most terrible thing about him was the way he managed to be murderous and animalistic and cruel while remaining fully and completely sane—

that it almost didn't occur to her to wonder what was carrying her until she happened to look down and see John Doe's upside-down and bandaged face bobbing right below hers. He was running the length of the corridor on the ceiling. Carrying her as he went.

When they passed the door to the supply room, he simply tossed her in and continued going. She landed on the floor with surprising gentleness—in fact, she landed on her feet. She turned and faced the door just in time to see the Hunter pass by, glance at her, evidently decide her not worth his time, and keep going. The sounds of battle resumed outside her line of sight: fists slamming against bodies, bodies slamming against walls, the grunts of air being driven by the combatants' lungs. Worst of all was the Hunter's laugh: "You're weakening, insect! You had some fight left in you, but not enough!"

For a moment Dr. Gwendolyn Harris merely stood there, un-comprehending. She'd not only come to believe in impossibili-ties tonight, but she'd also experienced one. Had it really happened? Had John Doe really carried her the length of the isolation corridor on the ceiling?

What were they?

Outside, John Doe cried out in pain. The Hunter laughed again. "See? I always love this moment—when all the futile strug-gling is done, and the beast finally loses its will to live. Can you feel it, insect? Can you admit that you're about to die?"

John Doe said nothing. And the Hunter's laughter went on, loud, and long. It was a sound capable of drowning out all the other sounds in the world . . . a sound that made Dr. Gwendolyn Harris realize that if help hadn't shown up yet, it could only be because there was nobody else left to help. The Hunter must have taken out every cop and security man in the hospital. It would have been easy for him. And the distant sirens she could hear slowly growing louder behind the laughter and the thunder and the rain and the beating of her own heart—they might have been coming with help, but they wouldn't arrive for long minutes yet, and the rescue they promised was an empty and contempt-ible lie. Because long before the reinforcements arrived, the Hunter would have finished what he'd come here to do.

When she left the supply room, several seconds later, the first thing she saw, looking at the aftermath of the battle—aside from cratered walls and dangling ceiling lights—was the Hunter, standing tall and triumphant at the end of the corridor. He stood ramrod straight, his back to her, with one bulging arm nonchalantly propped against his waist, the other holding John Doe off the floor by his neck. John Doe's hands both clutched weakly at the Hunter's wrist, trying to make him let go; but it was the last failing struggle of a man whose lights were finally going out.

Dr. Harris remembered what had happened to Gordy, and knew that in a second it would happen to her. But that didn't matter. As a doctor, she dealt daily with life and death, sanity and insanity, sickness and recovery. It also was more power than most people should ever be allowed to handle. And one of the first things she'd ever learned was that with great power comes great responsibility.

Fully expecting it to be the last thing she ever did, she ran forward and plunged two hypodermic needles filled with Thorazine into the back of the Hunter's neck.

He may have heard her charge, but he hadn't expected her to do that. He roared, whirled, and used his free arm to knock her the length of the corridor with a single backhanded slap. It was a lot like being run over by a semi, only worse. She hit the floor with fire in her side and blood on her lips, tormented by the knowledge that she'd accomplished nothing; because the Hunter still held John Doe at arm's length, squeezing the life out of him with nothing but the strength of his right hand.

The Hunter's eyes bored hate into hers. "Stupid woman! When I'm done with him, I'll break. . . . your . . . neck!"

The eyes behind John Doe's mask widened.

Dr. Gwendolyn Harris saw it. Understood it.

And in the instant before all hell broke loose, she knew that the Hunter had just picked absolutely the wrong thing to say.

The next sound was a snap. It came from the fingers on the Hunter's right hand, which all of a sudden didn't point in the right direction anymore. As the Hunter fell back against the wall in agony and disbelief, the suddenly wild-eyed and enraged John Doe dropped to the ground and screamed, *"No! Not again!"*

It was the turning point. The Hunter tried to defend himself against John Doe's fusillade of blows, but he would have been more successful trying to catch every raindrop in a thunderstorm; the hysterical and enraged John Doe was an engine of destruction, pummeling him again and again and again with too many punches to count. The Hunter went for a blowgun in his vest; John Doe smacked it out of his hand. He went for a bag of glittering powder in his belt; John Doe ripped it away and tossed it out of reach. He went for a curved ebony knife strapped to his thigh; John Doe took it away before the Hunter even got close to it. And while the Hunter reached for weapon after weapon, John Doe battered him again and again and again and again, keeping him too off-balance to fight back, denying him even the ability to fall.

A new expression entered the Hunter's eyes.

Helplessness. Terror.

The look of a deer caught in the headlights.

An unworthy part of Dr. Harris couldn't help taking satisfaction in that.

She had a bad moment when the Hunter batted John Doe away from him with a single roundhouse punch, but it wasn't the opening shot of a new offensive so much as the last effort of an animal desperate to escape. Even as John Doe fell to the ground and somersaulted back to a standing position, the Hunter was staggering away, his face bleeding, his fingers twisted, his good arm clasped against his side to hold together what were probably several broken ribs. Damaged as he was, he lurched away faster than most people could run—but he was less than he had been; both his awesome physical presence and impossible superhuman grace reduced to the broken gait of a man both defeated and humiliated. He did not glare at Dr. Harris as he passed by; nor did he look back as he plowed past the swinging doors. He just went, like any other terrified beast fleeing for its life.

John Doe didn't chase after him immediately, but instead stopped just long enough to kneel by the doctor's side. "Are you all right?"

She looked up weakly, to study the dark brown eyes that faced her from behind that inexpressive gauze mask. They weren't wild eyes, not anymore. They were calm, and compassionate, and concerned, and sane: the eyes of a person she would have liked to ask a lot of long and penetrating questions about the insanity that seemed to pass for his life. But this was not the time. And so she said, "Never better. You?"

But he'd already pursued the Hunter through the swinging doors.

After a few seconds of luxuriating in the awareness that her part in this nightmare was over, she hauled herself to her feet and began limping toward the outer office, to see if any of the others needed her help.

If there was much left to the fight after that, nobody saw more than a little of it. A cop came out of the elevator just in time to see the fleeing Hunter dive through a closed eighth-story window; Mother Nature chose that moment to provide a blinding flash of lightning, which made brilliant constellations of light out of the shards of broken glass that surrounded him on all sides as he plunged into the night. The same cop saw a half-naked man with a face wrapped in gauze leap half the length of the corridor to follow the other man into the darkness. The poor cop thought he'd just watched two consecutive suicides. But when he reported what he'd seen to Dr. Gwendolyn Harris (who, though looking pretty rocky herself, was busily tending to the injuries of four male hospital personnel in a room that looked like the aftermath of an explosion), she shakily expressed her opinion that no matter how diligently he and his fellow officers searched the alley below, they would never find any broken bodies. And she was right. John Doe and the Hunter had jumped out the window, but they had never hit the ground.

As she tended to the seriously injured Flack, he stirred, raised his head, and managed to say, "Are you . . . sure . . . you're not his Gwendy?"

Any other time, she might have laughed.

Tonight, she didn't have the slightest idea what to say.

Gordy and Flack recovered from their injuries and returned to their jobs. Willie the lab tech transferred to a hospital in New Mexico, where he quickly picked up everything he needed to know about snakebite. Bill The Guard took disability and became a taxi dispatcher. Sergeant Monaghan was killed rousting a drug den in the suburbs. Officer Ditmeyer wrote two novels that didn't sell before completing one that did. Dr. Gwendolyn Harris asked for the day shift and got it. The fingerprints and photographs taken of the perpetrator known as John Doe quickly disappeared from the filing room at the precinct house where he'd been booked—a locked room three stories up, with a single window that did not happen to be equipped with a fire escape.

Two weeks after the events in the Emergency Psychiatric Unit, Dr. Gwendolyn Harris came to work in the morning and found all her coworkers grinning at her. She didn't find out why until she made it to her little office and found a dozen red roses in a porcelain vase on her desk. There was a sealed envelope taped to its side. She hesitated, then peeled off the envelope and read the short, neatly typed letter inside.

It read:

Dr. Harris:

It's me. The mummy. See? I'm better. I'm not calling you Gwendy anymore.

I'm sorry I can't tell you my real name, or what that fight was all about. I have to keep my secrets, which is why, when I was capable again, I wasted no time relieving the police of my mug shots and prints.

On the other hand, I couldn't just disappear out of your life without letting you know that I'm all right. You don't know how much of that is due to you. All I saw was a terrifying mishmash of bad memories, swirling around me on all sides; there was nothing to hold on to, anywhere, and I might not have found my way back to sanity in time if I hadn't found somebody to depend on.

It was one of the worst nights of my life, which is saying a lot. I've had some bad ones, Doctor; you'll never know how bad. But this was one of the worst. And you were there for me. You kept me hanging on even when there was nothing to hang on to. And though part of it was your accidental resemblance to a friend long dead and gone, even that wouldn't have been enough if not for your strength, your courage, and your compassion.

I wouldn't exactly say that things are back to normal, but then, for me they never are. That's a joke. But I am back to my everyday life, among friends and family, and I'm doing fine, and I probably won't have to worry about the Hunter again for a long, long time. Next time he comes for me, I'll be ready for him.

Thank you.

There was no signature. None was needed.

Dr. Harris couldn't help wishing that he'd seen fit to thank her in person; she wouldn't have told the police, and there was so much she wanted to ask him, so much she needed to know. But life on the unit had been like that before; she didn't always get to find out what eventually happened to her patients. She'd have to be content with knowing that he was safe, and well, and ready to face the challenges that lay ahead for him. That was more than she usually got to know.

When she leaned over to sniff the flowers, something tickled the back of her hand. She looked down, and saw it: a spider. It must have been hitching a ride in the vase. As she studied it, the little thing froze in indecision, unsure which way to run.

*Tsk*ing with sympathy, she took it to a window and set it free.

CONTINUITY GUIDE

"Side by Side with the Astonishing Ant-Man!" by Will Murray takes place between *Amazing Spider-Man* #2 and #3 (May and July 1963).

"After the First Death . . ." by Tom DeFalco takes place in the general vicinity of *Amazing Spider-Man* #10 (March 1964).

"Celebrity" by Christopher Golden & José R. Nieto takes place shortly before *Amazing Spider-Man Annual* #1 (1964).

"Better Looting Through Modern Chemistry" by John Garcia & Pierce Askegren takes place a few weeks after *Amazing Spider-Man* #36 (May 1966).

"Identity Crisis" by Michael Jan Friedman takes place a few weeks prior to *Amazing Spider-Man* #39 (August 1966).

"The Doctor's Dilemma" by Danny Fingeroth takes place shortly after *Amazing Spider-Man* #42 (November 1966).

"Moving Day" by John S. Drew expands on the events of the last page of *Amazing Spider-Man* #46 (March 1967).

"The Liar" by Ann Nocenti takes place shortly after *Amazing Spider-Man Annual* #5 (1968).

"Deadly Force" by Richard Lee Byers takes place three weeks after *Amazing Spider-Man* #122 (July 1973).

"The Ballad of Fancy Dan" by Ken Grobe & Steven A. Roman takes place right after *Amazing Spider-Man* #146 (July 1975).

"Poison in the Soul" by Glenn Greenberg takes place around the events of *Amazing Spider-Man* #183–184 (August–September 1978).

"Livewires" by Steve Lyons takes place shortly after *Peter Parker the Spectacular Spider-Man* #45 (August 1980).

"Arms and the Man" by Keith R. A. DeCandido takes place right after *Amazing Spider-Man Annual* #15 (1981).

"My Enemy, My Savior" by Eric Fein and "The Stalking of John Doe" by Adam-Troy Castro both take place in recent Spider-Man continuity.